RASPUTIN'S
SHADOW

RASPUTIN'S SHADOW

RAYMOND
KHOURY

First published in Great Britain in 2013 by Orion Books,
an imprint of The Orion Publishing Group Ltd
Orion House, 5 Upper Saint Martin's Lane
London WC2H 9EA

An Hachette UK Company

1 3 5 7 9 10 8 6 4 2

Copyright © Raymond Khoury 2013

A CIP catalogue record for this book is
available from the British Library.

ISBN (Hardback) 978 1 4091 4380 2
ISBN (Export Trade Paperback) 978 1 4091 4381 9
ISBN (Ebook) 978 1 4091 4382 6

Typeset by Input Data Services Ltd, Bridgwater, Somerset

Printed and bound by CPI Group (UK) Ltd, Croydon, CR0 4YY

The Orion Publishing Group's policy is to use papers
that are natural, renewable and recyclable products and
made from wood grown in sustainable forests. The logging
and manufacturing processes are expected to conform to
the environmental regulations of the country of origin.

www.orionbooks.co.uk

For my fabulous Mia,
The last eighteen years have presented us with
good times and bad, but the one constant
has been the sheer delight that is you.

Man's most transcendental achievement
would be the conquest of his own brain.

Santiago Ramón y Cajal (1852–1934),
neuroscientist and Nobel laureate

PROLOGUE

As the high-pitched shriek reverberated against the walls of the copper mine, Maxim Nikolaev felt an unusual pinch deep in his skull.

The big man set down his pickax and wiped his brow just as the painful sensation subsided. He took in a deep breath, flooding his already-infested lungs with more toxic dust. He didn't even notice or care anymore. Right then, the mid-morning break was all he was thinking of, given that his working day had started at five.

As the last echoes of the whistle died out around him and with the army of pickaxes now at rest, Maxim heard the distant sound of the Miass River, out by the mouth of the open mine. It reminded him of when he was a boy, when his uncle often took him swimming at a secluded spot on the outskirts of Ozyorsk, away from the thick, putrid smoke that belched out of the smelting plant twenty-four hours a day.

He remembered the smell of the pine trees, so tall they seemed to touch the sky. He missed the tranquility of the place.

He missed the open sky and the clean air even more.

A voice rang out from farther down the tunnel. 'Hey, Mamo, get your ass over here. We're playing for a go on Pyotr's daughter.'

Maxim wanted to roll his eyes at Vasily, partly for the diminutive, which he hated, and partly for the man's general stupidity, but the wiry bastard took offense at the slightest provocation, so Maxim smiled at the group of men instead, hefted his pickax onto a broad, muscle-bound shoulder, and sauntered over to where the three other *mudaks* were already at their regular seats.

He sat down next to the unfortunate Pyotr and set his tool against the wall beside him. Maxim had laid eyes on the man's daughter only once, and though she was indeed strikingly beautiful, he had no doubt that she could certainly do a lot better than any of the pathetic losers around him toiling deep in the bowels of the earth for a less-than-meager wage.

Maxim fished out a small flask – a punishable offense – and took a long swig, then wiped his mouth with a grimy sleeve. 'Let's play, then,' he told Vasily. He might as well try to win some money from the leering idiot if he could.

Stanislav, the most pathetic of the foursome, went first, followed by Pyotr, then Maxim. Then Vasily's turn came around. He slammed his fist down onto a just-turned Queen of Hearts, rattling the half-broken wooden table around which the four men sat, then leaned back with a smug smile on his face.

Maxim didn't flinch. His mind was already drifting away. He felt another odd tingling in his head, like a little tickle really, deep in his brain. For some reason, he thought of how much he hated Ochko. Everyone pretended it was about skill when really luck was all you needed. He much preferred Durak, a game that seemed to be about luck, but was really about skill. He had never once been the last to hold cards in twenty-seven years of playing that game. It was probably why that leech Vasily refused to play the game with him.

Vasily's croaky voice broke through his curdled thoughts. 'Come on, Mamo, deal yourself a card before we all turn to stone.'

Maxim looked down and realized he had turned over his first two cards without even looking at them.

Stanislav turned a Seven of Clubs, unsurprisingly cutting him out of the game after three cards. Pyotr turned a Two of Spades, giving himself nineteen. He looked nervously at Vasily, whose expression didn't change. The bastard was leading with eighteen. That, and he was a very bad loser. Vasily gestured at Maxim to hurry up and take his turn, presumably so he could turn a Three and win the small pile of coins sitting in the middle of the table.

Maxim really didn't want to let him win. Not that day. Not there, not then. And as he was about to turn his card, he felt a piercing sensation worm its way through the back of his skull. It didn't last for more than a breath. He shook his head, shut his eyes, then opened them again. Whatever it was, it had gone.

He peeked at his card, then looked up at Vasily. The wiry creep was leering at him and right then, Maxim knew that the man was cheating. He didn't know why, but he was dead sure of it.

Not only cheating, but looking at him like – like he hated him. More than hated. Loathed. Despised.

Like he wanted to kill him.

And right then, Maxim realized that he loathed Vasily even more. His veins throbbing angrily against his skull, he managed to turn over his card. He watched as Vasily dropped his eyes to take it in. It was a Five of Diamonds. Maxim was also out. Vasily smirked at him and turned his own card. A Four of Hearts. Too many. He had won.

'That's us, *moi lyubimye*,' Vasily said, all smug and reaching out to gather his winnings. 'Four hearts, beating as one.'

Maxim's hand shot out to block Vasily, but just as he did, Stanislav turned away from the table and convulsed before throwing up, spewing the contents of his belly onto the cheat's boots.

'Fuu! Stanislav, you son of a whore—' Vasily lurched back from the retching man, then a pained look spread across his face and he fell off the wooden crate on which he had been sitting and hit the ground, clutching his head, knocking over the table and sending the cards flying off.

Pyotr shot to his feet too, flaring with indignation. 'Four? What four? I didn't see a four. You filthy cheat.'

Maxim swung his gaze back at Stanislav, whose eyes were bloodshot, as if the force of his retching had blown all the blood vessels in his face, and Maxim knew, knew for sure, that Stanislav had also been cheating. They all had, the swine. They were going to fleece him – then they were going to hurt him.

As if to confirm it, Vasily started to laugh. Not just a laugh, a demonic, deep-rooted laugh that gushed with contempt and mockery and – Maxim was sure of it – hatred.

Maxim stared at him, rooted to the mine's soil, feeling the sweat seep out of him, unsure of what to do—

He saw Vasily take a step in his direction – he really didn't look at all well – then the cheat's eyes went wild and the man stopped in his tracks.

Pyotr had just embedded Maxim's hack into the side of Vasily's head.

Maxim lurched back as Vasily hit the ground at his feet, a fountain of blood gushing out of the man's skull. Then he was aware that the pain in the back of his head was back, sharper than before. An intense fear washed over him. He would be next. He was sure of it.

They were going to kill him unless he killed them first.

He'd never been as sure of anything in his entire life.

Angry yells erupted from other recesses of the mine as he launched himself at Pyotr, blocking his arm while grabbing the hack and fighting the murderous cheat for it. In the dim light of the lone grimy lantern, he glimpsed Stanislav, back on his feet, going for his pickax too. Everything turned into a blur of claws and swings and shouts and punches until Maxim felt something warm in his hands, something he was absolutely compelled to squeeze until his hands met each other in the middle, and when clarity returned to his eyes, he saw poor Pyotr's eyeless, bloodied face turn a livid purple as he snapped the man's neck.

All around him, the air was suddenly full of screaming and the sound of steel cleaving through flesh and bone.

Maxim smiled and sucked in a big lungful of air. He had never heard anything so beautiful – then something flashed in the corner of his vision.

He leaned backward as the ax came swinging toward his neck and felt the displaced air blow across his face. He jabbed a fist into his attacker's ribs, then another. Something crunched. He stepped behind the groaning man, swung an arm around his throat – it was Popov, the shift manager, who had never even raised his voice the whole time that Maxim had worked there – and began to choke him.

Popov dropped to the ground like a sack of beetroot.

Maxim grabbed the ax from the dead man's hand and immediately buried it in the face of Stanislav, who already had the hack he was holding halfway through an arc toward Maxim's chest. Maxim tried to duck out of its path, but the hack still connected and gouged a large chunk out of his side.

Stanislav toppled backward and fell to the ground, the ax embedded in his face.

Maxim dropped to his knees then keeled over, grabbing his torn flesh with both hands, trying to push the two sides of the wound back together.

He lay there, writhing on the ground, pain shooting through him, his hands bathed in his own blood, and glanced down the mineshaft. He could barely make out the dimly lit silhouettes of other *mudaks* up and down the tunnels, hacking away at one another furiously.

He looked down to the wound in his side. His blood was rippling through his fingers and cascading onto the thick grime of the mine floor. He kept staring at it as the death cries echoed around him and the minutes slipped by, his mind numb, his thoughts adrift in a maelstrom of confusion – then a powerful explosion ripped through the air behind him.

The walls shook, and dust and rock shards rained down on him.

Three other explosions followed, knocking the lanterns off their mounts and plunging the already-dark tunnels of the mine into total darkness.

Everything went deathly silent for a brief moment – then came a cool breeze and an urgent, rushing sound.

A rush that turned into a roar.

Maxim stared into the darkness. He never saw the solid wall of water that plowed into him with the force of an anvil and whisked him away. But in those seconds of consciousness, in those last moments before the water overpowered his lungs and the force of the torrent slammed him against the tunnel wall, Maxim Nikolaev's final thoughts were of his boyhood and of how peaceful it would be to return to the river of his youth.

Standing by the detonator at the mouth of the tunnel, the man of science listened until all silence returned to the mountain. He was shaking visibly, though not from the cold. His companion, on the other hand, was unnaturally calm and serene. Which made the scientist shake even more.

They had made the long journey together, from the distant isolation of the Siberian monastery to this equally forsaken place. A journey that had started many years ago with the promise of great things, but that had since veered into savage, criminal territory. The man of science couldn't quite put his finger on how they'd reached this point of no return, how it had all degenerated into mass murder. And as he stared at his companion, he feared there would be more to come.

'What have we done?' he muttered, fearful even as the words snuck past his lips.

His companion turned to face him. For a man of such power and influence, a man who had become an intimate friend and confidant of the tsar and tsarina, he was unusually dressed. An old, greasy jacket, tattered around the cuffs. Baggy trousers that hung low at the back, like the *serouals* worn by the Turks. A farmer's oiled boots. Then there was the wild, tangled beard, and the greasy hair, parted down the middle like that of a tavern waiter. The scientist knew it was all artifice, of course, all part of a calculated look. A craftily honed image for a grand master plan, one in which the man of science had become an enabler and an accomplice. A costume designed to convey the humbleness and humility of a true man of God. An outfit so basic it also couldn't possibly detract from its wearer's hypnotic, gray-blue gaze.

The gaze of a demon.

'What have we done?' his companion replied in his odd, simple, almost primordial manner of speech. 'I'll tell you what we've done, my friend. You and me ... we've just ensured the salvation of our people.'

As always happened in the other's company, the man of science felt a numbing weakness overcome him. All he could do was stand there and nod. But as he began to digest what they had just done, a stifling darkness descended upon him and he wondered about what horrors lay ahead, horrors he would have never imagined possible back in that secluded monastery, where he'd first met the mysterious peasant. Where the man had brought him back from the edge, shown him the wonder of his gift, and talked to him about his wanderings among the hidden cloisters deep in the forests and the beliefs he had learned there. Where the mystic with the piercing eyes had first told him about the advent of 'true tsar,' a fair ruler, a redeemer of the people born of the common folk. A savior of Holy Rus.

For the briefest moment, the man of science wondered if he'd ever be able to extricate himself from his mentor's hold and avoid the madness that surely lay ahead. But as quickly as the thought had surfaced, it was gone, snuffed out before it could even begin to take shape.

He'd never seen anyone refuse anything of Grigory Efimovich Rasputin.

And he knew, with crippling certainty, that his will was far from strong enough for him to be the first.

1

Queens, New York City

PRESENT DAY

The vodka didn't taste like much, not anymore, and that last swig had scorched his throat like acid, but that didn't stop him from wanting more.

This was a bad day for Leo Sokolov.

A bad day coming close on the heels of many bad days.

He tore his eyes off the wall-mounted TV screen and gestured to the barman for a top-up, then returned his gaze to the live feed coming back from Moscow. Bitterness roiled inside him as the camera zoomed in on the coffin being lowered into the ground.

The last of us, he lamented in angry silence. *The last ... and the best. The last of the family I wiped out.*

The screen split to show another feed, this one coming from the city's Manezh Square, where thousands of protesters were angrily demonstrating under the walls and spires of the Kremlin. Under the very noses of those who had murdered that brave, noble – that magnificent man.

You can scream and shout all you like, he fumed inwardly. *What do they care? What they did to him they'll do again, and they'll keep doing it every time someone dares to speak out against them. They don't care how many they kill. To them, we're all just ...* he remembered the man's rousing words.

We're all just cattle.

A profound sadness seeped through him as the screen shifted to a close-up of the grieving widow, all in black, doing her best to appear dignified and defiant despite knowing, Sokolov was sure, that any lingering aspirations of protest would be relentlessly snuffed out of her.

Sokolov's fingers tightened against the glass.

Unlike other opposition leaders, the man they were burying hadn't been an egomaniac lusting for power, or a bored oligarch looking to add another trophy to his gilded life. Ilya Shislenko hadn't been a wistful Communist, a messianic environmentalist, or a raving leftist radical. He was just a concerned, ordinary citizen, a lawyer who was determined to try to make things right. If not right, then at least better. Driven to fight those in power, the ones he'd publicly branded as the party of liars and thieves – a label that was now firmly embedded in the psyches of those campaigning against the government. Committed to fight the rampant corruption and embezzlement, to get rid of those who'd stolen the country from the ones who'd enslaved it for decades, those who now ruled it with a gold-plated blade instead of an iron fist, those who'd pillaged its formidable wealth and stashed their billions in London and Zurich. Putting his life on the line to give his fellow countrymen some of the dignity and the freedom that many of their neighbors in Europe and elsewhere around the world enjoyed.

How proud Sokolov had felt when he first read about him. It had breathed new life into his weary, sixty-three-year-old lungs, seeing this charismatic young man fêted on the news channels, reading glowing profiles about him in the *New York Times*, listening to his rousing speeches on YouTube, watching as the protest marches he'd led grew and grew until the unheard-of started to happen, until tens of thousands of angry, fed-up Russians of all ages and means braved freezing temperatures and menacing riot police and started congregating in Bolotnaya Square and elsewhere in the capital to hear his words and shout out their agreement and express their having had enough of being treated like mindless serfs.

And if listening to his words wasn't exhilarating enough, if seeing those crowds back in the home country didn't make his heart thunder, what made it all the more rapturous was that this inspirational leader, this exceptional and courageous man, this savior of saviors, was none other than the son of Leo's own brother. His nephew, and apart from him, the last surviving member of his family.

The family that he had all but obliterated himself.

The screen cut back to footage of his nephew's last speech, footage that Sokolov suddenly found almost unbearable to watch. Looking at the young man's poised features and the irresistible energy he radiated, Sokolov couldn't help but imagine how that would have changed after he'd been arrested, couldn't block out the horrors that he knew had befallen the man. As he had so many times since the news of his death had broken, he couldn't avoid picturing his nephew – that beautiful, shining beacon of a man – thrown in some dark hole at Lefortovo Prison, the bland, mustard-colored detention center close to the center of Moscow where enemies of the state had been incarcerated since the days of the tsars. He knew all about its sordid past, about how dissidents held there were force-fed through their nostrils to get them to be more compliant. He knew about its dungeons and its 'psychological cells,' the ones with the black walls, the solitary twenty-five-watt bulb switched on 24/7 and the constant, maddening vibration that roared in from the neighboring hydrodynamics institute with such vigor that you couldn't even set a cup on a table without it skittering off. He also knew about its monstrous meat grinder, the one they used to pulp the bodies of its victims before they were sluiced into the city's sewers. Alexander Solzhenitsyn had been imprisoned there, as had another Alexander, the ex-KGB agent Litvinenko, who'd been given a chain-smoking informer for a cell-mate during his incarceration there – a thoughtful little gift from his former employers, given how much he couldn't stand cigarettes – before being murdered by way of polonium-laced tea after running off to London following his release.

The death of Sokolov's nephew hadn't been anywhere near as sophisticated. But, Sokolov knew, it was undoubtedly far more painful.

Undoubtedly.

He shut his eyes in a futile attempt to block out the wrenching images of what he knew they would have done to him in there, but the images kept coming. He knew what these men were capable of; he knew it well and fully and in all of its gory, inhuman detail, and he knew they wouldn't have spared his nephew any of it, not when a decision had been taken high up, not when they needed to get rid of a major thorn in their side, not when they wanted to set an example.

The screen shifted to another point of view, this one coming from somewhere much closer to the rundown Astoria bar Sokolov was slouched in. It showed a protest demonstration that was currently under way in Manhattan, outside the Russian consulate. Hundreds of demonstrators, waving signs, shaking fists, attaching bouquets of flowers and tributes to the gates of adjacent buildings – the whole scene watched over by New York's finest and a small army of news crews.

The screen then cut away to show other, similar, demonstrations taking place outside Russian embassies and consulates around the world before returning to the one in Manhattan.

Sokolov stared at the screen with deadened eyes. Within moments, he'd paid his tab and staggered out of the bar, vaguely aware of where he was, but dead certain about where he needed to be.

Somehow, he managed to make it from Queens to Manhattan and all the way to East Ninety-First Street and the big, noisy throng that pressed against the police barricades. His chest heaved with anger, fueled by the intense passion on display all around him, and he joined in, making his way deeper into the crowd, pumping his fist in the air as he took up the familiar resounding choruses of '*Izhetsy, ubiitsy*' (Liars, murderers) and '*Pozor*' (Shame on you).

Before long, he was at the front of the crowd, right up against the barricade that protected the consulate's gates. The chants had grown louder, the fists pumping the air more vigorously. The whole effect, combined with the alcohol swirling through his veins, turned almost hallucinogenic. His mind wandered in all kinds of directions before quickly settling onto a very satisfying image, a revenge fantasy that spread across him like wildfire. It warmed him up from within and he found himself nursing it and allowing it to grow until it consumed him like a raging inferno.

Through tired, foggy eyes he noticed a couple of men by the consulate's entrance. They were eyeing the crowd and conferred briefly before retreating behind closed doors.

Sokolov couldn't help himself.

'That's right! You run and you hide, you godless swine,' he hollered after them. 'Your time's running out, you hear me? Your time's running out, all of you, and you're going to pay. You're going to pay dearly.' Tears were streaming down his cheeks as he slammed his fist repeatedly against the barricade. 'You think you've heard the last of us? You think you've heard the last of the Shislenkos? Well, think again, you bastards. We're going to bring you down. We're going to wipe you out, every single last one of you.'

He spent the next hour or so there, screaming his tired lungs out and shaking his weak, tired fists. Eventually, his energy drained and he slunk away, his head bowed. He managed to make it back to the subway and then to his apartment in Astoria, where his doting wife, Daphne, was waiting for him.

What he didn't realize, of course, what he wasn't conscious of even though he should have known better and would have known better had it not been for those four last shots of vodka, was that they were watching. They were watching and they were listening, as they always were, especially at times like these, at gatherings like these where crowds of undesirables could be taped and analyzed and catalogued and added to all kinds of sinister lists. CCTV cameras mounted on the walls and roof of the consulate had been rolling and powerful directional mikes had been recording and, even worse, undercover agents of the Federation had been roaming the crowd, mimicking the protesters and their angry shouts and fists all while studying the faces around them and picking out those who merited a closer look.

Sokolov didn't know any of that, but he should have.

Three days later, they came for him.

2

I know they're called spooks, but this guy was starting to feel like a real ghost.

I'd been hunting him down for a couple of months already, ever since that day at Sequoia National Park, at Hank Corliss's cabin. The day Corliss blew his brains out shortly after telling me who he'd reached out to in the matter of getting my son Alex brainwashed.

My four-year-old son.

Takes a particularly vile specimen of humanity to do something like that. Corliss was damaged, I'll give him that. He was a living, breathing wreck of a human being. He'd been through a tragic, devastating nightmare while running the DEA's operations in Southern California and Mexico around five years ago. I was there at the time, part of a joint FBI-DEA task force. We'd been chasing Raoul Navarro, a barbaric Mexican drug baron known as El Brujo – 'the sorcerer' – and it had all gone pear-shaped. What went down had damaged me too, but what they did to Corliss that night – that was beyond barbaric.

Using my son, heinous as it was, came out of a twisted obsession Corliss had for revenge. They'd made him watch his daughter die before riddling him with bullets. It was a miracle he'd survived. Maybe the need to avenge his daughter had kept him alive. And thinking about it now, I wonder if I wouldn't have done what he did. If it had happened to me, maybe I would have been as obsessed as he was. I hope not, but who really knows? Reason and any kind of moral code can get easily pushed aside at times like that.

Regardless, Corliss paid the ultimate price for his misguided deeds, but the depraved sicko who'd actually handled the dirty work for him and messed with my son's mind – a CIA agent by the name of Reed Corrigan – was still out there. Even by spook standards, this Corrigan had to be seriously depraved. And as a badged federal agent, it was my sworn duty to make sure his depravity never darkened anyone else's life. Preferably by choking the life out of him with my bare hands. Slowly.

Not bureau standard operating procedure, by the way.

Problem was, I couldn't find the bastard. And the fact that my previous boss, Tom Janssen, was not the guy sitting here in his old office on the twenty-sixth floor of Federal Plaza and facing me from behind that big desk wasn't helping either.

Janssen I could count on.

This guy – the new assistant director in charge of the FBI's New York field office, Ron Gallo – well, let's just say that in his case, the ADIC acronym that came with the job was a really nice fit.

'You need to drop this, Reilly,' my new boss was insisting. 'Let it go. Move on.'

'"Move on?"' I shot back. 'After what they did?' I managed to avoid spewing out what I really wanted to say and, instead, settled for: 'Would you?'

Gallo took in a stiff breath, then gave me an even more exasperated stare as he let it seep back out, slowly. 'Let it go. You got Navarro. Corliss is dead. Case closed. You're just wasting your time – and ours. If the Agency doesn't want one of their own to be found, you're not going to find him. Besides, even if you did – what then? Without Corliss around to back you up, how are you gonna prove his involvement?'

He gave me his signature deadpan, patronizing look, and much as I hated to admit it, the ADIC had a point. I didn't have much to press my case. Sure, Corliss had told me he'd reached out to Corrigan to get it done. But Corliss was indeed dead. Which meant that even if I ever did manage to break through the CIA's impenetrable *omertà* and actually get my hands on the spectral Mr. Corrigan, in strictly legal terms, it would be my word against his.

'Get back to work,' he ordered me. 'The kind we pay you for. It's not like you don't have enough on your plate, is it?'

I tapped his desk hard with two fingers. 'I'm not dropping this.'

He shrugged back. 'Suit yourself – long as it's on your own dime.'

Like I said re: the custom-tailored acronym.

I left his office in a funk and, given that it was almost eleven and I hadn't yet had breakfast, I decided it would be a good time to get some fresh air and smother my frustrations in a sandwich and a coffee from my favorite four-wheeled restaurant. It was a crisp October morning in lower Manhattan, with a clear sky and a brisk little breeze whistling in through the concrete canyons all around me. Within ten minutes, I was sitting on a bench outside City Hall with a bacon-and-fontina omelet roll in one hand, a steaming cup in the other, and a whole lot of unanswered questions on my mind.

To tell you the truth, I wasn't really worried about the legalities involved. I had to find him first, him and the shrink or shrinks who'd messed with Alex's mind. It wasn't just out of my need for justice and, yes, revenge. It was for Alex's sake.

As we'd done earlier this morning, Tess and I had been taking Alex to see a child psychologist once a week since we all got back from California. The shrink, Stacey Ross, was good. She'd helped Tess with Kim, Tess's daughter, who'd been through a traumatic time a few years back, when she was around ten. They'd been caught up in the middle of a blood-soaked shootout at the Met. A cop outside the museum had had his head chopped off by a sword. It was there that I'd first met Tess, that same night, soon after the carnage. Stacey had worked wonders on Kim. We needed more of those wonders now, but Stacey needed to know what they'd done to Alex in order to figure out how to undo it properly. She knew everything we knew – I hadn't kept anything from her – but it wasn't much. Alex was improving under her care, which was heartening. But the nightmares and the nervousness were still around. Worse, I felt some of the awful stuff they'd planted in his brain about me – like making him believe he had a cold-blooded killer for a dad, and that wasn't even the worst part – was still lurking around in there. I could sometimes see it in his eyes when he looked at me. A hesitation, an unease. A fear. My own kid, the son I never knew I had, the son I was overjoyed to discover a few short months ago, looking at me like that, even for a second, when I would happily die for him.

It just obliterated me, every time.

I had to find these guys and get them to tell me exactly what they'd done to him and how best to flush it out of him. But it wasn't going to be easy, not without the support of a bureau heavy-hitter wielding a big, heavy bat. None of the monster databases I had fed Corrigan's name into – the public, commercial, criminal, or governmental ones – had given up a hit that fit the profile of the kind of creep I was after. Not that there were that many Reed Corrigans out there, anyway, but the few the system did cough up were relatively easy to check out and dismiss. All, that is, but one. A certain Reed Corrigan was one of three directors of a corporation called Devon Holdings. The company had a PO-box address in Middletown, Delaware, and little else on record. It had, though, leased a couple of Beechcraft King Airs, as well as a small Learjet, back in the early 1990s. When I took a closer look at Devon, it quickly became clear that the two other officers listed with Corrigan were also ghosts, shabbily crafted ones at that – their social-security numbers were registered in 1989, kind of unusually late in life for guys who were company directors two years later. Devon was a sham paper company that, upon further investigation, led me back to – *quelle surprise* – the CIA.

Peeling back the layers of such dummy corporations wasn't too complicated. We used them a lot, as did other agencies, including the CIA. They were handy for establishing cover personas for agents and, beyond that, for all kinds of covert activities, like chartering and leasing planes for rendition flights of terrorist suspects or ferrying agents quietly across borders, which is what I suspected might have been going on here. Reed Corrigan was the fake identity my ghost agent had been using while working on whatever the Devon assignment involved, and it was an identity that he had evidently long-ago discarded, which was standard practice once the assignment was completed or terminated.

No name. No face.

A ghost.

This didn't come as a huge surprise to me. Corliss had only muttered the name grudgingly, and it was suddenly clear to me that he had been a pro right to the bitter end by not giving up his buddy's real name. He had no reason to sink him, not when the guy had come through for him. And while the fake name gave me a bone to chew on, it also gave my ghost something far meatier: advance warning that I was coming after him. Somewhere, on some server in some basement at Langley, a flag would have inevitably come up as soon as I started digging into the Corrigan persona, and he'd have been alerted about that – and about me. Which meant it was safe to assume he already knew I was gunning for him, while I didn't know the first thing about him.

Kudos to Hank Corliss for the posthumous flip-off.

It had all got me wondering about how Hank Corliss knew Corrigan's fake name, and how he managed to dredge it up under pressure, when I'd confronted him at his cabin. He had to be real familiar with it. Then I wondered if maybe it was the only name by which he knew him. It had to be one of two scenarios: either he only knew him as Reed Corrigan, which meant that they'd met under shady circumstances while my ghost was using his cover identity and didn't feel a need to share his real identity with Corliss; or – and this seemed more likely to me, given that Corliss had reached out to Corrigan for help with his dastardly, off-the-books deed – he knew his real name, but they'd both been part of some assignment, some task-force bonding experience where my ghost had been using the name Corrigan.

Either way, I needed help accessing the CIA's operations records, and that's not something they share with outsiders, not unless there's a congressional hearing involved, and even then, I wouldn't bank on it. I had to find a way into their files, and I didn't have much in terms of where to start looking, not beyond the Devon link and the other thing Corliss had mentioned: that Corrigan had been involved with MK-ULTRA 'back in the day,' as he'd put it. I knew a bit about that program already, of course – we all did. But after Mexico, I knew a hell of a lot more about it, and what I discovered pissed me off even more.

MK-ULTRA was the code name of a secret, and highly illegal, CIA program that started in the early 1950s. It was all about mind control. The thinking was, the commies were doing it to our POWs, *Manchurian Candidate*-style, so we should be doing it too. Thing is, we didn't have a lot of Soviet or Chinese POWs locked up anywhere close to Langley, so the fine, upstanding scientists at the agency's Office of Scientific Intelligence decided they'd experiment on the next best thing: American and Canadian volunteers. Except that these folks didn't volunteer. They were just civilians and soldiers, a bunch of unsuspecting government employees, mentally ill patients, and hapless grunts – with a few hookers and johns thrown in – who had no idea about what was really being done to them.

In some cases, the doctors and nurses who were administering the treatments didn't know who they were really working for. The few we have on record claim they were told that the sleep manipulation, sensory deprivation, drugs, electroshocks, lobotomies, brain implants, and other experimental therapies that were taking place in rooms with cuddly names like 'the grid box' and 'the zombie room' would help their test subjects get better.

Several of those unwitting patients ended up committing suicide.

I'm guessing the pillars of the medical community who ran these experiments must have skipped class the day the Hippocratic Oath was being explained. Or maybe they were too starstruck with the Nazi scientists we'd recruited after the war to kick-start the whole program to ask too many questions.

The enemy of my enemy – maybe that was one way they justified it to themselves. But whatever. It's all history. At least, I thought it was. Until I realized a lot of these guys were still around, for the simple reason that none of them had ever been arrested for what they'd done.

Not one.

And there were a lot of them.

MK-ULTRA involved more than a hundred and fifty covert programs that were run in dozens of universities and other institutions across the country. And if that wasn't enough of a murky swamp for me to be trawling in, what complicated things even more was that all the MK-ULTRA files were destroyed a long time ago, long before digital trails and WikiLeaks made it pretty hard to permanently erase anything. Back in 1973, when CIA director Richard Helms ordered all those files destroyed, it was actually possible to do that. A stash of files did manage to survive, though – for the banal reason that they had been filed in the wrong place. They'd been recently declassified, and I'd spent a lot of time going through them. None of them, though, made any mention of my elusive scumbag.

And speaking of scumbags, it was looking more and more like Gallo's order for me to lay off wouldn't be too hard to follow, given that I was running out of veins to tap. Short of breaking into the CIA's server room and hacking into their database while hanging from the ceiling in a sleek black cat suit à la Tom Cruise, there was only one other route I could think of, but it wasn't a wise one to follow, not by any stretch. If you wanted to be a real nitpicker, you could also point out that it was highly illegal. It was an idea that had come to me one night a couple of weeks earlier, late, fueled by a few beers, in a moment when I was consumed by an anger that I couldn't shake off easily, the one that bubbled up whenever I thought about what they'd done.

Staring into the park and the steady flow of civilians wandering through their mundane and safe days, I suddenly found myself contemplating it again, wondering if I really had any choice in the matter, wondering if I already knew I'd be doing it and, perversely, starting to find some enjoyment in imagining how it would play out and what I would get out of it. And that was when my phone buzzed and snapped me out of my cunning, if highly ill-advised, scheming.

My guardian angel turned out to be my partner Nick Aparo, wondering where I was and telling me we had our marching orders. We were to drive out to Queens, pronto. Someone had taken a bungee jump out of a sixth-story window in Astoria. Without bothering with a bungee cord.

I tossed my wrapper into a garbage can and headed back to the office.

I could use the distraction.

3

'So how'd it go with Gallo?'

Aparo was behind the wheel. We were in his white Dodge Charger, lights strobing and siren wailing, rushing up the FDR on our way to the Midtown Tunnel.

'He's a prince,' I said, just staring ahead.

Aparo shrugged. 'Seriously, Sean ... how long are you going to keep this up?'

'Really?' I snapped back. 'You too?'

'Hey, come on, buddy,' he protested. 'You know I'm with you on this. All the way. But you've got to admit, we've kind of run out of bullets on this one.'

'There's always a way.'

'Sure there is. It's like me and the thirty-six double-D's in my spinning class.'

'Hang on, you're doing spinning now?'

He tapped his belly. 'I'm down nine pounds in two weeks, amigo. The ladies no likee the blubber.'

Nothing like a fresh divorce to make a guy get back into shape. 'And you just discovered that?'

'My point was, this chick,' he continued, 'I'm sure she'd rather be kidnapped and sold off into slavery in Sudan than spend a night with me. But does that mean I'm going to give up trying? Of course not. There's always a way. But then again, we both know how low I'm willing to stoop and how much I'm ready to humiliate myself in my hopeless quest for booty. The question for you, my friend, is: how far are you willing to go to get it done?'

I was asking myself the very same thing.

We soon hit Astoria and our destination was, predictably, a bit of a zoo. Despite how blasé one would expect New Yorkers to be given everything the city's seen, a public death like that still managed to attract a standing-room-only crowd.

The scene in question was a six-story brick prewar building on a tree-lined cross-street just off Thirty-First. The area had been cordoned off, causing some traffic mayhem, with irate drivers honking their horns and hurling disappointingly unimaginative abuse at one another. Aparo managed to cut through the mess with the assistance of blips from his siren and some deft maneuvering before parking down the block. We made our way past a scattering of media vans and patrol cars and badged through the taped perimeter to get to the first point of interest, the spot where our victim had met his demise. It was on the sidewalk right outside the building, which had a delicately detailed façade that was zigzagged by fire escapes and further defaced by a scattering of air-conditioning units that dotted some of its windows.

The forensics people had put up a large tent over the body to safeguard any evidence from tampering – accidental or otherwise – weather damage, and, of course, to ensure privacy. Judging by the amount of people looking down from their windows, I imagined there'd be a lot of canvassing to do and cell-phone photo and video evidence to collect. Canvassing and collecting, because the preliminary info we'd already been given was that the first cops on the scene had quickly ascertained that the dead man had come through a closed window before plummeting down to the sidewalk.

Suicide jumpers tended to open the window first.

My other question – why we were being called out to a potential murder in Queens, when that's pretty much the local homicide squad's exact job description – was also easily answered. The victim was a diplomat.

A Russian diplomat.

As we approached, I looked up and saw a couple of guys leaning out a window on the top floor of the building, directly above the tent. They were probably the local investigators. It was a safe bet they wouldn't be too pleased to see us. Also, it looked like our victim had missed the trees on his way down, which didn't bode well for what shape his body would be in.

Aparo and I stopped at the tent door. There was a handful of forensic technicians busily taking pictures and collecting samples and doing all the geeky things they do. I asked for the coroner. He was still there, waiting for the green light to whisk the body away to his windowless lair, and stepped out of the geek scrum. As we hadn't met before, we introduced ourselves. His name was Lucas Harding and he had the same unnervingly casual demeanor all medical examiners seemed to have.

Harding invited us into his fiefdom. We slipped some paper booties over our shoes, donned the requisite rubber gloves, and followed him in.

It was not a pretty sight.

No body that flew down six stories onto a concrete sidewalk ever was.

I'd only ever seen one similar corpse in my day from a big fall like that, and although I've witnessed my fair share of blood and gore, it was a sight I'd never forgotten. The sheer fragility of our bodies is something most of us tend to ignore, but nothing brought that fragility rocketing into focus with such brutal clarity than seeing someone sprawled on the sidewalk like that.

Despite a skull that was so pulverized it looked like it had been made out of plasticine before some giant baby had squashed it out of shape, it was still clear that we were looking at a white male adult with dark, short hair, somewhere in his thirties and in good shape, at least before the fall. He was dressed in a dark blue suit that was perforated in a couple of places – below his left elbow, and by his right shoulder – by shattered bones that had ripped through the cloth. There was a big puddle of coagulated blood around his head, and another to the left of his body, where it followed the slight angle in the sidewalk before pooling in a big crack in the concrete. Most gruesome, however, was his jaw. It seemed to have taken a direct hit and had been wrenched out of place, and was hanging off to one side like an oversized helmet chin strap that had been flicked off.

There were also shards of broken glass around the body that we avoided stepping on.

Harding noticed me glancing at them.

'Yeah, the glass matches what the body's telling us,' the coroner offered. 'The arms are consistent with him extending them to try and break his fall. Pointless, of course, but instinctive. And it confirms he was alive and conscious when he fell. The position where he landed in relation to the edge of the building also fits the story. Suicide jumpers tend to just drop down. No one does it enthusiastically; it's not like they're leaping off a diving board. They usually just step off a ledge, and if that were the case, I'd have expected him to land a few feet closer to the base of the building than he did. This guy left the building with some momentum. If this sidewalk hadn't been as wide as it is, he'd have landed on someone's car.'

'Do we have a positive ID?' I asked.

Harding nodded. 'First responders got it off his wallet. Hang on, I have it here.' He flicked a page back on his notepad and found it. 'Name's Fyodor Yakovlev. It was confirmed by the rep from the Russian embassy who's around here somewhere.'

'Confirmed, as in he knew him?'

'*She* knew him,' Harding corrected.

'What was the time of death?' Aparo asked.

'Eight twenty, give or take a minute or two,' Harding said. 'He almost hit a couple of pedestrians. They were the first to call it in.'

I checked my watch and knew what Aparo was getting at. It was almost eleven. Our victim had died around two and a half hours ago. Which meant that if this was a murder – which seemed kind of obvious at the moment – it meant we were coming to the party late, which was not an ideal place to start.

I looked around, then asked what had become the key question in a situation like this. 'Did you find a cell phone on him? Or anywhere around?'

The coroner's face scrunched up curiously. 'No, at least, not on him. And no one's handed anything in.'

Not great. But there were ways for us to recover what he had on his phone, once we had the number. Assuming the Russians gave it to us, which was unlikely, given that he was a diplomat. 'We need to make sure the area's properly searched in case it fell out of him on the way down.'

'I'll get the guys to do another trawl.'

We finished up with the coroner, left the tent, and headed into the building.

As we walked into the lobby, I noticed that there was a voice intercom by the front door, but no security camera. The lobby area was tired, but clean. No CCTV cameras in there that I could see, though I didn't expect there to be any in that building. There was a grid of lockable mailboxes on the wall to our right, some with names and others with just apartment numbers on them. We were going up to 6E. It was one of the ones that didn't have a name on it.

We rode the rumbling elevator to the top floor and were greeted by a uniform as we stepped out. The landing had three apartments on it, with 6E being the one farthest to the left. I imagined the immediate neighbors would have already been interviewed, although given the time of day it had happened, some of them may have already been at work.

We stepped into the apartment. The place was dark and had a kind of faded grandeur to it. Like many of the better prewars, it had some charming, old-world features – thick hardwood floors, high ceilings, arched doorways, and elaborate crown moldings ... stuff you didn't get in newer buildings. Its décor – all dark wood and floral and lacy and cluttered with knickknacks – even its smell instantly conveyed a strong sense of history. Its occupants had obviously been living there for many years. A framed photo on a side table in the foyer fit the place's aura perfectly. It showed a smiling couple in their mid-sixties, posing in front of some great natural arch, the kind you find in national parks out west. The man in the picture, short and round-faced and with a thin tuft of white hair around his balding pate, was clearly not the dead man downstairs. On the wall above it hung a trio of antique religious icons, classical depictions of Mary and a baby Jesus painted on small slabs of cracked wood.

There was also a woman's magazine on the side table, where one would normally leave the mail. I noted the name on its subscription mailing label – Daphne Sokolov.

The foyer led to the living room, where three guys – two suits and a uniform – and a woman were standing and chatting by the shattered window that looked out on to the street. It was immediately obvious there'd been a tussle of some kind in the room, as attested to by the broken coffee table, shattered vase, and flowers strewn on the carpet by the window.

Quick intros informed us the suits were indeed the detectives from the 114th Precinct, Neal Giordano and Dick Adams. The uniform was an officer by the name of Andy Zombanakis, also from the 114th. The three of them looked put out, which was likely, given that they'd probably been told to wait there for us and hand over what they no doubt considered to be their investigation. They also looked annoyed, like Aparo and I had somehow intruded on their little get-together. That was even more understandable and likely due to the lady they were conversing with, who looked out of place until she introduced herself as Larisa Tchoumitcheva, there on behalf of the Russian consulate.

She was gorgeous. Almost my height in three-inch-heels, slim but with rolling curves that challenged the tailored navy blue skirt suit and white shirt she was in, and the wickedest combo of lips and blue eyes I'd ever seen, the lot topped by perfectly coiffed light auburn hair that fittingly veered more toward fiery red than stately brown. I flicked a glance at my newly single partner and could just visualize the wet 'n' wild clips that were unspooling in his lecherous mind. In this instance, it was hard to blame him. Any man would have had a hard time keeping them in check.

Ever the perfect gentleman, I told her, 'I'm sorry for your loss. Did you know him?'

'Not really,' she replied. 'I met him briefly at some official functions, but our duties didn't really intersect.'

She spoke with the barest hint of a Slavic accent. And as if she needed it, her voice only made her more attractive.

Focus.

'Who was he?'

'Fyodor Yakovlev. He was Third Secretary for Maritime Affairs at the consulate here.'

Maritime Affairs. I hadn't come across that one yet.

I asked her, 'And you? You said your duties didn't intersect.'

She fished a card out from an inside pocket of her jacket and handed it to me. I read the small letters under her name out loud. "Counselor for Public Affairs."

Well, at least it didn't say 'attaché.'

I left the words hanging there and looked up from the card. Our eyes met and I just gave her a small, knowing grin. She obviously read me and my suspicions, but didn't seem fazed by it at all. It was a dance I'd danced before with, among others, Chinese, French, and Israeli 'diplomats.' But most of all, it was the Russians who never stopped hogging that particular ballroom.

The one for spies.

4

Even with the Berlin Wall down and the Evil Empire a relic of the past, we were still playing the same old games.

Russia was no longer the USSR, the head honchos of the KGB and their organized-crime kingpin partners now owned the country outright instead of just controlling its people, and Communism was lying in some shallow grave while a wildly perverted version of capitalism was dancing the *kalinka* on it. But that didn't mean we were friends. Even though we no longer had any ideological differences, we still pretty much hated each other's guts, and we both spent a lot of time and resources snooping on each other.

We had spies over there, they had spies over here. Mostly, the ones the Russians shipped our way were pretty much of the classic kind: some would be here under 'official cover,' meaning they'd have some mundane job at their embassy or consulate, typically an attaché, secretary, or counselor; others, the more adventurous ones, would be here under 'non-official cover' – the ones we call 'NOCs' – meaning they didn't have a government job as cover and, as such, they didn't enjoy the associated diplomatic immunity if they were caught. And given the stiff penalties sometimes handed out on espionage charges – execution, for one – being a NOC was by far the more hazardous of the two.

Then there was the new breed of 'penetration agents,' like Anna Chapman and her bumbling crew of social butterflies who we nabbed and expelled a few years ago. The media had giggled at the notion of a glamorous redhead and her Facebook-addicted posse posing any kind of threat to our great nation. The truth was, a Russian spy in our midst was far more likely to have a degree from NYU, start out as an intern somewhere, have an affair with someone who had an important position in an area of interest to the Kremlin – finance, industry, politics, media, among others – and end up working in some target institution and sending back insider knowledge about that sector.

It was no longer about destroying each other militarily. It was now all about making money and getting the upper hand economically. And if a terrorist attack or a war in another country helped to distract, weaken and bankrupt us while messing us up as a society – all the better.

We had a dead third secretary downstairs and a counselor here to assist us in the investigation.

More old-school. But potentially nastier.

I turned and took in the rest of the room. There was a sofa, well used and floral patterned, and a couple of plain armchairs on either side. There was a big old TV set facing them, and massive bookshelves all along one of the side walls. The shelves were crammed with books and held what looked like a pretty elaborate stereo system, with two beefy speakers sitting on opposite ends of the top shelves. There was the broken coffee table I noticed earlier. And there was the large window that gave onto the street. Its glass was mostly gone, and the timber frame was cracked and splintered.

'So where are we with this?' I asked the three of them, pointing at the damage. 'What do we know? This wasn't Yakovlev's place, right?'

'No,' Giordano answered. He handed me another framed photo. It was of the same couple as the picture in the hallway, only this time they were on vacation somewhere sunny. 'You're looking at Leonid Sokolov and his wife, Daphne. They live here.'

'So where are they?'

'Well, they ain't here, are they?' Adams pitched in.

His tone wasn't particularly friendly. Not that I cared. But I didn't have much patience for juvenile sulking or for a jurisdictional pissing contest. I'd seen it played out in too many bad movies to ever want to suffer through it in real life.

Giordano stepped back in. 'Sokolov teaches science at Flushing High. He didn't show up at work this morning.'

'And his wife?'

'She's a nurse at Mount Sinai. She was on the night shift last night, came off work at seven.'

'No sign of her, either?' Aparo asked.

Giordano shook his head. 'Nope. We had a look around the place. Toothbrushes in the bathroom, bed's been slept in, reading glasses still on the night table. There's a couple of empty suitcases tucked away in the hall closet where you'd expect them. Doesn't look like they're on a trip. Also, the toaster's got a couple of slices of bread still in it.'

Which was curious. 'An unexpected visit? An interruption?' I asked.

He shrugged. 'Maybe.'

I nodded and, avoiding the debris on the carpet, I stepped over to the window. I looked down. The tent was directly below us. Then I looked across the street. It might have been helpful if there had been similar buildings across from where I was standing. Maybe someone there would have seen something. But there was only a single-story row of shops. Great open view for the Sokolovs and their neighbors. Not so great for us.

'Anyone hear or see anything useful? Neighbors, people out on the street?'

Zombanakis said, 'We've got uniforms and detectives out canvassing, but nothing so far.'

I turned to Larisa. 'So why was Yakovlev here? What was he doing?'

'I don't know. I spoke to the first secretary for Maritime Affairs – his direct boss. As far as he knows, Yakovlev had no official business here.'

'Did Yakovlev know the Sokolovs?'

'Not that we know of,' she replied. 'But we need to talk to people who knew him.'

'Was he married?' Aparo asked. 'Any next of kin we should be talking to?'

'He was single,' she replied. 'Any relatives he has are back in Russia.'

'Girlfriend?' Aparo pressed on. 'Boyfriend? Sponsor?'

My partner, the king of tact. I shot him a small glare, to which he responded with his trademark, faux-surprised 'What?' look.

Larisa didn't flinch. 'None that he's bragged about,' she told him flatly. 'Look, this only happened a couple of hours ago, and as you can imagine, everyone at the consulate is pretty shaken up about it. We'll get some answers soon enough. Believe me, we want to know what happened here as much as you do.'

I nodded and glanced at the framed picture again. Leo and Daphne Sokolov. A sweet and harmless-looking older couple. On the face of it, the kind of folks we'd all like to have as neighbors. Only there was obviously more to them than that. That much was clear. But I doubted there was any point in pressing Larisa on it. If she knew anything more about them, she wasn't about to share.

Still, for the record, I asked, 'What about the Sokolovs? Anything else we should know about them? Any kids?' I hadn't seen any telltale pictures of kids and grandkids.

'Doesn't look like it, but we're not sure,' Giordano said.

I asked Larisa, 'Are they on your radar for any reason?'

'No. But then again, I wouldn't expect them to be. As you well know, there are hundreds of thousands of Russians in this city. We have no reason to keep tabs on them any more than you do. They only come to us if there's some kind of problem.'

'Which the Sokolovs never had – until this morning.'

She shrugged and nodded in agreement. 'So it seems.'

'Would anyone want to harm them?' I asked.

She looked at me curiously. 'What are you thinking?'

'Well, could be there was a confrontation and one of the Sokolovs ended up pushing Yakovlev through the window. But Yakovlev seemed like someone who was in pretty good shape and I'm finding it hard to imagine Leo or Daphne Sokolov getting the upper hand on him physically like that.'

'Unless Leo – or Daphne, for that matter – unless one of them had a black belt we don't know about,' Aparo threw in helpfully.

'Sure, there's always that possibility,' I granted him without too much sarcasm in my tone.

'Or they could have drugged him,' he added.

'Your coroner will look into things like that, won't he?' Larisa asked.

'Yes, we'll get a full tox report on the victim. But maybe the Sokolovs weren't behind this. Maybe they were in some kind of trouble and they turned to Yakovlev for help. Maybe they were friends and he showed up here at the wrong time and interrupted something and got shoved out the window for it.' He turned to the detectives. 'Either way, Yakovlev shows up here, there's some kind of a fight, he ends up taking a dive out the window, and the Sokolovs are gone. The key is to find the Sokolovs. That sound about right to everyone?'

'Hey, you guys are the pros,' Adams said sourly. 'We're just here to do the legwork.'

I let it slide and asked, 'You got a BOLO out on them?'

It sounded weird to say it. Not the word. The idea. To have an all-points bulletin out for a couple of sixtysomethings who seemed like your quintessentially harmless citizens felt odd. But the more I thought about it, the more it seemed to me like they might be in trouble. We needed to find them.

Adams, meanwhile, had feigned a deeply concentrated look, like he was racking his brain about it, before his face lit up in a eureka moment. 'Damn, why didn't we think of that?' He turned to his partner and pointed in our direction. 'Listen and learn, buddy. These feds, they're just magic. Listen and learn.'

He was obviously aching for me to give him an excuse to escalate things, and judging by the uncomfortable face his partner pulled, it wasn't a first. But I didn't feel like getting baited. Aparo was off to one side checking out the shelves and he turned too, but I shot him a look to make sure he kept his cool.

'All right,' I said. 'Until we find the Sokolovs, we've got a lot of questions that need answering. Let's start at the beginning. How did Yakovlev get here? Did he drive, did he take a bus or the subway or a cab? Did anyone see him arrive? Was he alone?' I looked pointedly at the detectives. They stayed mum. 'Was anyone else here already,' I pressed on, 'and if so, how did they get in? Also, what happened to Yakovlev's cell phone? You didn't find one here, did you?'

Adams shook his head.

''Cause there's no sign of it downstairs,' I continued, 'and he had to have one, right? And who else was here? Clearly, someone was. Was it the Sokolovs? Someone else? Either way, how did they leave? Is there a back entrance to the building, a service entrance? Did anyone see them leave? Do they have any cars and if so, where are they?' I let the barrage of questions hang there for a moment. 'So there's a whole bunch of legwork that needs to be done here,' I then added, eyeing Adams as I said it, 'and you can either lose the attitude and make yourself a couple of friends at Federal Plaza which could come in handy someday, or you can stop wasting our time and get your ass out of here and let us do our job. Your call. But make your play, here and now.'

Giordano glanced at Adams and said, 'We're cool here. And we're glad to help. As long as you keep us informed on what you find. It's gotta be a two-way street.'

'Sure thing.'

'And we'd like to share the collar,' he added.

'Not a problem. Though if we end up following this thing halfway across the planet, it might not work out that way.'

Aparo chuckled. 'These things do have a habit of turning out that way with him,' he said, referring to me.

I glanced at Adams. Giordano gave him a look.

He frowned, then nodded grudgingly. 'Sure. Whatever.'

Aparo cut the tension by remarking, 'Hey, was this open like that when you came in here?'

We all turned to see what he was talking about.

He was pointing at the stereo. I stepped over for a closer look.

The stereo was a stack of black, clunky, old-style components – amp, tuner, cassette player, and CD player. The cassette player had two decks in it, but it was the CD player that had caught Aparo's eye. It was one of those five-CD changers that stored the discs not in a stack, but on a tray the size of a twelve-inch vinyl album that slid out when you hit the Eject button, allowing you to place the five CDs in their respective slots around its rotating platter. The tray was in its out position. I took a closer look. It had four CDs still in it. The slot farthest out – the one that would start playing if you hit the Play button and it had a CD in it – was empty.

Which was curious, sure. But whether it actually meant something was doubtful.

Aparo was studying the names on the CDs with a smirk on his face. 'Whoa. Get a load of the opera and classical stuff they've got in here. And given the size of those speakers . . . the neighbors must love them.'

We all looked at him blankly.

He shrank back. 'I'm just saying.'

'What about the media?' Giordano asked. 'They're waiting for something from us.'

I thought about it for a moment, then handed Giordano the framed photo. 'Let's put it out. Say we need to talk to the Sokolovs, it was their apartment, but they weren't here when the tragedy happened. Choose your words and your tone carefully and make sure you don't paint them as suspects, that needs to be clear. Maybe we'll get lucky and someone will call in.'

Giordano nodded. 'I'll take care of it.'

I took in the room again.

A Russian diplomat had been pushed out a window after some kind of fight, and an older couple was missing.

Not exactly worthy of raising the threat alert level to orange. Or even beige, for that matter.

I had to admit I wasn't too excited about dealing with it. It was, well, a murder investigation, and as such, it was probably better left to the local homicide detectives, at least to start with. Even a jackass like Adams could probably put it to bed effectively. The only reason Aparo and I were there was because of the kind of passport the dead guy carried. And we had bigger fish to fry – not to mention the spook I was hunting. Still, there was no ducking the assignment. Besides, somewhere at the back of my skull, an irrepressible little voice was telling me that the Sokolovs needed our help. And after all these years, I knew better than to ignore that nag.

We needed to find them. And fast.

5

Dare County, North Carolina

The call came in as Gordon Roos was on his way back from his late-morning walk on the beach. He loved it out in the Outer Banks. The constant breeze coming in off the ocean, the salty taste in the air that did wonders for his sinuses, the Zenlike openness of the landscape – it was far more enjoyable than the confines of the Falls Church, Virginia, penthouse he used to live in before his retirement from the Company. A bit removed from the action, perhaps, but still close enough for him to be able to jump in when something juicy came up.

Something like this.

He checked the caller ID on his 1024-bit RSA key-encrypted cell phone, even though he knew who it was before he looked at it. Hardly anyone had that number, for besides being a retired agent of the CIA, Gordon Roos wasn't a social animal, not by any stretch. A couple of tried and tested high-class escorts were more than enough to liven up his nights when he needed company. Which was not unusual at all for someone who'd spent most of life running dangerous undercover assignments for his country. Not that he minded. Gordon Roos had never had much patience for small talk and cocktail parties, something his wife eventually decided she couldn't live without.

He took the call in his customary fashion, without uttering a word.

His caller knew the drill.

'Our Russian friends just heard from two goons babysitting Sokolov's wife,' the man said. 'One of them was waiting for their guy outside the apartment and saw him take the dive. He drove off in a panic and they called it in.'

Roos kept walking at the same leisurely pace. 'Where are they now?'

'They're babysitting her at some dive. A motel in Queens, near JFK. Russian-owned. The guys at the embassy are waiting to hear back from Moscow on how to handle it now that Sokolov's in the wind.' He paused, then added, 'Maybe it's time we move in and take her off their hands. It would give us leverage over Sokolov.'

Roos processed the suggestion in all of four seconds. 'No. Let's keep her there and let it play out. Sokolov seems to have some of that old pluck left in him. If she's there, there's a good chance it'll draw him in. Even if he doesn't find his way to the motel, she's the bait that'll flush him out. Better we don't rock the boat and spook him. We just need to be ready to swoop in when he shows up.'

'All right. I'll put a team on it.'

'Off the books, of course.'

'Of course.'

'Good. Keep me apprised. Day or night.'

'You got it, buddy.'

Roos hung up.

As he walked on toward his house, which appeared behind a wind-swept sandbank up ahead, his mind drifted back many years, to when it had all begun. To the initial, unexpected approach from the Russian. The excitement at the prospect. The meticulous planning. The green light. The adrenaline of putting the lift in motion.

The thrill of meeting the Russian for the first time.

Then came the little prick's stab in the back.

The damn Russian. He'd been a major snag in Roos's stellar rise at the agency. More than a snag. He'd almost derailed his career altogether. But Roos had overcome the defeat and the humiliation. He'd cleaned things up, he'd redeemed himself by shepherding other tough projects to success – and here they were again, more than thirty years later, playing the game again.

He smiled inwardly at the prospect of what the days ahead would bring. Maybe it would all finally come good, after all those years. He had far more options now that he was out on his own. 'Independent contractor.' It was the wave of the future, and a future with much greater promise than he'd ever counted on had suddenly dropped into his lap.

Sokolov could be a mighty prize indeed. The kind of prize that could bankroll a much more satisfying level of retirement. And he sure as hell wasn't going to let that prize get away from him a second time.

6

London, England

At about the same time, four thousand miles east of there, another man received a similar call informing him of similar developments, only this call originated a couple of thousand miles farther east from his own location.

From Moscow.

From the Center, to be exact.

The Center being a sprawling, cross-shaped concrete structure nestled in the middle of a large forest just southwest of the city.

The Center was also the headquarters of the SVR, the successor of the KGB's notorious First Chief Directorate. Officially tasked with foreign intelligence gathering and counterintelligence. Unofficially tasked with anything else that was deemed necessary to safeguard the Motherland's interests.

Anything.

And when a particularly tricky anything came up, the odds were it would be assigned to someone from its highly secretive Zaslon unit – the word meant 'the shield,' and not in its badge sense – an elite team drawn from the Spetsnaz special forces, whose members excelled in their physical and military prowess as well as their talents at deception.

And when the Zaslon unit was handed a particularly sensitive task, the odds were it would be assigned to Valentin Budanov.

Not many people knew that. For the simple reason that not many people knew Budanov even existed. They didn't need to. Budanov worked alone.

He worked in the shadows, only emerging when he needed a critical piece of information or some operational support from someone – usually a senior embassy staffer or a fellow SVR agent – who would have been ordered to provide him with anything he required. And when he did emerge, it was, of course, never as Budanov. Like other SVR agents, he traveled under a number of false identities. He also spoke many languages flawlessly – seven at last count – and could easily disguise himself so he would pass unnoticed. And on the rare occasions when he did break his deep cover, it was never as Budanov or as whatever ID he was using at the time.

It was as Koschey, a code name that inspired a deep-seated fear in those who heard it. A code name drawn from an old Slavic folk tale.

Koschey the deathless.

Just then, Koschey was in London. He'd spent a lot of time in the British capital in the last decade. London was where a lot of the Kremlin's enemies came to find a safe haven. It was also where a lot of its big hitters and their friends stashed their ill-gotten gains – billions that they parked safely in hedge funds, fabulous properties, and high-profile investments. The thinking was that, besides being a great place to live and to party, London provided a secure and stable hideaway for their fortunes. There, they would be unreachable by those running things back home if and when their old friendships turned sour.

But no one was unreachable. Not in London. Not anywhere. And certainly not with someone like Koschey on tap to reach them.

He'd been in London for six days, preparing to take out a GCHQ analyst who'd been recruited by Moscow eleven years earlier and who the SVR suspected had been rumbled by the British intelligence services. Then the call had come in on his encrypted cell phone.

The general told him he was to drop that assignment and fly to New York.

A file, also encrypted, had been attached to an e-mail and left in the drafts folder of a Gmail address that had been created specifically for that single task.

A file that Koschey retrieved and read immediately after terminating the call.

A file that Koschey found astounding.

The analyst had caught a lucky break. He would get to live a little while longer.

Koschey had a plane to catch.

7

The rest of the day didn't bring about any great revelations. We were covering all the bases on the Yakovlev case, but so far, we didn't have much to show for it.

Visits to the school where Sokolov taught and to the hospital where his wife worked didn't give us any leads. In the case of the former, he hadn't shown up for work, which we already knew. The principal said he'd ask around to see if anyone had noticed anything unusual in Sokolov's behavior of late, but as far as he knew, the Russian had been just as he always was: dedicated, pleasant, loved by his students, an all-round nice guy. Sokolov didn't seem to have any family that needed notifying or that we could interview. Daphne Sokolov, on the other hand, had a sister, Rena. By the time we got to Delphi Opticians, her store over on Steinway, she'd already heard the news and was, to put it mildly, concerned. Rena's maiden name, which she'd reverted to since her divorce, was Karakatsani, and her Greek blood was on full display.

Aparo and I calmed her down as much as we could, telling her there had been no evidence of foul play – a small lie, I know – and assuring her that all efforts were being made to find the Sokolovs and make sure they were safe. She eventually did calm down, and I finally got to the questions I needed to ask.

'Tell me, Rena. Your sister and Leo … is everything okay in their lives?'

'Yes, of course,' she said in her throaty, full-bodied voice. 'Daphne and Leo – they've always been drama-free, you know? They're like a fairy tale. He loves her to death and she's the same. They're like teenagers, which is weird, especially in this day and age.' She shrugged sweetly. 'Lucky them, right?'

'They've been together a long time?'

She rolled her eyes. 'Forever.'

'How long?'

Rena thought about it. 'Let's see. They got married in' – she ransacked her mind – 'eighty-three, I think it was. Leo was new to the city, he hadn't been here that long. Maybe a year or two. His English wasn't too good, and when she first introduced him to us, we were like, "Seriously? This guy?" I mean, he was a nice guy, but he was bussing tables in an Egyptian restaurant down on Atlantic Avenue. My parents, God rest their souls, they had bigger ambitions for their daughter. I did too. I was dating this E. F. Hutton guy at the time – don't get me started on him. And Leo ... lousy job, no prospects, and a drinking problem too. And boy, did he drink. Russian-style. He had a serious problem. But not violent, you know? No temper. He was just miserable, that much was clear. Sad, deep inside. But that didn't excuse the fact that he was still a drunk. And Daphne knew it. But she saw something in him, and she said, "Yeah, him. He's the one. He's a good man. You'll see." And you know what? She was right.' She paused, then her eyes darkened. 'Where are they? What's going on? What are you not telling me?'

'We don't know anything, we're just trying to figure out where they might be,' I replied truthfully. 'But go back a second to Leo. So he was bussing tables? How'd he get from that to teaching science at Flushing High?'

'I'm not sure. I just remember thinking he was clearly smart, from day one. Even with the booze, you could see it. Too smart to be bussing tables. That was obvious. But his English wasn't great, and he kind of kept to himself. Then Daphne got him off the bottle and they got married, and not long after that, I remember he was let go by the restaurant. Something about a cousin of the owner needing a job. So he got a job as a janitor at the high school. And we were like, yikes, you know? But then somehow, he started giving private lessons, here and there, bringing in some extra cash. God knows how he got that going. And through word of mouth, he got more and more work, and he got his teaching qualifications and ended up with the full-time teaching job, and that's pretty much how it's been ever since.'

I could see the *Good Will Hunting* wisecrack germinating inside Aparo's head, and headed it off with a follow-up question.

'And no big arguments, nothing going on that caused you any concern? Nothing that could lead to them leaving home all of a sudden like this?'

Rena's face crumpled with concentration. 'Not really. I mean, I always thought it was a bit weird that we never met anyone from Leo's family. He never talked about them. Daphne said any family he had were all back in Russia and it wasn't as easy back then, it's not like they had e-mail and Skype, right? But he was a quiet guy anyway. A loner, really. Which Daphne didn't mind. In our family, she was the quiet one too.' She softened, and a bittersweet smile warmed her face. 'She was his life.'

I nodded and wondered about the Sokolovs again. I didn't think Rena was hiding anything from me, which meant that whatever it was they'd gotten themselves into, they hadn't shared it with her. It was time to move on and dig elsewhere.

Then she said something that resonated with me.

'Maybe the one thing that did give them some hard times was when they were trying to have a kid and it wasn't working – they were shattered when they found out they couldn't. But with time, that sadness went away. Leo's students kinda took their place.'

I just nodded and said nothing. Tess and I had been through that. We'd been through that grinder, and I knew full well how brutal it could be. We had ended up facing that same disappointment, and it had almost torn us apart, only in the last few months, we'd been lucky to have my little Alex surface unexpectedly and fill part of that void. I understood what the Sokolovs must have gone through, and it explained the lack of kids' photos in their apartment.

'That's all I can think of, really,' she added. 'That, and a bad day for the Yankees. You don't want to be around Leo when they lose.' She smiled again, but it didn't really disguise the worry in her eyes. 'I know what you're thinking. Money problems, God knows we all have them these days. Gambling, maybe. The kind of stuff you guys must come across a lot. But there's none of that. Not with Leo. He's a sweet man and stand-up guy. Big on values, you know? Lives in a dream world. Like with Russia. He loves his homeland. We all do, right? But seeing it like that, even from this distance and after all these years. All that promise after the Wall came down and how it got all screwed up instead, all these gangsters running around, robbing the place blind ... that made him sad. The rigged elections ... he cared, you know? Like when that activist was killed last week, you know the one I mean?'

'Ilya Shislenko?' Aparo asked.

I gave him a look of surprise and admiration. He winked back, proud and cheesy.

'Yeah, him. Leo was so bummed about that.' She let out a small, wistful shrug. 'Daphne told me he even went to their embassy and joined the protesters. She said she'd never seen him like that. Really down, she'd said. And he'd taken a few pulls of vodka – one too many, according to her – which he didn't do, not anymore. You see what I'm saying? He's a decent guy.' She paused, then added, 'You've got to find them. Please.'

We left Rena's shop without much more to go on than we had going in. We'd need to follow up at the school and at the hospital and see if any of Leo's or Daphne's colleagues remembered anything else about the missing couple. The CCTV footage from the hospital's security cameras would be checked to see if anything unusual was going on around Daphne, especially at the time she had left. We'd also be checking any footage we could get from any cameras in storefronts or on ATMs close to the Sokolovs' apartment building, as well as video and still images taken on cell phones by bystanders who had been there when Yakovlev had taken his dive.

Beyond that, I didn't see that there was much more we could do. Not until we caught a break with some new piece of information, or if the Sokolovs decided to resurface. So Aparo and I headed back to Federal Plaza. I had a few loose ends to follow through on a couple of other files I was working on, then I was looking forward to going home to catch some quality time with Tess, Kim, and Alex, then mull over the plan that I was finding harder and harder to resist.

8

Little Italy, Manhattan

Without bothering to remove his shoes, Sokolov swung his legs up onto the creaky bed, sat back, and closed his eyes. He tried to master his breathing and slow his still-racing heartbeat, but all he could think was that his life, his second life, the one he'd built up over decades and had grown to love, was now over.

Out in the open, he had very deliberately kept his mind away from the circumstances of his flight and from that debilitating conclusion. Now that he was alone and – he hoped – safe, at least for the time being, his attention slipped back to earlier that day, back at his apartment, back when he merely thought his wife was late, rather than in the hands of those monsters.

They have Daphne.

They have my lapushka.

The thought forced Sokolov to sit up again, bolt upright. His lips were quivering, as were his hands. He looked around his crummy hotel room in abject panic. The sight was as grim and desperate as he felt. The walls were cracked, and two columns of dirty yellow light were leaking into the room through moth-eaten drapes from a streetlamp outside. He could almost hear the mites and roaches scratching and scurrying around beneath him. He shut his eyes again and tried to imagine that he was back at home in Astoria, listening to his beloved music with his even-more-be-loved Daphne curled up next to him on the couch, but his mind wouldn't play along and forced him to confront the reality of his situation: that he was hiding in a thirty-dollar-a-night dump in Little Italy, his wife was being held captive, and he had killed a man.

The apartment's entry buzzer sounded in the hallway, and Sokolov checked his watch. It could only be Daphne, of course – who else would it be that early in the morning? No doubt she was running late and her keys were buried at the bottom of her bag. Not the first time that had happened, nor would it be the last.

'Here you go, *lapushka*,' he said as he buzzed her in. 'I'll get the tea ready.'

Leaving the front door open, he hummed along to the Rachmaninoff coming from the living room as he padded back to the kitchen, thinking he didn't have that much time before he'd have to set off to work. He turned the kettle on and slipped a couple of slices of rye bread into the toaster, but as he waited to hear her walk into the apartment, something deep within clawed at him – and the unfamiliar, sharp footfalls he heard coming his way only confirmed his unease.

His body taut with apprehension, he stepped out of the kitchen and into the foyer, only to come face-to-face with a complete stranger. Sokolov immediately knew he was Russian. Not just Russian. An agent of the Russian state. He emitted that unmistakable combination of arrogance, resentment, and thinly suppressed violence, traits Sokolov knew well.

Traits he'd happily left behind many years ago.

They'd found him.

And given the ominous timing, it meant they also had Daphne.

Sokolov's heart imploded. He'd finally made the mistake of sticking his head above the parapet, just once, after all this time, and almost immediately, his wife had paid the price. Nothing was more Russian than that. Not even the unblinking eyes staring at him.

'*Dobroe utro*, Comrade Shislenko,' the man greeted him with a sneer of blunt irony as he pulled a handgun from his black leather coat and leveled it at Sokolov's chest.

Sokolov stared at the gun and backed away from his uninvited guest, as instructed by the sideways flicks of the gun in the man's hand, until he was standing in his living room.

'Thank you for alerting us to your whereabouts – and, indeed, to your intentions – in so unambiguous a manner,' he told Sokolov in Russian.

Sokolov was standing by the stereo. 'Where's my wife?' he asked as his fingers reached out and hit a button on his CD player, killing the Rachmaninoff.

The man's face soured. 'Why'd you stop it? I thought the concerto added a nice nostalgic ambiance to our little gathering, no?'

'Where's Daphne?' Sokolov insisted, his voice breaking.

'Oh, she's fine. And she'll stay fine as long as you behave,' the man told him as he sat down in an armchair facing the window.

He gestured for Sokolov to sit on the sofa adjacent to him, by the wall of bookshelves that were jammed with books and home to an elaborate hi-fi and a pair of expensive-looking speakers.

The speakers were positioned in such a way that the far armchair was the optimal listening point. Sokolov had spent many hours sitting in that very chair, reading the *Times* and listening to Scriabin preludes and Tchaikovsky ballets. Right now, it was precisely where he needed his guest to be sitting.

'We should charge you for all the resources we spent looking for you all these years, both here and back home. But no matter. We have you now. Once you've given us what we want – what you stole – we'll let your wife go free. I can't promise the same for you. That's out of my hands.' The man scratched one unshaven cheek with the muzzle of his gun. 'Does she even know who you are?'

Sokolov shook his head.

'Good. We suspected that would be the case. So her safety depends entirely on your actions,' the man said – then an odd, confused look flooded his face, and a thin film of sweat broke out across his forehead.

Sokolov watched nervously as the man switched the handgun to his left hand and back again as he shrugged himself out of his coat.

'Why do you keep the place so hot?' he asked. 'And what's that noise?' The man rubbed his ear irritably. 'Sounds like you have cockroaches in the walls.'

Sokolov leaned forward and, concentrating as hard as he could to stay in control, stared directly into the man's eyes.

'Don't worry about the *tarakanchiki*. They don't care about you. Tell me, Comrade. What is your name?'

The man furrowed his brow and winced, as if he had just stepped on a tack. He seemed to wonder about the question for a moment, then, his expression vacant, he said, 'Fyodor Yakovlev. Third secretary to the

Russian Consulate of New York.' He looked lost, as if he wasn't quite sure that this was the case.

Sokolov kept his eyes lasered on his captor, his concentration absolute. He knew his whole existence from here on depended on this moment, and with each sentence, he slowed and deepened his voice, accentuating seemingly random syllables.

'If they see the gun, they will be angry. You should place the gun on the table,' he told the man.

'Who? Who will be angry?'

'You know who will be angry,' Sokolov told him. 'They will be very angry. Now, why don't you show them you mean well and put your gun down on the table.' He tapped the coffee table with his fingers. 'This table right here.'

Yakovlev stared at him for a moment, then slowly placed his gun on the glass table between them. Sokolov made no attempt to pick it up.

After a moment, Yakovlev shifted in his chair, then made to retrieve his gun, as though he knew he'd just made a grave mistake.

'No,' snapped Sokolov.

Yakovlev withdrew his hand as though an electrical charge had just run through it. He looked like a child who'd just had his knuckles rapped.

Sokolov immediately reverted to the deep and arrhythmic intonation. 'They'll think you mean them harm. Go over to the window and see if they are still watching you.'

The man's entire face was now covered in perspiration. He stood, leaving the gun on the glass table, and wandered silently over to the window. He peered outside, taking several seconds to scan every element of the window's aspect.

Sokolov remained in the armchair, motionless. 'Do you see them?'

'Yes.'

'So now, you can understand why I need to talk to my wife. She will be worried. About both of us.'

Yakovlev nodded, then took out his cell phone and pushed a speed-dial button.

And then it happened.

At that exact moment, a fire truck's siren pierced the air outside. A blaring wail that ripped through their ears and kept coming. Yakovlev blinked twice, looked down at his empty right hand then swiftly located the gun on the glass table. But before he managed his first step away from the window, Sokolov had launched himself out of his chair.

He threw himself across the room and crashed his entire body weight into the off-balance target, sending the man smashing through the glass then shoving him over the window sill and out through six stories of New York air and onto the sidewalk below.

Sokolov heard the splat and the screams, but he didn't dare look out the window. His heart was kicking and screaming its way out of his chest. He looked around in desperation, then acted. He picked up the cell phone from the carpet where Yakovlev had dropped it, and slipped it into a pocket. He also picked up the handgun that had fallen from the Russian. Then he crossed to the shelves and hit the Eject button on the multi-CD player. While he waited impatiently, the tray slid out. He fished out the disc that was in the front-most position and slipped it into another pocket.

Then he rushed out of the apartment, wondering if he would make it out of the building alive and unseen.

Sokolov's mind snapped back to the present as his eyes settled on the '80s-style LED clock on the side table.

It read 10:5-. He assumed that meant ten fifty-something. He wished he had some of his sleeping pills. He wished he could lie down and just fall asleep. He wanted to burn away as much of the night as he could, to let the nightmare dissipate and allow a new day to rise and wash away this insanity and let his real life resume its normal course. He needed to delay, as far into the future as possible, the moment when he would have to make a decision.

But that wasn't the solution.

That wasn't going to get his wife back.

A siren – *another damn siren* – broke through the hubbub outside the hotel. And although Sokolov had a passion for sounds and what some would mistakenly call noise, he hated pointless, random cacophony, which is what was assaulting his senses through the hotel's loose-fitting window. When he had first come to America, it had taken him a long time to get used to the constant noise of the big metropolis. Moscow had been deathly quiet when he left, way back then. He knew everything had suddenly changed. For better, first – and then, for worse.

He rubbed his face and glanced at the side table again.

His wallet was there, with what was left from the thousand dollars he'd taken from an ATM not long after he'd slipped out of his building's service entrance. That was his daily limit, and he knew he needed to make it last, thinking it would probably be unwise to use the card again. The gun and the cell phone that he had taken from his unannounced Russian visitor were also there, beside the broken clock. He needed to hide them – he half expected that they'd be stolen during the night. He saw the TV remote and picked it up, stuck the single battery back inside the remote with the final few molecules of glue left on the frayed black tape, and switched on the pawn-shop TV that was pointlessly anchored to the wall.

He flicked through the channels until he found the local news.

An update soon appeared, about a Russian diplomat falling to his death in Astoria. The reporter said there were no witnesses and no suspect – but then Sokolov's face appeared, right there, on the screen for the world to see. His face, and Daphne's, side by side. Not as suspects, but as the occupants of the apartment the man had fallen from.

The nerve endings throughout his body flared with alarm.

He knew the bastards were only telling the Americans what suited them. Which meant the *siloviki* henchmen were in charge of the playbook, and New York's finest were watching from the sidelines.

He threw the remote at the screen in disgust, but missed. It split into pieces and fell to the floor.

What do I do?

I can't go to the police, he thought. A Russian agent just went through my window, for God's sake. What would I tell them, anyway? 'The KGB' – no, the FSB, that's what these gangsters call themselves today, even though they were the same people, the same sadistic thugs, just a shiny, new, supposedly democratized version of the same old murderous machine – 'the FSB took my wife?'

'Why would they do that, Mr. Sokolov?' the cops would ask. What answer could he give to that, what answer could he possibly give that wouldn't trigger an entirely different brand of pain from an entirely different brand of murderous machine, pain not just for him but for God only knew how many others ... all because of a futile, misguided attempt to save her. More than misguided. Pathetically naïve, really, because he knew that calling for help would end in dismal failure. He knew the Americans would never let him go either. They'd never leave him the freedom to carry on with his harmless little life and live happily ever after with his beloved Daphne. Not once they knew who he was. And certainly not after they got what they wanted from him.

Then another realization hit him.

If they don't know who I really am, then they must think I'm a murderer.

A wanted man. A fugitive, on the run – even if they're not saying it yet.

Were they just trying to lull him into handing himself in?

Maybe they know.

His quivering increased.

No, he couldn't go to the cops.

Which didn't leave him many other options. None at all, in fact. He was on his own, cast out of his home in the darkening city, on a citywide alert, the Costa Rica holiday picture they took from his apartment popping up on computer screens in police cruisers all over town, a man wanted for questioning in the suspicious death of a Russian government official.

He was on his own.

The thought tightened around him, and the city felt darker and meaner than it ever had before.

He had to make things right. For Daphne's sake. He had to do every thing he could to save her. Nothing else mattered. She was the one beacon in his life, the one good thing to have ever happened to him. An outlier in a life that had been plagued by bad choices.

He wondered what shape she was in right then. His imagination veered into horrific territory and he tried to rein it in. His throat tightened at the thought that Daphne would have no idea why she was being held. She would be scared, terrified even – though she wouldn't give her captors the gratification of showing it. Thirty-eight years as a nurse – the last eleven at Mount Sinai in Queens – had given his wife the toughened exterior of a Marine, even though Sokolov knew that inside she was still the delicate, sweet-hearted girl that he'd first met thirty years ago.

He needed to toughen up too.

He'd done it before. He needed to draw on those instincts again and make the impossible happen.

He'd brought this calamity upon himself. All of it. Right from the start. Right from the day when, as a curious fourteen-year-old, he'd made that fateful discovery in the cellar of his ancestral home.

The day that set everything else in motion.

* * *

It wasn't a grand home. There was no such thing in Soviet Russia, not unless you were part of the ruling Politburo. Sokolov's family wasn't anything like that. He had grown up in a farming lodge on a small plot of land in Karovo, eight miles away from the nearest village and a hundred miles south of Moscow.

His grandfather had lived and died in that same cottage. Sokolov knew all about their family history. At least, he thought he did, until that day.

His father had told him how Sokolov's grandfather Misha had arrived there shortly after the 1917 revolution. He'd settled there after a harrowing journey from St. Petersburg across a country ravaged by civil war. He'd found a haven in its idyllic landscape of birch forests, bluffs, and lush flood meadows that hugged the meandering Oka River. In better days, Karovo had been an estate comprised of a manor house, six villages, and good land. There was a gravity pump to bring water up from the spring; a steam mill where rye, barley, and buckwheat were ground; and a distillery where spirits were produced from potatoes. Then the Bolsheviks had taken over. The landowner was kicked out and his estate was turned into a *kolkhoz* – a collective farm. The manor house was turned into a teachers' training institute and, after World War II, it became an orphanage for the hordes of children who had been left homeless by the war. By the time Sokolov was a young boy, it had become a rundown weekend rest house for the workers of the giant turbine plant at Kaluga, some forty kilometers to the west, a far cry from its former glory.

Misha had worked the fields. He'd married a laundress, a former employee of the estate's owner. They'd had seven children, more able bodies to toil the land and feed the masses. Two of them had died during the hardships of Stalin's Great Purge, and the second world war almost finished off the rest. Four of Sokolov's uncles had died in various battles. His father, though, had survived, and he'd managed to return safely to Karovo, where he resumed working the fields, like his father. Men were in short supply after the war, and he'd had his pick of the town's prettiest girls. He'd ended up marrying the daughter of a schoolteacher, Alina, who had given him four children, all boys. The youngest of them was Sokolov, who was born in 1951.

As in the rest of Soviet Russia, life in Karovo was hard. Sokolov's parents worked long hours for little pay. He and his brothers had to work hard too, from a young age. Life under Soviet rule offered few treats, and there was little comfort to be had. The soil was tough and difficult to work. The huge wood-burning stoves were hard to keep alive. Drinking water needed to be brought over in buckets from a distant well. And at the cottage, the outhouse was mired in ankle-deep mud for most of the year. Food was scarce, the collective farm inefficient and badly run. The village shop was almost always bare. Frost-bitten potatoes, beets, cabbage, and onions were often the only nourishment available to stave off starvation.

Stuck in this harsh reality, Sokolov escaped into a fantasy life whenever he could. His mother, in particular, had been a wonderful storyteller. She was a fount of knowledge, and while his father would drink himself to sleep every night, she would regale Sokolov and his brothers with all kinds of stories and folk tales. In the centralized Marxist-Leninist education system Sokolov grew up in, the collective took precedence over the interests of the individual, and creativity and imagination were frowned upon. Sokolov's mother quietly disagreed and encouraged his whimsy and his ravenous curiosity. Sokolov's imagination was his escape from the dire conditions of his daily life, especially after the untimely death of his mother from tuberculosis when he was twelve.

One of the stories his mother had told them was about a grisly discovery at the Yusupov Palace, the former home of one of Russia's wealthiest families and once the home of Felix Yusupov, one of the self-confessed murderers of Grigory Rasputin. The discovery had taken place after the revolution, when the Bolsheviks had taken power and sent the Yusupovs, along with the rest of the aristocracy, off to rot in prison or face the firing squads. A secret room had been discovered in the apartment of Felix's great-grandmother, who had been reputed to be one of the most beautiful women in Europe. In the room, they found a coffin containing the rotting bones of a man who turned out to be a lover of hers, a revolutionary she had helped escape from prison. She'd kept him hidden in her palace for years, even after his death. Sokolov had heard stories about how secret chambers filled with chests of jewelry and all kinds of valuables were discovered in the homes and palaces of the aristocracy after the revolution, chambers they had hastily covered up with plaster and paint before fleeing the uprising. He would often sneak into the old manor house and look for such secret rooms, imagining what it would be like to find a hidden treasure of his own.

As it happened, what he found wasn't a treasure, and neither was it in the manor house.

It was in a small, hidden alcove buried deep in the cellar of his family's cottage. An alcove that looked like it hadn't been disturbed in decades. He'd stumbled upon it by accident while hiding from his brothers, and at first it didn't seem like much: not gold, silver, or anything like that. Just three rotting old journals, each bound in soft leather, the bundle wrapped tightly with a piece of string.

Sokolov had no idea that what he'd found would be far more valuable – and far-reaching – than any treasure.

He didn't share his discovery with anyone. Had his mother still been alive, he would have told her about it, without a doubt. But she was long gone, and his drunkard, cynical father wasn't worthy of it. He didn't tell his brothers about it either. Not until he knew what it was. It was his secret, and Sokolov knew he had something very special when, on the second page, a notorious name jumped out at him:

Rasputin.

He couldn't read it fast enough.

9

'Hey.'

It was, I don't know, three or four in the morning. Really late, in any case. I was lying with Tess next to me, asleep, or so I thought, her head still buried in her pillow, her voice no more than a whisper.

'Why are you still up?' Her tone was all warm and dreamy.

I didn't say anything. I just leaned over, kissed her on the shoulder, and drank in her delicate smell.

Tess was my oasis. My work at the Bureau, as you'd expect, took me to some pretty dark places. With alarming regularity, it exposed me to a side of the human psyche that most people were blissfully unlikely to encounter beyond their TV screens or e-readers – and, trust me, it's not even remotely close to actually living it. But no matter how repugnant my days were, coming back to Tess's lush embrace fixed me. She was my antidote, my deflector shield, the port I sheltered in when storms were raging around me. But this time, my mind was was still caught up in hurricane Corrigan.

'You worried about something?' she asked.

I gave her another kiss, softly. 'Go back to sleep.'

She moaned, equally softly. 'I can't. Not if I know you're awake.' She sat up a little, propping herself on one elbow, her buttery-blond curls half-covering her face. 'You thinking about Alex?'

I didn't answer.

She sighed. 'He's doing better, Sean. But it's like Stacey says. It's going to take time.'

I shrugged. 'More time since we don't know what they did to him.' I turned to face her. 'He only gets one childhood. He shouldn't have to have it ruined like this.'

'It's not ruined. He's got you now. And me. And Kim. He's settling in well at school. He's going to be fine.' She reached out and stroked my cheek, her emerald-green eyes somehow lighting up, even in the darkened room. 'I hate seeing you like this. Every week, it's like our visits to Stacey just bring it all out in you again. You've done all you can.'

I just nodded.

The plan – my ill-advised plan about how to find Corrigan – was still creeping around in my head, feeding on ideas. Growing.

Which Tess spotted.

She knew how my brain worked. We'd lived through enough wild adventures for that, right from the get-go, from the night we first met at the Met and the subsequent mad rush halfway across the globe to track down the secret of the Templars. Even though she'd now ostensibly given up the hotheaded archaeologist mantle and morphed into a supposedly more placid novelist, she was no stranger to danger, nor to the extreme measures that were sometimes needed to get through sticky situations.

It made her sit up a little more and give me that inquisitor's look.

'Sean. What are you planning?'

If I was going to go ahead with it, I sure as hell wasn't going to let Tess in on it. Or Aparo, for that matter. In both cases, I didn't have a choice. Not knowing would protect them, given that I was about to break the law.

With Tess, it was an easy decision. I didn't tell her everything about the job, and she didn't necessarily want me to. Like I said, I don't exactly work at Willy Wonka's, and there's no need to bring that ugliness into our private lives. We'd already had more than our fair share of that. In fact, her first books were based on some of those wild adventures. I hoped her next oeuvres would come out of her imagination, but knowing her and the kind of stuff she liked digging her nose into, I wasn't holding my breath.

With Aparo, it was a different matter. Nick was my partner. If and when I ever got to a place where I needed help, there was no one else I'd want riding shotgun with me. But at this stage, keeping him in the dark would also protect him if it all went belly-up. I knew that when I eventually did tell him, assuming I did go ahead with it, he wouldn't see it that way at all and he'd be all pissed off at me for not sharing with him from minute one. And I wouldn't have it any other way.

'Nothing you need to worry about,' I told Tess.

She gave me the narrowed eyes for a moment longer. 'Why don't I believe you?'

'Because your imagination's way too active and the wheels in there are always going loco,' I said, gently tapping her forehead. 'Go back to sleep.'

She leaned over so her face was inches from mine, and let her body curl into me. 'Too late,' she whispered.

I could feel her warm skin against mine – any kind of bedwear was verboten in our household, by mutual decree. It was a lovely and highly addictive feeling that never failed to get all kinds of endorphins going haywire inside me.

'You're not helping me fall asleep,' I said.

'I wasn't trying,' she replied as her hand reached over and settled on my chest. 'Far from it, truth be told.'

I chuckled, and was inching closer to her when I sensed something from the corner of my eye. Or, rather, someone. Standing in the doorway of our bedroom.

It was Alex. Just standing there, motionless, hugging the stuffed bunny Tess and I had bought him out in San Diego.

I looked at Tess. Her expression softened instantly, a bittersweet smile lighting it up.

'Hey, sweetie, what's up?' she asked.

He hesitated for a moment, then said, 'I had a bad dream.'

Another one.

Even in the darkness, I could see his little lips quivering. I could also see the unease in his eyes when they flicked my way for the briefest moment. And, again, my heart shattered, like so many times before, like someone had zapped it with a freeze gun before letting it drop to the ground.

'Aww, darling, there's nothing to be scared of.' She glanced my way and I nodded back as she pulled on a night dress she kept in a drawer of her side table, climbed out of bed, and hurried over to Alex. She knelt down so she was eye-level with him, then drew him in and hugged him tight against her and said, 'You want me to sleep with you?'

He nodded.

'Come on. Let's get you back to bed.'

My insides were burning up with acid as I watched them disappear into the hallway. How many nights would we live through this? How much longer would Alex need to suffer like this?

Any lingering doubt in my mind evaporated right there and then. I was going to follow through with my plan.

Regardless of the consequences.

10

'Who took this?' I asked.

It was around eleven in the morning on a fine Tuesday, and we were all huddled around Aparo's desk: Nick, me, and the two other agents assigned to the case with us, Kubert and Kanigher – a weird combo in that they looked like twins, what with their matching number-one hair cuts, their slick, rimless glasses and the merging, Borg collective-like, of their mannerisms – watching a video clip on my partner's laptop.

Someone called Cuppycake12 had filmed it on a smart phone outside the Sokolovs' apartment building and uploaded it to YouTube during the night. And a good thing they had, too, since so far, the clips and images we'd collected from our canvassing hadn't revealed anything new.

Background checks on Leo and Daphne Sokolov also hadn't kicked up anything noteworthy. The two of them seemed to be living normal, uncomplicated lives. Neighbors described them as a pleasant and reported no troubles. No runs-ins with the law, no financial problems. Nothing. The apartment was rent controlled, they'd never missed a payment. Credit scoring was fine. Bank statements didn't show anything out of place apart from a noteworthy, large ATM withdrawal yesterday morning. They seemed like model citizens in every way.

We'd also gone through the CCTV footage from the hospital, and hadn't spotted anything suspicious or helpful on it. Daphne had left the hospital and headed in the direction of her bus stop pretty much as she did on every other day. There was also nothing about her body language that indicated any kind of stress or furtiveness going on. The footage we'd collected off a few cams on ATMs and such hadn't yielded any epiphanies either, and neither had the statements that Adams, Giordano, and their troops had collected off the people at the scene.

This clip, however, was interesting – and gruesome. Gruesome, because whoever took it wasn't squeamish. It began at what must have been only seconds after Yakovlev hit the ground. The clip starts with the kind of frantic, shaky footage of someone who's just switched on his camera and is rushing across the street and down the sidewalk to get to the scene itself.

There, the image lingers on the dead man's body. You can hear horrified wails coming from other bystanders, a lot of sobs and 'Oh my God' and 'Is he dead' and 'Someone call an ambulance' – all of it punctuated by Cuppycake12's own breathless commentary. Cuppy – a young woman, by the sounds of it – also tilts up and pans across to show us the people standing around ogling the body, some turning away, others unable to tear their eyes off him, the whole thing filmed with the frenzied visceral energy that these off-the-cuff clips often bring with them.

'Right here. Watch this,' Aparo said as he hit the Pause button. 'This guy right here,' he added, tapping the screen.

He was pointing out a figure – adult, male. I couldn't really tell much more because the image was grainy due to the jittery cinematography. The man had appeared behind some of the people who had congregated around the body.

'Keep your eye on him,' he told us before resuming the playback.

The guy looks over the shoulders of the first row of bystanders. He lingers there for a beat. Then he looks up, toward Sokolov's apartment, which is where the body obviously fell from. Then he looks at the body again, and turns away and drops out of view behind the wall of people.

'He disappears for a while,' Aparo explained. 'But watch this.'

Cuppy gets bored of his gruesome shot and goes around to try to get a more comprehensive reportage of what had happened. She steps out onto the street and tilts the camera up, taking in the building before zooming in on the sixth-floor window that, from way down there, you can just about tell is broken. Cuppy has a good eye. Then a car surprises her, there's a nudge of a horn that makes her jump, and Cuppy's camera angle drops away from the window and goes all over the place as she hustles out of the car's way. Clearly, this doesn't go down well with Cuppy, who lets rip with some colorful language directed at the impatient driver before following him down the street with her zoom.

Which is when Cuppy captures the bit that caught Aparo's eye.

The guy he'd pointed out is also in the frame. We see him come around a parked SUV, get in, and drive off. In a hurry, just charging out and almost colliding with a passing car. Like he just wanted to get the hell out of there.

Which I thought merited closer inspection. Not because he was leaving in a rush. He could well have been distraught, freaked out by what he'd seen. Anyone would. That might even be considered a healthy response. But it was his body language that made us take notice. He was all business, focused. Not distraught. More like furtive. Which wasn't as wholesome, response-wise.

'Nice,' Kubert chortled. Or maybe it was Kanigher. I was never really sure anymore. 'Maybe the guy's squeamish. Maybe he wet himself.'

'Very likely,' I said. 'On the other hand, maybe he was waiting for Yakovlev and decided to bail fast when the diplomat took the shortcut down.'

'If he was with him, why not go upstairs and get whoever did it? Or at least call the cops?' Kanigher asked.

'Maybe their little visit wasn't official,' Aparo speculated.

'Maybe.' I nodded. 'Anyway, we'll know more if the lab can get a decent close-up of the guy's face and his license plate. And we need to try and marry it up with traffic-cam footage and see if we can get a fix on which way he went.'

'I'll ship it down to them,' Aparo said. 'Oh, and get a load of this. The couple who live just below to the Sokolovs in 5C? Seems their dog went loco that morning and bit the husband. Like, mangled him, got him in the forearm and wouldn't let go. Right about the time Yankovich—'

'Yakovlev,' Kubert corrected him.

'—took his swan dive.'

'Did they hear a fight?' I asked.

'No,' he said. 'Just a small thud, maybe the vase hitting the floor, then the screams from the street.'

'So what are they doing with the dog?' Kubert asked.

'Nothing. She's back to normal. They've had her for years, never bit anyone before.'

Kubert's face took on that familiar, pensive expression, like he was about to reveal another great secret of the universe to us. 'Dogs sense things, you know. They have these powers ...'

'What we know about how their minds work doesn't even begin to scratch the surface,' Kanigher added.

And before they both segued into another fascinating episode of their *Twilight Zone* take on the animal kingdom, I decided to take my leave.

The lab had some work to do on our little YouTube clip, and I had a date with a large man and a whole lot of maple syrup.

About a hundred blocks uptown from Federal Plaza, Larisa Tchoumitcheva stepped out of her boss's office on the third floor of the Russian consulate and pondered the crisis that had been thrust upon her unexpectedly.

It was a crisis, but it was also an opportunity. A chance for her to make a difference, which is why she had taken that job in the first place. But this situation had been sprung on her without warning. She hadn't had a chance to prepare, to think things through. Which meant she was vulnerable to something going wrong. In her line of work, that carried some serious health implications.

Further complicating matters was that her boss at the consulate, Oleg Vrabinek – officially the vice consul, unofficially the city's senior SVR operative – wasn't sharing. She'd been frozen out of what he and the now-deceased Yakovlev had been up to. All she'd been told before heading off to Sokolov's apartment was to deny, to deflect, and to report back. After what she'd seen, she'd decided this had to be her first priority: to get inside Vrabinek's circle of trust. She needed to know what was going on if she was going to have any chance at making that difference – to say nothing of staying alive.

One thing she did know, however, was that Sokolov was important. To her people, and to the Americans. They were both desperate to get hold of him. And Vrabinek had been less than forthcoming about Sokolov when Larisa had asked who he was.

'That's not relevant here,' was all Vrabinek had said.

When she'd prodded him – gently, deferentially, as was expected – he'd added, 'You'll get more information if and when it becomes necessary. Right now, it isn't.'

Which gave Larisa her next priority: to find out who Sokolov was and why he was so important. She needed to get access to his file, but she had to do it without Vrabinek or anyone else at the consulate finding out.

Easier said than done. And not great on the health-implications front.

Then there was the FBI agent, Sean Reilly. She'd been told he'd be like a Rottweiler in tracking down Sokolov, and in that sense he'd be very useful. She'd been ordered to get close to him and report back about his progress on everything he was working on. She'd also been warned about his intuitiveness. In the flesh, though, she found that he was different from the adversary they'd made him out to be. She sensed something else in him. An honesty, a decency that surprised her. Which was dangerous.

She had her orders. Her superiors knew what they were doing, and they had their reasons for setting her those tasks, regardless of what she saw in him. She needed to stay on target and see things through.

Vrabinek hadn't been any more forthcoming in the meeting she'd just had with him. She hadn't learned any more information about Sokolov. He had, however, generously bestowed one new piece of information on her, but it wasn't in any way reassuring.

He told her they were sending someone over. A special operative, flown in to deal with the situation.

That didn't sound good.

It sounded a lot worse when he told her it would be Koschey.

She'd never met him. Very few had. And though the little information she had about him was sketchy, one thing was certain: his involvement was seriously bad news on the health implications front.

For her, and for everyone else involved.

11

An hour after leaving Federal Plaza, I was in Newark, New Jersey, seated in a booth at a bright and cheerful IHOP, facing a leviathan of a man, still amazed that he'd managed to lever himself onto the double-seat bench.

He hadn't been too happy to see me when I'd showed up at his place – well, his mom's place, technically – and told him I needed a powwow. The last time he'd seen me was when Aparo and I were grilling him in a cold interview room. An invitation to join me for a bite – I use the word purely figuratively here – helped lower his defenses. Cheap trick, I know, but hey, I'm a firm believer in taking the path of least resistance whenever you can. And who doesn't love IHOP?

The triple-XL Advanced Idea Mechanics T-shirt stretched against the folds of his wobbling flesh as he grabbed the menu and started eating the entire thing with his eyes. I'd said it was my treat and he was obviously going to take me at my word as he waved the waitress over and started to order. About halfway through his list I realized I could probably eat too, though I normally went out of my way to avoid the cholesterol-and-sugar slamdown of a pile of pancakes. I interjected a garden omelet and let him go back to what was fast appearing to be some kind of record attempt.

Kurt Jaegers was thirty-two, weighed at least three-hundred-and-fifty pounds, and lived with his mother, a divorced psychotherapist who worked from home and specialized in addiction. That was cute enough. But Kurt was also number seven on the FBI's cybercrime watch list. He'd come close to being sent away for a couple of years, but the judge at his trial happened to be in a charitable mood. Which, ultimately, didn't disappoint me.

Kurt fascinated me. In his dreams, he probably had a string of glamorous girlfriends, drove a Rolls and cruised exotic beaches on a large yacht, Kim Dotcom-style. The reality was probably online porn and his mother's beat-up Volvo whenever he could heist the keys. But for some reason, I liked him. He had an inner honesty that I found weirdly admirable. And right at the moment, I didn't really care what his domestic arrangements or louche hobbies were. I just needed his help, which is why I decided to play nice.

'I said whatever you like and I meant it, but I may need to leave you after the first couple of rounds.'

'No worries, dude.' He'd finally finished ordering and sent the waitress on her way. 'You must try the stuffed French toast. It's incredible. But you'll need to order some of your own. I only got two.'

'I'm good, Kurt. But thanks anyway.'

His expression turned quizzical. 'So ... you're going to give me a get-out-of-jail-free card? Is that for real?'

'Something like that. Unless you're really naughty – NSA or NCIS or even NASA for that matter, anything with an "N" or an "S" in it and you're on your own.'

He chuckled. 'Hey, no sweat. JWICS is tight as a cat's butthole since Bradley Manning downloaded the whole enchilada. Even Anonymous have mostly packed up and gone home when it comes to SIPRNet. There's no more fun to be had with those guys. I spend most of my time playing WoW nowadays.'

Clearly, my face telegraphed what I was missing.

'World of Warcraft, dude. You don't know that?'

I shrugged. 'I'm a Neanderthal, what can I tell you.'

He waved it off. 'I'm really into my female Pandaren at the moment. She's called Chiaroscuro. Cause she's black-and-white, you know? Lately, though ... I think I want to do her. I know it's wrong, I mean she's a fucking panda, right? That's like zoophilia or something.'

'It's something all right, I'm just not sure I want to think about it.' My head was already spinning, and the food-fest hadn't even landed yet. 'At least it's good to hear you're playing safe these days.'

Kurt drank some coffee and grinned. 'There's fun to be had. Like sometimes, I'll add extra items to Mom's credit card bill just to mess with her.

Last week, she spent an hour trying to work out how she'd bought sexy lingerie from a store in Paris.'

'Well, that's the kind of blowback I can help you with.'

'Understood, dude.' His eyes took on a sad countenance. 'I know you're mocking me in your head, but ... thanks for not throwing it back at me. I appreciate people who can keep it off their face.'

I shrugged. 'Come on, Kurt. We're all screw-ups in our own way. You wouldn't believe some of the shit I've done.'

'Don't say that, dude. Now I'll have to hack your file.' He smiled, then laughed nervously and started to rearrange the first wave of dishes that our waitress was delivering to the table. 'Joke, man. Joke.' He looked up, finally happy with the positioning of the plates. 'So what do you need? And I assume it's you personally, otherwise you'd be talking to one of your in-house cyber squads or – shudder – the stormtroopers from DC3.'

He was referring to the Department of Defense Cyber Crime Center down in Linthicum, Maryland. These guys knew what they were doing, and they also knew Kurt. They had forensic, counterintelligence, and training divisions and were on tap to us and to all the other law-enforcement agencies. We'd crossed paths when Kurt had slipped inside the United Nations' server farm, which was how I'd first met him.

I took a bite of my omelet and decided to come right out with it.

'I need to find someone. Someone who doesn't want to be found.'

His eyes widened with interest. 'Where's he hiding?'

'Some file locked away in Langley.'

Kurt sputtered on a mouthful of French toast and raised his hands defensively. 'Whoa, dude. I'm not going there. Not for any kind of free pass.'

'I'm not going to ask you to, not directly anyway,' I said. 'I know you need to be careful and so do I. Thing is, I only have a cover ID for this guy. And yes, it's personal. Deeply personal.' I held his gaze for a breath, then I added, 'I just want you to find someone on the inside that I can lean on. Someone with the necessary clearance. Someone who works there and who I can visit in person and,' using his parlance, I went with, 'convince of the righteousness of my quest.'

Kurt held up his hand as he finished devouring plate one of his syrupy odyssey. Finally, he swallowed.

'What's his game? The guy you're looking for. It's a guy, right?'

'It's a guy. And I've got some threads to pull on. DEA, Black Ops,

Mexico, South America. I'm sure there's a lot more besides.' I had already decided not to mention MK-ULTRA. It was important that I at least appeared to be the sane one in this relationship.

'You'll need someone with at least a Level Two clearance, no lower than a "2-C."' He thought about it for a moment. 'There's got to be a few hundred CIA staffers with that level of clearance. A couple hundred of those are analysts.'

'So find me one who's not the fine, upstanding citizen he or she appears to be.'

His mouth widened into a grin that was disturbingly juvenile. 'Now, that could be fun.' His mind was almost visibly churning through various scenarios. 'I could go in through a government employee database. Health care, pensions maybe. Cherry-pick the departments we want. Cross-reference that with clearance-levels data sitting on a black hat site I use. Should be able to get you name, gender, age, address, Social Security, time on government's payroll, pension, medical, dental, disciplinary, sexual orientation—'

I cut him off with, 'I get it.' Too harshly, maybe. But listening to him, I was starting to wonder if I was taking the whole thing too far. Delving into the personal lives of people who had nothing to do with me or Alex and never would.

'Don't be squeamish, dude,' he said, reading me. 'Information wants to be free.'

'Unless it's the identity of hackers.'

He chuckled. 'Touché. But let's try not to dwell on that particular contradiction. Anyway, difference is we're not meddling in the affairs of sovereign nations or monitoring every single action performed by the citizens of a supposed democracy.'

I wanted to hit the ball back at him, but I didn't have time to get into a big Orwellian debate, so I just took another bite out of my omelet, slid the plate across the table, and followed it with a big sip of coffee instead.

I put the mug back on the table. 'OK. Good. Get me all that. Then go deeper and do your thing and find me stuff that doesn't stack up. Anything I can use to apply pressure.'

'You got it, dude. In my limited experience, the more upstanding you appear, the more screwed-up you are behind closed doors. At least I appear screwed-up.'

I couldn't help but smile at that. He knew himself pretty well, but that still didn't stop him from diving into a plate of blueberry pancakes.

I dropped a hundred-dollar bill on the table, then slid out of the booth. 'Call me when you have something.'

'Sure. It'll be from a VPN'd fake Skype account billed to an entirely random Japanese woman's credit card. You sure you don't want to get yourself a burner?'

'One phone's enough. Just keep it short and vague.'

'Wilco, my friend.' Then he paused the trajectory of fork to mouth, and his face took on a rare, serious sheen. 'Must have been something bad for you to be doing this. Like, risking your career and all that. You sure you don't want to just let it go?'

I shook my head. 'Funny how everyone keeps telling me that. But if I was going to drop it, I would have already done that. I guess we're the same in that way. Neither one of us knows when to stop.'

He shook his head, smiled, and deposited a mini-stack of syrup-drenched pancakes into his mouth. 'Yeah, but at least this stuff tastes great.'

At least, I think that's what he said.

As I drove back into the city, two interesting tidbits landed on my phone: A face, and a license number.

The face I didn't recognize, but I didn't expect to. It was the blow-up of the guy from the YouTube clip. They were running it through facial recognition software at that very moment. The license number was from his car. Again, no hits. The car was a maroon Ford Escape that was leased to a New York LLC. Records were being tracked down to find out more about the company, and a tri-state-wide APB had been put out on the car, with both Aparo and me, as well as Detectives Adams and Giordano, listed as investigating officers.

I thought it might be interesting to ask Ms. Tchoumitcheva if the You-Tube guy's face rang a bell, but I decided to wait until I had a bit more to go on – a name, or a Russian link to the company that had leased the car – before I made that call.

My thoughts glided back to my meeting with my favorite hacker, and thinking about it imbued me with a mixture of low-level fear and energizing satisfaction. I knew the balance of power between the hackers and the military-industrial complex was close to shifting dramatically in the favor of the latter. The next-generation encryption we'd been briefed about was supposed to be all but impossible to break into. Which meant that hackers like Kurt would find it increasingly difficult to boldly go where they weren't welcome. But at the moment, one geek with limitless time to burn and no sense of privacy other than his own could still beat the best firewalls out there. Which suited me fine. Finding the names of a few analysts shouldn't be too much of a problem for him – not yet.

Of course, the whole thing could blow up in my face. But then again, when did that ever stop me from doing anything?

12

S okolov stood quietly by the yellow cab and waited.

He was outside the Cooper-Hewitt Design Museum, near the corner of East Ninety-First and Fifth, about three hundred yards north-west of the Russian consulate. The whole street was bathed a drab gray, deep in the shade, what with the evening sun lying low in the Western sky. A small cluster of trees obscured his view of the consulate's entrance, but this was as close as he wanted to be for the moment. A first-time visitor would have never suspected that a mere three days earlier, the street had been full of protesters. Or that this was where, after all this time, Sokolov had been so stupid as to reveal to his enemies exactly who he was.

Or, rather, who he had been.

He had to make his move. And he had to do it quickly. After all, with Daphne in their hands, he didn't have a choice. He had to try to get her back, despite the potentially catastrophic consequences of his capture. And so he'd left his hotel at seven that morning and grabbed breakfast at a cheap diner that wouldn't put too much of a dent into his limited cash reserves. Then he'd walked three blocks to an Internet café, where he'd spent the best part of the morning researching the Russian consulate and its employees.

He knew that many of the job titles given to consulate employees were bogus – merely cover for what they *really* spent their time doing: intelligence-gathering, industrial espionage, recruiting agents, and hypo-critically luxuriating in America's plentiful embrace while nodding slavishly every time the Kremlin issued yet another edict condemning America and the West's interference in the sovereign affairs of Mother

Russia. He'd always thought it ironic that the consulate was housed in John Henry Hammond House, one of the most opulent private homes ever constructed on the island of Manhattan. It had been built in the early 1900s by Emily Vanderbilt Sloane and her husband as a gift to their daughter. The mansion next door, Burden House, had been built for her sister. Hardly standard bearers of the proletariat ideal, but then again, the rulers of Russia, past and present, had never intended to share the grim conditions they imposed on their people.

He'd spotted Third Secretary Fyodor Yakovlev's name on the list, his now-dead visitor of the day before, and seeing the name had sent a cold jolt up his spine. He'd moved on and kept searching until he'd settled on Lazar Rogozin, counselor for political-military affairs, who he'd seen on a recent circular from a New York–based NGO protesting the systematic attacks on gays and immigrant workers in Moscow by members of the Nashi, the Kremlin's modern take on Hitler Youth. The circular asked that everyone who took issue with this abhorrent and increasingly common practice in the motherland should bombard Rogozin with letters and e-mails, whom the organization had identified as having financial interests in at least two businesses that were known to fund Nashi's activities. The NGO activists had even been gracious enough to provide a photograph of him.

After grabbing some lunch, Sokolov had managed to find a phone booth, which he'd used to call the consulate. Using a disguised, soft-spoken voice, he'd asked if Rogozin was in. The answer had been yes. Sokolov had hung up while he was being transferred, then walked around until he'd found a thrift shop. There, he'd bought a heavy navy-blue coat that he'd shrugged on while he was still in the shop, a loose-fitting felt beret that he'd pulled down so it covered most of his ears, and a knitted scarf he'd wrapped around his neck.

He'd then taken the subway and walked across town to the corner of Fifty-Ninth and Fifth, where he'd spent almost an hour studying the faces and body language of various taxi drivers and mustering up the courage to go ahead with what he intended until, at about five, he felt confident and desperate enough to approach a driver for the task ahead. The cabbie he'd chosen was a black man in a Rasta hat who, unsurprisingly, turned out to be Jamaican. The man, Winston, was so laid-back he didn't bat an eyelid at what Sokolov told him he needed him to do. The only issue with Winston, as Sokolov soon discovered, was that he always drove with the window open, no matter the time of year. He said it kept the germs from breeding inside his cab, which, given the rickety state it was in, seemed like it should be the least of his worries in terms of his well-being. Still, he was ready to do Sokolov's bidding without asking questions, and that was all Sokolov required.

And so they'd driven uptown, motored past the consulate, and parked outside the museum.

And waited.

And as he waited, his mind drifted back to how it had all started. To the discovery he'd made in the cellar of his father's house. To the journals of his grandfather, the ones that would consume his future.

The ones he suddenly wished he'd never read.

13

Misha's Journal

DECEMBER 1899

Everything has changed.

My stay here, in this place, has been upended. I was here for a reason I thought I understood. I came here to put my old life behind me, to think about what I had done, and to find a noble direction for the future. But the future that is now before me is like nothing I imagined. Here, at the dawn of the new century, I feel the portents of an eventful time ahead, a time of which a lot is unknown at the moment, save for this feeling that great change is about to be thrust upon us all.

A change in which I feel I am destined to play a central role.

And yet, this has all come unexpectedly. That was not at all my plan. Far from it. It is for this reason that I have taken pen to hand and I am writing this journal while still closeted away here, at the Nikolaev Monastery, a sixteenth century cloister that sits crouched on a hillock close to the town of Verkhoturye in the Ural Mountains. No doubt you will have heard of it, as it is famous across Siberia for its relics: the bones of Saint Simeon, the mystic who wandered the banks of the Tura River and spent his days praying, fishing, and mending the clothes of the poor. Simeon had died in 1642, a young man of thirty-five, as a result of his fasting; fifty years after his death, his coffin was said to have risen out of the ground, with his remains astoundingly well preserved. Simeon's grave became a place of pilgrimage for those seeking to be healed, and after two and a half centuries of duty, his bones were moved to their new healing outpost here at the Nikolaev Monastery, where they continue to attract wanderers in need.

It is because of Saint Simeon that I find myself in this portentous situation. For I have recently met a man, here, in this remote place of contemplation and prayer, a man who also came here to seek Saint Simeon's guidance. A man who, I believe, will bring about this great change.

I came here myself seeking change, seeking to escape from my own demons. You see, I have done things that confound me. I have delved into secrets that terrify me, the unfortunate result of a life devoted to study and knowledge – knowledge that I now wish I had never gained.

I had considered myself fortunate to have enjoyed the benefit of a proper education. My father, a schoolteacher, had sewn the seeds of curiosity in me from my earliest days. My mind had been taken captive by the wonders of science ever since I was a child, and I remember gazing with equal fascination at the stars in the sky or at the veins in my wrist. But it was at university that the hidden truths of our nature started to be revealed to me. It was also there that chance – or misfortune – would introduce me to the work of Heinrich Wilhelm Dove, the illustrious Prussian physicist. It would, however, be disingenuous for me to blame him for my discoveries. It was my own curiosity, along with my selfish disregard for propriety and caution, that have led me this far and have now brought me here to try and atone for my digressions.

At first, the ramifications of my work were not manifest to me. I was simply intrigued, and thrilled, by the results of my first experiments. It never occurred to me that I should abandon my line of enquiry. I was blinded, driven by an unseen hand to explore further the secrets hidden inside us. Secrets that I should have left alone. Secrets that are laden with monstrous potential. And so I came here, to this remote, holy place, to pray for guidance. To try to veer away from my chosen path, to leave behind the science of the devil that had bewitched me, to try to find a more worthy pursuit for the rest of my years.

This man has changed all that.

He is an illiterate peasant, of average height, skinny, and with unusually long arms. He has a large, irregular nose, rich sensuous lips, and an unkempt, shaggy beard. His hair, which is combed across his forehead, is long and parted down the middle. He wears tattered clothes and never washes. His skin bears the marks of hardship, of years of harsh exposure to hot sun and cold winds, no doubt a result of many years of wandering the land. Since his arrival over two months ago, he kept to himself and spent most of his time in silent prayer and introspection. I had not given him much notice until the day he looked at me, and I saw his eyes.

They are impossible to ignore.

Peering out from under thick brows, they are gray-blue and unsettlingly hypnotic. They are bursting with life, at first gentle and kind, rich with dreaminess and contemplation. And yet, in an instant, they can turn fierce and angry. His speech is strange, too, almost incoherent, lulling, somehow primordial. It is clear that he has no education, and he speaks in breathless torrents of simple words. And yet, when he does, the effect of his impassioned words, combined with the intense gaze emanating from his deep-set eyes, is nothing short of mesmeric.

Over the last few weeks, we have spent many hours talking.

He told me he was born in Pokrovskoye, a small Siberian village on the banks of the Tura River, in January of 1869, thirty years ago. It was the day of Saint Grigory, after whom he had been named. For that is his name. Grigory Efimovich Rasputin.

His father drove mule carts and worked on the barges by the river. When he couldn't find work, he farmed the little land he owned, and fished. Grigory worked with him and still lived in the home of his parents with his wife and his two children. He tells me she is pregnant with a third.

There is a great hunger in this young peasant. He tells me he wasted a large part of his life, engaging in fist fights and drunken debauchery. He confesses to having a wild streak to him, an animalistic craving for violence and for women. I must admit that despite his crude ways, there is something inexplicably magnetic about him. I imagine that women must find him beguiling and irresistible. He tells me that back in Pokrovskoye, he had been caught several times with wenches and had suffered numerous beatings because of it. This does not surprise me.

'This peasant life is meaningless,' he told me early on. 'Backbreaking labor from dawn to dusk, only relieved by drunkenness and the release through the flesh of a woman. That is not the existence I seek.'

Eventually, he candidly told me how he had resorted to crime to fund his debauchery. He stole fences, horses, and cartloads of fur. He was caught, and he was beaten. His peers mocked and taunted him, calling him 'Grishka the Fool.' Strangely, he told me how he took pleasure in the beatings and the abasement. More than once, he referred to this 'joy of abasement.' And somewhere in this mad, wasted life, he discovered what had been missing in his life.

He started seeking God.

The search did not start well. The priest in his village, also uneducated by the sounds of it, failed to provide him with the spiritual guidance he was looking for. Dissatisfied with not finding the answers he'd been seeking, frustrated that his contemplation was not bringing him closer to God, he resorted even more to drink and to women. The beatings resumed. He decided to leave and search elsewhere. So began his life as a wanderer in search of enlightenment.

He has been wandering the land for many, many years.

He journeyed to the Tyumen and Tobolsk cloisters, the monasteries closest to his village. He didn't find the answers he was looking for there, so he ventured on. He visited more monasteries, farther afield. More churches, more villages, meeting countless people, praying with them. He had trouble with insomnia and spent many nights without sleep. And in his ceaseless wanderings along the meandering Tura River, he found inspiration in the glorious nature around him and began to have mystical visions.

'I woke up one night to see the mother of God before me,' he told me. 'She was weeping. She said she was weeping for the sins of mankind, and asked me go forth and cleanse the people of their sins.'

Inspired by this vision, he returned to his village and started holding prayer sessions, but those around him didn't trust him. They knew him as a libidinous drunk and laughed at him.

'Everyone watches he who seeks salvation as though he were some kind of robber,' he told me, an unsettling rancor festering in his eyes. 'All are too quick to mock him. But that is the suffering one must endure. It is part of the journey.'

So he left again. He told me it was then that he stopped smoking or drinking, stopped eating meat or sweets. He walked thousands of miles, from the Siberian hinterland to Kiev and Petersburg and back, with no more than a knapsack over his shoulder. He stayed in churches and monasteries or with peasants who admired his devotion and offered him shelter and alms. He spent time getting to know, and understand, many dozens of people. And his journeying had eventually brought him here, to this monastery, where he hoped to find salvation and healing from his inner torment through the relics of Saint Simeon.

I had been here myself for months, following the same quest. I was here to be saved, only I still hadn't found the salvation I was yearning for. I was still unable to let go of the notion that had been embedded into me from my earliest days: that God was to be found in the wonders of science. The science that had already caused me so much torment.

The more we spoke, the more this man bewildered me.

How could a man change like that? How could he go from a self-confessed thief and serial fornicator and become a sincere *strannik* – a pilgrim? For he is a sincere believer, of that I am certain. He tells me he dreams of God. He speaks of searching to understand the mysteries of life, of hoping to get closer to God. Of hoping to be saved.

As do I.

For unfathomable reasons, I found myself sharing my secrets with the man, despite the fact that I had sworn to myself that no one would ever know what I had discovered. And yet, here I was, telling this mysterious wanderer everything. I could not resist his will or the comforting inner strength that radiated out of his eyes. And when I was finished, I felt a great sense of relief knowing that someone else shared my burden.

My tale brought satisfaction to Rasputin as well, but in a very different way.

It lit a great fire inside him. I could see it in his stare, which rose even more in its unbearable intensity. Once I was finished, he remained quiet for an uncomfortably long moment, just studying me in silence.

'It is all very clear to me now, Misha,' he finally said.

'What is?' I asked.

'Us, here, you and me. There is a reason we are here.' He reached out and cupped my hands in his. 'God is that reason, Misha. God wanted us to meet. That's why He brought us both here. Do you understand? What other possible reason could there be for us to be sitting here, together. We are here because of His great plan.'

'What plan?' I asked, stupefied, my mind entranced by his commanding gaze.

'His plan to save the Russian people. That is His plan for me. And that is why He has sent you here, to meet me. Because you, Misha, are going to help me achieve it.'

* * *

This man is truly a gift from God, Rasputin thought as he studied Misha.

He wasn't sure if the man of science's brilliance would save all the people of Russia. What he did know, however, was that it would certainly be his own savior.

It would save him from the tedious, miserable existence he'd suffered so far.

He felt a deep gratification at his decision to come to the monastery. And while what he'd told Misha was partly true – that it had been the result of a hunger to find some kind of meaning to his life – his spiritual quest had also helped him to avoid a jail cell and a criminal record back in Pokrovskoye. He'd needed a credible excuse to leave his village, a reason that would make the townsfolk hesitate at holding him back. Announcing that he was to become a strannik *was the perfect way out.*

And the more he thought about Misha and his astounding discovery, the more he became convinced that his decision to come here, to this austere place, would reward him richly.

Perhaps Saint Simeon was, he laughed inwardly, working his miracles after all.

14

A loud car horn jolted Sokolov out of his reverie.
He was still standing by the cab, outside the Russian consulate.
Waiting.

He thought he had it all mapped out. The street was one-way, meaning that when Rogozin left for the day, he would have to pass the yellow cab, enabling Sokolov to follow him. But when the first car left the consulate shortly before six, Sokolov realized he'd missed a key factor: the official car that drove out of the metal security gate before turning right down Ninety-First Street and past his position was a gun-metal-gray Mercedes S-Class with blacked-out windows that made it impossible to tell who was inside.

As the car turned onto Fifth Avenue, Sokolov cursed loudly and slammed both palms hard against the roof of the taxi.

'Yo, brother, what you do that for?' Winston protested.

'Sorry, sorry ... My apologies,' Sokolov told him.

Winston shrugged, turned away, and resumed his gentle head bobbing to the music coming through his earphones.

Sokolov fumed in silence. *Who are you trying to fool, Leo? You're no longer the young man who outwitted them before. You're just a bitter old man who couldn't keep his bloody mouth shut after too many vodkas. A typical Russian, in fact. Not an American at all.*

He closed his eyes, sucked in a deep breath, and rubbed his hands across his face.

What the hell do I do now?

He could retreat back to another dive and spend another night feeling sorry for himself, or – excepting the flag-flying limousine of the consul general – he could just wait and hope they weren't all like that, or just randomly pick another car, whoever may be inside, and see where he ended up.

It wasn't really a choice at all.

He sucked in a deep breath and tightened his grip on the gun he had in his coat pocket. It was an alien piece of equipment to him. A primitive, vulgar weapon. But right at the moment, it was also useful, and he was grateful he had it.

He waited some more. Then things improved.

The next cars to leave were sedans, mostly pretty high-end, with standard windows. And the eleventh car to exit the gates, almost an hour later, was a dark-gray Lexus with none other than Rogozin at the wheel.

Sokolov watched him glide by, then hopped in the cab.

'That car,' he motioned excitedly to Winston. 'That's the one. Follow it.'

The yellow cab pulled into its wake.

Winston nearly lost the Lexus several times, but each time, he just managed to stay within sight of the shiny dark sedan. By the time they reached their shared destination, a towering apartment building on East Thirty-Sixth, it was just past seven and the light was fading fast.

The Lexus turned into an underground parking garage and disappeared inside, with the garage's metal shutters rolling back down behind it.

Sokolov knew he had to move fast.

'Stop here, let me out,' he yelled at the Jamaican.

Winston slewed to a stop just next to the descending barrier. Sokolov had already seen the meter showing a hundred and eleven dollars, and he shoved two hundred-dollar bills into the small flap in the security partition that separated him from the driver before bursting out of the car.

'Thank you, but I must go now,' he said as he darted toward the gate.

He got there as the edge of the barrier was less than three feet off the ground. Without hesitating, he threw himself to the ground and landed heavily against his left knee before dragging himself clumsily under the barrier like an injured crab and making it inside just as the gate slammed to a stop against the grimy asphalt.

He caught his breath while lying there on his back, instantly aware of the pain that had lit up in his knee. He gave it a quick rub with his hand, then ignored it and pushed himself to his feet, amazed at what he'd just done. He took a quick glance around him, then trotted deeper into the garage in pursuit of the Lexus.

Maybe you can do this after all, Leo, he told himself, breathing heavily and feeling heavy-footed yet enjoying the sensation of the adrenaline pushing the crippling fear away.

Maybe.

The sun was also setting on yet another day on the job for David Miller and Frank Mazzucchelli. Another twenty minutes and they'd be heading back to the 106th Precinct, dumping their white Chevy Impala squad car, getting into their own cars, and heading their separate ways until the whole routine started again tomorrow.

At least, that was the plan. Not a great one, not a particularly memorable one, but one they could usually count on.

But then Mazzucchelli, who was riding shotgun, had to spot the SUV. The maroon Ford Escape, parked down the side of a rundown motel on Howard Beach. The SUV for which an APB had been issued earlier that day. And their plans for the evening, they knew, had been scuppered.

Still, there was possible overtime to be earned. And that wasn't a bad thing. Not a bad thing at all. So Miller slowed down, pulled a U-turn, and drove back to check it out.

Then they called it in.

15

Sokolov slipped behind a column and gripped the gun in his pocket just as Rogozin walked past a glass enclosure and into the small foyer, where the Russian diplomat pressed the elevator call button.

He was right there, within reach – and alone.

Sokolov's entire body sizzled with apprehension.

Do it. Do it now.

Grab him. Take him somewhere quiet. Force him to call his people and arrange for Daphne to be set free.

Sokolov's fingers tightened against the gun as he emerged from behind the column, but he hadn't taken two steps before he heard a small telltale ping and saw his quarry disappear into the elevator.

No!

He rushed the foyer, moving as fast as his legs could muster – but he was too late. The elevator doors had already shut by the time he reached them.

He felt the throbbing of blood against his temples as the sequence of tiny bulbs rose through the bronze-effect Roman numerals until they finally came to a stop on the seventeenth floor. Inside the thick coat his right hand had sweated so much it had made the butt of the gun slick with moisture. He loosened his grip, took out his hand, and wiped it down the front of the coat, but it had little effect. He was sweating too much.

He hesitated for a moment, then he tapped the call button repeatedly with his other hand and shifted nervously from foot to foot while he waited. He pulled his sweat-stained hat and his scarf off as the lift arrived with a soft ping and its doors glided open. He hesitated again, then stepped inside. The doors closed after him.

He pressed the button for 17. Nothing happened. He tried again. Still nothing. Then he noticed a security-card slot above the floor buttons. A sign above the slot clearly stated: ENTER SECURITY PASS TO ACCESS FLOORS ABOVE L.

More blood welled up inside his skull.

His only option was to take the elevator to the lobby and try to use one of the main elevators – but there would inevitably be a concierge or a doorman he'd have to get by first. He didn't have much choice. He knew he'd never survive seventeen flights of stairs, and even if he did, the doors on the residential floors probably wouldn't open from the stairwell.

He pushed 'L' and suppressed a surge of bile as the elevator doors started to glide shut – and just then, he heard a voice calling out.

'Can you please hold the elevator?'

His hand struck out instinctively and intercepted the closing doors. As they receded into their slots, he leaned out and saw a fortysomething woman in high heels and a skirt suit carrying a couple of big Whole Foods paper bags and hurrying into the foyer.

'Thanks,' she said in a small fluster as she stepped into the back of the cabin. 'Twenty-four, please.'

His body went rigid. He tried to contain his alarm as his mind raced for a way out, with her staring at him and expecting him to hit that button.

Which he couldn't do. Not without a security card.

'Of course,' he blurted as he started patting his coat as if he were look-ing for his wallet. He smiled sheepishly at her and put on his meekest, most heart-warming old immigrant's tone. 'Let me just find my card for you, I was just going up to the lobby, you see. I needed to see the con-cierge before going upstairs. There's a package I've been waiting for and, anyway,' he kept patting his coat, 'where is that wallet of mine?'

She studied him curiously, then her impatience took over and she huffed and reached into her handbag and pulled out her own pass from her wallet.

'Here,' she said, her tone annoyed, 'this'll be faster.'

She slipped it in and out of the slot brusquely and hit 24, then stepped back, clearly bothered by the delay.

The elevator swiftly ascended the two floors to the lobby, where it stopped with another ping. The doors parted.

Sokolov had to get out. He peered out into the lobby. It was marble-floored, with walls that were paneled in dark wood and a huge chandelier dangling from the ceiling, beyond which he spotted the building's other elevator bank. A concierge's counter was between the two, positioned so that it protected the main lifts from unvetted guests, and the concierge, a tall man with stern features and gelled-back hair, was at his post.

Sokolov glanced at the woman. She eyed him curiously, evidently waiting for him to get out. He gave her a slight smile, his mind racing through his limited options. He couldn't get to the main elevators without getting by the concierge, and he couldn't think of how he'd be able to bluff his way past him. Then again, he couldn't stay put. Not when he'd said he was going to the concierge.

He had to step out.

And just then, as he took his first step and the elevator doors started to close behind him, Sokolov saw the concierge brighten up and heard him say, 'Good evening, Mrs. Greengrass,' just as a small, immaculately groomed terrier trotted into sight, trailing a small, immaculately dressed elderly lady.

'Hello, Diego,' she said as she went up to the desk.

Sokolov froze in place.

He spun on his heels and reached out just in time to catch the elevator doors. He slipped back inside and gave the woman an embarrassed half-smile.

'I'll come back down for it later. That Mrs. Greengrass … Once she gets going with Diego, they'll be chatting for hours.'

The woman didn't seem amused.

He gave her a sheepish nod, then reached out and hit the button for 17.

It lit up.

A bead of sweat trickled down his forehead as the doors slid shut and the elevator started moving.

He was on his way.

'Adams,' the detective grunted.

It was late, he was tired. A cold beer and a foot stool beckoned.

'Detective? Officer Frank Mazzucchelli here, from the hundred-and-sixth. You've got an APB out on a maroon SUV, a Ford Escape. As related to a suspicious death over in Astoria?'

Adams perked up. 'What about it?'

'I'm looking at it.'

Adams was already on his feet and waving his partner over as he got the rundown and took down the location of his caller.

Before hanging up, he asked, 'You already call the feds about this?'

'You're my first call. Figured I'd keep it in the family.'

'Appreciate the heads-up, Frank. We're on our way.'

Adams hung up and grabbed his jacket. 'The SUV the feds flagged from outside the Russians' place?' he told his partner. 'It's at a motel down in Howard Beach.'

'Let's go,' Giordano said, grabbing his own jacket. 'We can call it in from the car.'

Adams stopped and turned to face him, his arms spread open, palms out, his expression mystified. 'You kidding me?'

'What?'

'Screw the feds,' Adams said. 'Our backyard, our squad car, our collar. We can call them once we're done.'

16

Another soft ping and the elevator doors opened on the lobby of the seventeenth floor.

Sokolov gave the woman a quick, courteous bob of the head before stepping out. He glanced back and just caught sight of her studying him before the doors liberated him from her icy stare.

He took in his surroundings. The lobby, which was darkly lit and finished with a moody contemporary wallpaper that depicted a forest of thin tree trunks, led to two corridors, one on either side. A discreet sign indicated that apartments A through C were to the left, with D and E to the right.

Five apartments.

Sokolov cursed inwardly and choked his hat and scarf with his left hand. He had no idea which apartment housed Rogozin.

His eyes darted left and right, his mind struggling for an insight to grab hold of. He wandered about waiting for someone else to arrive on that floor, someone he could ask, then quickly dismissed the idea. People in buildings like these would be suspicious. They'd wonder how he got up there in the first place if he hadn't been invited up by a resident whose apartment number he would obviously have to know. His mind was overflowing with worry and counter-worry, and he decided he had to do something, so he just headed left and went up to the first door.

He swallowed hard and composed himself as best he could and, with his right hand clenched tight around the handgun in his pocket, he hit the apartment's doorbell.

No one showed up, and neither could he hear any movement in the apartment.

Sokolov wiped his sweaty hands on his shirt, then went up to the second apartment, but before hitting the buzzer, he leaned in and pressed his ear against the door to see if he could hear anything. He could hear something faint, he wasn't sure what it was – a TV set maybe? – then a ping from behind him startled him. He stepped away from the door and spun around just as a firm voice asked, 'Sir, you mind telling me who you are and what you're doing here?'

Adams slowed down and pulled up behind the parked squad car. The two officers were standing by their car, waiting. The maroon Escape was parked where they'd said it was, outside the tired motel. There were only two other cars in the parking bay, which wasn't surprising on a weeknight at this time of year. The place was enough of a fleabag to make Adams wonder who in his right mind would choose to stay there and what their reasons would be for doing it.

Had to be someone having a seriously skanky affair, he reckoned. That, or someone needing to lie low.

The two detectives conferred briefly with the uniforms. Mazzucchelli told them he'd been in and had a word with the receptionist.

'Based on where the car's parked, he thinks it belongs to the guest in 107,' Mazzucchelli informed them. 'Russian guy, according to the receptionist. Seems they get a lot of Russkie clients staying here. Anyway, our guy checked in this morning, early. Alone. Paid for three nights. Desk guy hasn't seen him since.' He gave the detectives a knowing grin. 'Our guy paid in cash, naturally.'

'Doesn't everybody?' Adams snorted. He reached out to shake the officer's hand. 'Thanks, guys. We've got it from here.'

'You sure you don't need us to stick around?' Miller asked.

'Nah, we're good,' Adams replied. 'Domestic dispute. Not a biggie.'

Miller didn't seem convinced. 'The BOLO had a FBI contact listing on it too,' he queried. 'Seems like a lot of manpower for a domestic.'

Adams gave him a confident wink. 'It's under control. Thanks again. Appreciate it a lot. You take care now.'

His body language was dismissive enough for Miller to get the unsubtle message. He gave Mazzucchelli an uncertain look. Mazzucchelli shrugged and made a slight nod of the head in the direction of their car. 'We'll see you around.'

* * *

The two men assigned to keep an eye over the motel watched from their car as the two cops climbed back into their cruiser and took off.

They kept watch as the two plainclothes detectives stood there for a moment while the squad car departed, then headed toward the motel's lobby.

'What do we do?' the first man asked. 'They're gonna mess this up.'

'Can't have them do that,' the second man replied. 'Our orders are clear. We need to keep Sokolov's bait in place.'

A quick glance was exchanged, then they both climbed out of their car and strode up to the lobby.

Adams had just shown the weedy receptionist his badge when he saw the two sharp-suited men come through the front door.

They looked completely out of place in that fleabag, but Adams didn't get too much of a chance to wonder about them. They had the sunglasses, the telltale bulges under their jackets, the swagger, the attitude, and one of them had his hands out in a halting gesture.

More goddamn feds, he thought.

'Gentlemen, please, a word,' one of them told the two detectives brusquely, motioning for them to join him to one side, away from the receptionist.

Adams's jaw dropped. 'Excuse me?'

'Call it a friendly intervention,' the suit told him.

'Come again? Who the hell are you?'

'I'm afraid that's above your pay grade.' The other suit took over. 'All you need to know is, you're interfering with an ongoing investigation. We need you to cease and desist, effective immediately.'

Adams glanced at his partner in amazement, then laughed. 'Can you believe these jokers? "Cease and desist"?' He turned to the agent. 'What planet are you from?'

The suits didn't seem amused. 'We need you to pack up and head on home, is what he's saying,' the first agent offered. 'You're about to mess up a sensitive op.'

Adams pulled open one side of his jacket, making a point of exposing his holstered gun. 'Well, how about you get your ass out of here before it ends up needing a different kind of sensitive op, if you get my drift.'

The suit smirked and reached under his jacket.

Adams went for his gun, the other arm out, fingers splayed, and yelled, 'Hands where I can see them. Do it!'

The suit quickly spread his arms wide and flashed the detectives an easy smile. 'Just relax, all right? I think you need to talk to someone.' He paused, then added, smugly, 'At Langley.'

This got Adams even more riled.

First the FBI, now the CIA?

'Hey, buddy, in case you haven't noticed,' he scoffed, 'this isn't Iraq or Iran or wherever the hell else you're supposed to be doing your snooping. You're a couple thousand miles off your jurisdiction.'

The suit slid his partner a wry look and was about to say something back to Adams when Giordano stepped in, his tone hushed and conciliatory. 'What's going on here, guys? What's this all about?'

Before the suit could answer, the front door jangled and swung open.

All four men turned to see who was walking in.

It was a man, alone. Tall, slim, fit. Bushy goatee, longish dark hair parted down the middle, tortoiseshell glasses. Charcoal-gray suit, black shoes, polished.

Also, wearing a glove on one hand. The one that wasn't behind his back.

The man didn't slow down, didn't stop moving. Just kept advancing fluidly toward the quartet, taking big strides. Expressionless, cool, calm, collected. Like he was riding on rails. And as he did, his other hand swung out from behind his back, elegant and lightning quick, rotating out until it was pointed right at them.

Like his other hand, it was also sheathed in a black glove.

Unlike the other, this one had a gun in it.

Automatic. Sound-suppressed. Twenty-round clip.

Sixteen more than he needed.

Fifteen, if you included the receptionist.

Koschey was not one to waste bullets.

17

The concierge came striding out of the elevator toward Sokolov, moving purposefully, a walkie-talkie in his left arm, his right arm extended, his index finger jabbing aggressively at the Russian.

Sokolov faltered, panicking.

'Sir?' the man bellowed.

The woman. The damn woman in the elevator. She must have called downstairs and ratted me out.

He swung a glance down the corridor behind him, but there was no movement coming from the far apartment.

'Sir!' the concierge called out as he came right up to him.

Sokolov pulled out his gun and waved it wildly at the concierge, cupping its grip in both hands.

'Stop right there. Don't come any closer. I'll shoot.'

The concierge stopped in his tracks and held up both his hands in front of him, open-palmed and defensive.

'Whoa, whoa, whoa, take it easy, all right? Take it easy.'

Sokolov took another step back, up against the wall, his eyes jumpy as they scoured the corridor in both directions. 'Dmitry Rogozin, from the Russian consulate. What apartment is he in? I know he's on this floor.'

'Sir, calm down—'

'Which one?' Sokolov yelled as he stabbed the air with the handgun.

'Sir, you should know I've already called the police.' He held up his radio. 'This thing's live. They can hear everything we're saying and they'll be here any minute now. So maybe you should think of getting the hell out of here before it's too late.'

'Shut up and tell me where he is,' Sokolov barked as he reeled under what the concierge had just told him. Was his radio really live? Would he have called the police already?

He stormed right up to the man, waving the gun excitedly just inches from his face. 'Tell me where he is!'

'Sir, you'd better get out of here,' the concierge insisted, his tone steady, his gaze leaping from the gun to Sokolov's eyes and back.

Sokolov was finding it harder to breathe. What good would it do anyway? Through the turmoil in his mind, he managed to see that even if he knew what apartment Rogozin was in, the Russian would never open his door. Sokolov would have to shoot his way in, and then what? The police would probably be there before he could force him out and he'd end up with a pointless, zero-sum hostage situation, with Daphne still held captive and him ending up in custody or dead.

He took one last look down the corridor, then blew past the concierge and rushed to the elevators. He found one of them there, its door blocked open. He didn't really understand why that was, but when he got in, he saw a set of keys in the control panel and realized the concierge had locked them open while he investigated what the stranger was doing there.

Sokolov turned the key, pulled it out, and hit the lobby button.

Less than twenty seconds later, he was scurrying up Thirty-Sixth Street, his hands in his pockets, his hat pulled right down over his face, hugging the buildings and hoping no one was coming after him.

Koschey didn't hesitate, didn't flinch.

Four pulls of the trigger, in quick succession. Four head shots, one after the other. The whole thing was over in less than four seconds.

He didn't even bother to stop and check the bodies. There was no need. He knew the damage his bullets would have made, given where he'd placed them. He'd done it many times before, and his aim had never let him down.

He didn't stop there.

He strode up to the receptionist's desk, stuck the gun right in the terrified man's face, its suppressor barrel pressed against his forehead. Koschey brought his other hand up to his mouth simultaneously, his extended index finger positioned in front of his pursed lips.

'Shhhh,' he told the receptionist. Then he moved the finger away from his own face for a more severe 'Be careful' gesture.

The man responded with some rapid-fire nodding.

'Room number?' he asked.

The man's eyes widened, like he wasn't sure.

'Room number?' Koschey repeated.

'Nine.'

Koschey rewarded him with a third eye.

Then he looked around, made sure the small lobby didn't have any security cameras – he didn't expect any in a dive like that – and walked out.

He hadn't anticipated running into any law-enforcement officers there. That had surprised him. Up until then, it had all gone flawlessly.

The Virgin Atlantic flight from Heathrow.

Breezing through immigration at JFK on the fake Croatian passport.

The Chevy Yukon SUV that had been left for him in the blue garage at Terminal 4 – not a rental, nothing that could flag up the fake ID he'd used to come into the country, not in this day and age when you were fingerprinted and photographed at immigration.

The gear that had been placed for him in its trunk.

The address he'd inputted into his Nexus phone.

All flawless.

Then he'd spotted the two operatives and decided they would need to be eliminated. Then the two cops and the two detectives had arrived, further complicating matters. Fortunately, the cops had been dismissed, or he would have had to deal with them, too.

Unforeseen complications – nuisances, really. He knew that killing them would raise the stakes and make things harder for him. American law enforcement officers didn't hold back when they lost one of their own. Four would make them go ballistic. Koschey knew that.

It didn't bother him.

Besides, he was pretty sure that before he was done, there'd be other reasons for them to go even more ballistic.

And that didn't bother him either.

Daphne Sokolov was huddled in a corner of the small bathroom, shivering.

Her day had turned into a personal hell before it had even begun.

She couldn't understand why this was happening to her. She'd worked through the night at Mount Sinai. It had been a decent shift, with all the patients under her care doing well. Then she'd signed out and left the hospital, anticipating a hot cup of tea and some thyme honey on toast with Leo before he set off to work. Then the insanity had plowed into her life.

The stranger – Russian, she knew – who had intercepted her as she walked to the bus stop, told her he had a gun in his pocket, told her to stay quiet and do as he said if she wanted to see Leo alive again, and forced her into the car that had been trailing just behind them.

The nylon handcuffs with which they'd tied her hands.

The big Band-Aids that locked her eyelids shut.

The sunglasses – they had to be, that's what they felt like – that they then slipped over them.

The drive, to a destination she couldn't see.

And, finally, being dumped here, in this grimy, windowless bathroom, of some hotel, she assumed from the look of the place, her hands secured behind her back with a clasp that was hooked into a water pipe that ran along the bottom of the wall, her eyelids mercifully liberated, her mouth incarcerated in their place, the Band-Aids swapped for a strip of duct tape.

She'd been in there all day, a day that had grown more terrifying by the minute, especially after one of her captors had returned from somewhere where things had gone badly wrong.

He'd come back all shaken and frantic, rambling breathlessly as he tried to tell his partner what had happened.

She'd understood a lot of it. Living with Leo for so long, she'd picked up more than a few words. And what she'd understood had terrified and confused her even more.

The Russian had, it seemed, taken someone he considered his superior to their place. To meet Leo. That, already, stunned her.

What did this have to do with Leo?

They were supposed to bring Leo back, then the Russian's superior, whom he referred to as Yakovlev, had crashed out of a window – *their window* – and fallen to his death. Pushed out by Leo, the Russian believed.

Pushed out? By my Leo?

The Russian had described Yakovlev's corpse in grim detail to his compatriot, and although the sight had spooked him, what terrified him even more, it seemed, was how their boss would react to this news.

Their boss, whom they referred to only as *kuvalda* – the Sledgehammer.

The Russian had finally calmed down and mustered up the courage to call his boss and inform him about what had happened. He'd been given a severe dressing-down – the Russian had recounted it to his partner, word for word. They were told to wait there for further instructions.

That had been hours ago. They hadn't spoken much since – at least, not in a high-enough voice for Daphne to overhear what was being said, especially not with the TV on. But one thing was clear. They were both clearly terrified of what that failure would mean for them. And their terror had infected Daphne and made her even more fearful. None of this made sense. Leo, pushing a man to his death. Not possible. And these men – as scary as they were, their boss was clearly far worse.

Daphne felt frazzled beyond anything she'd ever experienced. She tried to calm herself, but she couldn't think of anything that augured even remotely well. She found herself worrying about whether or not she'd see Leo again, whether or not anyone would ever hear from her again, whether or not this would be the end.

She had to do something, but there wasn't much she could do. Escape was out of the question, not with them on the other side of that door, not with her secured to the radiator pipe. Then her mind locked on a different notion – the thought of leaving some kind of record of what she'd been through, some kind of clue to anyone who came looking for her. She had to – she couldn't just disappear without a trace. But – how?

Then came the knock at the door.

Daphne froze – as did the two men. She could feel it, even with the door between her and them. She heard a few whispers. They hadn't been expecting anyone.

She felt confused – at first, fear took over, the fear of meeting her captors' boss. Then, mercifully, she felt a surge of hope. What if this was something good? Had the police found her? Was she about to be rescued?

She struggled against her bonds, desperate to at least be able to rip the tape off her mouth, to be able to scream out that she was in there, held prisoner by these two thugs. But it was no use. Her hands were tied firmly behind her back. She couldn't reach them.

She calmed down and listened again.

She heard movement in the room. One of the Russians – the one who'd been with Yakovlev – must have gone up to the door of the room. She heard him ask, 'Who is it?'

Then came a flurry of chaotic, frenzied sounds.

First, a sharp crack, like something had just punched through the door.

Then a thud, big and dull, something falling to the floor.

A loud crash immediately followed it – a destructive crash, like a door being bashed off its hinges.

Then a brief yell, a metallic snap, another thud.

Then silence.

Daphne's pulse soared. She was being rescued, she was sure of it. It was the police, or the FBI – had to be. They'd stormed in and incapacitated her kidnappers. Leo must have told them what had happened, and they'd tracked the men down. She was going to be all right. She was going to be reunited with Leo, and everything would be back to normal again.

She kept her eyes trained on the door, her mouth straining against the duct tape, her heart racing in anticipation, waiting for a hero cop to swing it open and untie her and take her out of that horrible prison.

The door did swing open. Only it wasn't a cop.

It wasn't anyone she knew. Just a tall, slim man with a bushy goatee and glasses.

And from the look on his face, she knew he was no hero.

18

S even bodies.

We had seven bodies and no witnesses and nothing but a lot of blood and a whole lot of questions.

Me, I just had one question.

What the hell were the detectives doing here?

It was around eight o'clock, and Aparo and I had driven over the second I'd received the call informing me about the shootings and telling me the two detectives we'd met the day before were dead. The scene outside the motel was lit up like a carnival, with cruisers and unmarkeds crowding the small building haphazardly like they'd been drawn in by a giant magnet. A string of media vans formed an outer perimeter, their satellite dishes deployed like a miniature SETI listening farm. The place was crawling with cops, techs, and reporters, as well as a small army of gawkers who'd come out of the woodwork for a closer look.

I got directed to the chief of detectives of the 114th, a tall African-American man called Byrne. He looked understandably grim, and angry. After the quickest of intros and dispensing with first names, I asked, 'What the hell happened here?'

'I don't know, but … it's brutal,' he said. 'I've been on the job for twenty-seven years. Bronx, Crown Heights. I've seen my share.' He paused, and his expression turned bewildered. 'I've never seen anything like this.'

'What do you mean?'

'See for yourself.'

He led us through the maze of cops and into the small, low-ceilinged lobby of the motel. Four bodies were strewn there, on the tiled floor, so close together that the pools of their blood had blended into each other. Crime-scene technicians were all over them. I recognized Adams and Giordano, but not the other two. And I saw what Byrne meant. Each one of them had a single-entry wound to the head. A couple of foreheads, one eye, and one upper cheek.

Four bullets. Four kills.

Which was stunning, for the simple reason that they couldn't have been fixed targets. Two of them were cops. Trained law-enforcement officers. With the requisite training and reflexes. They would have made a move. And yet there they were, their guns still holstered, lying there like fallen targets in a shooting gallery.

Which got me wondering about the other two.

'What do we know about the other two?' I asked him.

'Not much. Civilians, as far as we can tell. But they were packing.'

I looked again. They had shoulder holsters and automatics poking out from under their suit jackets. Handguns that also hadn't come out when needed. But the suits, the concealed hardware, the fact that they were in there having some kind of meeting with the detectives – these guys had government agency or private contractor scrawled all over them.

'What brought them out there?' I asked.

'They got a call about the maroon Ford Escape.'

My gut did a backflip. 'What, the one from our APB?'

Byrne nodded. 'A squad car spotted it parked outside. The officers called it in.'

'And they called them instead of us.'

He gave me a knowing look. 'Keeping it blue. You know how it goes.'

I did. And I could just see Adams electing not to call and let us in on it, deciding it could lead to some kudos for him and Giordano. Instead, it got them killed.

Stupid, I thought. Stupid and petty. But it happened. More than you'd think.

Still, it didn't tell us what these other guys were doing there. And given how these contractors tended to work, no one was about to just waltz in and fill us in.

I considered the crime scene again. There was a fifth victim, sign-posted by a big splatter of blood on the wall directly behind the reception counter. I took a look behind it and saw the body. Again, one slug, dead center of his forehead.

Another execution.

I cast my gaze around the lobby. I didn't see any bullet holes in the walls. It looked like no other shots had been fired apart from the ones that had ended these five lives. I tried to picture what had gone down here. Even with the element of surprise, even if it had been a sniper taking them out without them even seeing him, the other men would have reacted after the first bullet struck. No way they wouldn't. I mean, there were four of them, all armed. And this was no sniper. There was no angle, no broken glass. No, as I was sure ballistics would bear out, whoever shot them had to have walked in and just shot the four of them. In the face.

Which meant it had to be more than one shooter. Two, at least. At best. If they were both great shots and had the element of surprise. They pull out their guns simultaneously and take the first two out, adjust their aim, fire again. Four men down.

Doable. At a stretch.

'Two shooters?' I wondered aloud.

'Got to be,' Aparo said. 'Maybe more.'

This was going to get messy. I got a sense that a lot of suited people would be coming into my life very soon. Suited, attitude-laden, and not particularly pleasant to work with.

I asked Byrne, 'We were told seven dead. Where are the other two bodies?'

'This way.'

He led us back out and down the side of the motel to Room 9. Its door had been kicked in, but not before someone had fired a shot through its peephole. The lucky receiver of that slug was sprawled out right behind the door. It had gone straight through his right eye. Even with the damage of the entry wound, I recognized him from the YouTube footage as our unknown observer from outside the Sokolovs' apartment.

There was another dead man inside the room, by the bed. Looked like one solitary round, again, though this one was through the heart. Otherwise, the room looked undisturbed.

'Any IDs on them?'

'No,' Byrne said. 'But we'll have names and jackets soon enough. They're covered in ink.'

I leaned in for a closer look. The guy with the missing eye had tattoos on his fingers, hand, and I could see the edge of one on the base of his neck. The guy by the bed was the same. And from the designs and the Cyrillic letters, it was obvious we were dealing with Russian gangsters. The tats would tell us a lot, and fast. Russian criminals used tattoos to tell their life stories. We'd know where they'd been incarcerated, what gang they were in, what rank they had. A delightful and charming tradition, and a boon to law-enforcement agencies.

I glanced around the room and wondered if this was a place they often used to lie low. A chat with the manager was on the agenda.

I still didn't get what had happened here. Some shooters had showed up and gunned down the detectives and the other two outside, as well as these two. Why? To shut them up? What did they know that the shooters didn't want the detectives to find out? One of them was outside the Sokolovs' place. Was he there with Yakovlev, or was he just keeping tabs on him or on Sokolov?

Too many questions. Too many unknowns.

I walked into the bathroom to have a look. It was pretty basic. Sink, mirror, toilet, bathtub with a fixed shower head. Old-style column radiator, small window mounted high, white floor tiles. Reasonably clean. The bath's shower curtain was dry, its soap bar unopened, its large towels unused. The Russians clearly hadn't been there for too long, which wasn't surprising. I didn't think they were staying there.

'No luggage, right?' I asked.

'Nope.'

I was getting impatient with myself. We were playing catch-up while the bodies were piling up. I unconsciously stopped in front of the mirror and stared at myself for a moment, willing myself to figure this out before more bodies dropped, then as I turned away, something snagged my attention. A small glint, coming from behind the radiator.

I crossed over to it and bent down for a closer look. There was definitely something there, small and silver. It had been jammed in from the side. I took out my pen and nudged it around until it broke loose and fell to the floor.

I picked it up. It was a watch. But not a normal watch with a wristband. This was a fob watch, hanging from a short, two-inch chain.

A nurse's fob watch.

'Check this out,' I called out to Aparo.

He stepped in. I held it up to him.

'Daphne Sokolov?' he asked.

'Got to be. She was here.' The watch jump-started my mind, which had started screening various possible scenarios.

'So that's what the shooters were doing,' Aparo said. 'They came for her.'

'Or for them,' I wondered aloud. 'Maybe she and Sokolov were both being held here.'

'Or maybe she was being held here and Sokolov came for her,' Aparo offered.

'Our meek science teacher turning into the Terminator? I'm not sure I buy that.'

Aparo pursed his lips in agreement. 'Maybe he recruited some muscle to break her out.'

'Maybe.' I frowned, frustrated by what I felt we were getting sucked into. 'Here's our problem. We don't know anything about this Sokolov, and I don't think we're going to get anywhere until we do.'

I tried to take a step back and process what we knew and what we were seeing.

The one-eyed bandit is outside Sokolov's place while, up in the apartment, there's a scuffle that ends with a Russian diplomat going through a window and falling to his death. Were they there together – in which case, why was our dearly departed diplomat openly cavorting with a tattooed Russian gangster? – or was the heavy watching the diplomat? Then we have Sokolov's wife going missing that same morning. Cyclops ends up here, with another Russian wiseguy, and they've got at least Daphne Sokolov locked up in the bathroom. Maybe Sokolov, too. The detectives and two men in black show up here, and end up leaking all over the lobby. Then the killers take out our Russian heavies and leave with Daphne, and maybe her husband, too.

Too many maybes.

I bent down to look at the base of the radiator, wondering if she'd been held there, if she'd been cuffed to it and if anyone else had too. It was definitely the best option. The towel rail wouldn't handle anything with more muscle than a two-year-old. Same for the shower rail. And the base of the toilet, well, that would've been just nasty. And cumbersome.

Then I saw something else. On the base of the wall, above the row of tiles that skirted it. Something had been scratched into the paint.

I leaned in for a closer look.

They were letters. Cyrillic letters.

I looked at the watch again. It had a safety-pin fastener, like on a brooch. Which could easily have been used to carve the letters.

'There's something here,' I told Aparo. 'In Russian.'

Aparo got down on his haunches for a closer look. 'What does it say?'

'Hang on.' I pulled out my smart phone, launched the Google Search app, and went to Google Translate. I selected Russian to English, brought up the Cyrillic keypad, and typed in the word: Кувалда. It came back with what it sounded like, *kuvalda*, and what it meant in English.

I told Aparo.

He gave me an impressed nod. I nodded back. We both knew what this meant. Daphne Sokolov had definitely been held here. And to find out why, we now knew who to talk to. A Russian mobster who'd been on the bureau's radar for years. A smug slimeball by the name of Yuri Mirminsky, nicknamed *kuvalda*.

The Sledgehammer.

19

Leo Sokolov was back in his ratty hotel room, standing by the grimy window, staring out at the noisy, traffic-clogged street below.

He was angry at himself. He'd almost screwed everything up with his impetuousness, which wasn't like him. Sokolov wasn't a rash person. He normally thought things through, took his time. If anything, he was usually overly cautious and analytical. And yet here, faced with a crisis, he'd jumped into the deep end without checking the pool first.

He was lucky to be alive – and free. Very lucky. He thought back to his failed attempt at kidnapping Rogozin and realized how close he was to it all going seriously wrong. He caught a ghostly reflection of his face in the glass and felt a pang of shame and remorse. He chided himself again. He couldn't do this again. Not like that. He'd thought it would work out, his being brazen, as he had been all those years ago, when he'd outwitted his CIA handlers. But this was a different world, and he was a different man.

He couldn't afford to fail again. He'd need to do better.

And he needed to get help. He couldn't do it alone. Not anymore.

He didn't move for more than an hour. He just stood there, in the darkness, staring out into the night, oblivious to the bustle of the city outside his grimy window.

Remembering. Thinking. Searching for an inspiration, for someone he could turn to.

An ally.

Then, out of the confusion in his mind, a name came forth.

He didn't want to drag anyone else into the chaos of his now-exploded life, but he really didn't have a choice if he was ever going to see his

Daphne again. And who better than someone who, against all of Sokolov's advice, seemed incapable of doing anything else than dedicating himself to a life of crime.

Jonny.

He needed to find Jonny.

20

The Sledgehammer.

Yet another of the high-quality individuals we'd welcomed to our land of opportunity with open arms, only to end up bitterly, bitterly disappointed.

I'm not sure that he was tired, poor, huddled, or yearning to breathe free when we let him in. In fact, I can't imagine that the person who rubber-stamped his visa didn't have a pretty good idea of what kind of lowlife he really was. But we still let him in, and here we were, sixteen years later, wasting time and money investigating his sordid activities and looking for a way to either lock him up – and waste more time and money that way – or kick him back out.

Same old, same old.

Yuri Mirminsky came into the country on a business visa, indicating he'd be working in the movie industry. When we got our first taste of what he was really up to, we discovered that the real reason he'd left Moscow was because it had become too dangerous for him there, what with the savage competition between Mafiya mobsters after the collapse of the Soviet Union. Needless to say, Mirminsky never made it to Hollywood. He got busy right here in New York and was running one of the strongest ROC groups on the whole East Coast.

Yeah, we've even got an acronym for it. ROC. Russian organized crime.

Collateral damage from the fall of Communism.

I often wondered if we'd have been better off with the Evil Empire still in place.

The Sledgehammer's talent was much like Lucky Luciano's. He was an organizer. He took bit gangs of Russian bangers and stitched them together into one big crime corporation, with him running the show. And his talent served him well. His branch of the Solntsevskaya gang now had more than two hundred upstanding immigrants living among us and beavering away at drug-running, extortion, and a whole bunch of other fine pursuits.

The first time I heard of him, I remember wondering where he got the nickname. My wishful thinking was that he'd been a huge fan of Peter Gabriel. Maybe he was. I mean, back then, who wasn't? But this sledge-hammer was different. It originated from his early days in Russia, before he came to the States. After the Wall came down. Back when he was an out-of-work KGB 'niner,' an unemployed member of its Ninth Director-ate who'd gone from muscleman providing protection to the Kremlin's top dogs to up-and-coming *bratok* – a low-level Mafiya thug. Yuri got into a fight with some poor schmuck and he punched him so hard the guy's guts spilled out. Literally. The guy had recently had surgery and his stitches hadn't been out for that long, but still. One punch.

I don't know about the choice of nickname. I'd have gone with Drago. Or Popeye. But maybe that last one was too American. Besides, the *French Connection* movie had it locked down. For my generation, anyway.

The problem was, Mirminsky was insulated. I'd never met the guy, but the Bureau had been involved in a couple of cases over the years that linked back to him, the most recent of which was a colossal fraud where Mirminsky and his associates operated dozens of small medical 'no-fault' clinics and bilked car-insurance companies out of tens of millions of dollars for fictitious treatments of car-accident victims. We never got anywhere near taking him down. Mirminsky was a smart *vor* – what Russian Mafiya bosses were called, short for *vor y zakone*, meaning 'thief-in-law' – and he knew how to work the system. He never had any direct involvement with any of his cabal's dirty deeds. Nothing ever got tied back to him, which is how it was with most, if not all, of the Russian mobsters who'd left the old country for the security and due process of the West. They raped and pillaged, they partied, we watched.

Depressing stuff.

Still, he'd lost two underlings here, which was something to smile about. And he was also clearly involved in whatever had led to the death of two NYPD detectives, which was going to bring down some serious heat on him.

Maybe his days on our sunny shores were numbered.

I wasn't holding my breath. But I was happy to do everything I could to help bring that about.

'We ought to pay the Sledgehammer a visit,' I told Aparo as we hit traffic on the approach to the Brooklyn Bridge. 'Rattle his gilded penthouse of a cage.'

Aparo didn't answer immediately. I glanced across and saw that he had a little grin going.

'What are you smiling about?'

He put on a mock-pensive look, then said, 'I think we should. But before we do that, I think we need to rattle someone else's cage before she gets too much of a heads-up about what just went down.'

I knew exactly what he was thinking. And, in fairness, I'd been thinking the same thing. We also needed to know more about what seemed to be the key to all this: Sokolov. Which was why I called Larisa Tchoumitcheva right there and then and told her we needed to meet, pronto.

'J. G. Melon's in an hour,' I told Aparo after I hung up with her. Then I added, 'I don't have time to drop you off at the office. York Street subway station good for you?'

His face dropped for only a couple of seconds before he realized I was kidding, but those seconds were priceless.

Larisa hung up with Reilly, thought about it, then dialed another number.

Her boss took her call promptly.

'I just got a call from Reilly. He wants to meet.'

'Good,' the man answered. 'We need to know more about what happened at the motel. Have you heard anything new?'

'No more than we already know. Koschey took out the two *bratki* who were watching over Sokolov's wife.'

'Which means he's got her now,' the man said. 'And he'll use her to draw Sokolov out.'

'No doubt.'

Larisa's boss went quiet for a moment, then said, 'We can't let Sokolov slip out of our hands. Do you understand? This is imperative. I can't emphasize that enough.'

Still with the secrecy, Larisa fumed inwardly. But she knew better than to ask. They'd already made it clear that Sokolov's CV was beyond her need to know. And so far, her attempts to gain access to his file had failed.

She masked her frustration and said, 'I understand.'

'Call me back when you're done,' he told her. 'And Larisa?'

'Yes?'

'Get him to like you.'

21

Koreatown, Manhattan

The train rumbled into Thirty-Fourth Street, causing Sokolov to force his eyes open and pull himself to his feet.

He'd spent the whole ride thinking about the eager-to-please sixteen-year-old who had shown so much promise and, in particular, such a flair for science, when he first became Sokolov's pupil. Sokolov had done everything he could to encourage and help the boy – from after-school coaching to loaning him books from his own collection. But when the change happened, it appeared to take place overnight. Yaung John-Hee – or simply Jonny, without the 'h,' as he was known at school – had started off by skipping homework assignments and coming into school late. Then he started missing whole days, and he'd finally ended up getting expelled when a gun was found in his backpack.

How it had gotten there wasn't cut-and-dry. Not even close.

Jonny had consistently stuck to his story. He said he'd just happened to find the gun in Clearview Park. What complicated the matter was that the Beretta 9mm turned out to be free of prints – except for Jonny's – and the police to whom it had mandatorily been reported linked it to three deaths. They suspected it actually belonged to Jonny's older brother, Kim-Jee, a low-level dealer in one of the city's Korean gangs. And Jonny had a rock-solid alibi for the night of the killings, so the police had nothing with which to pressure him.

At each step, Sokolov had tried to talk the boy around, to try to turn him away from the violent and self-destructive black hole that was drawing him in. At each step, Jonny had pretended to listen, then he'd just continued down his own path. Sokolov had even put himself on the line. He had vouched for the kid with both the school's principal and the cops when Jonny had been suspected of dealing drugs at the school. He had assured anyone who would listen that Jonny was different from his brother. That the boy wanted to go to college and become an engineer. That he and Jonny had an understanding. Then, three years ago, there was this business with the gun and Sokolov couldn't protect him anymore. Nor did he really want to. He was left looking ridiculous. He was still angry about how Jonny had managed to deceive him so completely, still unsure about whether he had been played the entire time or whether Jonny had honestly tried to stay on the right side of the law but hadn't been strong enough to resist his brother's pull.

At the moment, it was that calculating ability to lie that Sokolov was counting on. It was a gamble to even approach the volatile young man, but to Sokolov, it was his best shot. He was certain he'd glimpsed a trace of remorse in Jonny the last time they'd spoken, remorse over how the student had manipulated his teacher and rendered him unreliable in the eyes of the school's board. So much about high school was the ability to read character, and Sokolov, who had always prided himself on his skills in this area, had proven himself fallible.

Sokolov dragged himself up the stairs at Herald Square and set off down Sixth Avenue. The shops were empty and the Empire State Building loomed overhead like a giant sentry. Sokolov tucked his hands deeper into his pockets, where he again felt the cool grip of the handgun. He found it oddly disconcerting that there he was, all that time later, coming to see Jonny, and that it was he who was carrying a gun. *Desperate times, desperate measures,* he reminded himself, and pushed the discomfort away as he turned onto Thirty-Third Street and followed it into the heart of Koreatown.

After the cops had raided the back room of the community center in Murray Hill where the brothers used to hang out, Kim-Jee and Jonny had begun to spend much more time in Koreatown. They'd eventually started working at their aunt's restaurant, the Green Dragon, which was right in the heart of Koreatown, between Thirty-Third and Thirty-Second Streets. Sokolov had heard that since then, Kim-Jee had risen through the ranks of the gang, with Jonny riding in his wake. Anything more than that would be a guess. Better to see for himself, now that he was there.

He walked past several small clusters of diners who'd stepped outside for a smoke and went in. He knew he was taking a risk just walking into the restaurant unannounced, but as he had already convinced himself on the way over, he really didn't have a choice. It was a fair bet that, whether he was a fugitive or not, Jonny's relatives would be reluctant to call the cops to their premises whatever the circumstances. Not after everything Sokolov had done for Jonny over the years.

The place was huge, and bustling. Even though it was almost two in the morning, the Green Dragon was almost full. Korean pop music was blaring from speakers and the din of multiple conversations fought for airspace with the sound of tables being cleared and food being delivered to customers. Almost the entire clientele was Korean, though a table by the window was occupied by a group of young tourists clearly enjoying the authentic atmosphere and cuisine.

Sokolov walked over to the hostess, a petite woman in her twenties wearing a white silk dress decorated with a single green dragon that looked like it was coiled around her torso.

'Is Yaung John-Hee here?'

The woman's expression didn't change at all.

'I'm his teacher. Well, I was,' he explained. 'I used to teach him science. At Flushing High School.'

The woman's eyebrows slid upward almost imperceptibly.

'I need to talk to him,' he pressed on. 'Tell him – tell him Mr. Soko is here. Tell him I need to see him. And tell him . . .' He hesitated. 'Tell him I saw Kim-Jee give him something. He'll understand.'

The hostess studied him for a second, then motioned to a waitress to cover the floor before she disappeared through the swing doors into the kitchen.

Sokolov watched her go, then turned around and sat himself down at an empty table by the back of the room. The table was still covered in half-eaten dishes, sauce-smeared plates, and empty Hite bottles. Without looking at the hostess, Sokolov removed his coat and hung it on the back of his chair, then grabbed a menu from a nearby table and started to read it.

He gazed around the large, crowded space.

He'd missed them when he'd entered because they were sitting in a booth, but the two young guys wearing leather jackets and vests over Uniqlo T-shirts had the unmistakable look of Kkangpae. One of them had the butt of a gun not-too-discreetly poking out from under his vest.

Sokolov looked away in time to see the hostess coming back through the swing doors. She beckoned for him to follow her. He grabbed his coat and followed the woman to the back of the restaurant and noticed that the two guys were following him with their eyes.

She led him through the swinging doors and into the kitchen, which was deafening and bursting with frenetic staff. The hostess cut straight through the center of it all without slowing, with everyone in there moving out of her way like a parting sea. Sokolov had a tougher time, narrowly avoiding a waiter carrying two huge plates of ribs but still managing to knock a pile of empty food containers from the edge of a counter. He left the kitchen to the sound of loud swearing in Korean.

The hostess entered a tight hallway with only two exits: one a set of fire doors, the other a narrow staircase leading up to the next floor. Without looking back at him, she continued up the stairs. Sokolov followed, already struggling for breath after the first flight. When he reached the very top – three floors above the restaurant – the hostess was waiting for him by a metal door. She watched him, blank-faced, as he joined her, then she turned and knocked at the door. Seconds later, it swung open. A cloud of smoke hit Sokolov. A Korean man, young, with green streaks in his hair, a lit cigarette in his hand, and intense eyes fixed on Sokolov, stood aside to let them in.

Sokolov followed the hostess in.

Yaung John-Hee lazed on a battered leather sofa inside the dimly lit, smoke-filled room, his cowboy-booted feet up on a glass coffee table, on which sat a wrap of what Sokolov knew had to be cocaine, a razor blade, a recently licked mirror, a handgun, several cell phones, and an open silver MacBook. Jonny looked just as Sokolov remembered him: the thick black hair, long, with wild shards of it cutting across his indifferent, cool eyes. Thin, too, but Sokolov knew it was all really coiled, tight muscle, waiting to lash out if and when called upon. He was dressed in a black bomber jacket that had a big Armani logo on it, over washed-out black jeans.

Opposite the sofa stood its equally worn-out twin. Green Streaks crossed back and took up his own slouch on it. A large plasma screen hogged the side wall, with an Xbox and an array of games and controllers strewn on the floor in front of it.

The hostess and the boys exchanged a few short words, then the hostess left the room, barely glancing at Sokolov before shutting the door behind her and leaving Sokolov with nothing but words.

Still standing, Sokolov pointed at the gun. 'I assume that one is yours.' The smoke was bothering him, but he did his best not to show it.

'In the sense that I'm using it for now, yeah.' Jonny gestured for Sokolov to sit opposite him.

Sokolov sat down, next to Green Streaks, careful to avoid knocking the low table. 'Not in my direction, I hope.'

'We'll see.' He took a long toke, then brushed the smallest trace of white powder from a lapel of his jacket. He blew the smoke out of his nostrils slowly, looked at Sokolov dead straight, and said, low and matter-of-factly, 'We never go up against the Russians.'

Sokolov nodded, a pained half-smile breaking through his lined eyes. Jonny was as savvy as he remembered. He motioned at the TV. 'You saw the news?'

Jonny nodded. 'Looks bad, Mr. Soko. Me, I'd say you pushed that Russkie out your window. But then again, what do I know.' He gave him a knowing smile, then his smugness faded and his expression shifted to betray a hint of unease. 'So what's that you were saying down there? Did you really see Kim-Jee give me something?'

Sokolov held his gaze. 'Of course not. But he did. We both know it.'

'No,' Jonny hissed as he sat forward, crushing his cigarette butt into an overflowing ashtray. '*I* killed them. All Kim-Jee did was make our aunt give me that alibi. All 'cause I didn't throw the gun fast enough. And now look at me, right?' He sounded both proud and full of regret at the same time. 'The boss-man is in Miami and we're running the show.' He swept his arm in a casual arc across the room.

Sokolov felt as though he were going to pass out from the combination of the smoke and the effort of maintaining his composure. He became conscious of his heart thudding against his rib cage. He closed his eyes, tilted his head slightly back, and took in a couple of shallow breaths.

Jonny was silent.

Sokolov opened his eyes. 'They took my wife.'

Jonny looked at his quizzically. 'What you say?'

'Daphne. They took her.'

Jonny sighed and shook his head from side to side, slowly. 'Aww, Mr. Soko. What did you do?'

Sokolov hated what he was about to say, but he couldn't think of any way around it. 'They're going to kill her if I don't pay,' he muttered. 'I owe them money. Three hundred thousand.'

Jonny slapped the table, his hand splayed out flat. '*Byung-shin-a*. What the hell were you thinking?'

'I don't know. Please ... I need your help. I don't want her to suffer because of my stupid mistake.'

'*Gaesaekki dul jokka ra kuh hae,*' Jonny rasped. 'Kidnapping an old woman like that. Fucking animals.' He grabbed the razor and starting cutting himself a fresh line. 'I'm sick of the *hule jasik* Russkies. They're all over the place. Acting like this is downtown Moscow.' He shook his head. 'Who has her?'

'I don't know exactly. I have a phone number. That's all.'

Jonny bent forward and hovered inches from the coke, a dollar bill rolled in one hand. 'You don't got the money, do you?'

'No, but—'

'Don't matter,' he interrupted just before he sent a line up his nose.

Sokolov watched, perplexed, as Jonny leaned right back, his eyes closed. After a moment, the Korean said, 'Tell them you have the money.'

Sokolov couldn't hide his shock. 'What?'

'Tell them you have their damn money.' Without looking at Sokolov, Jonny shook his head. 'You knew I would help. That's why you came.'

'I wasn't sure.'

'You can read people fine.' He snorted another line, then wiped his nose and fixed Sokolov with a hard glare.

'Talk to them. Say you have the money. Set up a meet. We'll take care of the *go-jas* and get your wife back.' He studied Sokolov for a moment, then asked, 'Where are you staying?'

'A small hotel. Downtown.'

'You safe there?'

Sokolov shrugged.

'You stay here,' he told his old teacher. 'We have room downstairs. You'll be safe here. My cousin Ae-Cha will take you down and get you what you need.' He motioned to Green Streaks, bobbing his head in the direction of the door.

Green Streaks got up and unlocked the door. Ae-Cha was still standing there. She stepped in without saying a word. Jonny blurted some orders at her. Ae-Cha nodded quietly, then beckoned for Sokolov to follow.

Sokolov turned to Jonny. 'What about Kim-Jee? Don't you need to ask him?'

'Kim-Jee? He's out. His girlfriend's expecting twins. Two girls. Living the dream, isn't that right?' He snorted derisively.

Sokolov nodded and stepped out, and the door swung shut behind him, drowning out Jonny's bitter laughter.

We all choose our own paths, thought Sokolov.

Jonny had chosen the power of violence.

He had tried to choose peace.

Until now.

22

Larisa had suggested we meet at J. G. Melon's, on Seventy-Fourth and Third. The restaurant was close to where she lived. I loved the place, and since she'd already had dinner while neither I nor my demure partner had eaten much all day, we snagged a quick table and ordered a couple of Swiss cheese burgers, skins, and Cokes.

'You gonna behave?' I asked Aparo.

He grinned. 'Why on earth would you ask that?' He looked pensive for a second, then he subtly raised his arm a bit and leaned his head sideways and took a quick whiff to check himself.

I made a mental note to see if there was anything I could start slipping him that would throttle back his testosterone a couple of notches.

We just about managed to get through our burgers by the time she breezed in. I stood up, caught her eye and waved her over. She threaded her way to our table, put her hand out for a businesslike handshake, and directed a warm 'Nice to see you again' at me with a look that lingered a second more than was strictly necessary.

'So what's going on?' she asked, straight to the point. 'You said it was important.'

'Did you catch the news?'

She nodded, then her expression changed into one of surprise as she made the connection. 'The shootings in Brooklyn?'

'Yes. Two of the victims were Russians.'

'Oh my God. Not—'

'No, not the Sokolovs. Just a couple of hired guns. I don't have names yet, but we think they're part of Yuri Mirminsky's crew. You know who I'm talking about, right?'

'Of course,' she said, not exactly upbeat about it.

A waitress dropped by, and Larisa hesitated, then ordered a Bloody Mary. Aparo and I stayed with our Cokes.

Aparo unlocked his phone, pulled up a photo from its picture gallery, and showed it to her.

'Do you know this guy?'

She looked at it, then shook her head. 'No. Should I?'

He made a hold-on-a-sec gesture as he pulled up another one. 'Wait, that was the before shot. This one's more recent.'

He showed it to her. She flinched – slightly. He'd just shown her two shots of the dead Russian hoodlum: a screen grab from the phone video taken outside Sokolov's building, the other with a bullet through his forehead.

Larisa gave Aparo a cold stare. 'Are you done?'

'Hey, I'm just wondering what the connection is between your dead coworker and a known *bratki*,' Aparo replied.

'Is there a connection?' she asked coyly. Then she turned to me. 'Is this what you asked me here for? Were you hoping to shock me into saying something I shouldn't and spill all our dirty little secrets?'

I smiled, took a breath, and leaned in. 'We've got seven dead bodies, Larisa. Eight, counting Yakovlev. Now, that's a big deal in this city. It's not something we take lightly. This is going to get noisy. The papers haven't even got started with Yakovlev, and the minute they hear two of the dead at the motel were *bratki* ..." I gave her a knowing look. "You can imagine the headlines. And the kind of attention you and everyone else at the consulate are going to get hit with."

She frowned.

'It's not going to be fun,' I pressed. 'And given the protests last week about what's been going on back in Moscow, I'm sure it's the kind of publicity you'd rather avoid.'

'So what do you want from me?'

'This is all about Sokolov.'

She looked at me quizzically. 'Why do you think the two are connected? The shootings and Yakovlev?'

'Come on,' Aparo said, holding his phone up. 'The "before" shot? That was taken outside the Sokolovs' apartment a few nanoseconds after your buddy took the quick way down.'

She eyed us thoughtfully, like she was wondering how much to say.

'What's Sokolov involved in?' I pressed.

'I don't know.'

Even though I doubted that, I really couldn't tell for sure whether she was being honest with me. I studied her for a second, then I half smiled. Not a warm kind of smile. A smile that said 'I know you have to play this game, and I know you know I know that.'

'Look, I don't know what's going on here, but whatever it is, it all goes back to Sokolov. It started with him. So we can either wait until this all spins out of control and you're running around doing damage limitation and rebutting every blogger and nutty conspiracy theory out there ... or we can work together to shut it down before it gets even messier. But to do that, I need you to level with me. I need to know what Sokolov was involved in and why all these people are interested in him. I need to know what your "third secretary for maritime affairs" – and yes, I did give her the air quotes – 'was doing out at his apartment.'

She flashed us both an amused smile and waited while the waitress deposited her Bloody Mary on the table and walked off before leaning in. "Third secretary'?' she asked, mimicking my air quotes. 'Should I take offense?'

Aparo spread his palms out. 'Seriously? "Maritime affairs"? "*Third* secretary'? Like we've got that many maritime issues that two diplomats aren't enough to deal with them?'

'We have plenty of outstanding maritime issues. Fishing rights and Arctic exploration and boundary agreements and all kinds of disputes going on all the time. Yakovlev had his hands full.'

'And yet,' I countered, 'for some reason, the first thing on his agenda Monday morning was to go to Sokolov's apartment and get pushed out of his window – which I'm guessing didn't have anything to do with depleted tuna stocks.'

She eyed me curiously.

'OK, fine,' I said, in a conciliatory tone. 'I know there's stuff you can't talk to me about. There's a lot we can't talk about either. But I'm telling you this is going to turn into a PR disaster for you. You want to roll with it, fine. You want to head it off and make it go away, then help us out here. Besides, it might be better for you to have us focused on the bad guys than casting our net all over the place.' I flashed her a knowing look. 'You never know what else we might drag up.'

She took a sip of her drink, then sat back and studied me and Aparo for a moment with her head tilted slightly. After a long second, she sighed with exasperation. 'We don't have anything on Sokolov, and that's the truth. Nothing. Which in itself is curious.' She paused, then asked, 'What do you know about his background? Do you know when he came to this country?'

I remembered what Daphne's sister had told me. 'He got married in 1983, and I don't think he'd been here that long. A couple of years, maybe.'

She nodded like it confirmed something that was burgeoning in her mind. 'So if he came to America in '81 or '82, the questions we need to ask are, where did he come from and how did he get here?'

Aparo said, 'His sister-in-law said he came from Russia.'

'Well, that's why I ask. Because it wasn't that easy to leave the Soviet Union back then. Under the Communists, no one was allowed to leave. The only people who made it here were dissidents and defectors who managed to escape and were granted political asylum after they got out – and they're all on record. We know who they are, and Sokolov isn't one of them. Then in 1970, after Kuznetsov and his gang of refuseniks tried to hijack their way out of there, Brezhnev agreed to allow some Jews, but only Jews, to leave – and only to Israel. But a lot of them never intended to stay on in Israel. They just used it as a way out and ended up here, in New York.'

Actually, I knew it wasn't a humanitarian move by the Politburo chiefs, nor were its consequences that great for us. This vast exodus wasn't just made up of innocent, persecuted Jews. The KGB simultaneously and quietly released thousands of hard-core criminals from the Soviet gulags, the ones who happened to be Jewish, and let them leave. In one swift move that probably gave rise to a lot of mirth in the Kremlin, the KGB dumped these ex-cons on an unsuspecting world – knowing most of them would end up here. We didn't know which of the immigrants we were taking in had been in jail and if so, for what reason, since the Russians never shared their criminal records with us. Still don't, for that matter. Fidel Castro, ever the faithful follower of his Soviet mentors, took a page out of the same playbook several years later during the Mariel boatlift, emptying a lot of his jails and shipping them our way, with the ensuing effect it had on crime in South Florida.

'And that policy didn't change until 1985,' Larisa continued, 'when

Gorbachev relaxed controls and opened the borders. But you're saying Sokolov came here around 1981, before Gorby's policy shift, and I don't remember seeing a mezuzah or anything like that in the Sokolovs' apartment. Do we know if Sokolov is Jewish?'

'I don't,' I said. 'I know his wife is Greek. And they had icons in the entrance hall.'

'Christian icons,' she noted pointedly.

'Yes.'

'Which matches the fact that he's not on any of our lists either. So if he didn't defect and if he wasn't part of the Jewish exodus, then how did he manage to get out of the Soviet Union at a time when no one was allowed out?'

I pondered her words and realized we needed to do a lot more digging into Sokolov.

Assuming that was even his real name.

'OK. We'll have a look at that.'

She nodded, then seemed to remember something. 'Oh, and I need your help on something. We can't get hold of the coroner's report on Yakovlev. Can you get them to release it to us?'

I couldn't see any harm in that. I glanced at Aparo, and he shrugged. 'Sure.'

'Did it show anything unexpected? Was he drugged?'

I smiled. Just the kind of thing a 'counselor for public affairs' would think of asking. 'Nothing unusual in his system,' I told her. 'He was clean.'

'Look into Sokolov's background. I'll keep digging on my end. But let's agree on something. If we're going to contain this and bring it to a swift and mutually agreeable conclusion, we need to work together. Even though, like you said, there will be things we can't tell each other. But we have to try and get past that. We need to be open with each other. Keep each other informed.' She leaned in and settled her gaze on me. 'If this is going to work, we need to share – maybe more than what would normally be considered acceptable.'

I wasn't sure if she was toying with us or not, if watching what effect she had on men was just a personal little thrill for her or if it was a deliberate tactic to get our brains steamed up and our tongues loosened. Either way, it was breathtakingly effective. On other guys, of course. Aparo's pulse had to have quickened by a couple dozen beats, easy.

'OK,' I finally said with staggering eloquence. And despite the tumult in my mind, one thing was becoming clearer by the minute: this was all about Sokolov.

They obviously wanted him.

Which meant we had to find him first.

Larisa watched Reilly and Aparo drive off, then pulled out her phone as she headed home.

'Where are they on Sokolov?' her boss asked.

'They don't know anything.'

'Did you help them along?'

'I gave them something. Pointed them in the right direction.'

'Good,' he told her. 'Build on that. And get closer to Reilly. We'll use whatever resources we have available to help track Sokolov down. But if the FBI manages to find him before we do, you'll need to make sure we have enough time to get there first.'

'I'll keep you posted,' she told him. Then she hung up.

She turned down Seventy-Eighth, feeling a bit hollow inside. This was definitely turning into the most significant assignment of her career, but not knowing the full story was really starting to grate at her. She hadn't signed up for this in order to just be a pawn in someone else's game, and she didn't like playing a role without knowing the full backstory. Her line of work was all about judgment calls, and she was starting to question why they weren't telling her the full story, with the obvious answer – the one that piqued her curiosity even more – being that they thought she might act differently if they did.

She had to get the entire story on who Sokolov really was. And given how her access to that information seemed to be blocked from all sides, she hoped Reilly would prove to be as good as they made him out to be.

Until then, she had no choice but to keep playing the game.

23

Daphne Sokolov flinched as she felt the man's presence close in on her. She was on a hard, cold floor, her hands tied behind her back and attached to some kind of pipe, a replay of what she'd been through at the hotel. Only this time, she was the prisoner of someone else.

Someone far scarier.

She'd heard him gun down the two men who'd kidnapped her, and he hadn't appeared to be even remotely flustered by it moments later when he'd taken the band-aids off her eyes. There was a coldness in his demeanor, an almost inhuman rigidity that was deeply unsettling. He'd also let her see his face, which was equally disturbing – not his face, but the notion that he'd just killed two men and didn't seem to mind that she knew that and could identify him if it ever came down to it. The fact that he wasn't worried about that worried her. A lot. She was no expert on crime, but one thing she did know was that killers didn't usually leave witnesses behind.

She felt the man bend down, heard his clothes crease as he leaned into her. She sensed his hands reaching out to her, then he was pulling off the balaclava he'd covered her head with. Her eyes quickly adjusted to the light, and the man's face came into focus.

He looked the same, only this time, up close, she could tell that the beard was fake and the glasses too clear to be anything more than a prop. She tried to take some comfort in the fact that he was concealing his true face behind the disguise, tried to cling to the fleeting notion that maybe it meant he didn't intend to kill her after all, but the comfort was short-lived. The iciness chiseled into his face quickly smothered any notion of possible mercy.

He stayed uncomfortably close, studying her.

Her eyes darted around to get a look at where he was keeping her. She was in a bare, windowless room, like an office in a light industrial warehouse that hadn't been used for a while. The floor wasn't carpeted, just a cold, bare screed. Then she noticed something on the floor next to her captor: a small toiletries pouch, the kind used for travel.

She didn't quite know why, but the sight scared her even more.

He stayed unnervingly silent. After a moment, she summoned up the courage to speak.

'Why am I here?' she asked, trying to control the quiver in her lips. 'What do you want from me?'

He just stared at her quietly, then his eyes dropped to his pouch and he unzipped it. He reached in and pulled out a couple of small plastic ampoules. They were like the ones used for eye drops, with the snap-off tips.

'I'm going to need to ask you some questions,' he told her as he snapped the top off one of the little tubes. He held it up to her. 'These will help you answer them. I ask you not to resist. They won't harm you, they'll only make you more … compliant. Make it easy on yourself and don't fight me. One way or another, I always get the answers I need.'

She was too terrified to answer.

He didn't wait for her reply. He just reached out and put one hand on her chin, tilting her head back against the wall and holding it in place.

'Don't fight it,' he told her, softly. 'Just let me put them in and we'll get through this as quickly as possible.'

She started trembling wildly, uncontrollably. But she didn't fight him. It was pointless. She just tried to take in deep breaths and control her rampant fear as he reached in and, as deftly as someone who'd done this many times before, titled her head so it was at a slight angle. Then his thumb and his index finger crept up and across her left eye and held it wide open, forcing her eyelid to stay up.

His gaze locked on hers as he brought up the small tube of clear liquid and held it in front of her for a torturous moment. Then he turned it and squeezed it, allowing its contents to drip into his captive's eye.

Daphne needed to blink, but she couldn't, not until the man was done.

He pulled back, studying her curiously, like she was a lab rat. He was clearly enjoying the dread and the confusion that had to be playing across her face.

'There,' he comforted her. 'That wasn't so bad, was it?'

He did the same to the other eye, emptying the other ampoule into it. Then he put the empty ampoules back in his pouch and got up.

'Let's give it a few minutes to take effect,' he said. 'Then we'll chat.'

The questioning didn't last long.

Code named SP-117 – the SP stood for "*spetsial'noĭ podgotovki*," or special preparation – the drops were a cocktail of barbiturates, alkaloids, and other psychoactive substances, and they worked. The world – and Department Twelve of the KGB's S Directorate, in particular – had come a long way since the days when alcohol, given as intravenous ethanol, was used to loosen tongues. But while so-called truth serums encouraged the talkativeness of their subjects, their weakness was that it was hard to tell what part of the subjects' blabbering was fact from what was fiction. The reliability of what was said while under the drug's influence was key. And that was what made SP-117 special. It subdued the imagination and made its victims focus on nothing but what they believed was fact.

In this case, though, the facts Daphne Sokolov had given him were worthless.

Sokolov hadn't told her anything. She knew nothing of his past, or of his work.

Which wasn't unexpected. Koschey anticipated as much. Still, having her here was important. Sokolov was a capable man, and they were clearly very much in love. Koschey knew the scientist would do everything he could to get her back. It was only a matter of time before he popped his head over the parapet again.

Koschey reclined his car seat as far as it could go and leaned back, running through possible scenarios of how things might play out from here. It was a discipline that had served him well. He hadn't failed yet. His whole career had been a string of successes, right from the beginning. Only things had changed. He'd grown bitter and disillusioned. And sitting there in the darkness of the empty warehouse, he wondered if this assignment was going to lead to a new beginning.

A rebirth for the deathless.

He'd grown up in a patriotic communist family in Minsk and had been recruited by the KGB while working in a factory alongside his father, making parts for military helicopters. He graduated from the KGB's Academy there after excelling in marksmanship and bare-handed combat, and was on his first mission in Riga, breaking into and bugging the British embassy there, when the Wall fell. His work wasn't affected. He was busy running audacious disinformation campaigns against the CIA, identifying and taking out Chechen rebel leaders, and seeding insurgency headaches for the West in places like Afghanistan and Sudan. He reached the rank of major six years after graduating, lieutenant-colonel five years after that.

And then it had all changed.

After the collapse of the Soviet Union, everything he'd been trained to fight for was suddenly gone. His role changed. It wasn't about helping to spread Communism and beating America at the game of global dominance. It wasn't about sneaking missiles into Cuba or arming Arab states or supporting South American insurgencies. Ideology was no longer relevant.

Instead, it was now all about money.

A tsunami of greed and corruption had swept up everyone around him. And while Koschey was out in the field, defending the values he'd had instilled in him by his father and his mentors at the Academy, fighting a dirty war against capitalism and the decadence of the West, those same mentors were jumping ship. His superiors at the KGB, even hard-liners like the general, jettisoned any allegiance to the founding concepts of the Soviet Union and threw themselves into the pursuit of wealth with embarrassing abandon. To a man, they scrambled to line their pockets and grab as much money as they could, shamelessly and ruthlessly – and there was a lot of it waiting to be grabbed.

Koschey, ever the perfect soldier, had stubbornly and naïvely clung to his values, only to find himself out to sea in a world that no longer existed. And with each passing year, he grew more disillusioned and more cynical. He took pride in knowing that he excelled at what he did – which was why they needed him, why they spoiled and cossetted him. Only, things were different. He knew he was being used. He was no more than a glorified enforcer, a foot soldier in a global battle that was about nothing more than greed, sent out to safeguard his superiors' cushy lives and their bank accounts. His missions were now all about controlling oilfields and gas pipelines and making sure turmoil in the Middle East kept the price of oil up – a major source of revenue for Russia, a lot of it ending up in the hands of those above him who'd raped the country. It was also about silencing any dissident voices or potential headaches for the regime, whether in Moscow, Georgia or in London, to make sure his superiors stayed in power and continued to enjoy their newly acquired wealth.

Koschey's disillusionment had taken time to set in. He'd been too focused on staying alive while carrying out his missions all over the world to notice what was happening back home. But the disillusionment was now well and truly entrenched, and he'd grown more bitter with each passing day. More than bitter.

His work made him feel dirty.

It made him feel used.

He needed to change. To adapt. To accept the new reality on the ground and redefine his life.

And the more he thought about it all, the more he sensed that Sokolov would be the key to his rebirth.

He just had to find him first.

24

I didn't sleep well.

It often happened to me when I was faced with too many unknowns on a case, when my mind had too much room in which to roam. So I got up earlier than usual, made myself a quick cup of coffee and showered in the basement bathroom so as not to wake anyone up. I crept back upstairs and as I was getting dressed, I saw Tess stir awake.

'What time is it?' she grumbled, still half-sleep.

'Sssh,' I said as I padded over quietly to the bed and kissed her on the shoulder. 'It's early. Go back to sleep.'

She studied me through droopy eyelids. 'Everything OK?'

'Everything's fine. Just go back to sleep. I'll call you from the office.'

I left the room and tip-toed upstairs to check on the kids. I peeked inside Kim's room. She was a heavy sleeper and, judging by the phone, laptop and iPad arrayed around her bed, she was probably up late Whatsapping and what-not and would be out of it until something major – usually Tess on round four of the Kim waking-up ritual – forced her out of her slumber. I slipped down the hall and looked in on Alex. He was also fast asleep, cocooned protectively under the sheets, hugging his bunny tightly. I wanted to move in closer and give him a kiss, but a part of me felt it was better not to do that. I didn't want to risk disturbing his sleep or giving him a stir, not when I couldn't be sure seeing me suddenly like that in a darkened room wouldn't scare him. How horrible is that – my own son, and I'm apprehensive about scaring the pants off him by giving him a peck on the cheek in his own bed.

Reed Corrigan has a lot to answer for. And I was going to make damn sure he did.

I drove through virtually empty roads all the way down to Federal Plaza, thinking I'd get a jump on the day and have some decent time to prep properly before our face-off with the Sledgehammer.

The news that greeted me was mixed.

On the one hand, the two dead Russian heavies had been positively identified and did, in fact, turn out to belong to the Sledgehammer's *organizatsiya*. That was enough for me to put our plan into motion. I called up the DA's office and made an appointment, then called a judge I knew would look favorably on what we were planning. We needed to get the paperwork sorted out and have everything in place as quickly as possible, before we went to see the *vor*.

The bad news concerned the two suits who had died with Adams and Giordano.

They weren't carrying any IDs, but we got hits off their prints. Problem was, the hits were for two Army grunts who'd been killed in Iraq back in 2005.

Which was worrying on many levels.

It wasn't that easy to swap people's fingerprint files around, even in an age where everything was stored on servers and it could be done remotely. You had to know where to find them, and – keyboard wizards like my friend Kurt notwithstanding – there were all kinds of authorizations and firewalls that were very tough to get past. Also, these guys were packing Glocks and were chatting to the two detectives when they were gunned down – and it was at the scene of an active investigation. All of which only confirmed to me that something dirty was going on here, and that the players involved didn't necessarily want us to know they had a hand in the game.

I'd need to look over my shoulder more often until this mess was put to bed.

I was back at my desk and trawling through the most recent NCIC entries on Mirminsky when Aparo came in looking uncharacteristically spooked.

'Ballistics came in from the shootings at the motel,' he said, holding up a file. 'You ready for this?'

He had my attention. 'What?'

'Same gun,' he said.

He wasn't making sense. 'What do you mean, same gun?'

'One gun. All seven vics.' He stared at me like he couldn't believe it either. 'It was one shooter, Sean. He took them all out on his own.'

I froze, right there.

One shooter?

I was still replaying what I'd seen in my mind's eye and trying to imagine how it might have gone down when my phone beeped. I glanced at the caller ID. It was an unidentified caller. For a second, I considered ignoring it – then I remembered my pet hacker and his penchant for the cloak-and-dagger. I raised an index finger at Aparo in a hang-on gesture and picked up the call.

'Tell me, briefly,' I said.

'I've got something,' Kurt replied, his voice echoey and disembodied from the Skype call.

'Great. But I'll need to call you back.'

'Not possible. Bat-phone's outgoing only. I'll call you back. Half an hour OK?'

'Perfect.' I hung up and parked my anticipation while I focused on Aparo again.

Fortunately, he seemed so mired in the ballistics conclusion that he didn't bother asking who had just called.

'That's ... that's some shooter,' I said.

'Yep.' His face furrowed even more. 'We're gonna need Kevlar balaclavas.'

I shrugged. 'No point. I don't think this guy would have much trouble putting his slugs through the eye sockets.'

'Well, that's comforting.' Aparo shook his head slowly. 'What if it was Sokolov?'

I wondered about that. Whoever it was, I couldn't say I was looking forward to meeting him.

I was outside the building at the pre-agreed time when my phone rang.

'Can you talk now?' Kurt asked. The echo on the line was disconcerting.

'You'll have to speak up, Mrs. Takahashi,' I told him. 'The line's terrible.'

His voice increased in volume and clarity. 'I'm almost eating the microphone, so you'd better be able to hear me now. And *konnichiwa* to you, too.'

'You said you have something?'

'Do I ever,' he said proudly. 'I've been on this nonstop since last night. I ran all the parameters as agreed. Cross-referenced several databases, including the Enrollment and Eligibility Reporting System and the RAPIDS credential issuing repository. Long story short, I've got seven names. All with the necessary clearance. All with disciplinary warnings. All company lifers. Two went through the internal alcohol-addiction program and have stayed clean. So far. One is currently on a course in London: 'Global Security and China: The Paradox of Capitalism.' Which sounds riveting. One was involved in a fatal car crash and now uses a wheelchair, so I suspect you don't want to mess with him. Three were warned about sexual harassment, so I figured they all had potential, and one of them I really like, a guy by the name of Stan Kirby.'

'Tell me more.'

Kurt was clearly thrilled by this undertaking. 'He's in his mid-fifties. Decent-looking guy, not that I'm into that kind of thing. His mid-level diplomat parents sent him to Vassar, after which his act of rebellion was to get himself recruited by the CIA. He's been there ever since – twenty-four years as of last November – and is currently a senior intelligence analyst with Level 2-B clearance. He's got full benefits and is line for the company's top-tier pension package.'

I still couldn't believe the information someone with Kurt's skill set could dig up so fast. 'So what's the leverage?'

'Almost every Thursday night, going back over seven months, he hits the same cash point after work. Sevenish. Pulls out three hundred bucks.'

'Maybe he's loading up on cash for the weekend?'

'Plausible, but here's the thing. He works at Langley, his home's in Arlington, and the cash point's in Georgetown. He's overshooting his house and going all that way to Georgetown to get some cash, then turning around and heading home? It doesn't make sense.'

'Maybe he's spending it on something local.'

'My very thought. And I kinda doubt he's handing it over to some homeless shelter. I think he's up to no good. And here's the kicker,' Kurt added. 'Same night? Every week? His wife's got an evening yoga class. Seven till nine.'

This made it sound a lot more promising.

'OK, see if you can find out what he's doing with the cash.'

'Already on it, my liege. I'll call you as soon as I have something.'

Then something clicked. 'Hang on, you said Thursday, right?'

'I sure did.'

Thursday. As in tomorrow. And from the way he said it, Kurt was clearly also on the same track.

'I'm on it,' he assured me. 'Keep your phone handy.' Then he clicked off.

Mirminsky's place was called Atmosphère, written the French way, with the accent, and pronounced 'atmos-*fair*,' as befitted any self-respecting high-end nightclub in the Meatpacking District.

It was the Sledgehammer's latest venture, the flagship of his burgeoning empire, and it was huge. Even during the day, with no pounding music or heaving bodies or dizzying light shows on display, you could easily feel what it must be like in full swing. The place was an opulent maze of black velvet, chrome, Swarovski crystals, and weird opaque glass that looked like something out of a sci-fi movie. It was unbelievably flashy, although surprisingly tasteful. It had to be, given the globotrashy clientele Mirminsky was after, the Aston Martin-driving European high-fliers and homegrown hedgies whose tabs ran to thousands of dollars a night and the models and Kate Middleton clones who orbited them.

A couple of Cro-Magnons in black suits and dark shirts led us to Mirminsky, and we found him seated at a large banquette, three associates around him. Judging by their furtive looks, I'm pretty sure they weren't discussing the DJ's playlist for the night. Mirminsky didn't exactly light up when he saw us, and his comrades withdrew as we arrived, wisely.

The Sledgehammer was heavier than I'd imagined from the surveillance pictures I'd seen in his file. He'd clearly been feasting on the bounties of life in America in more ways than one. His beady eyes, which looked more reptilian than human, studied us unblinkingly as he invited us to sit down.

He raised a full cocktail glass at us. 'Can I offer you a drink, gentlemen? I know you guys never drink on duty, but you really should make an exception in this case. This is very, very special. We call it a "Green Feeling." You try?'

I smiled. 'Love to, Yuri. It sure looks good. Thing is, if we did take you up on that, where do we draw the line? Some caviar canapés? Some of your lovely ladies? Maybe a couple of Es and some blow?'

Mirminsky smiled back, a forced, cold smile that so clearly had zero connection to what was really swirling behind those shifty slits. 'You just name your pleasure, my friend, and leave the rest to me.'

'You know something? I'm a cheap date. I don't need the Champagne and the caviar.' I pulled out two shots of his dead underlings from my inside pocket and laid them out in front of him, then tapped them with two fingers. 'All I need right now is to know what these guys were doing at a motel on Howard Beach yesterday and what's going on between you and Leo Sokolov.'

I studied his face as I said it, but I didn't expect to see anything. There was no tell there. Mirminsky was too much of a pro for that. He didn't even grimace at the sight of the dead men. Instead, his face tightened with concentration that was followed by confusion. 'I'm sorry, Agent—'

'Reilly,' I offered.

'—Reilly, I don't know these men. Should I?'

I gave him a dubious look. 'I think so, Yuri. They've got these tattoos on them. It's like they're animals that have been branded, and those brands lead right back to your ranch.'

The Sledgehammer laughed, making his eyes disappear altogether. 'My ranch? I like that. Maybe I'll call my next club that. Could be fun. A tribute to a great American tradition.' His face morphed into humble contrition. 'Maybe they did work at one of my clubs. The problem is, I have so many employees. Maybe they were waiters, or bouncers. Maybe we caught them stealing from the till, or worse even. Anyway, if they ever did work for one of my many enterprises, I have no doubt they were fired for being' – he looked for the word – 'undesirable.' He smiled smugly, like we were done.

'And Sokolov?' I asked.

He shook his head. 'It's a very common Russian name, Agent Reilly. Like Smith, or Jones. And my memory just gets worse by the day.'

'Tell you what, Yuri. Go see an herbalist and get some memory-boosting supplements. 'Cause you're going to need everything you have locked away in that cesspool of a brain when we haul your ass in for conspiracy to murder two homicide detectives. Because in this country, that's a crime we never, ever let slide. The file on this case – it'll never get closed, not until we've got whoever did this.' I let him stew on that for a moment, then I put on a more détente-esque expression. 'You lost two men out there, Yuri. So did we. So unless you enjoy having federal agents watching over every breath you take, you might want to cooperate with us on this one and help us get whoever did this.'

I gave him a pointed, questioning look.

Mirminsky frowned, like he was processing it all. Then his face broke out in another pervy-uncle smile. 'If I hear anything, anything at all, that can help you, I'll be sure to call you, Agent Reilly. You have my guarantee.'

There was no point in sticking around now that I'd delivered our message, so we followed our steroid-boosted tour guides back out into daylight.

Aparo and I walked past a van that I knew to be one of our mobile listening posts – the ones the judge had signed off earlier on that morning – and got into our car.

Mirminsky, I hoped, was about to discover that his privacy settings weren't anywhere near as robust as he imagined.

25

Sokolov sat on the creaky bed in the small bedroom of the second-floor apartment above the Green Dragon and stared at the cell phone he had taken from Yakovlev after shoving the man out his window.

He had tossed and turned all night, finally falling asleep not long before dawn. He wasn't used to staying up late. It was something he hadn't done with any regularity, not since first arriving in the United States. He and Daphne had found a way to make their lives dovetail, even with her recent move to alternating shift schedules. They had been comfortable in what seemed like perfectly complementary patterns. At least until his past had crashed right through his present with all the subtlety of an eighteen-wheeler.

He couldn't stop thinking about Daphne, couldn't stop wondering about where she was, whether or not she was all right. How scared she had to be. He shut his eyes and pictured her, his mind's eye conjuring up images of her in happier times, before all this madness. He remembered the deeply warming smile she gave him when he called her *lapushka*, remembered the first time he'd allowed himself to call her that, tentatively, uncertainly, that glorious day so many years ago when they were out walking along the beach that crisp fall day out at Rockaway, how he'd explained its meaning to her and how she'd melted at the endearment and snuggled up to him, they day they'd first kissed.

Would things ever be the same again, he wondered. Even if he did get her back – would their life ever return to any semblance of normality? Or had the firewall to his past been irreparably breached, sending them into new territory, into a life where Daphne would need to hear all about everything he'd lied about all those years.

The thought saddened him even more.

He pushed the grim thoughts away and concentrated on the task at hand, locking his attention on the phone in his hand. He had already established that the last call placed by Yakovlev was to a DDI number at the Russian consulate. Which wasn't surprising, given that he worked there. It was where Sokolov would start, but so far, he hadn't dared test the number. He didn't want to make contact until he was ready. He'd removed the SIM card and battery from the cell phone as soon as he'd put enough distance between himself and his apartment to stop and take a breath. He knew that nowadays, locating someone via a live cell phone was a relatively simple task. As an engineer and a scientist, the advent of cell phones had in fact fascinated him. He had become an expert on cell technology, something that had spurred him to renew his own research and advance his work into realms that would have sounded like science fiction a mere decade or two earlier.

Realms that, at the time, he couldn't resist exploring even though he knew they would only lead to trouble.

Ironically, his work could now prove to be crucial in saving Daphne – and himself.

After replacing the SIM card and battery, he powered up and immediately pressed the Dial button. The call rang through for four long rings, then someone picked up.

And said nothing.

Sokolov grasped the handset close to his ear, also saying nothing. He could hear some faint breathing on the other end.

He imagined that whoever picked up the phone was probably surprised as hell to see the caller ID displaying their dead colleague's name. And whoever it was probably figured it could only be one of two people: either a cop investigating Yakovlev's death, or Sokolov himself.

After a few drawn-out seconds, the male voice said, '*Da,*' flatly and questioningly.

Sokolov felt his throat tighten, then he said, '*Eto ya.* Shislenko.' *It's me. Shislenko.*

More silence.

Sokolov guessed that whoever was on the other end probably wasn't alone and was almost certainly starting a recording and initiating a trace.

'Prodolzhat,' the man then said. *Continue.*

Sokolov's heart was punching its way out of his chest. 'You have my wife,' he said in Russian. 'And I have what you want. So here's what we're going to do. I will call you back at exactly eight o'clock to tell you when and where we make the exchange. There will be no discussion.'

He clicked off and swiftly removed the battery and SIM card.

He stared at his shaking hands.

What the hell are you doing?

He sucked in some deep breaths and tried to calm himself. He could feel a headache galloping in.

The only thing you can.

He stayed like that, immobile, for a few minutes, questioning himself, second-guessing his actions. Then he pushed the doubts away and stood up.

He got dressed, collected the small number of possessions he had with him, and left his room.

He had an errand to run.

'He just called. He's going to call again at eight. He wants his wife back.'

Koschey listened as Oleg Vrabinek, the Russian vice consul and the city's senior SVR operative, relayed the little that Sokolov had said.

'All right,' he told Vrabinek. 'Call me as soon as he contacts you again.'

He killed the call and glanced in the direction of the small office, where he was keeping Daphne. This was good. Sokolov was feeling brave. He was offering a trade. He was willing to expose himself.

Koschey couldn't really ask for more.

He'd need more muscle, though. Just in case. Even though it was an added complication, he had no misgivings about killing the two *bratki* at the motel. He couldn't let them live. For one thing, they had been sloppy. Yakovlev had failed, and they had been compromised. Proof of that was how easily the Americans had found them. And despite the strict code of silence he knew any *bratok* would follow religiously, Koschey couldn't count on that silence. He needed that silence to be permanent, and there was only one way he knew of to guarantee it.

Beyond the risk of exposure, leaving those two *bratki* alive would have left him open to another, greater risk, one he was even more keen to neutralize: he didn't know how much they knew. They'd spent several hours babysitting Sokolov's wife. At the time, Koschey didn't know how much Sokolov had told her, nor did he know what she'd told them. And given what was at stake, given the potential involved, Koschey really didn't want anyone running around out there who knew, especially not a couple of lowlife incompetent *gopniki*.

He had a couple of potential sources who could supply him with the muscle he needed, but in a moment of inspired perversity, he decided to go back to the original source. Doing that opened up all kinds of interesting possibilities.

He pulled up the number he'd been given by Vrabinek, and, liking his plan more and more with each passing second, dialed the *vor* they called the Sledgehammer.

26

Aparo and I were in the A/V lab with Tim Joukowksy from our field intelligence group, our go-to agent on Russian matters who was, as you'd expect, fluent in the language. The listening van outside Mirminsky's club had been feeding audio files back to home base when they came in, and Joukowsky would listen in on the ones the guys in the van thought merited close attention. He'd alerted us about a call that had just taken place.

It involved Mirminsky and another Russian – a Latvian native, according to Joukowsky, who was an accent and dialect expert. He played the tape for us, stopping it after every noteworthy sentence to explain what had been said.

The mystery caller starts by introducing himself as Afanasyev.

'We have any hits on that?' I asked, knowing it would be a fake.

'Nothing, apart from it being the name of a very prolific author of folk tales. Kind of a Russian brother Grimm,' Joukowsky said.

Aparo said, 'I'm impressed.'

Joukowsky snorted. 'Thank Wikipedia, comrade. No one needs to know anything anymore.'

A caller using a pseudonym like that. It sounded promising. If anything, the guy had a sense of humor.

A sense of humor that disappears right after he introduces himself.

The call continues rather bluntly. Not many words are exchanged. The caller tells Mirminsky he needs some help moving some heavy furniture. Says it's going to happen tonight. Says he's gonna need four movers.

The Sledgehammer demurs briefly, then grumbles that he's already 'down two movers on this' and gruffly asks if the caller has any idea what happened to them. The caller then does something unexpected. He tells Mirminsky, 'That's not what I called you about. I called to tell you to get four movers ready for me for tonight.' Just like that. Coldly. Bluntly. Without raising his voice, though the threat in his tone is hard to miss. Even without speaking Russian, I got that. And looking at Joukowsky as we listened to it, he clearly got that too.

Then the Sledgehammer does something even more unexpected. He says nothing for a beat, then he just says, flatly and in a resigned, submissive tone, 'It won't be a problem. They'll be ready whenever you need them.'

The caller says he'll get back to him with a time and a place. Then hangs up.

We were stunned.

'A man of a few words,' Joukowsky said.

'Few, but ... effective,' I added.

'Did this guy just turn Mirminsky into his bitch or what?' Aparo asked. 'I mean, what the hell was that? Who talks to a *vor* like that?'

'Only two possible answers,' Joukowsky offered. 'Either this is someone higher up in the *organizatsiya* than the Sledgehammer—'

'They don't really come any higher than him around here, do they?' Aparo asked.

Joukowsky shook his head. 'Not really. There are others as big as him, other kingpins. But no one with that level of supremacy.'

'What's option two?' I asked, already knowing the answer.

'Option two,' he continued, 'would be someone with the kind of backing that would make Mirminsky – or any other Russian for that matter – sit up and take notice and do as he's told, no matter how powerful, how rich, or how connected he is. Someone he wouldn't dare disobey under any circumstance.'

Meaning someone with the backing of the boys back in Moscow.

Someone doing the Kremlin's bidding.

If it was option two, my local homicide investigation was going to get even nastier.

We left the A/V room in a fog of unease. Forensics would run the tape for a voice-print match, but I doubted they'd get a hit. I didn't think this guy would ever allow himself to be identified that easily. Whoever he was,

I sensed he was a new player in town. Which made me think back to the motel.

As if reading my mind, Aparo asked, 'You thinking what I'm thinking?'

'We've got two new players in the game. The Olympic gold-medal shooter – and Ivan the Terrible.'

'Two new players,' he questioned, his tone dubious.

'Or just one,' I said, finishing his thought.

'Exactly. But if he's the same guy from the motel, why'd he kill the two tattoos?'

'Because they screwed up,' I speculated. 'They couldn't handle grabbing a sixty-year-old high school teacher, one of them died in a very public way, they used a car that could be traced back to their hideout. Everything we've seen and heard about this guy tells us he's not just a real bad-ass, but he's an incredibly efficient bad-ass. And guys like that don't tolerate screw-ups.'

'Harsh,' Aparo noted.

'It gets results. It also means that maybe he has Sokolov's wife.' The more I thought about it, the more convinced I was that this was the same guy. 'Makes you wonder if the Sledgehammer knew the guy he was talking to had just taken out two of his men – and he was now asking for four more.'

'If he did, if he even suspected as much – Jeez, Sister Sledge must be just burning up inside.'

'Maybe we can use that. OK,' I said, 'if he's the guy from the motel shooting, then whatever's going down tonight has to be about Sokolov. Which would also mean it's about his wife.'

'What if it's a trade?'

'Could be. Either way, we'd better be ready. Let's get a handle on where and when this is happening. You, me, Kubert and Kanigher, plus a SWAT team and local backup on standby. We need to shut this thing down before it gets even more out of control.'

'Shame the Sokolovs are mixed up in this. We could have just sat it out and let these no-necks slaughter each other and be done with it,' Aparo suggested. 'In case you forgot, this guy's a pretty decent shot.'

'Yeah,' I replied glumly. 'We're gonna need a whole lot of Kevlar.'

27

Over in a rundown industrial park behind Webster Avenue in the Bronx, Sokolov stood in front of a lock-up single garage and looked around.

It was quiet. There was no one around. There rarely was. This was a place where people came for cheap storage, whether for cars or, more likely, for junk they usually forgot about. They didn't visit often. Back when Sokolov had paid for his first rental – in cash, as he had done ever since – it had been less of a dump than it was now. Whoever owned the place hadn't bothered to do much to it over the intervening twelve years. Maybe a quick lick of paint, once, without bothering to burn off previous layers or fill in the cracks. It suited Sokolov perfectly. He needed somewhere quiet, discreet, and cheap. Somewhere he could come and tinker without anyone noticing or asking too many questions.

He scanned left and right again, making sure there was no one around, then he unlocked the two large padlocks and rolled up the bolted aluminum door. He stepped inside and rolled it back down, and hit the light switch.

The white panel van was there, of course. It was a Ford Econoline, the refrigerated model with the bulky roof-mounted condenser. It was almost twenty years old and looked too tired for anyone to consider stealing. Which was exactly what Sokolov intended. The last thing he wanted was for someone to steal it and make off with the culmination of all his efforts, the end result of a lifetime of study and research.

The obsession that had taken over his life from the age of fourteen.

* * *

The fourteen-year-old boy couldn't stop thinking of his grandfather's journals.

By this point, he'd read them several times. The story contained within their tattered pages was remarkable, and it fired up his imagination.

It also terrified him.

It scared him so much that he kept it to himself. He wasn't going to share it with his father, who was rarely sober after sunset. He thought long and hard about sharing it with his brothers, particularly with Pavel, the third of the four boys and the one he was closest to. But he decided against it. Somehow, although it scared him, it also excited him. In a world of little – if any – possessions, it felt good to have something special, something no one else had or even knew about. Something he could call his own.

The more he reread it, the more he wanted to understand what it was and how it worked. But his grandfather had been very cryptic. The little he'd mentioned about what it actually was didn't explain much at all. Sokolov understood the reason for this. His grandfather Misha didn't want his discovery known. He didn't want anyone else to be able to do what he'd done. He'd mentioned it repeatedly in his diary: his remorse, his horror, his desire to bury his secret forever. And he'd almost managed it. Sokolov had found the journals by pure luck, but his grandfather's warnings had only served to stoke his curiosity.

It became his obsession. And it coincided with the fact that at fourteen, Leo Sokolov was about to complete his compulsory seven-year general education. Like his peers, his choices were dictated by the state. He could begin employment, go to a vocational school for manual labor, or try to enroll in a *technicum* – a specialized secondary school. Much against his father's will, he chose the latter. It wouldn't be easy, given the remoteness of where he lived, but Sokolov was determined and fought stubbornly until he managed to snare a place at an engineering technical school in Tula, fifteen miles away.

Once there, he threw himself into his studies. He demonstrated a curiosity and a fascination with science that greatly impressed his teachers. His appetite for physics and biology was ravenous. And in the highly centralized government-run educational system that was designed to feed the planned economy, nothing went unnoticed. Sokolov's intelligence and his hunger for learning soon caught the attention of the regional education committee. Engineering was a priority for the Soviet Union, which concentrated its vocational training resources in areas such as aerospace and military technology, and Sokolov was soon offered a place at Leningrad University.

While advancing his studies in science, Sokolov quietly sought out everything there was to know about Rasputin, especially about the monk's years in Petersburg, when he'd become a close confidant of the tsar and tsarina. Written information about that period wasn't plentiful, and most of it was tainted by a propagandist approach, so Sokolov traveled the country whenever he could to try to get to the truth.

He started at the State Historical Archive in St. Petersburg, where he studied the records of the Extraordinary Commission of Inquiry for the Investigation of Illegal Acts by Ministers and Other Responsible Persons of the Tsarist Regime, a commission that was set up in 1917, after the fall of the tsar. In particular, Sokolov was interested in the findings of its Thirteenth Section, the one concerned with understanding the activities of the 'dark forces' – political jargon, back in 1917, for Rasputin, the tsarina, and those close to them – that were believed to be controlling the tsar.

The commission's investigators held intensive interrogations of everyone in the tsar's inner circle, most of whom were by then languishing in prison. Sokolov also read the reports of the investigators' travels to Tobolsk, where Rasputin had spent his youth and where they'd interviewed his fellow villagers. All these investigations had been very thorough, but Sokolov knew the reports and transcripts weren't completely reliable; they were the result of a political witch hunt, seeking to discredit the monk in order to further justify the uprising against the royal family.

But some of the reports would prove useful in other ways. Sokolov got hold of the testimonies of monks from distant Siberian monasteries, where Rasputin's mysterious wandering had taken him and where his transformation had begun. He found references to the monastery at Verkhoturye, where his grandfather had first met Rasputin, but as much as he scoured the records for any mention of his grandfather, he found none.

Clearly, Rasputin had kept his friendship with Misha a secret.

The commission's archive also held Rasputin's unpublished diary, but Sokolov knew enough to not give it much attention. Rasputin was virtually illiterate, and this 'dictated' diary was widely assumed to be a fake – one concocted by the playwright and science fiction author Alexei Tolstoy as part of an effort to further discredit tsarism and promote the Bolsheviks.

He pored over the reports of the secret police agents who had been assigned to watch Rasputin, but much to his frustration, he discovered that they were very incomplete. He learned that entire batches of the reports had been destroyed in a fire that burned down the tsarist secret police's headquarters during the February Revolution, two months after Rasputin's murder. Other files were destroyed by the police officials who had fraternized with Rasputin and had scrambled to keep any association with him out of sight after the fall of the tsar. Again, there was no mention of his grandfather. Sokolov knew from the diaries that his grandfather and Rasputin had a very close association, but the monk had managed to elude his watchers whenever they had met – which probably saved the life of Sokolov's ancestor.

There was no record of Misha anywhere.

Sokolov also studied the testimony of Badmaev, a mysterious *emchi* – a Tibetan healer – at the service of the court. Badmaev was Rasputin's friend, another supernatural healer in the tsarina's orbit. Sokolov thought he might find something useful there, but again, it was not to be.

Eventually, Sokolov gave up and decided to focus on what he knew best: science. He committed himself to focusing on replicating his grand-father's success, using the cryptic hints Misha had – perhaps inadvertently, perhaps out of hubris – scattered throughout the long and detailed text.

It would take him years to figure it out.

28

Misha's Journal

Petersburg

SEPTEMBER 1909

He has done it.
Or, rather, we have done it. Together.

Rasputin – or Father Grigory, as his admirers everywhere call him, even though he is not a priest of the Church – is now the empress's indispensable friend. The healer, spiritual guide, and adviser she can not be without. And the tsar himself, her devoted and loving husband, has embraced my master's presence as much as she has.

Everyone in St. Petersburg speaks of it. It is the sensation of the salons and the teahouses. The crude, semi-illiterate peasant from Siberia with the incoherent speech, the monstrous scrawl, and the louche habits, is a regular guest at the glorious imperial palace out at Tsarskoye Selo.

He now calls the tsarina and the tsar 'Mama' and 'Papa' – the mother and father of the land of Russia. In return, they refer to him warmly as 'Our Friend.'

They know nothing about me, of course. No one does. That is how my master wills it to be, and as in everything else, I trust his judgment. For despite the simplicity of his manner, he is truly wise. Wiser, I would venture, than any man who has walked this land. A bold claim, but one I believe to be true.

Our journey together, the one that began in that faraway monastery all those years ago, was always destined to bring us here, to the capital. To

St. Petersburg. It was a long road and an arduous one, but one that was necessary to lay the groundwork for our enterprise. For that is why we are here.

To save the empire.

Before meeting Rasputin, I was oblivious to the unease that was simmering across our beloved Mother Russia. My life had been too insular, and I had been too focused on my research to notice the changes going on outside my laboratory. It was during our long discussions at the monastery in Verkhoturye that my master opened my eyes to what he had seen in his travels and told me about this great unease that needs our attention.

The peasants, downtrodden and oppressed, have grown jaded and cynical. Their worsening conditions have eroded their faith in the royal family, which seems lost in its own world. Our new German-born empress, Alexandra of Hesse, is haughty, stern, and domineering. The young tsar, Nicholas, is a physically slight, weak-willed, and anxious man who is in thrall to his imposing wife. They don't even live in the capital, preferring to stay at their palaces at Tsarskoye Selo, twenty-five versts to the south – a tiresome journey by carriage, or even by motorcar, for anyone who was fortunate enough to be granted an audience. They seem to be detached from the problems sweeping our country and are oblivious to the resentment that the populace, and much of society, feels for them. I remember my own shock and revulsion at what had happened when the tsar finally ascended to the throne. The newly married tsar and tsarina had set up an outdoor festival to celebrate their coronation; the intention had been to extend a helping hand to the poor by offering them a grand day out and free food. They hadn't planned for the hundreds of thousands of wretched souls who turned up. In the ensuing chaos, several hundred of the poor folk had died, trampled to death. The tsar and his young bride hadn't seen fit to cancel their grand ball that same evening. The dead were still being taken away by the cartload while the court toasted the royal couple and danced the night away.

Worse still for the state of our great nation is that the people have lost their faith in our Church. This is through no fault of their own. With its pomp and its doctrinal introspection, it is the Church that has lost its connection to the people. A connection Grigory understands better than anyone.

'The mystical and the prophetic are the true essence of Christianity, and these things matter greatly to the people,' he told me in one of our long discussions at the monastery. 'But the Church's officials and its preachers have forgotten it.'

My master told me about the time he spent in the pagan cloisters, deep in the Siberian forests. In theses 'churches of the people,' as he called them, he learned the ways of the elders. It was there that he was taught the art of healing through potions and prayer. It was also there that he'd first heard prophesies of the downfall of the Romanov dynasty and of a bloody revolution to come.

'The monarchy needs saving,' Father Grigory told me. 'The devil's agents are everywhere, even in the halls of government, plotting to topple the tsar and undermine the faithful. We will need to be cunning if we are to save the people from themselves. That is why God gave you his divine inspiration to design and build your machine. We will need it if we are to overcome the formidable forces of the Antichrist that are allayed against us.'

My master understands these matters with great perspicacity, and I am grateful to be accompanying him on this sacred mission.

We began our journey in the provinces, far from the capital. We needed to build on the work Father Grigory had already begun on his own and embellish his reputation as a prophet and a healer. I say embellish, for the man would be a prophet and a healer even without my assistance. He is gifted by God with such powers.

We moved from village to village, from monastery to monastery. I accompanied him as a humble, loyal follower. I quickly discovered that Father Grigory understands people with uncanny perceptiveness. He is a shrewd and unerring judge of character. All those years spent wandering the land before we met, sitting in prayer and discussion with countless people, gave him a veritable fount of insights. Even without the use of my discovery, his tremendous instincts and his hypnotic gaze allow him to divine the hidden desires and fears of those he meets. The most subtle of hints don't go unnoticed.

Of course, with the aid of my device, he was able to fathom all their secrets. Secrets that he put to good use by turning them into revelations that astounded his gullible, superstitious audience.

On a few occasions, when faced with more stern resistance and cynicism, Father Grigory felt that more memorable interventions were needed. I remember one such incident, in a village near Kazan. It was in the dead of winter, and our request for food and shelter had been brutishly rebuffed. The local priest, an oaf of a man whose name I have long since forgotten, was unmoved by Father Grigory's offers of spiritual enlightenment. It was only through the good graces of a reluctant blacksmith that we ended up in a small barn while the snow fell outside. The local townsfolk weren't any more amenable the next day, or the one after. Father Grigory's mood soured, and a vicious hunger for retribution took hold of him.

'Listen to me, Misha,' he told me that night. 'Something malignant has these peasants in its grip. I have seen it before, and I fear my words won't be enough to help them overcome it. We will need to be more cunning if we are to save them.'

I listened carefully as he outlined his plan, then nodded my acquiescence.

The next night was bitterly cold, and at the allotted time, I stood in the shadows as Father Grigory ran through the village with nothing but his shirt on, screaming like a madman.

'Repent,' he hollered, 'repent before the calamity strikes.'

He had been warning the villagers of something terrible all day. The peasants watched in shock as Father Grigory reached the edge of the village and collapsed into unconsciousness.

By the time he awoke many hours later, half the village had burned down.

Needless to say, those peasants were turned into fervent believers. Little did they suspect that it was I who had set the place aflame.

With prophesies, healing, and small miracles, we traveled the land and built up his reputation over the course of many months. On a couple of occasions, we returned to Pokrovskoye, his home. I met his parents, his wife, and his children. They seemed greatly relieved and impressed by his burgeoning fame. I heard stories of how, as a youngster, he spent hours staring at the sky and asking probing questions about life. I also heard about the early manifestations of his talents: how as a child, he'd correctly identified the thief who'd stolen a neighbor's horse, how he'd predicted another villager's demise, how he'd healed a horse that had gone lame.

The doubters and the suspicious, however, remained. And on our third visit back to Pokrovskoye, they were ready for us.

A bishop had been dispatched to Pokrovskoye by the Tobolsk Theological Council, and he had already interviewed the village's local priests before we arrived. By this time, my master was fond of traveling with two or three female companions – fellow pilgrims in search of enlightenment. I would follow on, a humble disciple. During our visits to the village, Father Grigory and his followers would customarily meet in a makeshift chapel in a cellar that had been dug under the stable next to my master's home. They would read from the Gospels, then he would explain the hidden meanings concealed within them to his riveted audience.

The inquisitor, a gruff man by the name of Father Arkady and assisted by an equally saturnine policeman, accused my master of having joined the Khlyst heresy and spreading its falsities through his 'ark,' the name the Khlysti apparently used for their communities. I didn't know much about the Khlyst sect. All I knew was that it was a banned doctrine that combined elements of Orthodox Christianity with paganism. Its adherents, mostly the poor who lived outside the cities, held their meetings in secret chapels that were often hidden deep in the forests, away from curious eyes. Many of its leaders had been executed over the years, its followers exiled. An accusation such as this was highly dangerous.

Father Grigory and I moved fast to defuse it.

I hid in the stable and set up my device in one of the stalls. At the pre-agreed time, my master invited the bishop and the policeman to join him in the chapel.

Once they were settled in the cellar, I stuffed the protective wax pellets in my ears, connected the wires, and switched on my device.

I could hear their voices. They were cordial at first. Then their tones changed. My master's voice rose in intensity as he probed the inner demons of his guests, while their own voices stumbled and stuttered in confusion. With each exchange, Father Grigory's voice rose in intensity until, by the end of his interview, his words were thundering down on them.

The townspeople, along with Father Grigory's family, were all waiting anxiously when the three men emerged from the stable. The inquisitor looked disheveled and shaken. The local priest who had summoned the inquisitor ran up to him, asking for his verdict.

'There is no heresy here,' the bishop announced. 'This man truly understands the scriptures. Heed his words.'

The policeman, for his part, turned to my master, bowed his head, and said, 'Forgive me, Father, for my transgression.' Father Grigory extended his hand to him. The policeman kissed it.

It was time for us to enter the capital.

* * *

We arrived in Petersburg in the winter of 1904. It was a tumultuous time. The empire was mired in the war against the Japanese, an unpopular war that we would lose the following year. The people were starving and angry. There was talk of revolution in the air, and within weeks of our arrival, in January of 1905, a march of protesting workers turned into a bloody massacre after the tsar's army opened fire. Over many months, more armed rebellion would follow until the tsar would be forced to sign a constitution limiting his powers to appease the populace.

Not all of the tumult was bad news for the royal family. After producing four girls, the tsarina had finally given birth to a long-awaited heir a few months before our arrival.

The young tsarevich would play a pivotal role in our adventure.

By the time we reached the capital, Rasputin's reputation as a prophet and a healer of exceptional gifts had already preceded us. Armed with a letter of introduction from another abbot we had beguiled in Kazan, my master soon had an audience with Bishop Sergius, the rector of the Petersburg Theological Seminary.

I managed to set up my device outside the window of the room at the Alexander Nevsky Abbey, where my master was to meet the bishop. Under its influence, the bishop was even more impressed by Father Grigory's impassioned words. He soon introduced him to other highly placed officials of the Holy Synod, and my master's ascent through the corridors of influence was under way. Bishop Feofan; the brutish anti-Semitic monk Iliodor; and Hermogen, the bishop of Saratov who dreamed of restoring the Patriarchate – one that he would head – all became his friends. The nobility began to seek him out for spiritual guidance and healing. Within society, word spread of how this crude peasant never failed to demonstrate a perspicacity that bordered on second sight and a wisdom that comforted all those who were distressed.

Of course, no one knew what was helping him obtain these insights into people's lives and unveil their innermost secrets.

It wasn't long before Rasputin's circle of admirers grew to include members of the tsar and tsarina's inner circle. We were now well on the path to the palace and to meeting the royal family. And it was then, through one of these close confidantes of the royals, that my master first heard whispers of what would prove to be the key to his influence over them.

He had moved into the luxurious home of the Lokhtins. Olga Lokhtina, the striking wife of a senior official in the government and one of St. Petersburg's most fashionable hostesses, was by now besotted by Father Grigory. She fawned over him publicly and gushed about him to all her society friends, and it was in her elegant salon that he became privy to all of the city's gossip.

'The tsarevich is sick,' he announced to me one day, at one of our clandestine meetings, away from his entourage. 'He could die very easily. It is a closely guarded secret. It is also an incalculably valuable opportunity.'

I was stunned by the revelation. The heir – the long-awaited heir, the sole heir to the throne, gravely ill?

'What is his condition?' I asked.

'The young child suffers from hemophilia,' Father Grigory informed me, his expression already clouded with machinations. 'His veins are too fragile to contain his blood. Even the smallest fall or the smallest wound could cause him to bleed to death.' He paused, thinking things through, then turned to me, his face tight with concentration. 'The empress is beside herself with blame. She will do anything to keep him safe.' A chilling vibrancy danced in his eyes. 'Anything.'

My spiritual mentor proceeded to tell me what Olga Lokhtina had told him about the empress. The tsarina was widely known to be highly religious. She was also, it transpired, a fervent believer in the mystical. Before the birth of her son, she had longed desperately for some kind of divine intervention to help her produce an heir to the throne. At a time when her resentful, impoverished populace was turning away from religion, she embraced it more and more, surrounding herself with icons and holy relics and seeking out miracle workers. Much to the dismay and ridicule of the capital's society and of the royal court, 'Men of God' were introduced to her, elders who were believed to be endowed with a special gift from God. One after another, they failed to help her produce a son. And yet, with each daughter she gave birth to – four in all – the empress kept firm in her belief that God would hear her prayers and send her a holy envoy.

'The last of these "miracle workers" was a French magus they called Monsieur Philippe,' he told me. 'He told the empress he could speak with the dead and said he lived between our world and the spirit world, and she believed him. He claimed he could heal all illnesses, even syphilis. And, of course, after insinuating himself into her world – Olga even heard he shared a bedroom with the royal couple – he assured her she would become pregnant and give birth to a son.'

'But she did,' I interjected.

'No,' my master corrected me. 'She did fall pregnant when under the care of this Monsieur Philippe, but it was a phantom pregnancy. It was simply a testimony to his powers of conviction and to her gullibility. He was banished back to France long before she conceived the tsarevich. But you know what his parting words to her were? He told her he would die soon, but that he would return "in the shape of another." And still she awaits her emissary from God.'

'But she has Feofan. She has Iliodor and Hermogen and Father Ioann,' I said, referring to the senior members of the Church.

'They won't do,' Father Grigory told me. 'They are rigid, trite Orthodox priests. The tsarina is waiting for a true mystic, and what's more, she believes this starets will come not from the capital, but that he will arise from among the common folk in some distant village – a true Russian who loves God, the Church, and the divine Romanov dynasty.' He nodded solemnly to himself. 'I will be that emissary, Misha. And we will rescue the tsarevich and, with him, the monarchy.'

I could not have hoped for a more noble, and a more redemptive, use for my discovery.

Saint Simeon was truly walking alongside us.

My mentor's unshakable faith, his intense passion, and his formidable inner strength had all combined to make a remarkable healer out of him, but this would require everything at our disposal. The life of a young child hung in the balance, and not just any child. This was the heir to the throne. Failure would mean a shameful end to our crusade.

In October of 1906, and through the championing of Olga Lokhtina and other members of the court, Father Grigory was finally granted an audience with the royal couple. For this occasion, I wouldn't be able to accompany him. I wouldn't even be able to be close by. We had anticipated this moment, of course, and I had been hard at work devising an alternative to my machine that my master would be able to carry with him. I was able to produce a small version that could be carried in a low-slung pouch under his coat. I ran a wire up the inside of each of the sleeves of my master's coat. The wires ended at two small transducers that I sewed on the inside of his cuffs. The whole apparatus was powered by four small dry-cell batteries such as those that Gassner had demonstrated years earlier at the World's Fair in Paris. I had first seen them for myself in the laboratory of Akiba Horowitz, who had since found fame and fortune in America under the new name of Conrad Hubert, of course, with his 'Ever Ready' Flash Light devices. The alternative Father Grigory would be taking with him was not anywhere near as powerful as the larger version, of course. It would only really affect anyone sitting right next to my master, and it would only have one setting.

We hoped that it would suffice. And, as providence would have it, it proved wondrous.

I watched anxiously from the nearby corner as one of the tsar's attendants, a slim man in royal livery and topped by a flat hat festooned with tall red and yellow ostrich feathers, came to fetch my master from the Lokhtin residence. My master appeared, wearing the coat I had prepared and carrying the gift we had carefully sourced. The canvas-topped motorcar disappeared in a belch of smoke, and I could hardly wait until they returned to hear how it went.

The Alexander Palace, he told me, was magnificent. He had never seen anything like it. The reception rooms were enormous, paved with acres of the finest marble and illuminated by dazzling chandeliers. The chambers had sumptuous gilded furniture, walls that were teeming with glorious paintings and ceilings bedecked with the most exquisite moldings. And in one of those rooms, the tsar and the tsarina awaited him.

His audience with the royal couple lasted far longer than had been anticipated – over an hour. He sensed their nervousness immediately. He began by presenting them with his gift: an icon of Saint Simeon, the miracle worker of Verkhoturye, the monastery where he and I had first met. He astounded me by telling me he did not make use of my device, not then. He decided he would simply use his own acumen and the powers of insight he had honed for so many years.

The royal couple were, he told me, enchanted by his words. The empress, in particular, seemed giddy at the prospect of miracles. He spoke to them of the sin of pride and prophesied a great future for the dynasty.

'You should have seen the delight in the empress's eyes when I told her she and her husband should simply spit on all their fears and just rule, as God had intended,' he told me.

It was then that Father Grigory asked for permission to see the child. They did not resist.

He was led to the children's wing, where he met the nurses looking after the baby and the heir himself. The tsarevich, now a little over two years of age, was unwell and in pain. He hadn't been able to sleep.

'How long has he been like this?' he asked them.

'Five days,' the empress replied, pain cracking through her polished veneer.

'And the doctors?'

She shook her head. 'They say there is nothing they can do. He is in God's hands.'

'You are right,' Father Grigory replied. 'He is in God's care now. But he will be fine. Of that I can assure you.'

Without asking for permission, Father Grigory approached the crib, leaned over it, and began praying. The room fell silent. He prayed hard, as he did in these situations, sweat breaking out across his face, his limbs shaking. After many minutes, he reached out and placed his hands on the baby boy's temples. The royal couple watched in astonishment as their son calmed down visibly, then fell asleep.

The next morning, Madame Lokhtina received an excited phone call from Tsarskoye Selo. The heir had woken up without crying. He seemed in perfect health.

Saint Simeon had smiled upon us. I struggled to understand what had happened – had it simply been my master's gift of healing at work, or did my device contribute to the miracle? After much deliberation, I determined it to be an effect of both. There is no doubt that my master possesses a magical power of his own, and in the case of the tsarevich, the calming effect of my binaural beats had slowed his pulse rate right down as intended, allowing the blood time to coagulate. It was this serendipitous combination that would remain the miracle cure for the ailing prince throughout his short life – and turn my master into the royal couple's untouchable man of God.

Over the following months, my master became the royal couple's intimate friend and counselor. He is particularly close to the empress, who is prey to many anxieties and suffers from migraines. Father Grigory's words of comfort about her future in this life and the next soothe her. By getting her to divulge all her innermost fears and desires, he knows everything about her. Then, when she is fully conscious, he regurgitates these secret wishes of hers, presenting them to her as prophesies of his own. Then he schemes to make them come true.

They summon him every time the prince is ill, and each time, my master restores him to good health. They believe he is the key to their son's survival, which, in truth, he is. Moreover, he has convinced the royal couple that their own survival, the very survival of their dynasty, depends on his presence and his prayers on their behalf.

They cannot imagine a life without him.

Of course, there are many detractors. Tongues throughout society are wagging about this crude peasant and his unsavory influence over the royal couple. It is mostly jealousy about his growing power, of course. But it is also about the women.

The women are becoming a problem. I worry that this will cause our downfall and prevent us from accomplishing the divine mission I have been blessed to participate in.

I shall never forget the first time I got wind of the gravity of this situation. It happened late one morning, when I went to visit him for tea at the Lokhtin apartment. There was a screen in his room there, behind which sat his bed. As I entered, I heard what sounded like loud slaps accompanied by moans, then I heard my master hollering, 'Who am I? Tell me who I am.'

'You are God,' a woman replied meekly. 'You are Christ, and I am your lamb.'

I stepped around the screen to witness the most disturbing of sights. Madame Lokhtina, wearing a loose, white dress that was extravagantly decorated with ribbons, was kneeling in front of my naked master. She was holding onto his erect manhood while he beat her mercilessly.

'What are you doing?' I shouted to him as I tried to intercede on her behalf. 'You're beating a woman.'

He pushed me aside and did not interrupt his beating. 'Leave me be. The skunk, she won't let me alone. She demands sin. She needs to be cleansed.'

I left in shock.

He is frequenting many women. Duchesses and wives of the highest officials fawn over him and kiss his hands openly. They are constantly at his side, whether at the apartment he now occupies here in St. Petersburg or on his trips to Verkhoturye or to his newly built home in Pokrovskoye. They even accompany him to the bathhouses. And that is not all. Aside from spending all this time with these high-placed ladies, he is frequenting prostitutes. He takes them to hotels or to the bathhouses. There have been occasions when I have known him to hire several of them in a single day.

Accusations are being voiced more and more openly, questioning his morality, claiming he is a scoundrel and a 'wolf in sheep's clothing,' even accusing him of being in a state of spiritual temptation.

When I questioned him about this, he shrugged and said, 'Don't believe what these people say, Misha. They'll never understand.'

'I don't understand,' I told him, fearful of the answer.

He fixed me with his deep-set eyes, then he said, 'Sin is a vital part of life. We cannot ignore it. God put it there for a reason.'

'I thought sin was the work of the devil,' I countered, confused.

'Sin is a necessary evil, Misha. There can be no true life, no joy without profound repentance, but how can our repentance be sincere without sinning? Do you see? We cannot be true to God without sin, and it is my duty at the command of the Holy Spirit to help these women rid themselves of the demons of lechery and pride that live within them.'

And that was when I started to understand. Father Grigory drives out sin with sin. The crude peasant is taking these poor women's sin onto himself, selflessly toiling and debasing himself for their redemption and for their purification. These women know to heed my master's cautions and not say anything to their confessors, whom he considers simpletons. He has warned them that it would only confuse the poor men and, worse, make them commit a mortal sin by passing judgment on the Holy Spirit.

'Each of us must bear his own cross,' he told me, 'and that is mine. So pay no heed to these wicked tongues. The impure will always stick to the pure. They shall answer to God. He alone sees everything. He alone understands.'

My master's understanding of God's will is truly beyond compare, or reproach.

He is God's emissary. The empire, and the royal family, are lucky to have their 'Blessed One' as their protector.

*   *   *

Yes, the monarchy needs us, Rasputin mused after he left Misha.

The royal couple need saving if they are to remain my patrons and my conduits to power and gratification.

He thought back to the times that had shaped him, back when he was a precocious, impatient young man in Pokrovskoye. He had seethed with jealousy and contempt every time the gilded aristocrats thundered by in their sumptuous carriages, on their way to some distant monastery for a frivolous cleansing of their souls. He'd heard about the riches in the big cities, about the motorcars and the ostentatious parties and the lavish lifestyles of the court. It had all festered within him after he'd left his village, during his travels, and it was still with him when he'd heard about the empress's problems and superstitions. She was the most religious, and the most credulous, of them all, even more so than the wretched souls who flocked to Saint Simeon's grave and rubbed themselves with its crusty soil in the belief that it would cure whatever ailed them.

It was a credulity that was begging to be exploited. And the insights he'd gleaned from the myriad encounters he'd experienced during his wandering years had turned him into a master of exploitation.

One chapter had marked him most of all, and that was his time with the Khlysti in a remote corner of the Siberian outback. He would always remember that first ritual among the sect of resurrected 'Christs' who believed repentance was pointless unless it was about repenting for a major sin, which usually took the form of fornication. The chants, the dancing, the frenzied whirling, all of it culminating in the rite of 'rejoicing' – the wild orgies, during which the Holy Spirit would, they were told, descend upon them. It was all mind-boggling.

What a concept, he thought. Rejoicing through group sinning. Abstention through orgies. The purification of the soul through wanton copulation. The boundless debauchery that, according to their beliefs, allowed every man the potential to turn into a Christ and every woman into a mother of God.

It was so twisted and ingenious, it was no wonder the Orthodox Church had moved quickly to stamp it out. But it survived, in the dark corners of the empire, its 'arks' connected to each other by secret messengers – the 'flying angels,' or seraphs who wandered the land.

For a while, Rasputin had become one such seraph. And with Misha's assistance, he would take the rituals of the secret sect of the poor from the forests of Siberia and unleash his own version of them on the high society *of St. Petersburg and its polished, unsuspecting women.*

It was a far better life than any the illiterate peasant of Pokrovskoye had ever dared dream of.

29

Sokolov unlocked the van's back door and swung it open.

The rear compartment was empty inside, except for a large metal box. It was a bit smaller than an under-counter fridge, and it was bolted to the van's floor behind the partition. It had a metal bar across it with a large padlock holding it shut. He checked the padlock. It was still locked and seemed undisturbed, as did the rest of the equipment in the back of the van.

He closed the rear door, popped the engine lid open, and reconnected the battery. Then he climbed in and turned the ignition key. The engine churned to life, sounding far healthier than it looked. Sokolov had always been fastidious with its maintenance. He pumped the gas pedal gently a couple of times and let the engine warm up a little, then he got out and opened the roller door, backed out, and lowered and locked it again.

Within minutes, he was on his way, headed for the Triboro Bridge, thinking about the phone call he would soon have to make, and not feeling any more confident about what the night would bring than he had been before collecting his van.

Shortly before eight, Sokolov pulled his panel van into the alleyway behind the Green Dragon. The refrigeration unit bolted to its roof made it look like any other vehicle delivering supplies to the back doors of the restaurants that lined the block.

Jonny sized it up with a sardonic look, then he lit up a cigarette and asked, 'So what's with the meat wagon?'

Sokolov shrugged. 'It was cheap. Get in. We should go.'

Jonny climbed in and took the outside seat of the two-passenger bench that was next to the driver's seat.

Sokolov slid a small, sideways glare at the cigarette, then pulled out and turned into Thirty-Second Street.

Jonny looked around the cabin. There was a partition behind the three seats. It had a narrow door built into it that reminded Jonny of the lavatory doors on commercial airliners. The door had a small window cut into it, about ten inches square. Everything else was pretty standard for an old van like that, apart from a small panel on the dashboard that had a couple of switches on it and seemed slightly out of place.

He settled in, pulled out his gun, and started checking it. 'I just hope no one sees me like this. Not good for my reputation. Not good at all.' He grinned when he said it, but it was clear he wasn't kidding.

'The only thing I care about is my *lapushka*'s safety,' Sokolov told him as he glanced at his gun. 'You do whatever you have to do to keep her safe. You understand? She's all that matters.'

'It'll be fine.' Then he added, '*Lapushka*. You always call her that. What's it mean?'

'It's like ... my darling. It's special.'

Jonny nodded. 'Cool. I like it. Has a nice ring to it.'

Sokolov said nothing for a moment, then added, 'You know I don't have the money, right? I'd pay them if I did. But they're going to want something instead, and that something's going to have to be me.'

Jonny shrugged. 'It's not going to come to that.'

'Well, if it does, I'm okay with it.'

'You're going to be fine, Mr. Soko. I know the docks. We do a lot of business down there. It's a wide-open space, so we can control this thing like we want. And it's nice and quiet, and far from prying eyes.'

'Sounds like it's better for them than for us.'

Sokolov stared ahead as he motored on, deep in thought. Then his eyes narrowed, deepening the creases in his face.

'I just hope the *ublyudki* haven't hurt her,' he added, almost under his breath. 'Because if they have, you're gonna need to control me, too.'

Jonny grinned. 'Now, that I'd like to see, teach. But it won't come to that. You'll see. Jonny'll take care of everything.'

'I hope so.' Sokolov went quiet for a moment, then he turned to face Jonny. 'Thank you. For doing this for me. I had no one else to turn to.'

Jonny didn't reply at first. He just sat there and took a couple of long drags on his cigarette, then he flicked it out the window and turned to Sokolov. 'You did the right thing, coming to me. Like I told you before, you can read people well.' He paused, gauged Sokolov, then decided to carry on. 'I wanted to go to college. Like you said. I did. Then one day Kim-Jee steals three keys of heroin from a local Jamaican crew and they mark him for dead. Almost killed him twice. But Kim-Jee wouldn't do anything about it. He couldn't call the cops. He was too humiliated to tell his boss. He was just waiting for them to take him out. And he's my big brother, you know? I'm watching him just waiting to die. And I couldn't just sit back and let that happen. No way. Not Kim-Jee. So I made my move. I took them out first. But from that moment on, there was no turning back. I was in. For good.'

Sokolov nodded slowly.

Jonny glared into the night. 'Just don't tell me it's not too late to change, all right? It's too late for that, and I've had enough of that bullshit.'

'I won't,' Sokolov told him. 'Especially not tonight.'

Jonny shrugged and let out a slight chuckle. 'Yeah, I didn't think you would.'

It was oppressively dark and quiet all around us as Aparo pulled us up behind the waiting SWAT truck, which was parked about five hundred yards from the entrance to the deserted shipyard. Kubert and Kanigher pulled in behind us.

I glanced at my watch. It was quarter to nine.

Fifteen minutes till kickoff.

Aparo and I got out and walked over to the SWAT-team leader. Kubert and Kanigher joined us. We were out in Red Hook in South Brooklyn, virtually facing Governor's Island. The location had been texted to the Sledgehammer, along with its GPS coordinates in a message we'd intercepted. They hadn't given us much time to get here, but it looked like we were all set anyway.

The area around us was bleak and desolate. Rotting docks, old brick warehouses with rusting roofs, rickety chain-link fences, clusters of aging eighteen-wheelers and containers dotted around. I was surprised there wasn't any tumbleweed rolling at our feet. The place had that kind of post-apocalyptic feel to it.

The SWAT honcho was a new guy. I'd pretty much worked with them all, and he wasn't familiar to me. Which wasn't ideal, but there's a first time for everything. I flipped my creds at him, and we did the quick intros. He said his name was Infantino and we shook hands, then went over the situation on the ground and the engagement protocols.

He pointed at the image on the laptop. It was a grainy, green-hued, night-vision live feed coming from a two-man advance team he had deployed to monitor the target site. It showed a big SUV with two guys standing beside it, one on each side. They were carrying.

'We're dealing with four guys,' he explained. 'Two standing, waiting for something to happen. They're carrying MACs.' Which wasn't great news. Machine pistols like MAC-10s or -11s could spit out close to twenty rounds in a single second. They weren't necessarily the most accurate weapon for a face-off, but if handled by someone who knew how to curb his enthusiasm, they were very deadly.

'Two still inside the SUV,' he continued, 'pissing themselves to Chris Rock's *Bigger and Blacker*. They've got it on so loud they must be half deaf.'

I didn't know what was harder to take in – that the heavies were into Chris Rock, or that the SWAT-team leader could tell one of his sets from another.

'Great. Let's hope the drop stays as casual as their choice of CD.'

'They all seem to love this shit,' Infantino said. 'That and Wu-Tang. It's how they learn English.'

'And attitude,' Aparo added. 'Wish they'd listen to Seinfeld or Justin Bieber instead.'

He got some weird looks, then we went over some specifics about the terrain. It was all flat and open, with old freighters and water on one side and stacks of containers on the other. When we were done, I tapped on the copy of the photo of the Sokolovs that he'd been given and reminded him, 'If Sokolov or his wife show up, their safety is priority one. We want them breathing.'

Infantino adjusted the night-vision rig on his helmet. 'Don't worry about it. But you know how these things can play out, especially with these vodka chuggers. They shoot, we shoot back.'

I tapped the photo again. 'They're the mission. I don't give a rat's ass about Russian mobsters or whatever else is going down here tonight. This is about them.'

'Copy that,' Infantino said.

One of his guys handed us our comms sets. We slipped our earpieces in and confirmed comms-channel settings with the SWAT team's tech inside the van – then the four of us fanned out to take up our positions. Kubert and Kanigher went right. We went left.

Aparo and I reached our position, the squat office building next to the open gate. There was no security at all. No passing cars. No cops or private security patrols. The place was a ghost town. Easy to see why they'd chosen it.

I peered out for a closer look and could see the SUV and the two armed *bratki* as described. I could even hear the faint laughter coming from inside the big car. Clearly, these guys weren't too stressed about whatever was going down tonight. Which I took to be a good sign.

We hunkered down and waited for the other party to arrive.

30

As Sokolov eased the van past the large oil-storage tanks and across to the edge of the vacant lot, he saw a dark Cadillac Escalade emerge from behind a stack of containers on the opposite edge of the shipyard. The big SUV advanced so it was just visible, then rolled to a stop.

Sokolov hit the brakes and stopped too. They were about a hundred yards across the clearing from the Escalade.

The Escalade flashed its headlights three times.

Sokolov returned the signal, as agreed. Then he turned to Jonny without turning off the engine.

'Listen to me. Keep the engine running. And I want you to take these. You're going to need them.'

He reached down under his seat and pulled out two pairs of industrial ear protectors. They were the kind workmen use when manning pneumatic drills, only they seemed to have extra layers of mesh and other materials welded onto them.

Jonny looked at him questioningly. 'You're kidding, right?'

'As soon as you have Daphne safe,' Sokolov said, 'put these on and get her to put them on too.' Then he pointed to one of the metal toggles that was on the small panel that had been screwed into the dashboard. 'And then hit this switch.'

The Korean seemed completely lost, and uncomfortable with it. 'Why? What is it?'

Sokolov hesitated, then said, 'A distraction.'

'What, like a siren?'

Sokolov shook his head. 'Not exactly. But it's strong, and it'll give us an advantage. Look, trust me on this. Just hit the switch, but make sure you have the earmuffs on. You and Daphne. Make sure.'

He studied the Korean, looking for confirmation that the kid would do as he asked. Jonny eyed the ear protectors with revulsion, then nodded with an indifferent shrug. Sokolov nodded back, then pulled out a couple of small earplugs from his pocket. He gave them a quick check before slipping one into his left ear. He put the other one back in his pocket. Jonny stared at him curiously, but Sokolov ignored him and glanced at his watch.

It was nine sharp.

Before Jonny could take the matter further, Sokolov climbed out of the van. He stood there at the edge of the clearing, glowering at the dark SUV up ahead, gleaming and still, like a shark that defied the laws of nature and sat motionless while waiting for its kill.

His guts were all twisted up, his skin bristling with apprehension.

After a few tense seconds, the Escalade's driver-side door finally opened and a man emerged. He was wearing a baseball cap and mirrored glasses. His face bore at least a week's worth of beard. The lapels of his leather jacket concealed most of the bottom half of his face. It was all but impossible to gain a sense of what he actually looked like, and even worse once he took a few steps so he was standing in front of the car's blinding headlights.

Jonny swung his door open and nimbly climbed down from the van, tucking his gun into the back of his belt in the same smooth motion. He stood by the open door.

Two thick-set men emerged from the Escalade's rear bench, one on each side. The one on the passenger side then pulled someone out after him. It was a woman. She had some kind of black hood covering her head. He had her by the arm and brought her across to the bearded man.

The bearded man pulled her hood off.

Sokolov shielded his eyes with one hand to get a clearer view.

It was Daphne. No question about it.

His pulse flew out of the park.

'Lapushka,' he muttered.

He could see that her hands were bound in front of her.

Even across that distance, Daphne's eyes locked with Sokolov's, and time seemed to stop. A moment of such intensity passed between husband and wife that even the bearded Russian appeared to be aware of it, though he seemed to experience it as if he were a visitor from another planet entirely – one where emotions did not officially exist and those who felt them always died before they reached adulthood.

Sokolov swallowed, tried to wet his lips. His mouth was so dry he felt completely unable to speak. He tried anyway.

'Let her walk toward me,' he bellowed in Russian.

The man in the baseball cap stood impassive.

'She walks toward me and I'll walk toward you,' Sokolov pressed.

The man in the cap nodded and waved him over, the flick of his hand reeking of contempt.

Sokolov turned to Jonny. 'Remember what I told you to do,' he said. 'My *lapushka*. She's all that matters.'

Jonny nodded.

Sokolov held his gaze, then turned and started moving toward the Escalade at an even pace. After he'd covered about ten yards, he stopped.

The bearded man just stood there for a moment, then he nudged Daphne forward. She started to walk toward her husband – slowly at first, then her pace quickened.

As she did, Sokolov's heart rose – then it seized up as he saw the man pull out his gun.

The man then straightened his arm and aimed the gun squarely at Daphne's back.

I could hear the seconds ticking away inside my head, but it was all quiet on the eastern front.

We were all set. A perimeter had been set up around the yard. There was enough light to render night-vision gear unnecessary, probably to the immense chagrin of the SWAT-team leader. We had the Russians in our sights. But something was wrong. I could sense it.

They were still there, alone, waiting.

It was well past nine.

We were still missing one of the two parties.

Mirroring my feelings, the two Russians standing out in the open were looking increasingly agitated. They kept looking at their watches, then at each other. The yard was silent. The guys in the SUV had already killed the comedy routine.

There was no sign of anyone else coming to join in.

I glanced at Aparo and caught his eye. He gave me a WTF shrug.

I had a sinking feeling we were missing something.

Nothing of any note had happened since we'd arrived and my relentless little internal nag was telling me we may have made a mistake. I quickly tracked back over how we'd got here. The two dead *bratki* at the hotel. Daphne's carved letters. Meeting the Sledgehammer. The wiretap. The call requesting – no, ordering him to provide the muscle.

If whoever was pulling the strings was smart – and it was beginning to look like they were – they might have assumed that we'd ID the dead *bratki* in time to connect them back to their ringleader. Which meant they might assume we'd put eyes and ears on the Sledgehammer. Which meant they could feed us any misdirection they wanted. And send us to the wrong location.

A bait and switch.

We'd been played.

31

Sokolov froze at the sight of the bearded man's gun, its sight lined up with Daphne's back.

But the man didn't fire.

Instead, he called out to Sokolov, in Russian. 'Don't think of double-crossing me, you *sooka*. Just keep walking.'

Somehow, Sokolov managed to get his legs to cooperate. He started moving again, picking up his pace gradually, fear still rippling through him.

As he drew level with Daphne, they both stopped. He reached out and pulled her in, and she nestled her head in his shoulder for a brief moment. He stroked her hair, burying his nose in it, finding solace in its familiar feel and smell. Then she pulled back and stared at him with eyes that were filled with such anguish and confusion that Sokolov felt all the life drain out of him.

'Leo . . . ?' She muttered.

He reached out and cupped her cheeks. 'It's going to be fine, *lapushka*. Just keep walking and do as Jonny says.'

He saw her glance furtively across the yard, to where Jonny was standing by the van, and the confusion written across her face only increased.

'Jonny,' he told her. 'You remember. From the school.'

She still looked mired in confusion for a moment, then she nodded, uncertainly. 'Yes, yes. But—'

He pulled her in and gave her a brief kiss. 'You must go. Please.'

Her eyes welled up as she nodded again, then she took a couple of steps back before turning and continuing on toward Jonny.

'I love you,' he called out after her.

Sokolov felt an icy bleakness engulf his heart, and with absolute clarity he knew that he would never touch his wife again. He tried to console himself by thinking that at least he had seen her one last time. At least he had said good-bye.

He was still rooted to the spot.

'Keep walking, old man,' the Russian barked.

Sokolov glared at him. The man impassively waved him over with his free hand, the other still holding the gun, still aimed at Daphne.

Sokolov reached into his pocket, pulled out Yakovlev's gun, and pressed it against his own chin.

'She leaves here alive or I blow my own brains out,' he yelled out. 'You hear me? She leaves here safe or you never get what you want.'

Koschey's lips curled into the faintest smile.

Of course he had no intention of letting anyone leave the clearing alive, other than himself and the scientist. And of course, the old man would know this was the case. The traitor had as cunning a mind as any, as evidenced by the fact that long ago, Sokolov – or Shislenko, as he was known back then – had managed to outwit some of the most capable operatives of his generation, on both sides of the Iron Curtain.

This caused a curious thought to spring to life inside Koschey's mind.

Did Sokolov actually build it? And if so, had he brought it with him? Did he have a way to use it? Even here, out in the open?

He shook his head.

Possible, he thought. Koschey knew that very few things were impossible, and that most of those came down to the laws of science rather than human will.

Possible, but unlikely.

No, what Koschey was after was tucked away in the folds of the man's prodigious brain. And Koschey needed to ensure Sokolov's brain was unscathed if it was going to unveil its secrets.

He opened his arms out welcomingly, so the gun wasn't threatening Daphne anymore.

'Just keep walking,' he ordered Sokolov. 'Keep walking and she'll be just fine.'

* * *

We'd been played.

They suckered us here with these bozos while the real meet was taking place somewhere else. At that very moment. While we were standing around like morons.

As if to pile-drive that infuriating thought home, I heard Mirminsky's name in my ear.

'Say again about Mirminsky?' I hissed into my mike.

A voice crackled in my ear. 'This is Grell. We're still at the club, but the bastard's given us the slip. There must be another way out of here, one we weren't covering.'

'Great. That's just great,' I fumed. Aparo and I would ream him out later. In private. And at great length.

'This isn't happening,' Aparo said.

'The heavies must have called it in and told Mirminsky that they're standing around with their thumbs up their butts and whoever it is they're waiting for is a no-show,' I told him. 'The Sledgehammer realizes he's burned and decides to duck out until he can figure things out and regroup.'

'Well we know how rattled Sister Sledge was by the guy who set up the meet. The last thing he'd want is for us to lean on him to get him to reveal who his mystery caller was. He'd be signing his own death warrant whether he told us anything or not.'

Aparo was right. I was more alarmed that the real meet was probably taking place right then and we'd missed it. The only option left for us at the moment was to grab the four guys in the big Escalade for illegal possession of automatic weapons and see if we could squeeze anything out of any of them.

'No one's coming,' I said into my mike. 'Let's take these clowns and wrap it up.'

Infantino gave the command and we all moved in.

I glimpsed Kubert and Kanigher up ahead, snaking around the containers, big bold letters on their backs, weapons drawn.

I moved out from behind the small office hut in a low crouch and went up their other flank, looking for a better angle on the Russian. Aparo was right behind me.

Kubert was closest to the SUV, about thirty yards away.

He huddled behind a container. He looked back and checked to see that we were all in position. I saw Kanigher nod to him, then I gave him the go signal too.

He leaned out from his cover, holding out his creds. 'FBI!' he hollered. 'Drop your weapons and put your hands on your head now.'

The two heavies by the car went rigid and took a step back, looking left and right as they scanned their perimeter, pulling their weapons in tighter.

'Drop the guns now!' Kubert yelled out.

The *bratki* inched back some more, then they seemed to relax and their arms spread out, away from their bodies, with the guns no longer aimed threateningly.

And then Kubert made his mistake.

He leaned out a bit more, exposing more of himself, thinking they were giving themselves up. And that was when a burst of bullets shot out from the Escalade and punched right into him.

About three miles southwest of Reilly's position, in the old docks across the parkway from Owl's Head Park, Daphne reached Jonny. He was standing by the van with his gun in his hand. She collapsed into his arms.

'Come on, Mrs. Soko, let's get you inside,' he said as he shepherded her toward the passenger door.

She hung on to him and started to weep. She had forced herself over to him, but now that she was safe, all the bottled-up pain, exhaustion, and fear just flooded out of her. Jonny had to take her entire weight while trying to keep his gun firmly in his grip.

'It's OK,' he told her. 'It's gonna be OK.'

And as he guided her toward the van's open door, his eyes caught sight of the ear protectors on the bench, and he smiled.

Sokolov twisted his head to see Daphne join Jonny.

He was almost at the SUV. Its headlights were stronger up close, assaulting his eyes as they lit up the silhouettes of the man in the baseball cap and his henchmen from behind.

He'd already slipped the second earplug into his hand, and as surreptitiously as he could, he slipped it into his other ear and jammed it in tight. It wouldn't provide him full protection, of course. He knew that. But it would dampen the effect a little, giving him a bit of an advantage over those who had no protection.

He kept moving, slowly, waiting for it. Waiting for Jonny to hit the button. Waiting for the tables to be turned. But before he'd even reached the Escalade, the bearded man took two lighting-fast strides up to him and wrenched the gun out of his hand while landing a savage punch across his cheek.

Sokolov faltered, his knees buckling from the force of the blow. Before he could fall, his adversary grabbed hold of his jacket and shoved him toward the open car door.

Through unfocused, concussed eyes, Sokolov glimpsed the man tuck Yakovlev's handgun into the back of his belt before raising his free hand to give his henchmen a signal.

In response, the shaved-headed *bratok* next to him reached into the vehicle and pulled out a fearsome-looking machine gun. And it wasn't an ordinary machine gun. It had a big cylinder under its barrel, like a fat black flashlight – which Sokolov knew to be a grenade launcher.

Sokolov let out a silent scream as he saw the man aim it at Jonny and Daphne and pull the trigger.

32

Kubert had immediately gone down with what looked like a chunk missing from his left calf. Then gunfire erupted from all around as the other Russians and the SWAT team let loose.

I saw one of the two heavies who'd been standing there get mowed down almost instantly. The other one was firing as he scurried backward to get into the SUV, and red muzzle flashes were also flaring out from the two guys inside. I leaned out and laid down some covering fire while Kanigher darted out into the open to help his fallen partner. He managed to get to him and dragged him to safety as bullets punched the metal container beside him.

We rushed in closer, taking shots at anything that moved. I saw the Escalade's headlight blink and heard its engine roar to life.

Time to go.

The big SUV lurched backward in a rightward arc as the shooter who was still on the outside was trying to climb inside the now-moving vehicle. He was firing from his hip with one hand and hanging onto something inside the car with the other as he backed up alongside the Escalade, but before he could pull himself in, a round from one of the SWAT snipers found a path into his upper chest, incapacitating him. His body fell half out of the vehicle, one arm still entangled in what had to be the seat belt.

The SUV kept hurtling back toward the far end of the yard, dragging the *bratok* along the ground until the driver executed a wild 180-degree turn that jettisoned the poor bastard's body from the vehicle entirely and sent it rolling along the ground. I saw it recede from view, then saw its brake lights flare up as the Russians encountered fire from the SWAT guys who'd been covering that side of the perimeter. White lights took their place as the SUV screamed backward, pulled another 180, and then barreled straight back toward me.

The guy riding shotgun had his window down and was indiscriminately sweeping arcs of automatic fire in the direction of the office hut and the gate – my direction. As I ducked for cover, I glimpsed what must have been a sniper's round punch through the windshield and take out the passenger, but from what I could see, the sniper had no angle on the driver, nor did anyone else.

We needed to grab one of these dirtbags alive. And so far, three of them were toast.

Which is why I stepped right into the path of the SUV.

Jonny's eyes hadn't left the bearded Russian for a second. And as he saw him make his move on Sokolov, he muttered one solitary word into the tiny, LED-free Bluetooth headset that was squatting under his mop of hair.

'Go.'

An instant later, he saw the shaved headed man pull out a weapon and take aim – then a shot ripped through the night and the man's head just exploded like it had no skull in it, like it was nothing more than a blood and brain-matter-filled balloon that had just been pricked, just as some kind of round blew out of his weapon and exploded against a container to Jonny's left.

Jonny pushed Daphne's head down as debris rained around them. He looked out and caught a glimpse of the shooter, who had slumped to the ground as more shots echoed across the yard.

'Quickly,' he told Daphne as he hustled her into the van, 'and put one of these on,' he added, pointing at the ear protectors.

Koschey swung around just as the shooter next to him collapsed to the ground, the back half of his head missing. His eyes raked the landscape across the clearing from him as he yanked the gun out of his belt and spun Sokolov so he was in front of him, facing the van and shielding him from where the bullet had come from.

'*Ukryvat'sya. Snaiper,*' he barked at the surviving *bratok. Take cover. Sniper.*

More bullets rained down around him, punching holes into the Escalade's front wing and grille before shredding one of its tires. The *bratok* responded with several bursts from his MP-5, pummeling the area facing them with bullets.

Sokolov screamed, 'No! Daphne!'

'What, you brought an army with you, you *sooka?*' Koschey rasped at Sokolov in Russian. 'Well, let's just see how good they are, shall we?'

He shoved Sokolov closer to the car, then with one hand tight around Sokolov's neck, he reached in and pulled out another MP-5 machine pistol. Then he yelled out, '*My dolzhny ikh avtomobil, speshite ikh*' – We *need their car, rush them* – to the heavy on the other side of the crippled Escalade.

And using Sokolov as a human shield, he started to advance toward the van, firing at Daphne and Jonny while scanning the surroundings for the sniper's likely position.

Jonny was pushing Daphne into the van when a few rounds raked the windshield, punching spiderwebbed holes through it and blowing the headrest into smithereens inches from her head.

Daphne screamed out and Jonny pulled her right back as he pivoted his head and raised his gun.

The sight sent a bolt of terror through him. The Russians were advancing across the empty lot toward them, with the one on the left, the bearded man, pushing Sokolov in front of him.

'What are you doing?' he rasped into his headset. 'Take them out.'

Three shots snapped out from his right, and he saw the Russian heavy drop to the ground. But the other one was still coming, moving fast and unloading his weapon their way, shielded by Sokolov.

Jonny pushed Daphne into the van and clambered in behind her. Another round punched through the windshield as he struggled to get into the driver's seat. In the manic frenzy of the moment, he lost sight of the ear protectors, and just then, his only thought was to get them both the hell out of there.

'Stay down,' he told her, breathless, aiming his gun out the window at the approaching Russians but not daring to fire so as not to hit Sokolov.

'What about Leo?' Daphne protested. 'We can't leave him.'

'We don't have a choice. They'll kill us. They'll kill us all,' he blurted back as the engine groaned to life.

'If you can't get the shot, pull out,' he yelled into his headset as he swung his gaze up to the top of the oil tank. He knew that his buddy Jachin, up in his vantage point, was having trouble getting a clear shot at the Russian. He also knew that if he pulled out of there, he'd be abandoning Jachin, leaving him to fend off the Russian who was still moving in, unimpeded, firing away, like a cybernetic creature from a sci-fi movie with only one directive.

He had no choice. Sokolov had been clear.

You do whatever you have to do to keep her safe.

He threw the van into reverse and hit the gas.

The big SUV was screaming straight at me.

I anchored my feet, took aim, and emptied a clip into the front wheel well before throwing myself to the ground and rolling out of its way.

I must have shredded the tire because the car veered off its path and rammed the securing stanchion of one of the huge cranes. I watched as it flipped up onto two wheels before slamming into the base of a second crane. There was no fireball, just the smell of cordite and burned rubber and that strange, intangible heaviness to the air that only death can bring.

The echoes quickly died away and everything fell silent.

I saw a couple of SWAT guys moving toward the crashed Escalade, their guns leveled at what was left of it. I stood up and brushed myself down, then set off to join them. They reached it before I did, and a moment later, one of them turned to me and said, 'He's alive.'

I nodded, then looked across the yard. Kubert was still on the ground but sitting up, one hand pulling on his belt, which Kanigher had already tightened just above his knee. Other SWAT guys were at the body of the shooter Kanigher had taken down. The guy didn't look like he was getting up again. Neither did the mangled body of the *bratki* who'd been dragged a hundred yards by the big car. His limbs were sticking out of his torso like someone had given up halfway through drawing a spider.

Aparo was walking toward me shaking his head. I was going to get yet another lecture on the dangers of my impulsive nature.

Didn't matter. My mind was elsewhere.

It was with Leo Sokolov and his wife, wondering where they were at this moment and what was happening to them.

It was also with the bastard who was pulling the strings with such ease that we had no idea who he was, what he wanted, or what his next move would be.

Koschey pushed Sokolov harder as he saw the van pulling away, but he knew it was a losing gambit. He had a sniper to deal with and couldn't waste bullets on trying to disable the van. Besides, he had what he had come for. Sokolov wasn't going anywhere.

With the science teacher still in front of him and shielding him from the sniper, Koschey took cover behind a stack of containers and caught his breath. He was in the shade, away from any light. It would make the sniper's job harder, unless the shooter had a night-vision scope. He pushed Sokolov to the ground, gave him a stern, warning finger wag, then threw himself down into a crawl position himself. He set down the MP-5 and pulled out his handgun. He snapped in a round, then gave himself no more than two seconds to steady his mind before rolling out into the open, the gun locked in a two-handed grip.

His eyes scanned the outline of the massive oil-storage tanks as he ran his gun sight right and left, panning across the top edge of the most likely drum, looking for the smallest tell.

He spotted it. A lumpy shape that seemed extraneous to the clean structure underneath it, rising off it.

Koschey locked his sight on it and loosed his remaining six rounds in quick succession. A fresh clip was in the Glock before the last shell casing from the previous one had hit the ground, but he didn't need to draw from it as he saw the lump flinch up with an audible grunt, then watched as the dark silhouette rolled sideways and dropped off the edge of the drum, falling more than a hundred feet before bouncing off a metal ledge and hitting the asphalt with a dull thud.

Koschey waited a moment to make sure no other threats were in store, then he got up and pulled Sokolov to his feet. He looked around, a scowl darkening his already-tenebrous stare. The Escalade was out of action due to its burst tire, and they were in the middle of nowhere. Which made him vulnerable.

Koschey didn't do vulnerable.

He herded Sokolov across the yard to where the sniper had fallen. He knew the man had to be dead, if not from his bullets, then from the fall. Which he was. He was lying in a crumpled heap, on his front, his head a mess of blood, hair, and green streaks. Koschey rolled him over using his foot, for a better look. The man was Asian – Korean, Koschey thought – and young, somewhere in his twenties. One side of his skull had been caved in by the fall, and his face was a mess of blood-slicked hair. His upper torso had taken at least three bullets.

He looked at Sokolov, who was staring at the young man with dread.

'Friend of yours?' Koschey asked.

Sokolov shook his head. 'No. A friend of a friend.'

Koschey nodded, thinking it through for a moment. Then he rifled through the dead sniper's pockets and found a set of keys.

The ring included car keys. For a Toyota.

Koschey glanced around. On the ground, a couple of yards away, was the sniper's rifle. Koschey recognized it as a Dakota T-76 Longbow. A solid weapon. He picked it up, gave it a cursory check, then turned to Sokolov.

'*Davaite*,' he ordered him. *Let's go.*

They walked away from the sniper, heading out of the yard, the way the van had left. They found the lime-green Toyota Supra sheltering in the dark behind the farthest oil drum.

Koschey hit the key fob. The lock bleeped open.

'Time to go home, comrade Shislenko,' he told Sokolov as he gestured for him to climb in. 'You've been sorely missed.'

33

Jonny peered into his side-view mirror as the big storage tanks faded into the night. No one was following.

Not the maniac Russian. But not Jachin, either. Which didn't bode well.

If his buddy had made it out, he'd be somewhere behind him already. The streets were dark and deserted, and Jonny knew he'd have seen his car's lights, even in the distance. But there were no lights, and the phone link to Jachin had also gone dead.

He wondered whether Jachin was still alive, whether or not he'd be calling Jonny at any moment to tell him he'd picked off the Russian and was bringing Sokolov back.

For the fifth time that minute, he glanced at his cell phone. It stayed dark. And deep down, something told him he wasn't going to get that call.

He wanted to go back, to try to help him. But he couldn't do that. Not with Daphne.

A wave of vengeful rage crashed against his heart as he kept his foot on the gas, wrangling as much pace as he could from the old van and missing his souped-up Mitsubishi. Why he'd ever agreed to use his teacher's lousy old van, he didn't know. He couldn't wait to dump it once he'd dropped Daphne off. More than dump it. Feed it to a crusher, maybe, or just torch the damn thing to hell.

Daphne was in the seat next to him, gripping his left arm so tightly it was starting to hurt. He gently uncurled her fingers and turned to face her. She was sobbing, but bravely trying to stifle the sound.

Jonny gently squeezed her hand and kept driving, in silence, not knowing what to say, even though he felt he had to say something. She needed it.

'We'll get him back,' he finally said to her. 'One way or another, we'll get him back. This isn't over.'

Daphne gasped a lungful of air and tried to take control of her emotions, but her body wouldn't stop shaking.

'They must want him alive, Mrs. Soko. Otherwise, they would have killed him there and then.'

She nodded, staring ahead, and straightened up. 'What's going on, Jonny? What is all this about?'

'I'm not really sure.'

She looked haunted. 'We ... We have to go to the police, Jonny.'

He'd been wrestling with the same thought. Much as he hated to have anything to do with them, the cops needed to be alerted to Sokolov's abduction. The events of that night were beyond both his comprehension and his firepower, and one of the reasons he was still alive was because he could back out of something just as quickly as he could burst in. But he didn't know the first thing about what was really going on, who the Russians were, or what beef they had with Sokolov. The cops needed to be brought in.

But not by him.

He wasn't used to having so little control over events in his life, and he wasn't enjoying the feeling at all. But he didn't want to upset Daphne.

He reached over for his smokes, lit one up, and took a deep pull. He offered one to Daphne, who declined.

'Do you know who took you?' he asked.

'You mean now, or before?'

Jonny wasn't getting it. 'What do you mean?'

'The men who grabbed me outside the hospital were Russian. They worked for a man they called *kuvalda*. It means sledgehammer. Does that mean anything to you?'

Jonny nodded. 'Sure. He's Russian Mafiya. Big.'

Her eyes flared with fear. 'Mafiya? But ... how? What's Leo gotten himself into?'

Jonny gave her an uncertain look.

'The man you saw back there,' she said. 'The one who brought me there – he came to the motel where they were keeping me and he killed them and took me with him.'

'And you don't know who he is or what he wants from Mr. Soko?'

'No,' Daphne said. 'Not at all. This is all just – it's madness.'

Jonny frowned. 'I'll drop you off at the precinct by the school, OK? But you can't mention me when you talk to them. I need you to tell me you won't. There's nothing I can tell them anyway. I've told you all I know. I was just trying to help keep you both alive.'

She dabbed at her cheeks with a sleeve. 'And I appreciate that,' she told him. 'A lot. I won't say anything about you if that's what you want.'

He thought for a moment, then said, 'I'll hang on to the van for a while, if you don't need it. Make sure it doesn't have my prints on it or anything. Is that okay with you?'

Daphne looked confused. 'Why wouldn't it be? It's your van.'

'No, it's not. It's Mr. Soko's.'

Daphne seemed genuinely surprised. 'It's Leo's?'

'You don't know?'

'No. I've never seen it before.' She twisted around and glanced back at the partition and the narrow door, then looked at Jonny. 'Why would Leo have a van? He doesn't need a van.'

'I don't know,' Jonny said. 'Why didn't he tell you about it?'

Daphne's expression clouded over, and she started to sob again. Jonny decided not to take it any further. It was painfully obvious that whatever Sokolov was involved in, his wife knew nothing about it.

'I'll take you to the station now,' he told her.

She didn't reply.

Larisa was at her apartment on East Seventy-Eighth Street, restlessly waiting for news, when her phone lit up.

She snatched it and checked its screen, then took the call.

'Have you heard anything?' the man asked bluntly.

'Should I?'

'There's been a shoot-out in Brooklyn. Several *bratki* dead. One in the hospital. The FBI's got a man down too.'

She felt a prickle of concern. 'Reilly?'

'No. Someone else.'

'What about Sokolov?' she asked.

'Gone. Taken.'

A rush of variables tumbled across her mind.

'This is bad,' the man said. 'More than bad. It's a fucking disaster. You need to find out where he is.'

'I'm being kept out of the loop,' she said. 'Strictly need-to-know. I can't get inside this, not since Monday night.'

'You're going to have to. 'Cause right now, it's looking like we might have lost him. For good. You have to find a way in. Find out where he is. Do whatever you have to do, but find him. At all costs. And I mean all costs. Do you understand?'

'Got it.'

She clicked off, stared at the screen, and brooded over her next move in silence.

She didn't like it.

She'd been walking a tightrope for years, treading carefully across a ruthlessly perilous landscape. And it sounded to her like her handler had just asked her to jump off.

Seven dead at the motel last night. Three dead, one mangled up, and a fellow agent with a chunk of his leg missing in this godforsaken wasteland tonight.

I wasn't too crazy about this new nightly routine we seemed to be settling into.

A bunch of paramedics were already on the scene. They were tending to Kubert, stabilizing him and getting ready to move him into the ambulance. I was with a couple of others, who were busy with the guy who was driving the SUV when I'd shot his tires out from under him. He was a mess of blood and bruises and looked like he'd been mauled by a Transformer.

'I need to talk to him,' I told the brunette who seemed to be running the show.

'And you probably will,' she snapped back tersely as she worked on him. 'Just not right now.'

'When?' I asked.

'Does it look like he's in a chatty mood?'

She had a point.

I stepped away and took in the scene around me. This was a disaster. While we'd been lured out here for an evening at the O.K. Corral, the real meet was probably taking place somewhere else. With consequences unknown for all involved. I wondered if we'd be finding more bodies there, and if they'd each also have one round through the forehead.

I was crossing over to where Kubert was being treated when my phone rang. It was a detective by the name of O'Neil, calling from the 114th Precinct. Adams's and Giordano's precinct.

'I think you need to come down here,' he told me. 'We've got a walk-in here you'll want to talk to. Daphne Sokolov.'

34

It was just after ten o'clock when O'Neil and another detective showed Aparo and me into the interview room where Daphne Sokolov had been settled.

She was the same woman I'd seen in the framed holiday pictures at the apartment, only any trace of that happiness had been sapped right out of her features. She looked scared, tired, and several years older as she sat hunched on the uncomfortable chair, her hands cupped around a steaming mug of coffee. But she wasn't shy. Before we even got to tell her who we were, she said, 'They've got my husband. They've got Leo. You've got to find him.'

I reassured her and tried to calm her down, but she ignored me and launched into her tale, her words frantic but precise and to the point. This was a woman who was used to being around life-and-death situations, although, admittedly, not ones that involved her husband of thirty years. So we listened as she told us about how she'd been abducted on her way home from work; tied up at the motel; grabbed by the other Russian; taken somewhere she couldn't identify, as she'd been blindfolded and locked up in the trunk; then finally driven to the docks, where they grabbed Leo just before the shooting broke out.

Which was where I stopped her.

'Where was this? What docks?'

'I'm not sure. I was also blindfolded on the way there.' She paused, concentrating, then added, 'Not far from Prospect Avenue. I could see on the way back.'

'Be more specific,' I pressed her. 'What else do you remember seeing?'

She thought about it for a brief moment, then said, 'There were these big tanks, like oil drums. You know, the kind they have at refineries.'

O'Neil said, 'There's an old fuel depot on Gowanus Bay, just before the IKEA. I can't think of any other ones in the area.'

I felt a stir of acid in my gut. It couldn't be more than a couple of miles from where we'd been faked-out. The bastard hadn't bothered sending us halfway across town. He was cool enough to have us that close. Sending us a message, showing us how in-control he was. Toying with us.

'Let's get some people out there,' I told O'Neil, knowing we'd probably be too late. Then I turned back to Daphne. What she was telling us pretty much tallied with what we suspected, that she was an unwitting part of this mess. I gave her a comforting nod and asked, 'What happened after that, Mrs Sokolov?'

Koschey took another look outside the front of the warehouse and made sure no one had followed them there, then locked the door and walked back to where he'd left Sokolov.

The Internet had made his life much simpler. There was no need to rely on local intermediaries to arrange safe houses for him and others like him, not anymore. Websites like Craigslist made it incredibly easy to find and secure all kinds of last-minute, short-term rentals at a day's notice. Which is what Koschey had done as soon as he knew he was coming to New York. In addition, arranging his own safe houses made them far safer, since no one but him knew their location.

Hotels were not an option for him. Too many people going in and out. Too much potential interaction with other guests and hotel staff. Not ideal, especially when you were carrying weapons or ferrying a hostage or two. A suburban house was good. The more secluded, the better. Or a ground-floor office space in some kind of second-tier commercial development. Those were better, as they tended to be deserted at night, which was when Koschey did a lot of his work. In this case, he'd gone with a bottom-tier warehouse by Jamaica, Queens. One month's rent paid in advance, not too many questions asked. It had electricity and a bathroom with running water, and it was big enough for him to park inside. And right then, in the middle of the night, it was totally quiet, with no one else around but him and his guest.

He'd dumped the sniper's garish road racer where he'd left his Yukon before the Sledgehammer's men picked him up in their Escalade en route to the shipyard. The black Chevy had been safely stashed inside the warehouse, facing out. Behind it, in the office, Sokolov was on the floor, his wrists tied behind him, the nylon restraint looped around the wall mount of a low radiator.

Koschey went up to the back of the SUV and popped its lid open. He pulled out his travel case and set it on the floor, by the wall. He unlocked it and retrieved his toiletries pouch from it, as well as a couple more zip ties, then he went into the office and got down on his haunches, facing his captive.

Sokolov glared at him defiantly. 'Was Daphne here?' he asked him in Russian. 'Is this where you brought her?'

Koschey nodded, slowly, as he set the small pouch on the floor. 'She was. She doesn't know where it is, though. So I wouldn't get my hopes up too high about any cavalry charging in here soon to rescue you.'

He studied Sokolov and his immediate surroundings for a second. He suspected the scientist wouldn't be as compliant as his wife had been, and decided he'd need to use a different method. He reached behind the teacher's head and tied one of the nylon restraints to the radiator. Then he picked up the other, and, without warning, his left arm lashed out and clasped Sokolov by the chin, jamming his head right back against the radiator and holding it there with such firmness that Sokolov couldn't move his head left or right.

'So tell me, Comrade Shislenko,' Koschey asked as he calmly picked up the other zip tie and slipped it through the other cuff and around Sokolov's neck. 'I've read your file with great fascination. To think of what you were able to achieve … it's remarkable.' He pulled on its loose tip, its teeth clicking tighter until it was almost choking Sokolov. 'Miles ahead of anyone else's work in that field. But then you disappeared on us.' Koschey released Sokolov's head. The teacher looked at him with wide eyes, clearly in shock at being pinned against the radiator and hardly able to move his head an inch. 'How long has it been now? More than thirty years … and a lot can happen in thirty years. A hell of a lot. Especially with all the advances in technology we've seen. Isn't that so?'

Sokolov remained tight-lipped as sweat drops materialized across his forehead.

Koschey smiled. He could see the fear seeping across his prey, whose eyes widened to see what he was doing as he unzipped the small pouch, fished out two of his small plastic ampoules, and held them up to give them a quick check.

'So, what I'd like to know is, what have you been doing all these years? Did you just forget about your old life and all the revolutionary work you were doing for the motherland and turn into a boring middle-class American? Or was your scientific curiosity too hard to ignore?'

He twisted one of the small tubes off its row, put the others back in the pouch, then snapped off its tip.

'Frankly, I'd be surprised if you were able to put it all out of your mind. Someone with your brilliance ... it's hard to put that genie back in the bottle, isn't it?'

He leaned in closer, then his left hand reached out to pin the teacher against the radiator again. His splayed fingers were squashing both of Sokolov's cheeks while his palm smothered the man's mouth. Then his fingers crept up and held his eyelid open while he poured the clear liquid into Sokolov's eye.

Koschey did the same to Sokolov's other eye, then put the empty ampoules back in his pouch. 'I thought you might like to sample the creation of one of your former colleagues at the S Directorate, comrade.' He paused, then added, 'Department Twelve,' and let it sink in, enjoying the heightened fear that mentioning the KGB's top-secret biological weapons research group brought out in Sokolov. 'Not as sophisticated as your masterpiece, of course. But still, it gets pleasing results.'

He picked up the pouch, pushed himself to his feet, and headed out of the office.

'Let's give it a few minutes to take effect,' he told Sokolov. 'Then, when you're ready, I want to hear all about what you've been up to all these years.'

We were going to find more bodies. At least a couple, according to Daphne. Maybe more.

Maybe even her husband's, although from the sounds of it, the man who took him clearly wanted him alive.

By this point, I wanted him too. Not Sokolov. The other Russian, the one who had Sokolov. And I wasn't too concerned about the alive part. Although, in some perverse way, maybe I did want him alive. I was curious about him. I wanted to know exactly who he was and why he was doing this and who he was doing it for. I wanted to look into his eyes – the eyes of probably the most impressive and ruthless shot I'd ever come across. I wanted to have some words with him and see how his mind worked before I put him away. Not that it would be easy. I wasn't under any illusions there. So far, he hadn't made a single misstep.

I was momentarily excited by the prospect of getting his description out of Daphne, but it wasn't to be. We got as much from her as we could on that front, but it wasn't too useful. The guy she saw at the motel had a goatee, glasses, and long hair that was parted down the middle. When she saw him again at the fuel depot, he had a beard, mirrored sunglasses, and a baseball cap pulled down low. We had the basics in terms of height and weight, and the artist we'd bring in would be able to sketch out something more specific, but for the moment it didn't look like we were going to get the glossy headshot I'd been hoping for.

Throughout, Daphne had avoided mentioning the person who'd driven her back to the precinct by name. She'd kept referring to him as 'some guy' and 'Leo's guy,' that kind of thing. But watching her, I knew she knew more than she was saying. I also knew why she wasn't telling us who he was.

'Listen to me, Daphne. From what you've told us, the person we really need to talk to is the guy who showed up with Leo at the docks. Leo brought him for a reason. He brought him there to protect you. Which means Leo trusted him. And if he trusted him, he might have told him what was going on, and that's something we need to understand if we're going to have half a chance of finding him. 'Cause right now, we don't know anything, and we don't have much to go on either. Right now, Leo is out there somewhere, and there's not much we can do besides wait and hope for the best. Which isn't how we do things.'

She frowned, opened her mouth to say something, then hesitated, 'I told you everything there is to know,' she said. 'Leo's friend doesn't know any more. He told me so.'

'There's bound to be more,' I insisted. 'And sometimes, even the smallest thing can make a huge difference. This is what we're trained to do. It's our job. And every minute we waste here is putting Leo's life more at risk.' I studied her for a beat, but she still seemed unconvinced. 'From what you've told me, whoever it was out there with you was there to protect you. I don't have an issue with that. I don't care about him gunning one of them down. I'm not after him, all right? I just want to get your husband back and lock up the guy who's got him. That's all.'

Her eyes darted around to the other faces in the room before settling on mine again, then she nodded. 'His name's Jonny. Well, people call him Jonny. His real name's Yaung John-Hee. He's Korean.' She paused, then added, 'Leo taught him. At Flushing High. Before he got into trouble.'

I got her to expand on that a little. What she said told me Jonny had a rap sheet. I asked O'Neil to pull it.

'What about his friend?' I asked Daphne. 'The one who was covering you?'

She shook her head. 'I don't know who that was.'

'Where can I find Jonny?' I pressed. 'Where is he now?'

'I don't know. He didn't say where he was going.' Her expression softened. 'Promise me you won't be hard on him. He was only trying to help.'

'Don't worry about it,' I said, then looked across to O'Neil. 'He's also got the van. We need to put an APB out on it.' I turned back to Daphne. 'Do you know what the license plate is on Leo's van?'

'No,' she said, her tone bewildered and somewhat cross. 'I didn't even know he had a van until an hour ago.'

35

It hadn't taken O'Neil long to pull Jonny's file.

Yaung appeared to have risen through the ranks of his gang at warp speed and now seemed to all but run the entire show. He was still listed at his parents' address in Murray Hill, but the jacket suggested he spent nearly all his time at his aunt's restaurant, the Green Dragon, where his cousin Ae-Cha was the hostess. Jonny's aunt also owned the three apartments above the restaurant, one of which she lived in. The file indicated that Jonny was more likely to be found there than at home, though it also made it clear that in more than three years of on-off investigation, neither vice nor narcotics had been able to make anything stick on anyone in Jonny's gang. While the Russians used fear and intimidation to keep their *bratki* loyal, Kkangpae relied on a close-knit family loyalty that was almost impossible to unravel.

As he turned the car off Thirty-Third Street, Aparo's phone rang with the *Dragnet* theme tune. He made me proud so often. He took the call, said 'Aparo,' listened for a long moment, grunted a couple of uh-huhs, then ended the call with a laconic 'Got it.'

'Three dead at the docks,' he informed me. 'Two Russians. One Korean. The no-necks are covered with ink and the Korean kid had no ID. They're running all the prints. They also found enough shell casings to suggest a major firefight – 10mm, probably from an MP-5; point 338s, that's a specialist sniper caliber; and some custom nine mils.'

'Jesus. Sounds like Jonny and his friend took on Ivan the Terrible and his goons.' Which was impressive, if foolhardy. 'Anything else?'

'An Escalade. Grounded. Its front tire was hit.'

Just to rub it in. He'd faked us using an identical SUV.

I said, 'We need to find out how Ivan got away.'

'Maybe the dead sniper had a car?'

'Possibly. They sending the tats to Joukowsky?'

'Yep.'

We parked across the street from the Green Dragon, but made no move to exit the vehicle.

Aparo looked at me. He knew how I got when something was nagging at me.

'Spit it out. I'm hungry.'

'It's the van. I know it's stupid, but ... none of it makes sense. Sokolov hides it from his wife. Then he takes it to the docks. We're missing something.' I shook the thought away. 'Any sign of it?'

'Kanigher's pulling up any CCTV and traffic-cam footage he can find around the area. Maybe we'll pick up a trail.'

It would have to wait. 'OK. Let's get you some kimchi before you pass out.'

We got out, walked past the ubiquitous bunch of smokers huddled outside the restaurant, and went in.

The place was surprisingly huge. It consisted of one long, high-ceilinged room, dimly lit and elaborately decorated. It felt old and authentic, without the merest soupçon of fusion. Even this late, it was packed with wall-to-wall diners crammed around small tables and an army of waiters and waitresses navigating the narrow aisles between them while ferrying massive platters of food. The clientele was overwhelmingly Asian, young and old, and they all seemed like they were having a good time.

We'd barely been standing there for a few seconds when a young Korean woman wearing a silk dress with a green dragon print on it spread her arms with a welcoming smile.

I smiled back while Aparo and I flashed her our creds.

Her expression soured. 'We've already had our inspection,' she said, moving me discreetly to one side. 'We have a Grade B. Only seventeen points.'

Aparo grinned. 'Sweetheart, right now, I'd eat here even if they'd given you a D minus.'

I asked, 'You must be Ae-Cha?'

She looked surprised, then nodded cautiously.

'We'd like to talk to Jonny.'

Her expression didn't alter to acknowledge the name. 'Jonny isn't here. Try him at home.'

Aparo nodded. 'We will.'

I gestured deeper into the restaurant, toward the kitchen. 'But while we're here, we'd also like to have a chat with your mother. She in there?'

Ae-Cha fluttered her eyelashes at Aparo. 'You look hungry, yes? What would you like? Some *Kal-bi*? We have a *Son-sol-lo*. Today's is with pork and grass carp. The fish is flown in all the way from Seoul.'

Aparo was clearly having some trouble keeping his mind on the investigation, so I stepped in. 'We won't take up much of her time.' I maneuvered around her and headed in.

Aparo smiled at Ae-Cha, shrugged, then continued after me.

The hostess called up after us, 'Okay, okay, wait up.'

She led us through the swinging doors and into the kitchen, where a swarm of cooks and waiting staff were busy shuffling plates around while firing off orders at each other. We cut through to the left, where a door led to a dark stairwell.

'Third floor,' she said.

We headed up.

Aparo called it first. 'Jonny's here,' he mumbled. 'And definitely not all the way up there.'

I said, 'Not a bad poker face though.'

Aparo chortled. 'As long as she doesn't say anything.'

Her face may not have changed, but her voice had lost all its color when she lied. Jonny was in, and he was probably already aware that we were on our way up. A quick call from Ae-Cha would have seen to that.

We hit the first floor with Aparo already out of breath and went for the apartment door off its landing in deliberate contradiction to what we'd just been told. We crept up to it and drew our sidearms, neither of us willing to take a risk with a trigger happy gangster who'd been in a gun battle only a couple of hours earlier. Regardless of which side he was supposedly playing for.

Aparo checked my readiness, then he knocked.

After a beat, the door opened, revealing a sprightly fifty-year-old Korean woman. She was dressed in a plain navy-blue tunic and cream-colored slacks. Her hair was cropped short. Her face gave the dual impressions both of having seen too much and of having the innate strength to deal with even more.

'Mrs. Yaung. I'm Special Agent Sean Reilly. This is Special Agent Nick Aparo. We'd like to talk to your nephew, Jonny.'

'He's gone to bed. He work very hard today.' Then, almost on auto-pilot, she added, 'He's a very good boy. Never any trouble.'

Aparo cut in, 'Please wake him up.'

Mrs. Yaung peered down at our drawn weapons with a high school principal's look, then padded down a short hallway and said something in Korean through the door at the end.

We all heard the studied groan from behind it. Aparo caught my eye and we re-holstered our sidearms.

As we waited for Jonny to emerge, we took a quick look around the apartment, which was all but bare except for a top-of-the-range 3D plasma TV and a large statue of the Buddha.

Eventually a tall, slim, black-haired young man appeared. He was dressed in gray track pants and a white T-shirt and his hair looked un-kempt. Even if he hadn't been sleeping, he had certainly put the effort into appearing as if he had been. He said something lightning fast to his aunt – who immediately disappeared – then casually ran a hand through his hair and slumped down into an armchair, swinging one leg over an arm.

We followed suit, though without the trailing limbs.

'We're—'

Jonny interrupted before I got any further, 'Special Agents Reilly and Aparo, FBI, and I have no idea what you want or why you're here.'

I opened the betting. 'We know you were at the docks. Daphne Sokolov told us.'

He gave us a confused-amused look. 'She could have been with any one of us. We all look the same, don't we? I assume you don't have me on camera, or we'd be talking at the precinct.'

Aparo raised, 'Why would she lie?'

'I didn't say she lied. I'm suggesting that maybe she is confused. Trauma is well known to have this effect.'

He glanced over at his aunt, who had come back into the room un-noticed. She was holding a tray that had a teapot, cups, and a plate of Korean pastries on it.

'I was here all night. Me and my *ee-mo* watched a *CSI* rerun.' He paused, then added, his tone flat and sardonic, 'It was the one where someone killed a prostitute.'

He flashed us a grin. I couldn't fault his sense of humor, but his arrogance was starting to piss me off.

Mrs. Yaung insisted on serving everyone with green tea and a sticky bun. Once the cups and plates had been distributed – Aparo eyeing his bun greedily – I decided it was time to cut to the chase. Mrs. Yaung interjected before I could speak. 'Jonny definitely here all night with me. Grissom find killer like always. Neighbor also here for three-player mahjong. You ask him too.'

Aparo asked, 'Isn't mahjong played with four players?'

Jonny smiled. 'As I said, you people think us Asians are all the same. We play Korean three-player mahjong. It's played by the old rules but with one less player. The Chinese don't like it, but we Koreans, we're pragmatists. Why wait for a fourth player if you can play with three?'

Mrs. Yaung and her nephew shared a smile while Jonny took a bite of his sticky bun.

Jonny didn't rush his mouthful, clearly attempting to show that he had nothing to fear from me or the FBI. Aparo had his face buried in his phone.

Finally Jonny swallowed.

I also couldn't fault their alibi wrangling. Jonny not only had his aunt lying on his behalf, but their neighbor, too. The benefits of being equally feared and loved.

I set my plate down. 'Jonny, I have no interest in stress testing your alibi. As far as I can tell, you were looking out for a friend and his wife. Daphne is alive, most probably thanks to you.' I took a bite of the bun. It tasted like cotton candy. 'Can we talk hypothetically?'

Jonny gave the slightest nod of his head and his aunt immediately got up from her chair and left the apartment, quietly closing the door after her.

Jonny pointed at the lacquered table in the center of the room.

'Take out your phones and put them on the table, and we can talk as hypothetically as you like.'

Aparo immediately acquiesced, his other hand already busy with a second bun. Jonny picked up Aparo's phone and pulled out its battery.

Choking down my natural dislike of being told what to do, I also complied, taking out my cell, sliding off the cover and pulling the battery out. For good measure, I stood, took off my jacket and showed him that I wasn't wearing a wire either. Reseated, I tried to catch Jonny's eyes, but he had a frustrating habit of looking away the second eye contact was established – a trick he probably learned after a few successive police interviews.

'So, if you *hadn't* been here watching unrealistic lab montages, if you *had* wanted to help someone who you obviously care about, what *might* have happened?'

'Sokolov might have told me he had gambling debts, but that would have been bullshit. No way has Sokolov gambled one time in his life. Not with money, anyway.'

Aparo swallowed a mouthful. 'Any idea what it was really about?'

'Theoretically?' he asked, smiling.

'Come on, Jonny,' I pressed. 'We're trying to save his life here.'

Eye contact or not, Jonny's face suddenly took on the unmistakable expression of someone trying to decide whether something was important. 'No idea. But he did say he would die for his wife.'

I leaned in. 'Sokolov told you that?'

'He told me that he'd swap himself for Daphne. He just wanted her to be safe.'

'When did he say that?'

'When he came over last night.'

'Did he say where he was staying?'

'Some hotel downtown. But he stayed here last night. He looked like he'd been through hell. He was here until he went to get his stupid van.'

I wondered about that. 'Tell me about this van.'

'It was weird, man. He insisted we take it to the docks. I didn't get it. Lousy getaway car if we got into trouble. But he insisted. Said he had some kind of siren in it that would help us. So loud you had to wear earphones. Like for construction workers. He had a couple of them in there and some chunky earplugs for himself so the Russian wouldn't spot them.'

'A siren?'

'That's my guess. I never heard it.'

I asked, 'Do you know where he went to get it?'

'No idea.'

Aparo asked, 'Where's the van now?'

'After I dropped Mrs. Sokolov outside the precinct, I drove off and dumped the van on Shore, somewhere across from Randall's Island. I think. It was late and my mind wasn't on geography.' He shrugged. 'It's probably up on some bricks by now.'

Aparo placed his cup and plate back down on the table and turned to Jonny.

'You haven't asked us about Jachin Kim.'

Jonny's expression hardened a touch. I could see he was struggling with what words to use.

Aparo put him out of his misery. 'Your friend's dead.' He gestured at his phone. 'They just got a match on his prints.' He paused, studying Jonny. 'That's gotta hurt. Seeing as how you got him killed.'

Aparo really was the master of misdirection. From greedy cop to no-nonsense interrogator in a heartbeat. And he got a reaction.

Jonny sprung up and flipped over the table, sending the pieces of our handhelds scattering to the floor. Then he froze in place, taking control of himself. In a low grumble, he said, 'I have no idea what the fuck is going on. Sokolov may seem like a sweet old man, but he's also a liar. He knows exactly what this is about. He just isn't talking. Maybe he's talking now, though. You should find him before that motherfucker cuts him into pieces.'

I stood and calmly collected the pieces of my cell. Aparo did the same.

'Tell us about him. The Russian.'

Jonny described the scene. There wasn't much he could tell us about what the Russian looked like, but his take on the man's moves sent a chill down my spine. Jonny wasn't exactly a wallflower, and yet, despite everything he'd been through, it was pretty clear that even thinking about the Russian gave him the creeps.

We were done here. We got up, but before we headed out, I turned to Jonny. He preempted me.

'I'm not going anywhere,' he said. 'And why would I? I wasn't there, right?'

'Right,' I told him as we walked out.

I sat in the car while Aparo collected his take-out, and one image kept monopolizing my thoughts: the Russian, charging forward, using Sokolov as a shield, firing away relentlessly.

If we ever got to that point again, the guy wouldn't hesitate to go down fighting, even if the outcome was clear.

Aparo appeared holding a brown paper bag packed with Korean delicacies and climbed in.

'Any sign of the guys?' he asked.

We were waiting for an unmarked with a couple of SSG's – meaning members of the Bureau's Special Surveillance Group team – to show up. Front and back of the restaurant, one SSG for each. I wanted to keep an eye on Jonny from here on out. Besides being the only live lead in this mess, he was angry and was probably thinking about some kind of retribution right about then. Which I preferred to avoid. The city didn't need any more body bags.

I said, 'They're five minutes out.'

Aparo nodded and offered me a Korean dumpling, which I took, the maxim holding true as it always did: never pass up an opportunity to eat while on the job.

As I bit into it, an unremarkable panel van drove by, and it reminded me of Sokolov's odd move. I wondered why a brainiac like him needed a van. We needed to figure out what his movements had been during the day, and I made a mental note to check with the DMV for a listing of the van in the hopes of finding out where he kept it.

36

Jonny waited a few minutes to make sure the agents were gone, then he hurried back into the bedroom and changed.

As he emerged into the living room, his aunt came back in. She looked at him sternly.

'You stay here,' she said. 'Police is one thing, but FBI? We don't need that kind of trouble.'

Jonny placed a consoling hand on his aunt's shoulder. 'Don't worry, *ee-mo*. I'm only going out to get some air. I need to clear my head. Besides, if I stay here, I'll just have Ae-Cha pestering me about Jachin. Again.'

It wasn't a total lie, but the thought of it pained him. He didn't know how he was going to tell his cousin that her boyfriend – her intended, as far as she was concerned – was dead.

He managed to suppress the ache in his heart enough to give his aunt a half-wink, then he hurried out, leaving the woman with a stoic expression lining her face.

He took the stairs up two flights and unlocked the door to his apartment. He stepped around the glass table, scowled at the sofa as he remembered inviting Sokolov to sit there when he first came to the Green Dragon, then went into the bedroom. He raided his stash and pulled out a Sig 9mm auto. He checked its magazine, tucked it away in the small of his back, then opened the window and climbed out onto the fire escape.

He rode the metal stairs up to the roof, moving quietly, aware of potential surveillance in the alley down below. Once there, he walked across the roofs of two other buildings before taking the stairwell of the third back down to the street. He paused in the building's front doorway and glanced out, made sure no one was watching, then stepped out into the night.

Even that late, there was still enough life on the sidewalk for him to not stand out. He turned a corner and headed for the heliport parking lot four blocks east of him, down by the river. He knew several of the watchmen who worked there, and they had an arrangement regarding discretion and the erasing of CCTV footage that often came in handy that he kept alive using crisp hundred-dollar bills. Tonight, he'd need one of the motorcycles he kept there. And as he made his way there, he realized that his aunt was probably right. Business was good. His position in the gang was solid. The last thing they needed was heat. And for what? A crappy old heap? It made absolutely no sense. But then again, Jonny had always listened to his instincts, and right then, his instincts were telling him that there was more to this van than one would assume from looking at it. Taken together, Sokolov's insistence and his evasiveness, the hard-core nature of the bastard who took him, Daphne's surprise at the vehicle's existence, and those weird heavy-duty ear protectors all pointed to something more.

He just didn't know what.

It was enough to persuade him that he had to get the damn meat wagon and take it somewhere quiet so he could look at it properly. Maybe even take the whole thing apart if he needed to. Luckily, he had lied to the feds about where he'd left the van. Not through luck, actually. It was more like second nature.

A second nature that was kicking into gear and baying for blood.

Koschey was dumbstruck.

The eye drops had done the trick. Just as they had many times before.

Sokolov had told him everything. And it was way beyond what Koschey had read in the brief the general had sent him.

As he sat there facing Sokolov, he felt exhilarated. The man sitting across from him was a bona fide genius. Not in the sense that people used it these days. Koschey hated that. It was a term that was grossly overused, especially in the West. Everyone was a genius there when, by any reasonable standard, they were not even remotely so. But Sokolov certainly was. And what he'd achieved made Koschey's head spin.

It also fired up his own brand of creativity in all kinds of ways.

There was huge potential here. Opportunities to be exploited. Plenty of them. Taking Sokolov back to Russia, back to his superiors, as per his assignment – maybe that was no longer the best play.

He needed time to think. To plan. To strategize. He knew that this was the opportunity he'd been waiting for. This was his chance to even the score. To make things right. To slam down his two-faced comrades in a way that they'd never forget.

Sokolov had handed him something unique. Something that could achieve all kinds of things for all kinds of people. People who would be willing to reward such achievements very, very generously. People Koschey knew and had done business with in the past.

The best part was that right at the moment, no one else knew what he had. Sokolov had guarded his secret well. Not even his wife knew about it. The Americans certainly didn't know about it. And the general and the select few back at the Center and the First Directorate who knew about Sokolov's work were way behind the curve. Decades behind. What Sokolov had achieved back then was already staggering. What he'd done with it since was nothing short of astounding. Koschey reveled in his handlers' ignorance. His contempt for them only bloomed when he imagined them back in Moscow, at the Center, all smug and self-important and drowning in corruption while being clueless about what he had just uncovered.

Which meant he had a free hand. A free hand for the foot soldier to turn into the kingpin.

But before anything, there was a major hitch he needed to address.

He could see Sokolov's eyes flagging – subjects who'd been administered SP-117 fell into a prolonged, deep sleep after their interrogations. And he needed one more piece of information from Sokolov before he allowed him to drift off.

He reached out and clasped Sokolov's chin tightly in his hand, forcing him to focus on him.

'Tell me more,' he told Sokolov, 'about this "Jonny" and where I can find him.'

37

Jonny turned left off Crocheron onto 169th Street and slowed his Kawasaki down to a crawl. He circled the entire half block at walking speed, scanning left and right for any sign of cops, and saw none.

The van was still where he'd left it – parked in an alleyway behind the tree-lined suburban street, the rear license plate backed against a wall and the front one hidden by a Dumpster that he'd pushed against it. He hadn't wanted to drive across the bridge or through the tunnel in the van, not with its partly spiderwebbed windshield or its other assorted bullet holes. He figured that if there hadn't already been an APB out for the van before his conversation with the feds, there had to be one now.

He needed to get the van off the street, fast.

He was also eager to see what made it so special to Sokolov. But that would have to wait. Regardless of how desperate he was to flick the metal switch and see what would happen, this wasn't the place to fire up a siren that was so loud it required ear protection.

He chained his bike to a solid iron fence at the mouth of the alley, then walked back and rolled the Dumpster away from the front of the van.

He climbed inside and started the engine.

His first thought was to find somewhere around the mess of access roads where the Cross Island and Grand Central Parkways met by Alley Pond Park, but he immediately dismissed the idea. Although the traffic noise would mask the sound of the siren – or whatever the hell it was – he knew there were traffic cameras there and he couldn't afford to be spotted.

The other option was much better. His gang had a warehouse off Powells Cove Boulevard, close to the water. There were no houses on the block, just a lumber yard on one side and a waste-management company on the other, both of which would be deserted at this time of night. He also knew there were no cameras at all on the side of the lumber yard that faced Long Island Sound.

He set off, and given how late it was, the streets were empty. He was there in no time.

He parked the van alongside the graffiti-covered warehouse and gazed out across the water. If the siren was seriously loud, it might even be mistaken for a boat's foghorn. Certainly, unless they were standing right next to the van, no one would suspect the battered white panel van with the refrigeration unit bolted to the top. Besides, the place was quiet as death.

He gazed at the button for a long time, then without further thought, grabbed a pair of ear protectors, slipped them on his head, and flicked the switch.

Nothing.

Not even the faint sound of a siren.

Only total quiet.

He pulled off the headphones.

Still nothing.

He flicked the switch back to off and shook his head.

He could feel a headache coming on. Little wonder, considering the way things had gone since Sokolov had come to see him two days earlier. And now his blood brother, the boyfriend of a cousin who was more than a sister to him, was dead, and he was in the crosshairs of the feds. Now that his brother was no longer running things, Jonny was supposed to be keeping everything ticking over while his boss was in Miami, not dragging the gang into an unwanted spotlight.

He cut himself a couple of lines and snorted them. One of the benefits of being so high up the supply chain was near-constant access to high-grade product, and this was certainly a privilege he didn't want to lose.

He took a few breaths and let his heartbeat go back to normal after the initial hit of the powder.

The whole thing was ridiculous. Surely the switch had to do *something*.

He had the key in the ignition and there was definitely power to the electrics.

Then he realized that he still hadn't looked properly inside the van's main compartment. He'd been so preoccupied – first with Sokolov, then with his wife – that he hadn't even opened the back for a good look.

It was time to remedy that.

He climbed out of his seat, opened the cabin door, and squeezed through the narrow doorway.

The rear compartment was neat and tidy. It was lined with a hard white plastic surface, like the inside of a fridge. It was mostly empty, apart from a big metal storage box that was bolted to the cabin's floor. Along the opposite wall were four low black boxes that were also firmly attached in place. These looked like old PC towers, but they seemed new and had small panels with red and green LEDs and digital displays on them. A thick but tidy stream of wires linked everything. More wires ran up the inside of the van and into the refrigeration unit, while others disappeared into the base of the partition behind the driver's position.

The storage box was secured by a bar and a large padlock, but there was no key for it on the van's key ring.

Jonny left the van and went looking for something with which to force the padlock.

It didn't take long. A length of rebar was lying on the ground about twenty feet away, probably from the waste-management yard.

He brought it inside the van and used it to bust the padlock. On the third attempt and to the soundtrack of him cursing out loud in Korean, it popped open.

The box was stuffed with elaborate electronic gear. It was like some kind of mega-stereo that someone had built themselves, a metal rack covered with dials, meters and sockets. An abundance of wires crisscrossed between them.

Apart from a laptop secured to the top of the stack, he had absolutely no idea what any of it was. Whatever it was, it was complicated.

After a few minutes spent staring at the boxes' contents and trying to divine what they were there for, he decided to bring in an expert.

He took out his cell, dialed, and waited.

A sleepy voice answered.

'Shin,' he said, 'get your ass over to the chop shop. There's something you need to see.'

38

I was back at Federal Plaza, feeling on edge and antsy. Not a great feeling, especially when it's coming up on one in the morning and I'm still at the office instead of annoying Tess with my alleged snoring.

On one level, it felt like the game had been played out, and we'd lost. Our mystery Russian – who we'd all started referring to as Ivan – had Sokolov and had pulled back into the shadows. Maybe that was it. Sokolov seemed to be what Ivan was after. Now that he had what he wanted, maybe they were gone for good. But if so, it left a lot of unanswered questions. I don't know why, but I couldn't help feeling that this was just a lull before the real storm.

As you'd expect, everyone was burning the midnight oil on this. We'd had three incidents with a total of eleven deaths in less than seventy-two hours. No one was going home just yet. I made a quick call to Tess to say I didn't know when I'd be back and not to worry. That last bit was, of course, kind of pointless. By now, she knew it meant we were dealing with something seriously nasty and worrying was entirely reasonable. But what else could I say?

Information was streaming in from various corners. All five of the dead Russians, as well as the one at the hospital, were confirmed to be part of Mirminsky's outfit. The Sledgehammer had lost seven men, with another out of action and in custody. We'd picked up a couple of calls informing him of this, but rather than going ballistic over it as you'd expect, he seemed oddly subdued. This lined up with the unexplained reverence he showed toward Ivan.

I wanted to know how we'd missed tracking the other two *bratki*, the ones who'd been at the real meet with Ivan. We'd put as tight a lock on all of the Sledgehammer's comms, and yet Ivan was still able to get through to him and arrange for his escort. Our surveillance guys were reviewing all the video, audio, and data from Mirminsky's club to try to figure out how Ivan had bypassed us. Ultimately, I doubted it would lead to anything. The key, as it always was, was Sokolov. Which was what the more intriguing bit of information that came in was about.

A background search on Leo Sokolov – or *Lev* Sokolov, to use what would have been his real Russian name according to our resident guru Joukowsky – didn't turn up much. His prints were clean. The little on record confirmed that Sokolov lived a straightforward, uncomplicated life. Then the search threw us a major curveball: it kicked up a Lev Nikolaevich Sokolov who was born on the same day as our Leo, back in 1952 – but who died nineteen years later. Which could be an incredible coincidence. Or, and this was far more likely according to my finely honed detective intuition, Leo – our Leo – wasn't really Leo Sokolov at all. He'd somehow got hold of Lev's birth certificate and used it as a breeder document to get himself a social security card and build a fake identity from it.

Which threw everything into question.

Leo Sokolov wasn't really Leo Sokolov at all.

Jonny arrived at the chop shop on Cross Island Parkway fifteen minutes after he'd broken into the metal locker. Shin was already there, leaning against the double doors, smoking a hand-rolled cigarette. He was dressed in a tattered old tracksuit and faded sneakers, with the hood of his top almost obscuring his entire face.

As the van turned onto the lot, Shin slapped one of the big doors three times with the flat of his hand. They both swung open with the grating sound of metal being dragged over concrete, then Jonny drove the van straight into the large space inside. Shin followed on foot and the doors immediately creaked shut behind him.

The chop shop was a twenty-four-hour operation. At present, there were four guys remodeling a Porsche Panamera and a Bentley Continental, readying them to be shipped out to Moscow or Beirut, where they would end up with new owners who weren't particularly bothered that their new cars had been stolen from someone a couple of continents away.

As Jonny jumped down from the cab, one of the crew working on the hot cars pointed at the van with his wrench.

'Hey, Jonny, nice wheels. You want us to drop a five-seven-two and some nitrous tanks in it? Or just fix your eight-track player?' He cracked up, as did his friends.

Jonny's face didn't even crease into a smile.

'Jachin's dead. Some Russian *gaejasik* took him out.'

The laughter died instantly.

The team's top dog, a muscle-bound Kkangpae called Bon, wiped his oily hands on a cloth and walked over toward Jonny.

'That's rough, man,' he said, running a finger along one of the bullet holes in the front windshield. 'So what are we gonna do?'

'Something, that's for sure. I don't know what just yet. Meantime, I need to figure something out.'

Shin appeared from behind the van, causing Bon to sneer.

Bon said, 'With *that*?' Meaning Shin.

'Yeah,' he told him. 'Now, get back to work. I've got to take care of this.' Then he remembered his bike. He fished out his keys and chucked them to Bon. 'I need someone to bring back the Kawa. It's on 169th. The alley by the laundromat.'

Bon spat to one side, shrugged, and headed back to the Bentley. 'No problem.'

Shin approached Jonny and pulled down his hoodie, revealing a crew-cut atop a skinny, haggard face.

The sight surprised Jonny. 'What the hell is wrong with you? You look like shit.'

'I'm living off fucking food stamps, man. Fucking PhD's not even good for wiping my ass.' He shook his head ruefully. 'They keep feeding me the same dog shit that I'm overqualified. No jobs. No teaching posts. Nothing. Why? 'Cause I'm overqualified. How fucked-up is that?'

He looked close to tears.

'So lie,' Jonny told him. 'You can't live like that.'

'It's Nikki, she ...'

Jonny spared his old school friend the humiliation of having to admit that he was pussy-whipped within an inch of his life. 'You could come back to work,' he told him. 'This new guy we've got takes twice as long to scan and code an RF key, and then when he's done, half of them don't work.'

'I promised Nikki, man.'

'It's good money.'

'Maybe I should. I don't know.' Shin didn't sound very convinced. He nodded toward the van. 'What's this worth?'

Jonny's eyes narrowed.

'I'll let you know when you tell me what it is.'

Jonny gestured for Shin to follow him through the van's rear doors. Inside, he opened the metal storage box and moved back to sit on a wheel arch while Shin moved in for a closer look.

The postgrad went quiet for a moment as he examined its contents, then he let out a long whistle and turned around.

'*Mwuh-ya yi-gae*, Jonny. Where'd you get this? Area 51?'

39

Who the hell was he?

I didn't have a clue.

None of us did.

Was he a sleeper? If so, what had he been up to all these years? Or was he running from something? If so, what was it and who was he hiding from? And why was this all happening now, thirty years or so after he'd taken on the Sokolov name?

It was easier to pull off back then. Things weren't that computerized, you didn't have the level of electronic databases we have these days. It wasn't that hard to get yourself a driver's license, Social Security card and bank account, either by getting a doctor to sign a fake birth certificate or, as seemed to be the case with Sokolov, using the identity of someone roughly the same age who died as a young child.

We didn't know who he was. We didn't know where he was from. We didn't know why he was valuable, valuable enough for someone to kill this many people over him without hesitating. There was a hidden history here that we knew nothing about. Old secrets that had sprung back to life with a vengeance. And the most frustrating thing about it was that maybe it was all over before we even got started. Now that Ivan had him, maybe that was the last we'd ever hear of Leo Sokolov, and we wouldn't know what the hell it was all about.

I hated this feeling.

I hated having so many open questions, not just about Sokolov, but about Ivan. We knew our shooter was either a high-level Mafiya enforcer, or a state-sanctioned operative. I was hoping for the former. If it was the latter and if this wasn't over, then things were going to get complicated, politically. A Russian agent gunning down several American agents on our soil – not exactly a misdemeanor. Either way, we'd need to bring in other agencies to find out more about Sokolov's background: CIA and ICE, for starters. There wasn't much we could tell them beyond giving them a set of his prints that we'd sourced in his apartment. Maybe that would be enough. If he had a secret Soviet history, they might know. Whether they'd want to share it with us was another story.

Then, of course, there was the lovely Ms. Tchoumitcheva. If Ivan was one of theirs, I wondered if she was now taking part in a private celebration deep within the consulate, now that Sokolov was in their hands. I was convinced the Russians had to know who he really was – but whether she was fully in the loop was another matter.

I'd also need to ask Daphne about this, although my gut told me that it would come as much as a surprise to her as it did to us.

As I stood by the floor-to-ceiling glass and looked down across Foley Square from our twenty-third-floor offices at the magnificent criminal courts buildings, I found myself churning over everything from the very beginning, yet again, and wondering how a high school science teacher ended up being the centrifugal force of an escalating situation with a body count that was already in double figures. And why an unassuming and quiet guy in his early sixties would trust a young Korean gangster over New York's finest with his wife's safety. And why he'd insisted on using his old van for their rescue mission.

Kanigher's voice broke through the synaptic maelstrom that was raging inside my skull.

'Check this out,' he said as he rushed over, waving a couple of sheets in his hand.

They were printouts from some kind of traffic camera. The grainy pictures showed a panel van driving toward it. 'We've got Sokolov's ride. I figured they'd have taken either the Brooklyn Bridge or the Battery Tunnel to get from the restaurant to the docks. Location and time stamps match, and that sure as hell looks like Jonny boy in the passenger seat.'

I took a closer look. I could make out Jonny, no question. Then I noticed the air-conditioning unit on the roof. 'You sure? It's a refrigerated van.'

'I know.'

I studied the picture more closely and got the distinct feeling I was missing something. 'Why would he need that?'

'Who knows. Maybe it was just a cheap buy. Especially if the A/C's shot. It's not exactly fresh off the showroom floor, is it?'

I was still baffled by it when Aparo appeared and cut in. 'I just got a call from the NYPD guys we sent to bring back the van,' he said. 'They can't find it.'

'Jonny said he only left it there, what, a couple of hours ago?'

Aparo said, 'If that.'

It didn't compute. In fact, nothing about that van made sense. And it sounded like Jonny had been less than forthcoming about it too. Everything about that van was suddenly bothering me. Everyone seemed to be lying about it. And right at the moment, it wasn't a lot, but it was all I had, and I didn't feel like spending the rest of the night lost in my own questions.

'Put out a priority APB on the van,' I told Kanigher, handing him back the printouts. Then I turned to Aparo as I grabbed my jacket. 'Let's get some Korean take-out.'

40

Jonny felt dizzy.

Shin had just finished an extended discourse on microwave technology and the mathematical principles behind cell-phone networks, but Jonny still didn't have a clue what he was talking about.

'Just, please, tell me in plain English what you think it is,' Jonny implored, 'before my head explodes.'

Shin rolled his eyes.

'Someone with a weird hobby and lot of free time on their hands seems to have stripped down a cell-phone tower, taken off all the juicy bits, and used them to turn this van into a mobile microwave transmitter. That's what the refrigeration unit on the roof is. He's just using it as a cover for the drum.'

Jonny frowned. 'So what's it do?'

'No idea. I doubt he's just after some unlimited 4G, though. Nice as that would be.' Shin looked stumped. 'I really don't know. I've never seen anything like it before.' He pointed at something that looked like the equalizer of a high-end stereo among the stack of electronics in the metal locker. 'He's got a custom-built modulator in there. Kind of thing that can tune the waves within infinitesimally small degrees. It's linked to the laptop, which must control it. And he's running the whole thing off the car's engine, which acts like a power generator. That's why he asked you to keep the engine running. This thing must eat up a lot of juice.'

Jonny spread his hands open questioningly. 'That's it? Look, I don't care about the technical mumbo-jumbo. I just want to know what it does. And here I was, thinking you were one of Mensa's finest.'

'I am. But this guy is some kind of meta-geek. Sergey Brin-level.'

'Funny you should say that,' Jonny said. 'The guy who built this is also Russian.'

Jonny decided not to burden Shin with any further information on that front. The last thing the poor guy needed was more stress on his plate. Instead, he asked, 'What about the earmuffs?'

Shin thought about it for a moment. 'You said the guy said it would give you some kind of advantage in a tough situation. The ear protectors must be some kind of shield against it.'

'But from what? When I tried it, I couldn't hear anything, even when I took them off.'

'You wouldn't necessarily hear anything. The wavelengths could be so short that they're outside the audible spectrum. Kind of like a dog whistle. The protectors are probably meant to shield your inner ear from the oscillation caused by the waves.' Shin thought about it. 'You know they've got these things for crowd control now. Sonic weapons. They blast out loud noise that's very focused, like a spotlight. Kinda like what they did at Waco. They had these things deployed around the Olympic stadiums in London last year. I'm thinking maybe this is in the same ballpark, only it's a different technology. And what effect it'll have exactly ... I can't say. I can tell you it's probably not gonna be very Zen.'

'How bad can it be?'

'The cell-phone towers, like the one this guy's jacked? They're microwave transmitters. Same basics as in the oven. A microwave oven cooks food using microwave radiation. A cell phone can do the same if it's turned up high enough. That's why there's all this research into cell phones: do they cook our brain cells and give us cancer, all that stuff. I don't buy into it. But it all depends on the frequency of the waves – and how much power is feeding them.'

Jonny felt a stir of excitement. 'You think this thing could fry someone's brains?'

'It's possible.'

Bon had sauntered over and started listening in while eyeing Shin disdainfully. Shin did his best to ignore the pile of muscle looming over him and kept his eyes on Jonny.

Jonny asked, 'What about the laptop?'

'It's got to be the command and control unit, but I can't get in it. It's password-protected. Must be rigged to go to sleep when the power drops, then comes to life when you hit the switch on the dashboard.'

Jonny said, 'Try "Daphne."'

'Why "Daphne"?'

'Just try it,' Jonny ordered.

Shin typed it in, then shook his head. 'No go.'

Jonny frowned, frustrated at being so close to something he felt held big potential. Then he remembered something Sokolov had said more than once. 'Try "*Lapushka.*"'

Shin's eyebrows rose. 'Seriously?'

'Try it.'

'How do you spell it?'

'How the fuck should I know? Like it sounds.'

Shin went to work. He typed in a few letters, hit the Return key. Hit a wall. Then he tried again using another spelling.

The screen came alive.

His face lit up with an ear-to-ear grin. *'Bil-eomeog-eul.' Goddamn.* 'We're in.'

The screen showed another synthesizer, only this one was virtual. It had banks of controls and digital readouts on it, as well as several buttons that had Cyrillic writing under them.

Jonny sat patiently as Shin's studious eyes explored the screen, the electronic deck and all the wiring, back and forth. Finally, he looked up. 'I think he's picked out several specific frequencies and saved them to these buttons, like you save FM stations on a car stereo. The first one's preset as the default frequency. That's the one it would have broadcast when you were going to use it. But beyond that – I can't tell you what effect it has or what it'll do.'

Jonny went all quiet and thoughtful for a long moment. Then he said, 'Let's go try it out.'

Shin objected, 'What, now?'

'Right now.'

'We don't know what it does.'

'Exactly,' Jonny said. 'Only one way to find out.' He turned to Bon. 'You up for that?'

Bon grinned from ear to ear. 'You bet.'

Jonny pointed at the van. 'And better slap some fresh plates on it. These ones are hot.'

Bon went off to do it. Jonny turned to Shin. 'This should be fun. Come on.'

Shin hesitated. 'You did hear what I said about microwaves, right?'

'Every word.'

Shin seemed bewildered.

'Let's take it down to Brighton Beach,' Jonny said. 'Try it out on some Russkies. Seeing as one of them invented it.'

Shin took a couple of steps away from the van.

'Not for me, man,' he said, his finger doing a wiper blade. 'No way. I'm outta here.'

Jonny stepped closer to him. 'Come on. I need you for this. Besides, what the fuck else you got to do tonight, you and that piece-of-shit PhD of yours? You'd rather go home and stare at your nice framed diploma while Nikki finds new ways to call you a loser?'

He put his arm around the gaunt man and headed him back to the van. 'Come on, bro. Where's your scientific curiosity? You, me, and the Pulgasari,' he said, pointing at Bon and using his favorite nickname for him, that of the Korean Godzilla-like monster. 'Let's go fry us some Russkie motherfuckers. What do you say?'

Shin hesitated, then nodded. Then he remembered something. 'The earmuffs,' he told Jonny. 'You said there were two sets?'

'That's right.'

'There's three of us going,' Shin pointed out. 'Maybe I'd better sit this one out.'

Jonny thought about it for a moment, then grinned. 'You and I can wear them. See what you can rustle up for the Pulgasari. I wouldn't be too worried about him. It takes a lot to get through his thick skull.'

Koschey slowed down as he drove by the restaurant on his first recon pass, his eyes surveying the place's entrance and its immediate surroundings and picking out points of interest with the speed and precision of the best multipoint autofocus software.

There was a gaggle of people outside the Green Dragon's double doors, smoking and chatting away in small cliques. The Asian community, he knew, were heavy smokers, and all the way there, he'd noticed huddles of smokers outside bars and restaurants. He spotted an armed bouncer closer to the doors, standing alone, staring down the sidewalk at nothing in particular. He was wearing a black T-shirt under a sleeveless black leather vest that didn't do a great job of hiding the shiny grip or holster strap that was peeking out from underneath it. Koschey also spotted a man in a parked car two spots away from the restaurant's entrance, clearly keeping an eye on the place. A cop or a federal agent, no doubt. Koschey assumed it would be the same out back, at the service entrance.

He didn't think he needed a second pass.

He drove the Yukon around, selected a strategic place to leave his car, and pulled in. Then he got out, walked around the block, and headed toward the restaurant, slowing his pace, timing his approach.

He'd adopted yet another look for the occasion, a smooth, metro-sexual combo of gelled-back hair, jeans, charcoal-gray turtleneck, beige corduroy jacket, and trendy black-rimmed glasses. He could have been an architect or a graphic designer, except that an architect or a graphic designer wouldn't have an unsheathed fixed-blade boot knife balanced up his sleeve.

He pulled out his cell phone and feigned taking a call while pausing until a suitable target walked by. He didn't have to wait long. Three Asians he'd spotted moments earlier passed him unawares, two guys and a girl, strolling together, talking and laughing loudly, out on the town.

Heading toward the restaurant.

With no one coming up behind them.

No one to witness anything.

Still faking a casual late-night chat on his phone, he tucked in behind them.

Kept their pace, moving right up so he was merely a couple of feet behind them.

Selected one of the guys, the one walking alongside the shop fronts.

Timed it so he was behind him when they were about twenty feet from the Green Dragon, maybe ten from the first of the smokers.

Allowed the blade to slide down his wrist and into his hand.

And struck, lighting-quick.

His arm moved unnaturally fast, lashing out for a nanosecond, the powder-coated three-and-a-quarter-inch-long blade aimed to perfection, stabbing the man's flank below his rib cage – a clean, deep in-and-out, the blade back up his sleeve before his victim had a chance to scream.

Which the young Asian did after stumbling and rag-dolling to the ground.

His friends leaped to his aid as he writhed on the ground, howling, his face a cascade of confusion and pain, the three of them in a sudden panic. They were all freaking out in loud outbursts of Korean and English, frantically trying to figure out what was wrong with him. The sudden commotion made the cluster of smokers outside the restaurant stir and take notice too, their curiosity drawing them in close to the fallen man.

It also drew in the bouncer, who threw a quick glance around the street before edging away from his post to see what was going on.

Koschey kept going, moving fluidly.

With the phone still stuck to his ear, he used the chaos to slip past the smokers and the bouncer and duck inside the restaurant just as a couple of patrons were leaving.

We were churning rubber heading uptown on Sixth Avenue in Aparo's Charger when my phone rang. I glanced at the caller display. It showed private call. I took it, heard her voice, and frowned. I hadn't expected to hear back from her this late in the night, or in the game for that matter.

'Miss Tchoumitcheva,' I said as I took the call. 'You're up late.'

Aparo's face lit up and he flashed me a juvenile, suggestive grin.

She said, 'I heard there's been some trouble in Brooklyn? More dead Russians?'

'You've got good ears.' Said with a side of sarcasm.

She didn't flinch. 'What, you think you're the only ones with a finger on Mirminsky's pulse?' A real pro.

But I didn't like being played, and right at the moment, I wasn't really in the best of moods. I decided to shake things up a little. 'No, I'm sure we're not. But I'm still surprised to hear from you.'

She seemed taken aback. 'Why's that?'

'Well, you really don't need to keep up this pretense any longer, do you? You got what you wanted. Mission accomplished. Or are you just calling to gloat?'

Aparo swiveled around to face me, eyes wide, mouth forming a silent, surprised 'What?'

She went quiet for a breath. 'I'm not sure I know what you're talking about,' she insisted, sounding put out.

'Come on. All that hogwash about us needing to work together. You were just pumping me for information about Sokolov. Well, you've got him now. What more do you need from me, aside from an update on how we're doing in tracking your man down? 'Cause you know this isn't over, right? You know we're not gonna stop until we take him down. Him and everyone connected to him.'

I was tired and I was angry and I wanted to prompt a reaction, but I knew I might be venting pointlessly. Even if she was part of this, she and her colleagues at the consulate had diplomatic immunity. Getting to any of them would be tricky and frustrating, if not downright impossible. And even if we did take them down, they'd probably get traded for someone we wanted back and end up as pampered cheerleaders for the regime back home.

'I understand why you might think that,' she countered. 'But you're wrong. I was actually calling to see if you wanted to talk about us leaning on Mirminsky together. Seeing as he's connected to this shooter. Maybe use him to flush him out. But hey, if we're on opposite sides, then maybe it's a bad idea. Anyway, think about it, and if you want to talk it through, give me a call in the morning.'

Then she hung up.

I stared at my cell for a moment in stunned silence. I glanced sideways at Aparo. He was looking at me like I needed a straitjacket.

He said, 'Your chat-up lines need a lot of work, compadre.'

I was still wondering why she called. The big question was whether Ivan had Kremlin backing at some level, whether he was here doing official wet work or just freelancing for some mobster. If it was the former, then the consulate – and Larisa – had his back. It would also make them accomplices in the murder of American law-enforcement officers. And yet, something in her tone was off. I got this weird vibe like she was genuinely rattled. Which didn't make sense, unless she and Ivan weren't on the same team. Which meant he was a wild card. Working for forces unknown.

I'm not sure which scenario I preferred.

The *Dragnet* theme hooked my attention. Aparo picked up the call, listened for a quick beat, then floored the pedal and glanced over at me.

'Something's going on outside the restaurant.'

41

Koschey scanned the busy restaurant with laserlike efficiency, his trained eyes quickly locking onto the pretty, petite figure in the green-dragon dress that Sokolov had described to him.

Ae-Cha. Jonny's cousin.

Heading toward the back of the place.

He streamed through the tables, his movement smooth, his body language unhurried and discreet. He knew how not to attract attention and pass unnoticed, regardless of how crowded a place was. He caught up with Ae-Cha just as she entered the kitchen. Before she even sensed his presence, his blade was pricking her lower back, his other hand clasped firmly around her upper arm.

'Keep smiling and don't make a noise or a lot of people will die and you'll be the first of them. You understand?'

Ae-Cha froze, then nodded nervously.

Koschey shepherded her forward, his stance casual despite his viselike grip on her arm, directing her toward the stairwell, smiling at her and at a passing waiter.

'Let's go see Jonny,' he added, low and to her ear.

She nodded again, more controlled this time, as they passed another waiter and pushed through the doorway and into the stairwell.

'Quickly now,' he hissed.

She led him up to the top of the stairs and knocked on the metal door. There was no answer. She glanced at Koschey, who knocked on the door himself, mimicking her tap.

Still nothing.

He pressed the fiberglass-reinforced-plastic blade to her neck. 'Where is he?'

'I don't know,' she stammered. 'He must have gone out.'

He pressed the blade harder as he studied her, ascertaining whether she was telling the truth. 'Try harder.'

'This is his place,' she insisted. 'If he's not in there, he's gone out.'

She was shaking too much to be lying.

He asked, 'You have his number on your phone?'

Ae-Cha nodded.

'All right. Let's go.' He herded her back toward the stairs. 'And let's hope you mean a lot to him.'

Jonny was glad to have Bon along for the ride.

Bon was exactly the company he needed on the drive down to Brighton Beach. Someone who didn't ask questions and did what he was asked. Most of the time. Plus the big guy was useful in a fight and knew how to party. Since Shin had swapped Colombian powder for formula powder – another member of the crew lost to trivial domesticity – he was no fun at all. Jonny could almost hear Shin's teeth chattering nervously from the far seat, by the passenger window. But at least the bookworm had been useful tonight. If the van proved effective in some way, then it had to be worth something. Or maybe he'd just keep it. Ask Shin to break it down in his own time so he had a better chance of understanding it.

But first Jonny wanted to see what happened when he threw the switch with people around.

They took Van Wyck and then Belt and Shore, covering the twenty miles to Brighton Beach in less than half an hour. They followed Ocean almost to the water, then took the off-ramp back around to Brighton Beach Avenue.

Jonny knew all about the Sledgehammer. Mirminsky had a reputation for being as brutal as he was greedy. Deals with the *kuvalda* were always completely one-sided – honored or broken on a whim with no shame and apparently no fear of any retaliation. His guys may not have been the last ones to have Daphne – or maybe there was some kind of power play going on within Mirminsky's crew – but either way the fat fuck had taken Daphne in the first place and was clearly up to his weasel eyes in the whole thing. Whatever the van did – if it did anything at all – was no less than the beetroot-eating bastard and his followers deserved.

It was Bon who had reminded Jonny about Mirminsky's original bar-restaurant, Lolita, which sat at the top end of one of the streets that ran south from Brighton Beach Avenue. Atmosphère was way too hot at the moment. There were always paparazzi camped outside and Jonny had no interest in unwittingly frying the brain of a Knicks star and his reality-show starlet girlfriend, especially not since he was an avid fan. Lolita was an entirely different proposition, the clientele leaning more toward meat-heads and past-their-prime platinum-blond gold diggers. Not that they'd find much gold on Brighton Beach Avenue other than what the local *bratki* wore around their necks.

They parked almost directly opposite the bar, which appeared to be full, even though it was midweek. Large windows on either side of the entrance gave a clear view of a crush at least seven deep facing the bar and several oversubscribed tables. A sizeable throng of customers stood outside, smoking and laughing. A small, wiry Uzbek-looking man wearing a black leather jacket, black jeans, and white leather boots was keeping the hard-core nicotine addicts amused – most likely with jokes that would make Louis C. K. blush. A tall, raven-haired woman teetering on six-inch heels was flicking her tresses from side to side, desperately trying to attract the attention of a young guy in a white T-shirt and fashionably torn blue jeans, who nonetheless appeared to be more interested in the short guy's comedy routine. The rest of the group looked like gym-ripped thugs or low-level Mafiya enforcers – guys who would never pimp, run numbers, or distribute product across more than a few city blocks.

Jonny waited as Shin squeezed between the seats and went through the narrow doorway into the rear compartment before following him through, a pair of ear protectors already slung around his neck. He kept the cabin door open so he could see the restaurant from the back.

'Get behind the wheel,' he told Bon. 'In case we have to make a quick exit.'

Bon did so. He then stuffed a couple of earplugs into his ears before slipping on a crash helmet. It was the best that Shin could manage at short notice.

'All set, Pulgasari?' Jonny asked him.

Bon always smiled when people used his nickname. He loved being compared to the giant, metal-eating beast of the infamous North Korean monster movie. He whacked his helmet hard with both hands, then nodded and gave Jonny a thumbs-up. Jonny couldn't help but laugh at Bon's antics as he donned his own ear protectors. Bon pulled out a small case from a pocket of his cargo pants and started to chop out some lines.

The van really was the perfect cover story, Jonny thought. Who was going to question a food-delivery vehicle anywhere near shops or restaurants?

Bon snorted a couple of lines and passed the remaining powder to Jonny, who sent them up his nose with minimal fuss.

'We ready?' he asked Shin.

Shin nodded, visibly jittery, and pulled on his ear protectors.

Jonny tapped Bon's helmet and shouted out, 'Let's do it, *oppa Brooklyn-style*,' mimicking Psy's Gangnam dance moves.

Bon made a big show of counting down with his fingers, like a TV producer, then flicked the switch to On.

With Jonny still bopping to an imaginary beat, they all stared out at the restaurant.

Nothing happened.

They waited ten, fifteen seconds. Nothing. Jonny turned to Shin and gave him a 'What gives' gesture. Shin grimaced back an 'I don't know.' Jonny pointed at the laptop and mouthed, *'Try another setting.'*

Shin highlighted another preset button on the laptop's screen and clicked it.

Still nothing.

At least, not for the first ten seconds or so.

Then it started.

I could see the small crowd outside the restaurant as we got there and pulled in.

We climbed out and were met by the SSG who'd called us moments earlier, a young agent by the name of Jaffee.

'There's an ambulance on the way,' he told us.

'What's wrong with him?' I asked.

'He's bleeding badly. He's got a big cut on his side,' he said, pointing to the back of his left flank. 'He was walking with his friends and he just fell. If I didn't know better, I'd say he'd been stabbed.'

I muttered a curse and bolted toward the restaurant's door, yanking my gun out and hoping we weren't too late again. 'Inside,' I told him, and Aparo as I rushed ahead. 'It's our guy. He's here.'

42

We charged into the restaurant with one thought ringing through my head.

We're late. We're too damn late.

'Call Gaines,' I told Jaffee as we paused at the door, referring to his partner, the SSG who was watching the Green Dragon's service entrance in the alley out back. 'Make sure he's got the back covered. And tell him to stay sharp.'

I quickly took in the huge room as he alerted his partner. It was still rammed with people, even this late. I tried to avoid causing a panic and held my gun down by my thigh, its barrel running along my leg, minimizing its profile. It still made the patrons closest to me recoil at seeing it. I had my other hand out and flat in a stilling motion, flicking them a 'Keep calm' look while trying to stay alert to anything threatening coming my way.

'He's on post and clear,' Jaffee said.

I nodded through my concentration. It was tough to pick out anyone suspect through the crowd, so I just pushed forward through the narrow aisles, heading for the swinging doors and the stairwell in the kitchen, Aparo and Jaffee close behind.

I was just going through the kitchen door when I saw them coming out of the doorway that led to the stairs: Ae-Cha, her face locked in stoic concentration, and a well-dressed guy with gelled-back hair and glasses right next to her. She didn't look like she was having a great time, which might have had something to do with the firm grip he had on her upper arm.

Her eyes caught mine in the same instant his did.

The few seconds that followed were a blur.

It was unreal, though it didn't start out as such.

The first minute or so after Bon had first flicked the switch was notable for nothing more interesting than the Uzbek grabbing his head as though he'd just gotten a migraine and the tall woman almost toppling to the ground and falling into the arms of the younger guy.

Bon had burst into hysterical laughter at that, but then, in Jonny's experience, Bon had a pretty low entertainment threshold.

Jonny tried to process what he was seeing.

'What the hell's going on?' he shouted to Shin.

'I don't know,' Shin answered. 'But it's messing them up.'

Jonny watched in fascination as the crowd took on a confused, lethargic stance. Some of them sat down and stared out, others looked around as if they were lost. Jonny wondered if Sokolov's aim at the exchange hadn't been some kind of disorientation, and though it was interesting, it wasn't the kind of damage he had in mind. After a moment of watching the crowd squirm with discomfort, he turned to Shin.

'Try another one,' he yelled to Shin.

Shin hit the second setting.

Nothing happened at first, then one by one, the people outside Lolita were clutching their stomachs and curling up with pain. Jonny watched in rapt attention as a woman dry-retched like a demented cat trying to heave up a mammoth hairball. It was beyond freaky. After a few moments, he tore his attention away and excitedly told Shin, 'Another one.'

Shin hit the third preset.

Then things got interesting.

The crowd outside the restaurant looked like they were coming out of their discomfort. They were straightening up, talking to each other curiously, clearly mystified by what had happened. Then an argument started between the young guy in the ripped jeans and the wiry Uzbek. The ripped guy poked the Uzbek in the chest, the Uzbek pushed him back – then the ripped guy unleashed a ferocious right hook out of the blue onto the head of the wiry Uzbek.

Next to them, the dark-haired woman had launched herself at the shorter man's attacker, raking two sets of nails down his face and driving a knee full-force into the poor bastard's groin.

Other fights were brewing quickly, and within two heartbeats they escalated wildly. A bald, middle-aged pimp stubbed out his cigarette on the tall woman's back while her nails were still embedded in the young guy's face. At the same time, a huge steroid-bodied thug had swung a lump-hammer fist into the stomach of the tattoo-necked guy standing next to him.

Jonny already had one leg swung over the seats from the back of the van as he clambered into the front seat for a better view, more than happy with the preset for the time being. On the bench next to him, Bon was clapping in delight and laughing uncontrollably, while in the back, Shin was watching it all through the open doorway in silent terror.

Lightning-fast, Neck Tattoo pulled out a knife and jabbed it into the big lug's kidney. Meanwhile the young guy had managed to fight off the woman and land a vicious kick between her legs. She collapsed to the ground, her screams so loud that Jonny could hear them – albeit faintly – through the ear protectors.

Her screams were muffled completely by the long-haired guy, who came crashing through the left-hand window and landed directly on top of her, blood pouring from a deep gash in his face.

Jonny couldn't believe his eyes.

I swung my gun up just as I shouted 'Everybody down!' as loud as I could.

Ivan was just as fast. He had his gun out before I'd even finished the second word, his arm pivoting up like it was on a spring release and locking onto us without overshooting by a single degree.

In that split second, I couldn't shoot. Not with Ae-Cha there. And he knew it. I also knew he wasn't prone to qualms or partial to having a chit-chat before he started firing, so I dove to the right while shouting out my warning and took cover behind a food-prep counter just as the first bullet whizzed past me and plowed into the back of a heavily laden waiter who had paused to let me through before delivering his platter. I heard the rattle of his tray's contents crashing through the swinging doors and the first panicked shrieks from inside the restaurant just as two other rounds pounded the side of the unit behind which I was crouched.

The kitchen staff freaked out and scrambled for cover as our shooter rapidly moved on to his other targets. Pots and plates were crashing to the ground as I turned and saw Jaffee take one in the shoulder by the base of his neck as he was darting to safety. I couldn't see Aparo anywhere, then I heard him yell, 'Everyone stay down!' followed by 'Sean, you OK?'

'Still in one piece!' I yelled back as I gripped the gun in two hands while pumping air into my lungs, debating when to stick my head out from behind the counter and risk having Ivan carve me that third eye he seemed to relish.

'Jaffee's down,' Aparo rasped.

'I saw,' I shot back over the pandemonium of screaming and fleeing patrons coming from the restaurant.

'I'm calling it in,' he said.

We needed an EMS team here pronto, but backup wouldn't help with Ivan. This was going down right now, fast. I felt shackled. There was no point in me swinging out firing – I wasn't going to risk hitting Ae-Cha, and all I'd be doing is presenting Ivan with my non-Kevlar-balaclavaed self.

I heard noise from their direction, and risked a peek to see the shooter hustling Ae-Cha toward the exit. I lined up a shot, desperately looking for just a couple of clear inches of any part him – head, shoulder, arm – any flesh of his that I could hit to unravel his tight hold of the situation, but he was being too careful to give me even that. I only got about three seconds to find that shot before his eyes spun back toward me, saw me, and his gun came back up and spat another careful volley of rounds at me, hammering the counters in front of and behind me a split second after I dived for cover.

I had war drums going off in my ears, and my breaths were coming in short and fast. I caught a glimpse of Aparo behind another counter, where he was tending to Jaffee. Frustration burned through his face, mirroring mine. I gestured to ask about Jaffee, he nodded positively. Then the ruckus from the other end of the kitchen got more intense and I gritted my teeth and swung back out, my Hi-Power choked by a two-handed grip.

Then Ivan was at the back exit, Ae-Cha still shielding him from my aim. He saw me and let off a couple more shots before disappearing out the door and pulling her out behind him.

I sprang up and rushed the exit, flying down the aisle past huddled, cowering kitchen staff and dodging pots and spilled food all over the tiled floor. My heart spiked as I heard two shots before I even reached the door. I burst through it just as Ivan was tearing down the alley in Gaines's bureau sedan, with Ae-Cha next to him.

The SSG himself was lying on the ground, bent in permanent repose in front of a Dumpster with a big green dragon stenciled on it, a small dark hole in his forehead.

43

'Call him,' Koschey ordered Ae-Cha.

He kept checking the rearview mirror of his Yukon while he drove on without a particular destination. He'd quickly swapped cars less than three blocks from the restaurant, dumping the bureau car and hustling Ae-Cha into the SUV he'd left there. It had been a calculated gamble that had paid off. Bureau cars and police cruisers had trackers on them, complications he preferred to avoid if given the choice.

He didn't know where Jonny was at the moment, but his mind was already thinking ahead, evaluating possible venues for what he was planning. He selected a couple of options as Ae-Cha pulled out her iPhone and called Jonny.

Jonny was having trouble processing the astonishing sight he was witnessing.

Lolita had descended into a mad frenzy of extreme, unbridled violence. The huge thug – seemingly oblivious to the knife wound in his side – had beaten Neck Tattoo's face to a bloody purple mess and had started pounding the back of his head into the sidewalk.

A table had smashed through the right-hand window, followed by two young guys trading blows with broken bottles.

The long-haired guy had staggered to his feet only to be knocked down again by the Uzbek. The two of them were rolling around on the ground – a blur of gouging, biting, and punching.

The tall woman had removed her heels, dragged herself upright, and begun to rain down stiletto blows on the pimp's bald head, which already looked like a ball of vanilla ice cream covered in raspberry sauce. Then a miniskirted woman wearing a cheap fur coat emerged from the bar, took a snub-nose from her purse, and shot the young guy in the stomach at point-blank range.

Bon was ecstatic – reveling in the kind of sustained excitement he usually reserved for watching Chan-wook Park's vengeance trilogy back-to-back. He was laughing hysterically and pounding away at the steering wheel.

Jonny was mesmerized, but not by the blood and the violence. He was already thinking about all the things he could do with this technology at his disposal. Then he noticed Bon's pounding of the wheel – the big man was now really having a go at it.

'Hey,' Jonny called to him, tapping his helmet.

Bon turned, his face twisted in a ferocious look of aggression that startled Jonny, so much so that it pushed aside his empire-building fantasies. It also made him fail to notice the incessant vibrating and pulsing blue-white light of his Samsung smart phone as it sat on the cabin floor by his feet and rang away.

'He's not picking up,' Ae-Cha told Koschey, fear raising her voice to a higher pitch.

'Try him again,' he rasped, his eyes resonating with deadly intent.

Ae-Cha nodded tensely, and hit the Call button a second time.

An onslaught of questions battered me as I surveyed the chaotic aftermath of the shoot-out at the Green Dragon.

A team of paramedics was already here and tending to Jaffee, who was going to be all right. Gaines, on the other hand, was probably dead before he hit the ground. The waiter, too. Some patrons had been injured in the mad scramble to get out of the place, but none seriously. And, of course, Ae-Cha was gone, which had caused her aunt and several of her relatives who worked there to freak out with worry.

I tried to block out the cacophony and focus on what had just happened and why it had happened. I hadn't expected our shooter to show up. He had Sokolov. Why had he come here? Why this late, this urgently? What the hell else did he want?

He had to be here for Jonny. But Jonny wasn't part of this. He'd only helped Sokolov. He wasn't a threat to him, in the sense that he couldn't ID him. I didn't think Ivan was petty enough to come out here for revenge, either. And he took Ae-Cha. Only reason for that would be leverage over Jonny.

Had Sokolov given Jonny something to hang on to for safekeeping? Something Ivan was after?

Then it hit me.

The van.

Jonny had lied about where he'd dumped it. Then he'd gone out soon after we'd questioned him about it. And now this.

It had to be the van. Sokolov had hidden something in it.

I grabbed my phone and called Kanigher.

'That APB on the van. Send it out again, priority one, Tri-State. That's what our shooter's after. We have to find that goddamn van before he does.'

The sound of automatic weapon fire punched through Jonny's ear protectors, forcing his mind away from Bon's sneering face and back to the side street off Brighton Beach Avenue.

There were now at least a couple dozen people out on the sidewalk, all involved in one, large, messy, lethal fight – either one-on-one or locked in a *Grand Theft Auto* version of a bar brawl. Inside the bar was no different.

Jonny was enjoying the spectacle, the sensation amplified by the cocaine lighting up his neurons, but Bon was getting too agitated. Jonny knew it was only a matter of time before the cops arrived and that the wise move was for them to leave before that happened, but he was finding it hard to tear himself away from the show.

He scanned the street ahead and checked the van's mirrors, scrutinizing the night for any telltale sign of spinning lights, when the blue light inside the van caught the corner of his eye.

His phone was glowing.

The display said: AE-CHA.

Jonny stared at it, uncertain about whether or not to take it. This was really going to mess up his high and kill the moment. He felt a chill as he imagined what she was probably calling about, this late at night: Jachin. Maybe she knew. Maybe she'd heard. And if so, he could just imagine the state she might be in, given how she felt for his now-dead friend.

He hesitated, then decided not to take the call.

He stared at it with a heavy heart as it droned on in silence, its blue light coming on and off hauntingly inside the dark cabin of the van, its ringtone muted by the big ear protectors on his head – then Bon lashed out, twisting around and slamming his big fists into the partition wall behind his seat like a caged animal on a rampage.

Jonny flinched and shouted to Shin, 'Kill it!'

Shin punched in the first preset, the one that hadn't had a discernible effect, just as Jonny grabbed the phone. And at that same moment, a police cruiser came around the corner, lights spinning.

'Get us out of here,' Jonny barked at Bon.

The big man looked at him with a dazed expression.

'Pulgarasi, we need to move.'

Bon stared at him for a second, then sat back down, threw the van into gear and floored the pedal.

Jonny looked back, watched as the police car pulled in outside the restaurant, then breathed out and answered his call. 'Ae-Cha.'

It wasn't Ae-Cha.

It was a voice he'd heard before, out on the docks, that night, with Sokolov.

'Where are you, Jonny?'

44

Officers Kaluta and Talaoc pulled in across the street from Lolita and scrambled out of their squad car. Kaluta froze as his mind registered the sheer horror of the scene outside the restaurant.

It was unlike anything he'd ever witnessed before.

People were trading blows or facing off with one another with knives and broken bottles, but they were outnumbered by those who either lay dead or dying on the sidewalk. Men and women who'd clearly dressed up for a night on the town were on the ground, writhing pathetically or limping away, their clothes ripped to shreds, their faces locked in expressions of confusion and silent terror. Blood was everywhere and on everyone, a tableau from a zombie movie come to life.

'What do we do?' Kaluta asked his partner as he drew his gun.

Talaoc didn't answer immediately. Something else had caught his eye, just as they were rushing up to the restaurant. A van had just stormed away and was turning off onto another street. A white panel van, with a refrigeration unit on its roof. Same kind of van that was on the priority APB that had just flashed up on the squad car's computer screen.

Talaoc hit the Call button on his radio just as two other squad cars swarmed in.

'You hurt one hair of—'

'Shut the fuck up and listen,' the Russian hissed. 'I don't care about her. You'll get her back in one piece. I just want the van.'

Jonny's mouth dried up.

The Russian didn't leave him time to even think about how to handle it. 'I know you have it. Don't lie if you want her to live. I can make things very long and painful for her. Then I'll come for you.'

The Russian's words, the coke, the emotions of the whole damn night – Jonny's mind was frazzled. He could barely think straight. Yes, of course, his first instinct was a desperate urge to hang onto the van, at any cost. But this was Ae-Cha the bastard was talking about. Ae-Cha, his aunt's only daughter. His Ae-Cha.

He couldn't lie.

'I've got the fucking van here.'

'Where are you?

'Brooklyn.'

The Russian went silent for a moment, then said, 'Drive to Prospect Park. You know where that is?'

'Yeah, I know where it is, motherfucker.'

'Good. When you get there, go in from the Ocean Avenue side. Take the drive down to the ice rink. I'll meet you there, in the lot.'

Then the line went dead.

Jonny cursed, shut his eyes to try to let some clarity seep back into his brain, then ordered Bon to change direction.

I was already moving for the exit, with Aparo hot on my heels.

'Put me through to the cruiser,' I blurted as I hit the sidewalk. 'We need eyes on that van. Don't let them lose it.'

Within seconds, we were pulling away from the mess outside the Green Dragon when the dispatcher put me through to the squad car.

'Who's this?' I asked, switching the phone to speaker.

'Officer Mike Talaoc, Sixtieth Precinct. I'm riding with Officer Kaluta. You?'

'Reilly and Aparo, FBI. You got the van?'

'We're about two blocks back from it,' Talaoc told him. 'It just turned right on Neptune.'

Aparo hit the gas harder now that he had a clear idea of where we were heading.

'OK, stay back but don't lose them,' I told Talaoc. 'Just tail them and don't let them spot you. I'm gonna call in some backup. Our shooter's coming after the van, and I want to be there when he does.'

* * *

The Sledgehammer was savoring a tumbler of limited-edition Iordanov Vodka when his prepaid cell phone rang.

'*Chyort voz'mi,*' he cursed to no one in particular before he grabbed it and took the call.

Mirminsky hated to be interrupted while enjoying the rewards of his efforts. He felt he'd earned the glass of five-thousand-dollar-a-bottle vodka, what with all the bullshit he'd had to suffer from the SVR enforcer – Afanasyev, or whatever the hell he'd called himself – as well as the accompanying increased heat from the feds. If he were entirely honest with himself, he couldn't taste the difference between what he was drinking and a glass of Russian Standard, but appearances counted for almost everything in his world and if he was unable to savor the taste, then he could at least savor the price.

Appearances also meant that he didn't enjoy being seen as someone's lackey, especially in the eyes of the cops and the FBI.

'You need to hear this, boss.'

'Put it through,' he groused.

After a couple of clicks, the incoming call was connected to Mirminsky's cell, which he knew was clean because it had been removed from its packaging less than three hours ago.

'Ditko here. We've got trouble.'

Mirminsky's mood went from dark to pitch-black. Ditko was with the vice squad at the Sixtieth Precinct, out in Brooklyn. He'd been on the Sledgehammer's payroll for seven years now, helping keep Lolita and Mirminsky's crew out of trouble.

'The lines are going crazy here. Some major bust-up at Lolita. It's bad. We've got some dead, Yuri. I'm on my way there now.'

Mirminsky's veins flared, then settled back. There had been brawls at the place before. Even a death or two. Lolita had navigated through the turmoil before, and it would do so again. Mirminsky's lawyers would see to that.

'Is that it?' he grumbled.

'You're not listening, Yuri. This is really bad. You need to get down there and see it. And that's not all. The feds are involved.'

That made Mirminsky sit up. 'Why the feds?'

'I'm not sure. We got a report of a white van at the scene. Some kind of meat wagon. The feds have a priority APB out on it.' The line went quiet for a moment as Ditko tapped a few keys on his computer. 'Wasn't there a refrigerated van in the shoot-out at Owl's Head Park? When your guys were gunned down?'

The Sledgehammer's blood was boiling now. 'And I lost two more at Red Hook. All because of the same *súka blyad*.'

Mirminksy knew most of what had happened at the docks. He had sources on his payroll at other police precincts throughout the city. This sounded like a definite lead on the bastard who had cost him six men and set the feds breathing down his neck.

He wondered why no one at the bar had called him. It wasn't a good sign.

'Where's the van now?' he asked.

'I can find out. We've got a squad car tailing it, but the fed in charge told them not to intercept.'

Mirminsky was already in full tactical planning mode. 'I want to know where the van is. Call me direct with updates. Petr will give you the number.'

He hung up and knocked back the rest of the Iordanov, then he opened a drawer in his desk and took out a Desert Eagle .50 Action Express. On each side of the customized handle, a sledgehammer had been embossed in gold.

He'd had enough of being told what to do. Of assholes destroying his property and treating his foot soldiers like they came off a production line.

Why Lolita?

The bar was close to his heart. It was his very first place. It was where his business grew from. His niece's fiancé ran it.

What if he were among the dead?

He tried Stefan's cell. It immediately went to voicemail.

He tried the bar. It rang out.

That sealed it.

This is America, not Russia.

The *sluzhba vneshney razvedk* – the SVR – didn't run the show here.

Enough was enough.

He was *kuvalda*. He was the Sledgehammer.

And it was high time he showed those *ebanatyi pidaraz* why they called him that.

45

The van fishtailed as it turned left out of Brightwater onto Coney Island Avenue and headed north. Bon ran a stop sign then jumped two sets of lights, but the traffic was so sparse at this time of night that it barely made a difference.

Next to him, Jonny had his head stuck out the open window, his eyes focused behind them, trying to see if they were being followed.

'*Jen jang,*' he cursed. *Dammit.* He pulled back into the van. 'There's a cop car tailing us. Can't this piece of shit go any faster?' His pupils were the size of quarters, his blood hosting an escalating concentration of adrenaline and endorphins.

The van lurched forward as Bon floored the gas and ran another set of lights. This time they made it over the intersection a split second before a short line of cars filled the cross street.

Bon turned right onto a side street, then immediately took a left.

Jonny peered out of the window. He waited until they'd done a few more turns before facing forward and taking a deep breath.

'I think we've lost them,' he told Bon. He slapped him on the arm three times. 'Good job, Pulgasari.'

He stared ahead. It was past two in the morning, and the roads were empty. He tried to keep a lid on his emotions and concentrate on reaching the ice rink, but he knew he'd gone too far this time. He knew there was no deceit or manipulation or charm that could extricate him from the spiraling violence in which he found himself trapped.

Ae-Cha had never wanted to be part of his world, but once she'd fallen for Jachin – it was Jonny who had introduced them – it was only a matter of time before she was dragged into their wake.

Jonny felt a surge of fury that was coupled with a parallel burst of sadness, and for the first time, he began to wonder if his brother and Shin had perhaps made the right decision after all.

Koschey was already over the Manhattan Bridge and heading down Flatbush Avenue toward Prospect Park.

Major cities were easy for him. In between assignments, he often spent weeks in solitary lockdown, most recently in a rented villa just outside the tiny village of Mougins on the French Riviera, usually with no more than an encrypted satellite Internet connection for company. He used that time wisely, to prepare, to explore, to compile useful lists – including lists of discreet locations to stay at, or to meet in. Even though the entire apparatus of the Russian intelligence service was at his disposal, he preferred to work alone, and for no one – not even his direct superior – to know anything more than what they told him. It was safer that way, both for him and for them.

He'd previously identified the lot next to the ice rink in Prospect Park as one of a handful of suitable locations for a meeting away from prying eyes, something that wasn't especially easy in a place as crowded as New York City. While most of the city was increasingly covered by CCTV, the park itself had minimal coverage, and he knew where the cameras were and where they pointed.

A pained grunt came from the seat next to him. Ae-Cha was struggling against the plastic strip that bound her wrists together, but had only succeeded in gouging a layer of skin from one wrist. A trickle of blood had stained the seat beneath it.

It didn't matter. The car wasn't long for this world.

Neither was its passenger.

Chewing gum vigorously like a coach watching a final, the Sledgehammer sat in the cushy backseat of the Mercedes GL450 and checked his Desert Eagle as the black SUV pulled away into the night.

His lieutenant, Petr – a thin man with a tailored suit, cowboy boots, and a mop of blond hair that failed to conceal a vivid scar running horizontally across one cheek – was behind the wheel. Two indistinguishable thugs in leather jackets were riding with them. None of the heavies sported the usual tattoos of the lower-rung *bratki*. They were Mirminsky's personal entourage, all ex-Russian Army Spetsnaz, specifically veterans of some of the most brutal Special Forces incursions into Chechnya. All three of them now earned more from him in a week, and with much better perks, than they'd received from the Russian state in a year.

Mirminsky's cell rang.

It was Ditko.

'Prospect Park,' the cop informed him. 'The lot by the skating rink.'

The Sledgehammer grunted. 'Keep me posted.' Then he clicked off.

He'd make sure the cop got something extra for his trouble. Mirminsky always rewarded those who helped him. It was one of the reasons he had risen so quickly. He believed in the old saying: *knut i pryanik* – 'the whip and the gingerbread.' Only, his whip had barbs.

He directed Petr where to go, then ran his fingers over his Desert Eagle, a savage impatience rising through him.

Aparo hung a left as I grabbed the radio handset and squawked for comms.

'Do you still have them?'

After a moment, Talaoc's crackly voice replied. 'We do. We lost them for a few blocks, but we've caught up with them again. We're on Ocean, still heading north.'

I glanced at Aparo and pictured a map of the city in my mind's eye.

He asked, 'Where are they going?'

'Ivan must have told them to head someplace where they can do the trade. Ae-Cha for the van. Somewhere quiet. But at this hour – could be anywhere.'

I lifted the handset back to my mouth. 'All right, just hang back, but don't lose them again. We're about ten minutes out. Backup's on the way too. Be advised the van might be hooking up with our shooter. Might be a hostage-exchange situation. This guy is armed and extremely dangerous.'

Talaoc took a second, then his voice came back. 'Copy that.'

As I replaced the handset, Aparo shook his head. 'Why do I feel real lucky to still be alive?'

I scowled into the night. At least I'd finally seen our shooter's face, and I knew a bit more about what we were dealing with. It helped to see him.

It helped demystify him and change him from a mythical monster into just another psychopath who enjoyed killing people. But I sensed something else.

'I think this could be our last chance to get him,' I told Aparo. 'He gets the van and disappears, that's it. He's gone.'

'Let's make sure we get him then,' Aparo said.

I just said 'Yeah' and left it at that.

46

Koschey turned into the lot.

Aside from a long box hedge facing the entrance to the rink, it was completely surrounded by trees. You couldn't even see Prospect Park Lake, which was only a couple of hundred yards southwest of the deserted expanse of concrete.

The Yukon came to a stop in the very center of the lot, then he killed the engine. It was deathly quiet, except for the intermittent calls of geese.

It wasn't long before he saw the van. It drove into the lot and crawled toward his SUV. He could just distinguish two figures inside. It stopped about fifty yards away, with the engine still running.

Two guys climbed out. The thinner one was obviously Jonny, whom he recognized from the docks. The other guy was at least six feet tall and built like a shot-putter. He had to assume that Jonny hadn't found the time to enlist any additional help, but regardless, he was careful to watch his lines of sight as he exited the car and dragged Ae-Cha out of the passenger seat.

His gun was aimed at her head.

Koschey felt a familiar rush, the rush that came with the culmination of a difficult assignment. The rush of victory.

In a matter of minutes he'd have the van and what it contained – technology that had so far eluded the CIA, the US military, and the entire apparatus of the Soviet state. And once he had it, there was no limit to what he could – and would – do with it.

'The Deathless' would leave his indelible mark on an unsuspecting, and helpless, world.

* * *

Jonny sensed Bon's hand inching toward the Beretta 9mm tucked into the back of his belt and placed a restraining hand on his arm before the big man could draw the weapon.

He spoke so only Bon could hear him. 'Wait till Ae-Cha's with us. And don't trust anything he says. I've been here before.'

'He's alone,' Bon whispered. 'We can take him.'

Jonny raised his hands palms out and flicked his head for Bon to do the same. After the sound of air sucked between teeth, Bon complied.

Jonny took a couple of steps toward the Russian. 'How do we do this?'

'Simple. I want the van,' Koschey yelled across the empty lot. 'So we just swap cars. And don't even think of hitting that switch.'

Jonny stiffened. As he expected, the bastard knew what the van could do

Poor Mr. Soko. He wondered if the crazy genius was still alive.

Jonny took another step forward. 'What about Ae-Cha?'

Kaluta killed the cruiser's lights and coasted in silence right up to the edge of a low wall that ran alongside the approach to the lot.

He and Talaoc got out and crept alongside the wall, keeping low, their sidearms drawn, their comms turned down.

They paused at the edge of the wall and surveyed the scene beyond the trees.

'Reilly,' Talaoc murmured into his mike. 'They're in the lot by the ice rink. The van's here, and an SUV too. How far out are you?'

Aparo spun the wheel and rocketed us into the park. I couldn't say for sure, but I'd swear we were on two wheels.

'We're in the park. What do you see?'

Talaoc said, 'Two guys by the van, Asians. One of them's big. A guy and a girl by the SUV.'

'She's the hostage,' I told him. 'Just stay where—'

'Both of you walk toward me,' Koschey ordered them. 'I'll let her go when we meet. But first the big guy loses the gun.'

Jonny turned to Bon.

Bon didn't move. Didn't take out his gun and toss it aside, as ordered.

The Russian didn't make a big deal out of it.

He just casually lowered his gun to the ground and pulled the trigger, drilling a hole into Ae-Cha's foot.

'Fuck, he shot her,' Talaoc's voice burst through the speaker. 'The guy by the SUV just shot the girl in the foot.'

I turned to Aparo. 'Floor it.'

47

Even through the tape covering Ae-Cha's mouth, the scream was loud enough to rip through the park. Her knees buckled, but the Russian had a firm grip on her arm and kept her upright.

'I don't ask twice!' he yelled out.

Jonny felt a flood of acid rush up his throat.

He knew the Russian would kill them all no matter what went down. He also knew the only way for any of them to leave the park alive was for them to take the initiative. He guessed Bon would react to the Russian's provocation – especially in his coke-fueled state – which gave him a split second to act himself.

Bon managed to draw his weapon, but Jonny had already pulled his own gun and fired a shot at the Russian. Both were too late. Bon's head flapped back and he collapsed to the ground, a bullet hole in the center of his forehead. And Jonny's shot had missed its mark.

The Russian let go of Ae-Cha and loosed two quick shots as Jonny ran for cover. The first shot sheared a slice off the side of Jonny's head, ear included. The second hit him in the back. Jonny staggered for a moment, trying to stay on his feet, willing his body to turn around and his arm to raise the gun so he could shoot back, but his body refused to comply. He fell forward and smashed his jaw against the concrete as he landed.

For a moment it felt like the deepest winter. He saw Ae-Cha lying on the ground, the Russian walking toward her for the kill shot. Then there was nothing but darkness.

*　*　*

We hurtled through the trees, beelining at the cruiser and, beyond, the empty lot. An instant later, the lurking silhouettes of the van and the SUV took shape.

'Go, go, go,' I spurred Aparo, whose shoe was almost going through the footwell.

We were almost level with the cruiser when I saw muzzle flashes lighting up the night ahead, then I saw one of the figures drop and another start running.

'Keep going,' I blurted as we rocketed past the cruiser before bouncing onto the lot, heading straight at the two vehicles and a lone figure walking toward a lump on the ground a few yards in front of him.

'He's gonna kill her. Take him out!' I yelled as I drew my gun and chambered a round. Not that I needed to say it. Aparo had the same idea and had aimed the car right at our target without taking his foot off the gas.

As we closed in on him, Ivan spun and started firing at us.

We both slid down in our seats as bullets punched through the front windshield, Aparo barely poking his head over the steering wheel, me keeping my head down while I stuck my gun out the window looking for a shot. I saw him bolting away a second before we plowed into him and watched him slam onto the hood of the car, crunch into the windshield before bouncing over the roof and hitting the ground behind us just as Aparo stepped on the brakes and slewed the car to a stop next to the Russian's SUV.

I shot a quick glance at Aparo. 'You OK?'

'Fuck yeah,' he said, already shoving his door open and drawing his gun.

We both scrambled out of the car with our weapons leveled at the shooter.

The bastard wasn't out of it. He was moving, righting himself, pushing himself to his feet. He didn't look like he had anything broken and was no more shaken than a gymnast who'd just hit the mat after a couple of flips on a pommel horse.

'Christ,' Aparo blurted, 'this guy really is the fucking Terminator.'

I rushed right up to him and kicked his feet out from under him, causing him to spin on himself and fall flat on the asphalt. 'Don't move,' I ordered him. 'Hands where I can see them.'

I put a knee on his back and patted him down. I pulled a knife and sheath from his belt and a Glock 26 from an ankle holster, both of which I threw behind me.

'You're ours now, comrade,' I told him as I pushed my gun into the back of his neck.

He turned his head to face me and gave me the thinnest, coldest smile I've ever seen, but he said nothing.

'I'll check the girl,' Aparo said.

He headed over to her, and as I was moving to cuff Ivan, I heard Aparo say, 'We've got company.'

I looked up. He was right.

Another dark SUV was approaching through the trees, coming straight for us.

48

I pulled Ivan to his feet as the dark Mercedes SUV drove onto the lot and came to a stop behind our two vehicles.

Four men climbed out.

One of them was Mirminsky. The other three consisted of a tall blond guy with a dark scar across his cheek and two crew-cut soldiers. All three were armed with machine pistols.

The muscle covered us while Mirminsky stood front and center. There was about twenty yards between them and us.

'What do you think you're doing?' I asked him, my Browning leveled at his head.

Aparo had his gun drawn too.

'Relieving you of a headache,' he said, glaring at Ivan. 'Now, put your guns down, both of you. There's no need for this. Besides, there are too many of us for you to handle.'

'He's not a headache. He's what I get paid to do. So how about you put the toys away, get back in your pimpmobile, and get the hell out of here so we can get the girl looked after,' I said as I gestured at Ae-Cha, who was still where she'd fallen. 'And if you're lucky and I'm feeling generous, maybe we can all forget this ever happened. Either way, I can tell you one thing: this asshole's not walking away from this.'

The Sledgehammer smiled and shook his head. 'You think I'm here to help him go free?'

I'd missed the nuance of his body language before then, but I wasn't missing it now. Mirminsky was out for blood.

'He's ours, Yuri.'

'What does that mean?' he asked. 'You know what it means?' he continued, without giving me a chance to answer. 'It means he'll sit in some comfortable room while a bunch of guys in suits ask him a lot of questions, and given what he knows and who he is, he'll end up making a deal. He'll either get traded back to Moscow, where he'll live like a king, or he'll get a nice condo on Miami Beach and a big fat bank account in the Cayman Islands for telling you and your friends at Langley all kinds of fascinating things that will make you think you have an advantage in the pointless games you all play.'

'He's not going to walk,' I insisted.

'Oh, please. You're smarter than that, Reilly. You know how these things play out.'

I had to admit, he wasn't spouting nonsense. Deep down, something within me squirmed with revulsion at the thought that what he described might actually happen. The idea was so repugnant to me, especially now, in the middle of night, in this deserted lot, knowing everything the bastard had done. But I didn't fully trust Mirminsky, and either way, there wasn't much I could do about it, short of putting a bullet through the psycho's head myself.

'Doesn't change the fact that he's coming with us,' I said flatly.

Mirminsky stared at me for a moment, then his expression soured, like he was really disappointed. He turned to the blond guy with the scar and tilted his head while murmuring something inaudible. Then, calmly, the blond swung his gun away from me and fired a short burst into the front tire of Aparo's car, shredding it to ribbons. Then he pivoted around to face Ivan's SUV and did the same.

The Sledgehammer meant business.

He gave me a bleak smile. 'You're not going anywhere.'

The soldiers continued to cover us while the blond walked out toward the van, no doubt to cripple it, too.

I swung my gun up so it was squarely aimed at Mirminsky's head.

'We'll take your car then,' I said. 'Move aside.'

The blond stopped and turned as Mirminsky raised his hands. 'Or what? You're going to shoot me, an unarmed civilian? You're going to shoot us all? Come on. Stop being stupid. Give him to me and walk away. Let me do to him what you know you can't do.'

We were cornered. With seriously limited options.

Then Ivan finally spoke up.

He hissed something in Russian at Mirminsky, and though I couldn't understand any of it, it sounded nasty and ominous. Mirminsky spat something back at him, uncowed.

The thought that maybe I should just let the Sledgehammer have Ivan and walk away crossed my mind. But I couldn't do it.

'Yuri, think about what you're doing. We'll make your life hell.'

Mirminsky smiled. 'Well, this last week hasn't exactly been one big party for me, has it? And I have some very expensive lawyers who are really worth every penny.' His smile morphed into a dead-serious glare. 'OK, enough of this. What's it going to be?'

Crunch time.

I studied their relative positions, then glanced over at Ivan. He was standing stock still, his face expressionless.

Aparo looked over at me. We knew each other well enough to know what the other thought. We should out-bluff them, wait for backup, and take them all in. We had two cops huddled close by, probably unsure about what was going on and debating what move to make and when to make it. Backup had to be very close by now. But until they got here and gave us an undeniable advantage, I wasn't keen on triggering a shoot-out. I didn't want to lose more lives over that scumbag.

Mirminsky read me and nodded at the blond, who sauntered over to where I was holding Ivan. He stared down at Ivan haughtily. Then just as he reached us, three shots came out of nowhere and tore through the night.

I don't know where two of them ended up, but the blond was hit from behind and folded to the ground, pulling Ivan down with him.

All eyes turned to the source of the shots, which was an indistinct shape a hundred yards away, up on its knees, handgun in a two-handed grip.

Jonny.

Teetering at the very edge of life.

The next minute was over in seconds.

One of Mirminsky's soldiers fired two bursts at the young Korean, cutting him down – and the patrol car chose that exact moment to charge onto the lot.

Aparo and I both hit the ground, Aparo taking down the closest of Mirminsky's goons as he rolled.

The cops exited the squad car, guns out, yelling at the other shooter to lie on the ground. He ignored them and unleashed furious bursts in their direction, hitting one of them in the shoulder. The cops dived for cover behind their vehicle as they fired back.

I looked over to where Ivan had been just a couple of seconds earlier, but he'd vanished.

I fired several shots at the second goon as he ducked for cover behind the Mercedes. None of them found their mark. Within seconds he popped out from behind the big SUV and unloaded most of a clip, first at me, then at the cruiser, peppering its grille with multiple hits and punching out its headlights.

Still pinned behind Aparo's car, I heard the van's engine churn to life. I glanced out to see the vehicle lurching forward.

Ivan. Had to be.

Mirminsky turned and fired several rounds into the van, but none hit the driver – and with the surviving goon still pinning us down under carefully timed bursts of fire, I could only watch as the van charged forward, headed straight for Mirminsky.

It hit him full force and swallowed him up under its front wheels like a vacuum cleaner. After about ten yards, the body broke loose and the van's rear wheels bumped over it with a sickening squelch.

I aimed at the rear tires and emptied my clip to no avail as the van careened out of the lot and disappeared between the trees.

I couldn't let him escape like that, but we were still taking heat from the fourth shooter.

'Go after the van, we'll cover you,' I shouted to the cops.

And with a big 'Go!' I rose from behind my cover and unloaded a clip at the SUV, with Aparo doing the same – only for us to be gutted by the sound of a starter motor in severe distress.

The cruiser's engine had taken one hit too many.

'Call backup,' I hollered, roiling with frustration. 'Get them to seal off the park.'

Then I turned toward the shooter who was still huddled behind the Mercedes. I was desperate to get my hands on the SUV. As far as I could tell, it still looked operational, and it was the only way I could go after the van.

'Game's over!' I yelled out to him. 'It's all over. You understand me? Throw down your weapon and come out with your hands up.'

It took him a tense minute to do so. A minute that felt like forever.

Because by the time he finally chucked his weapon aside and came out with his arms up, it was pointless to go after the van.

We'd lost him.

Again.

And this time, we'd let him take exactly what he came for.

49

Koschey checked outside the warehouse, made sure all was quiet, and locked the door.

He wandered across the large space, headed for the small office, deep in thought.

He knew he'd almost lost it all during his excursion to recover the van, but the thought didn't bother him. It was a risk he always carried. Especially on assignments like this one, where uncertainties couldn't be avoided and he had to make quick decisions without the benefit of advance planning. But that was part of what had made his legend: the fact that he could improvise better than most, and that somehow, he always came out ahead. This night had been a major test of that skill, a test he'd come through again with no more than a bruise or two. He'd learn from it, add it to the large repertoire of experience he'd inevitably draw from at some point in the future. More important, he now had everything he needed: Sokolov – Shislenko – and the van.

He checked on his captive. Sokolov was still firmly cuffed in place and asleep, the latter courtesy of the SP-117. Koschey knew the scientist wouldn't be coming out of it soon, although it was a process he could accelerate with some smelling salts. But he didn't need to do it just yet. While he didn't have too much time to waste, not with the kind of resources that must have been allocated to tracking him down, he had to get himself a new ride before waking up Sokolov.

He didn't have his SUV anymore, and the van was certainly too hot to use again.

He also needed to think. He already had a plan, one he'd started formulating as soon as he understood what he was dealing with, one that became much more immediate and irresistible after hearing Sokolov's revelations.

He needed to refine it, put it through the wringer, make sure it stacked up.

The event was soon – perhaps too soon. It had stood out from the list of major American events that the Center always kept track of. High-target-value events. But even if it was too soon – only a day away – it was the perfect venue for what he was planning. It was too good an opportunity to pass up. Besides, he couldn't hang around much longer. He was on enemy territory, and he needed to act quickly, before the net tightened in around him.

He needed to contact the key players – the backers, and the patsies – all of whom he knew, all of whom he also knew had the appetite and the means for what he envisaged. Then he'd put the plan in motion and he'd rock the world in a way that would never be forgotten, before disappearing to a comfortable outpost while waiting for the next opportunity to strike, the next occasion for him to flex his newfound muscle and lift himself even further up the podium of history.

The timing couldn't have been better. Along with everyone back in the corridors of power in Moscow, he'd also been watching the events shaking the Arab world. In country after country, people were rising against their oppressors. Dictators were being toppled, their ill-gotten gains and gilded palaces confiscated before they and their cronies were dragged into court or strung up from lampposts. A new mind-set was gripping the oppressed corners of the planet, a desperate and angry yearning for freedom and retribution, and an accompanying unease was rippling through the Kremlin. The protesters in Moscow were getting louder and more ballsy, and there was a deep-set concern that the 'Arab Spring' could spread to the motherland. If that happened, it would pull the rug out from under those in power. It would also deprive Koschey of any chance he might have at carving out the slice of notoriety and wealth he now felt he deserved, the one he felt he was owed for all his years of service.

Well, he thought, maybe his time had come. Maybe he'd start carving it out right here, in America, and not in some oil field or gas field in Siberia.

The thought of striking at America only made the prospect sweeter. For despite it all, Koschey was still, deep down, a patriot. A proud, staunch patriot. And the Americans, he felt, were too smug about their success.

Yes, the collapse of his motherland's old political ideology was inevitable. Yes, his superiors had proven to be greedier and more predatory than the worst of Wall Street's corporate raiders. But the Americans needed to be humbled. They were the only superpower left, and the way they wielded their power, with such arrogance and impunity, really grated on Koschey. They needed to be brought down, and Koschey relished the potential infamy that would be bestowed on the one who would do it.

With that prospect in mind, he took a corner of the office and lay down on the concrete floor.

After running through his plan one more time in his head, he finally allowed himself to drift into sleep.

Still crouched in the back of the van, Shin barely dared to breathe.

He was frozen in place, huddled against the partition, in the corner behind the passenger seats, a bundle of shivering sweat, listening intently while trying to make himself as small as possible.

He wasn't sure what had happened out at Prospect Park. He was still in the back when they'd stopped, and out of sheer terror, he'd decided to stay there. Through the small window in the cabin door, he'd glimpsed Ae-Cha and the Russian standing across the lot from them, seen him shoot her in the foot, witnessed Bon going down – then he'd hit the cabin floor and stayed there for cover. Before he knew it, there had been a frenzied firefight, then the van was moving again – not just moving, but charging, plowing into something and bouncing over it, taking a series of sharp turns that had him hanging on to the metal box for dear life before the van finally settled into a reasonable pace.

He'd risked a very angled peek through the window, barely creeping out of his hiding place, just to see who was driving. And he'd almost had a heart attack when he'd glimpsed the Russian who'd shot Ae-Cha and Bon and probably Jonny, too, in the driver's seat.

He'd slunk back into his corner and curled up there, trembling and sweating like he had typhoid, his mind locked in silent panic. He'd debated flinging the back doors open and jumping out while the van was in motion, but he couldn't bring himself to do it. He'd remained in that pathetic state until, some time later, the van had slowed down and pulled in somewhere echoey before its engine was killed.

Shin had never been as terrified as he was in the moments that followed, waiting helplessly in the back of the van, staring at the rear doors, expecting them to swing open at any moment, expecting to see the Russian's surprised eyes lock onto his before the man dragged him out, shot him, and dumped his lifeless body in some ditch.

His heartbeat had pounded out the seconds against his ear drums, but the doors didn't open and the Russian never came.

Instead, he could barely make out some footsteps walking away, then back, then past the van in the other direction. Then there was silence.

And more silence.

Shin waited, as immobile as a wax figure. And waited. Then, after about an hour, maybe more, after not hearing a single sound for all that time, he decided he'd risk it.

Using extreme care, he opened the cabin door and peeked out. The van was parked inside some kind of garage. Faint light was filtering from somewhere, allowing him to make out some walls beyond the windshield, but none of the lights inside the space were on.

He climbed onto the passenger bench, then slowly, very slowly, he pulled the door handle until it clicked and cracked the door open. He waited. Didn't hear anything. He pushed the door open farther and looked out.

An empty space, like a warehouse. Bare and basic.

He climbed down and gently set his feet on the ground, then pushed the door back against its locking mechanism without clicking it shut.

He hugged the wall and tiptoed toward the front of the large space, where moonlight was seeping in through some high clerestory windows that ran along the top of the wall.

There was a single door next to the large roller door of the warehouse. He tried it. The handle wouldn't budge.

It was locked.

He cursed inwardly, then retreated and tried the first space he found to his left. It was a small room, also empty.

His spirits soared when he spotted a small top-hung window up in one of its corners, its sill around eight feet above ground level.

Moments later, he was scuttling away from the warehouse, keeping low, hugging the walls, hoping against hope that this wasn't one of those tortuous bad jokes that life often liked to play, one where he'd soon find himself right back where he started, in the clutches of the murderous Russian and moments from a painful and very final death.

50

I was running on empty.

This thing had had us in its grip since we'd first stepped inside Sokolov's apartment Monday morning, and here I was back at Federal Plaza, three days later, bright and early, having managed all of a blissful two hours of sleep and a decadent ten-minute shower. Which is something I wouldn't normally complain about, but after the previous night's shootout at the docks, the restaurant, *and* Prospect Park, my body was threatening an insurrection.

The good news was that Ae-Cha was going to be OK. The foot would take a while to heal; the PT would take far longer to get all those tendons and bones to move seamlessly and do what they were meant to do, but at least it was time she still had.

The bad news was everything else.

The flak was coming in from all corners: the governor's office, the mayor's office, the chief of police, all of it fog-horned to us through my own esteemed boss. We spent a good part of the morning in his office: Aparo, me, the ADIC himself obviously, Kanigher, a couple of NYPD liaisons, and a couple of Bureau lawyers. After the requisite dressing-down for the massive body count and the fact that Ivan was still on the loose, Gallo wanted a detailed run-through of everything that had happened since our last little sit-down – which was only yesterday morning, after the shoot-out at the motel the night before. Sitting there and watching my boss frown intensely and purse his lips ever-so-thoughtfully as he questioned and second-guessed every move we made was truly painful, especially given the state I was in, but I'd decided to get through it as passively as I could in order to move on and get back to trying to figure out what was going on.

Because the one question I kept coming back to was this: what the hell happened at the Russian restaurant in Brighton Beach?

That was something no one had really explained.

It was still too fresh, but questions were being asked, particularly by the news media, who were all over the story. We had nine dead there. More than forty in the hospital, several of them critical. Men, women, young, old. The press and our own people were describing the massive brawl as a freak incident. Most of those who'd taken part were Russian. Theories were bouncing around that it was a gang thing. But it didn't make sense to me. I'd never heard of anything like it, not involving women, not un-related to a heated sporting event like a boxing match or a political event like a protest march. There was no rhyme or reason for such a savage out-burst. It just seemed insane.

The early information we had from the cops on the scene was that the victims themselves couldn't really say what had happened. They didn't know why they had done what they'd done, which was a useful defense, of course, though in this case, it felt like it was too widely consistent to be a cynical ploy from the guilty. A couple of them, however, had mentioned a rage, an aggression that had suddenly swelled up inside them, one they couldn't explain. They said it was like they were in a trance, or drugged. And I couldn't get that out of my mind.

The van had been there too, of course.

The van that Sokolov had hidden and lied about, the one Ivan had been so desperate to get his hands on.

By eleven, Aparo and I were back in his Charger, heading out to an industrial park near Webster Avenue in the Bronx. It was where the DMV records for Sokolov's van had it registered. Maybe we'd know more when we got there.

'What is it with this van?' I asked as I stared at the picture of it that I was holding, a printout from the traffic cam. 'What's Sokolov got in it?'

'Maybe he's like Goldfinger and it's made of gold,' Aparo said as we sped up the FDR. 'Or it's loaded with drugs. Or maybe,' he added, all excited, his index finger up in the air to press his point, 'maybe he's come up with some radical new kind of engine that runs on a super-cheap alter-native fuel and the Mystery Machine's his secret prototype.' He paused, then, undeterred by my dismissive look, he continued. 'Seriously. The guy's a bit of a nutty professor, isn't he? Maybe he's cooked something like that up. The Russians want to keep it under wraps so they can safe-guard their oil exports. We want it. Everyone's after it.'

He looked at me again like maybe he actually had something there.

I wasn't really listening to him anymore, as a weird and nutty idea of my own had just sprouted in my mind.

I hadn't just been staring at a photo of the van. My attention had been drawn to the refrigeration unit on its roof.

It got me thinking about why the unit was there. What one used refrig-eration for.

Meat. Ice cream.

Bacteria.

Viruses.

My mind went all kinds of places with it. And suddenly it didn't seem as weird or as nutty anymore. And it started to explain a lot about what had been happening.

Aparo spotted it on my face. 'You've got that look,' he told me.

I was too concentrated to retort.

'Come on, Sherlock,' he prodded. 'For the cheap seats.'

'This thing,' I told him, still pensive, tapping my finger against the unit on the van. 'What if it's not for refrigeration. What if it's the opposite.'

'A heater?'

'No. A diffuser. Something to blow air out rather than suck air in and cool it. And what if the air it was blowing out wasn't just clean air. What if it had something else in it?'

Aparo wasn't getting it, and his face clouded up. 'Like … ?'

'What if this is some kind of nerve agent?'

Larisa Tchoumitcheva took a deep breath and straightened her back, then stepped inside Oleg Vrabinek's office and closed the door behind her.

'We need to talk,' she told him.

He motioned for her to sit. She took a seat facing him.

'I'm getting a lot of pressure from the FBI and the mayor's office over everything that's been going on since Yakovlev's death,' she told him.

Vrabinek studied her in silence, but said nothing.

'What is going on, Oleg? You've kept me in the dark about this since Monday, but it's getting way out of hand and I don't know what I'm supposed to say anymore. All these shooting victims ... What's happening? Do we have him yet?'

Vrabinek's face clouded, then after a moment, he said, 'I think so.'

'You "think" so? According to the FBI, we do as of around ten p.m. last night.'

He frowned, the worry creasing his forehead. 'I think we do,' he said gruffly. 'But I can't say for sure for the simple reason that I haven't heard from our man in over twenty-four hours.'

'How come?'

'He was supposed to let me know when he had Sokolov so that I could arrange their extraction.' Vrabinek was clearly unhappy about the implication that the agent hadn't done so. 'I don't know where he is.' He thought about it for a moment, then asked, 'Could the Americans be playing us? Do you think they have them?'

Larisa considered it briefly, then shook her head. 'I can't see why they would. What do they have to gain from it? Besides, I think Reilly was genuinely frustrated and angry about their failure so far.' She paused, then added, 'Can't you reach him?'

'I've tried. He's not picking up.' Vrabinek pushed himself to his feet and walked over to the platter of bottles that sat on a low cabinet by the large window overlooking the consulate's rear garden. 'The thing about Koschey is, he's his own boss. He does things his way and answers to no one but the general himself. I can't order him to do anything.'

'So what do I do?'

He opened the small fridge that was built into the bar unit, took out an ice-cold bottle of vodka, and poured himself a tumbler. He knocked it back, then grimaced from the burning feeling it shot down his throat. 'Keep doing what you've been doing,' he told her. 'Mirminsky's dead. If Koschey does have Sokolov, then I don't think you'll be having much more trouble with this. It's over.'

Larisa nodded and walked out. And as she stepped into the hallway and headed back to her office, a worrying thought clawed at her gut.

Koschey's reputation was that he was a loner who played by his own rules. Which meant that he might be making his own travel arrangements. If he did, she would have failed at her task.

With, as her handler had warned her, disastrous consequences.

51

'A nerve agent?' Aparo asked. 'You serious?'

My thoughts were cartwheeling ahead with it. 'Think about it. Sokolov, or whatever his real name is – he's a scientist. A Russian scientist. We know he's very bright. Maybe he came up with something that can turn people aggressive. Something airborne that can set off their most primal instincts. Something he didn't want anyone to know about.'

'A gas that turns people aggressive?' Aparo repeated, looking distinctly unconvinced. 'You have the gall to say that with a straight face after blowing off my theory about alternative fuel?'

'I don't know if it's a gas or a spray or what, but maybe it's some kind of drug,' I countered. 'One that can go airborne. Like inhaling secondhand smoke. The way pot has an effect on the brain. Maybe this is something like that. The opposite of Prozac. Instead of calming you down, it makes you real angry. Angry and paranoid. So you lash out at the merest provocation. Everything feels like a threat.'

I felt a rush of energy. The more I thought about it, the less outlandish it seemed. A nerve gas would go a long way to explaining why the crowd at Lolita went from party animals to bloodthirsty savages and back within a matter of minutes.

'We've got to run tox tests on the Lolita crowd,' I said.

Aparo turned serious. 'Hang on a sec, that doesn't stack up. What about the docks?'

'What about them?'

'Sokolov went out of his way to get the van and take it to the docks when he and Jonny went to get Daphne back,' Aparo said. 'Why take the van all the way there but not hand it over in exchange for her? That had to be the deal, right?'

'Maybe that was the plan,' I agreed. 'Maybe Ivan wanted the van all along, but maybe something went wrong and he got Sokolov instead.'

Something about that felt wrong, but I still thought the diffuser/nerve-agent idea merited a closer look.

'So how come Jonny and his buddy weren't affected by it out at Lolita?' Aparo added. 'Gas masks?'

'Maybe,' I said. I mulled it over some more, then asked, 'What do you think?'

'Not to take anything away from my brilliant alternative-fuel theory – but, could be. And if that's the case – shit, we've got to get it back.'

'We've got to get him back too. He designed it.'

Aparo nodded as he sped up. 'Let's see what we find at the garage.'

Twenty minutes later, we turned into the rundown industrial park and pulled up by the small management office just inside its rusted gates. No one was there. We got back in the car and drove in until we found the unit that was the registered address for Sokolov's van. I wasn't sure what I expected, but it wasn't the small lock-up garage it turned out to be.

We had two padlocks to get past, and they proved tricky, but not insurmountable, with Aparo besting me by half a minute or so. We pushed up the roller door about an inch, and while Aparo held it open, I crouched down and had a look to make sure it wasn't booby-trapped. I didn't really expect it to be, and I didn't see anything suggesting it was.

We pulled it open.

The garage was empty. It was of a decent size, big enough to store the van, with about four feet to spare all around. I hit the lights. It was clean and tidy. No big oil stains on the concrete floor, no odds and ends left to rot there for years. There wasn't much in it, aside from one shelf hanging at shoulder level all the way down the left-hand wall. It had a couple of cardboard boxes stored on it.

We took them down and opened them up.

They had all kinds of electronic parts in them. Wires, cables, switches, rolls of flat copper-colored metal in different gauges, small plastic boxes filled with miniature circuits and connectors, and a collection of square metal tubes of different lengths and widths – some hollow and some filled with what looked like conducting material. There was also what looked like an old pair of jeweler's magnifying glasses.

They weren't car parts, that much I knew. Beyond that, I had no idea what they were or what they could be used for, but I sure as hell wanted to find out. I took several photos of them with my phone and e-mailed them to our in-house computer analysis and response team. It wasn't necessarily the specialty of the guys at CART, but I knew that their geekiness extended beyond digital data, and if they didn't know what these things were, I was sure they knew who to ask.

I had a sinking feeling about what they would tell us.

I was e-mailing the last of them when I got a call from an unidentified number. I snatched my phone off the desk, knowing it had to be the pancake-loving hacker I had tasked with my private dirty deed.

'Gimme a sec,' I told Aparo as I stepped away to take the call.

'*Konnichiwa,*' Kurt's voice echoed. 'You sitting down, boss? I have news.' He paused for effect, then proudly announced, 'Target acquired.'

'I'm listening,' I said evenly, not wanting to encourage him too much.

He sounded excited. 'So I got into the CCTV cam of the cashpoint, and I found our guy pulling out last week's cash. Then he kind of glances around like he's making sure no one's watching before he walks off.'

'Maybe he's just making sure no one's waiting to mug him.'

'Maybe. But no. It gets better. I found a personal credit card of his with no paper trail. Statements and everything else only comes through to him by e-mail. And not his main Gmail account. I looked through the last three months' worth of statements and you could say the card use doesn't really fit that of a married guy with two kids. There are multiple charges to trivial-sounding businesses, but when you dig into who they are, they're billing names for a lingerie shop called Sylene, a chocolate place called Cocova, and a flower shop called Gilding the Lily. They're all down in the DC area. Plus he had a single charge of over three hundred dollars to something called L'Escapade. It's an upmarket sex shop on U Street. Four and a half stars across the board.'

'So maybe he loves his wife. Maybe they're meeting away from the house to share some private time. Or trying to spice things up with some role-playing.'

He snorted. 'You talking from experience?'

I dropped my tone. 'Careful, Kurt. Let's remember the parameters of our relationship.'

He went silent, and I could sense all kinds of pressure valves popping inside his fragile physique.

'I'm kidding,' I told him. 'Go on.'

'Well, he has another credit card, the one he shares with his wife. In the last month he's charged all kinds of stuff on it. Car repairs, a plumbing contractor, his son's braces, horse-riding lessons for his daughter. Personally I prefer my mount mammoth-shaped and a hundred percent digital. Less chance of real-world injury.'

'Focus, Kurt.'

'Yeah, sorry. My point is, he would have used that card if it was on the up and up. But he's not. He's using it cause it's not with the wife. And here's the good news. The card was used to guarantee a hotel booking for tonight.'

My skin bristled. 'Cashpoint Thursday.'

'Exactly. And his disciplinary warnings were for arriving late to work on three Fridays in the last couple of months. You know anyone who arrives late at work so he can hang out longer with his wife?'

I wasn't about to argue with someone whose profound insights into married life were gleaned while living with his mother. 'So he books the hotel with the card, but pays the bill in cash.'

'And the authorization for the guarantee to hold the room is wiped clean. It never shows up on a statement. And you want the clincher?'

'Boggle me.'

'The hotel's right next to the ATM he uses.'

Kurt had come through for me, massively – pun wholeheartedly intended.

I said, 'He might be seeing her tonight.'

'I'll bet he is. Remember, that's when his wife has her weekly yoga class. Seven till nine. Meanwhile her husband's putting a hundred dollars'-worth of edible lubricant to good use.' He chuckled. 'And there I was, thinking field agents had all the fun.'

This sounded more than promising. 'OK. I need the hotel's details and a photo of Kirby.'

'Done. And I'll get into his alibi. Give you even more leverage.'

'Great.'

'He's lucky he managed to snag a room tonight. The whole town's booked solid.'

Which was curious. 'Why?'

'The White House Correspondents' Dinner. It's tomorrow night. It's like the Oscars these days. Huge.'

I wondered if it would make my getting a flight down there more difficult. 'OK. What time does he usually arrive?'

'I went through the hotel's card-issuing records. I found Kirby checking in last week and three weeks ago. Always between seven forty-five and eight.'

I glanced at my watch. It was almost noon. Tricky – but doable. Very doable.

I told Kurt, 'Nice work, man. Seriously. You'd make a good cop.'

He chuckled. 'With this body? I think not. Now, I've got a five-way *Halo* game starting in ten, so I'll bid you *sayonara*.'

The line went dead, leaving me to wonder about how I was going to make it down to DC and back undetected given everything else that was going on, and questioning whether cheating on one's wife would give me enough moral grounds for blackmail.

Then I remembered what they'd done to Alex, and any misgivings I was feeling were smothered into submission.

'Everything OK?' Aparo asked, giving me a curious look.

'Just peachy,' I told him.

I was going to need his help with this, but I wasn't going to mention it just yet. Everything was moving so fast that my plans could change at any moment.

I just hoped they wouldn't change enough that I wouldn't be able to meet our wandering lothario in a few hours.

52

Koschey didn't need the smelling salts. By late morning, he'd returned from his shopping-and-renting expedition to find Sokolov awake.

The scientist looked rough. Which was expected. On top of everything he'd been through, he hadn't eaten or had anything to drink for hours.

Koschey had what it took to remedy that. He'd bought supplies – food, drink – as well as everything else he thought they'd need.

He'd also rented a car. Being close to the airport, it wasn't too far to get to the big agencies there, where he found a large selection to choose from. Using a Greek passport and matching credit card – the upheavals in Greece had turned it into the European country of choice when it came to obtaining fake identities – he'd driven off with a black Chevy Suburban with tinted windows that had less than a thousand miles on the clock. He was pretty sure the SUV would do the trick. The fact that it was the vehicle of choice for government agencies was an added bonus that could always come in handy.

He peeled the tape off Sokolov's mouth and freed his hands from the radiator mount, then he cuffed them together again, only in front of Sokolov this time, so he could use them to eat and drink. He gestured at the sandwiches, bananas, and the big bottle of water he'd placed on the floor next to him.

'Eat. Drink. We have work to do.'

Sokolov eyed him hesitantly, then reached out and did as ordered.

'Daphne,' he asked after sipping some water. 'Is she all right? The truth?'

'She's fine. Probably in protective custody at the moment. I told you – I have no interest in her.'

Sokolov nodded, forlorn. 'If you're taking me back to Russia ... will I be able to contact her from there? Just to let her know ... why?'

Koschey nodded, thinking about it. 'Let's take things one step at a time. Cooperate. Do as you're told. And we'll see.'

He waited until Sokolov had finished half the big sandwich, then he got down to business.

'We need to move it out of the van,' he told Sokolov. 'I have an SUV with a big trunk area. I want you to put it in it. How long will it take?'

Sokolov frowned.

'And please, comrade,' Koschey added. 'Don't lie and make life any more difficult for yourself or for Daphne. The sooner we do this, the sooner we can all move on.'

Sokolov shook his head in defeat. 'I need to dismantle it.'

'I want it operational,' Koschey clarified. 'Not in crates.'

Which surprised Sokolov. His face crunched up with concern. 'You're going to use it?'

Koschey just looked at him, his face as expressionless as a slate of marble. 'Just do as you're told. For Daphne's sake.'

Sokolov held his gaze for a moment, then nodded in defeat. 'That'll take longer.' He paused, thinking about it, then added, 'I'll need tools. It has to be mounted into place.'

'I bought everything I thought you might need. Anything else you need I can also get. From what I can see, the only connection it has to the van itself is to get its power, correct?'

'Yes.'

'So you could take it out and put it anywhere, really. As long as it has a power source.'

Sokolov nodded. 'It's powered by four rechargeable fuel cells in the back. The engine charges them when it's running. They're very heavy.'

'Not a problem.'

He asked Sokolov more questions. About the device's other settings. About range. About whether it could go through walls. Windows. Three-inch-thick bullet- and blastproof glass.

The answers he got were all pleasing.

'Finish your food,' he finally told Sokolov. 'Then let's get started.'

Then he left him and went out to make the first call that would set things in motion.

Sokolov's spirits sank even lower as he watched his captor walk away.

The bastard was going to use it. An insidious new weapon was about to be unleashed on an unsuspecting world. Pain and suffering to innocents would inevitably ensue. There would be all kinds of ramifications, all kinds of uses Sokolov hadn't even dreamed of yet, but that others would. They always did. There were many out there who were more than happy to let their imaginations take them to the darkest corners of the human psyche, who didn't need to be paid to dream up new ways to inflict pain.

Things would never be the same from here on, and it would be because of him.

He considered not doing what his captor had asked, even if it meant the Russian would torture him to try and force him to do it. Which the Russian would. Sokolov didn't doubt that. And he doubted he'd be strong enough to endure it. In the end, he'd wind up doing it anyway.

He thought back to his grandfather's darkest hour. The man's misguided intellect had caused so much damage, and he wondered if he was now destined to cause more of it. Facing his own darkest moment, Sokolov contemplated killing himself, assuming he could find a way to do it. But he quickly dismissed it as the wrong way forward. The Russian had his device already. It was too late. The genie was out of the bottle.

More important, there was Daphne.

He had to keep fighting. He had to try to overcome it all.

For Daphne.

53

Misha's Journal

Petrograd

SEPTEMBER 1916

Things are spiraling out of control, and I fear the worst.

And yet, it was all going so well.

The mystic peasant from Siberia was well entrenched as the royal couple's irreplaceable healer, soothsayer, and stalwart. He was influencing virtually all of their major decisions. The empress was and remains his supreme protector and defender. Over the last few years, anyone who made threatening rumblings against him was swiftly removed from his position and neutralized.

That has all changed.

Madame Lokhtina is long gone. The poor woman was banished by her husband a few years ago after he found out about her scandalous dalliances with my master and stripped her of everything she owned. I hear this former beauty, once regarded as a beacon of St. Petersburg's high society, now roams the back roads of Russia like an escapee from a lunatic asylum, begging for alms, barefoot and still in her filthy white dress, with a strap around her forehead on which the word 'Hallelujah' is scribbled barely legibly.

There is no shortage of replacements for her. Rasputin is comfortably settled into his spacious new apartment on Gorokhovaya Street. And although he no longer needs to take his aristocratic beauties or his prostitutes to bathhouses or seedy hotels, he still cavorts openly with his coterie of female companions, causing his vilification to keep rising in intensity and in dangerousness.

He has gone from being the subject of hushed rumors to being paraded disparagingly across newspaper articles on a daily basis. The newspapers are obsessed by him. Only the sinking of the Titanic managed, briefly, to divert their attention from him. The press hounds are fascinated by stories of his incessant debauchery and revelry. There is even talk of rape, such as his having forced himself upon the heir's nurse at the royal palace.

The nobility and the bourgeoisie are in an uproar. Because of the blind faith and unshakable devotion the tsarina and her doting husband extend to Rasputin, the people have lost all respect for the royal couple. There are even rumors – ill-founded, I would hope – that he has bedded the tsarina herself.

Much to my frustration, Rasputin doesn't seem to care. While I toil away in secret at perfecting my device and exploring the extent of its powers, he spends his time seducing and partying with the gypsies. He parades his women without shame and flaunts his lecherous ways without apology while the tsar and tsarina reject any criticism of him and shut down any investigation that threatens to give credence to what they deem as nothing more than malicious lies or misinformed ramblings.

There is also a lot of contempt at Rasputin's meddling in high political affairs. He is openly interfering, going so far as to dictate appointments at the highest level of government and in the Holy Synod.

And then there is his stance against war.

It first flared up when the Austro-Hungarian monarchs, backed by their German protectors, decided to annex Bosnia and Herzegovina. The Russian bourgeoisie and the nobility were enraged and demanded war to defend their Slav brethren. The press was also calling for it. The military, eager for a chance to avenge their defeat in the Russo-Japanese war, wanted it. The tsar himself, educated in a military school and keen to endear himself to Russian society, was also on a war footing.

The tsarina, however, was against it. She hadn't forgotten the bloody revolution that followed the defeat against the Japanese. She is half-German – the kaiser, Wilhelm II, is her uncle – which made her position even more difficult.

Rasputin stepped in to help. He was passionately against war. As a man of God, it was natural for him to be in favor of peace, but as the empress's miracle worker, it became a mission at which he couldn't fail.

He spoke to the tsar repeatedly, warning him of defeats and revolution. The tsar listened – and backed off. War was averted.

I was delighted by this, of course. It was a noble, glorious achievement. Others were not as pleased. In the corridors of power and in the salons, all of St. Petersburg was incensed at how an uneducated and degenerate peasant had blocked a just war and brought down humiliation on their great nation. Powerful voices rose up against Rasputin – first the prime minister, Stolypin, then the Church's hierarchs, Feofan, Hermogen, and Iliodor.

Stolypin, infuriated by Rasputin's inexorable influence over the royal couple, unleashed a relentless persecution campaign against him. He spoke out against him in the Duma. He got the newspapers to run vicious stories about his scandalous behavior. He had him followed by agents of the Okhrana secret police, making our meetings more difficult to arrange. The surveillance men even gave Rasputin's women code names: Winter Woman, Dove, Owl, Bird, and so on. They were only too happy to leak their findings to the reporters who were on Rasputin's trail.

I was greatly worried by these developments, but Rasputin was unperturbed.

'Do not worry, Misha,' he assured me. 'He'll be out of our hair before long.'

'But he's the prime minister,' I replied.

'Yes,' Rasputin agreed, his tone flush with conviction. 'Which is why the tsar will listen when I warn him that this man has seized too much power.'

And so it happened, as he had said it would. The insecure tsar did listen, and his self-esteem was immediately threatened. When Stolypin went to see him, armed with a thick dossier on Rasputin and demanding he be exiled, the tsar rejected the findings and told Stolypin his agents were too simple-minded to understand what they had witnessed. Rasputin's true motives, he told his prime minister, were beyond their grasp. Then he threw the dossier into his fireplace.

Reports of Stolypin's being reassigned to the Caucasus didn't come to fruition. He was assassinated by a known leftist radical at the Kiev Opera House a month after his fiery meeting with the tsar. Rasputin was rumored to have had a hand in arranging the murder. A year earlier, I would have said that was a blatant lie. Today, I am no longer sure what to believe. I do know two things for certain: Rasputin was in Kiev on the day of the killing, and the tsar did put a stop to the investigation into his prime minister's murder.

Stolypin's death, and the rumors of Rasputin's involvement, made things worse. Attacks rained down on him from all corners, including one that would prove far more vicious.

It all came to a head on a moonless night, that of the sixteenth of December. Rasputin told me his friend, the monk Iliodor, whom he'd met when we first arrived in St. Petersburg, would be picking him up and taking him to an evening gathering at the Yaroslav Monastery with Bishop Hermogen and a handful of his friends.

It all went horribly wrong from the moment he set foot in the cloister.

Rasputin told me they were barely inside and taking off their coats when one of the assembled guests, the publicist Rodyonov, started mocking him openly.

'Look at the starets's humble rags,' he scoffed to the others. 'What's that fur coat worth? Two, two and a half thousand rubles? And that hat. It must be worth at least four hundred.'

'A true testament to self-denial,' Hermogen answered before leading them into the monastery's reception room.

Rasputin, unsettled by their open taunts, took a seat. Hermogen launched into a demented tirade almost immediately.

'You are a godless scoundrel,' he lambasted Rasputin. 'You have offended countless women and cuckolded their husbands. You're even sleeping with the tsarina. Don't deny it. We know you are.'

The others joined in, jabbing him angrily in the chest and shouting, 'You are an agent of evil, peasant. You are an Antichrist.'

Rasputin was frozen in his chair, stunned and surprised by this unexpected outburst. Then the bishop grabbed Rasputin by his hair and started punching him savagely across his face. 'In God's name, I forbid you to touch any more women,' he barked at him. 'And I forbid you to see the tsar or the tsarina. Do you understand me, you scum? I forbid it.' His blows kept raining down on Rasputin, who was too shocked to try to defend himself. 'The rule of the tsars is sacred, and the Church will not sit back and allow you to destroy it. You will not set foot in the royal palace again, do you understand? Never again.'

Hermogen let go of the bloodied Rasputin and nodded to Rodyonov. The nobleman unsheathed his sabre. With its blade pressed against Rasputin's neck, they forced him to swear on a big bronze cross that he would never set foot in the palace again, bashing him on the head with the cross as he made his oath.

I could not believe my eyes when I saw him bruised and battered like that. I have never seen him as shaken – and as enraged. He was livid with anger. He refused to see anyone until his wounds had healed, but he did dictate a telegram that I sent to the royal palace.

The tsar and the tsarina were furious. Not only had the bishop threatened the life of their special friend; he had insulted the tsarina by accusing her of committing adultery.

Hermogen and Iliodor were exiled from St. Petersburg, but they refused to leave. The tsar balked at removing them forcibly, not wishing to turn them into heroes. And so their sniping continued. Pressure was mounting against Rasputin from all sides. We needed a miracle.

True to his wily nature, Rasputin devised one.

It happened in autumn, when the prince fell ill again.

The royal family were vacationing at their hunting reserve at Spala, in the Belovezh forests of Poland. The prince slipped in his bathroom and knocked his thigh. The injury caused him internal bleeding, which spread through his groin and developed into blood poisoning.

The secondary hemorrhages spread, and the young prince was gravely ill. The doctors gave up hope and told the tsarina to prepare for the worst. The royal couple were frantic and desperate. And this time, Rasputin was nowhere in sight. He was back at his home in Pokrovskoye, too far to attend to the tsarevich in the flesh.

I was in Spala, of course. With my device. Waiting.

We had planned everything to deal with such an eventuality. Rasputin had prepared me as well as he could, but there were many unknowns. I had felt a grave trepidation at what we were doing. We were placing the young heir in mortal danger.

'He will be fine,' Rasputin had assured me, his unendurable gaze anchoring his words in my consciousness. 'You will see to that.'

I was too perturbed to mention the fear I felt for my own safety. I would, after all, be stalking the royals on their own grounds.

Rasputin had previously visited the castle on one of the royals' hunting trips, and knew it well. With a primitive hand, he had sketched out a plan of its layout for me and pointed out the location of the nursery. It was on the first floor and had a large window, which would suit our purposes reasonably well.

I took the train to Spala, shadowing the royals. Once there, I acquainted myself with the clerk at the town's telegraph office before venturing into the forest at dawn one morning to take stock of what might await me if I needed to act. It would not be easy. My device was rather bulky and difficult to carry, especially through the dense, overgrown forest. Bison and boar roamed the land, and I was not much of an adventurer. At least, I wasn't until I met Rasputin. I think that has all changed.

Still, if anything did happen to the tsarevich when they were there, it was a golden opportunity. And when the empress sent Rasputin an urgent telegram, imploring him to save her son, I was ready to step in.

The next dawn, I ventured into the forest again. This time, I had my machine with me. I managed to reach the periphery of the castle undetected, and huddled under cover, behind some bushes. I set up my machine and directed it at the tsarevich's bedroom, and activated it when I saw the messenger riding in with the mail pouch.

Rasputin had sent back a telegram from Pokrovskoye. In it, he told the tsarina, 'God has heard your prayers. The little one will not die. Just tell your doctors to leave him alone.'

I crouched in the bushes for three days, shrouded by an unnerving quiet due to the protective wax pellets in my ears, I lived off the meager supplies I was able to carry with me, wary of the wildlife scurrying in the wilderness around me, hoping the guards wouldn't spot me, hoping even more that my machine would be just as effective as it had been before without having Rasputin's own healing powers to complement it.

At first, I could hear the young child's wails of pain and his screams of 'Mama, help me!'

But after the first few hours, the cries stopped.

Much to the astonishment of the doctors, the tsarevich soon recovered. And lived. Just as Rasputin had predicted.

He had cured the heir to the throne without even being there.

No one could ignore that miracle.

Rasputin was now truly untouchable.

Rasputin could now do anything he pleased and was impervious to criticism. He strutted around the city in his leather boots and coats with splendid brocade lining and expensive silk shirts embroidered by the tsarina, brazenly reveling in his adoring circle of aristocratic beauties and prostitutes while openly steering the tsar and the tsarina's affairs of state. Akilina, his secretary, was taking in piles of money from all the supplicants who rushed to his doorstep, asking him to exert his influence with the royals on their behalf. I now had the resources, and the peace of mind, to carry on with my work and perfect my device. I rented a new laboratory and was advancing in leaps and bounds. My mentor, Heinrich Wilhelm Dove, who had first discovered the magic I was exploring, would have been most proud.

The festive year celebrating the Romanov dynasty's three hundred years on the throne came and went peacefully. And then the calamities starting raining down on us again.

I had just discovered a frightening potential for spreading the effect of my device using a piezoelectric transducer and a dynamo. The potential was truly terrifying – and it was then that two separate catastrophic events occurred on consecutive days, two assassinations that would affect the lives of countless millions and redraw the map of the continent.

In Sarajevo, on a Sunday in June of 1914, a young Serb murdered Archduke Franz Ferdinand, the heir to the Austro-Hungarian throne. A monstrous war now seemed inevitable. As before, the tsar, the military, the old aristocracy, and the young bourgeoisie were all aching for battle. And as before, the tsarina didn't want it. Rasputin intervened once again and sent the tsar several urgent missives, only this time, the dire prophesies of God's emissary were rebuffed by the tsar. Even worse, Tsar Nicholas, now firmly on a war path, refused to see Rasputin and instructed him to go back to his village, 'for the sake of social calm,' as he put it.

And it was there, on the very next day, in Pokrovskoye, that the mad woman knifed him.

I wasn't with him, of course. I had to remain in St. Petersburg, in case the tsarevich fell ill again and needed our help.

'I was walking back from church when this disfigured beggar approached me, asking for help,' he told me. 'I reached into my pocket to give her a coin, and the devil woman just pulled out a dagger through a slit in her shirt and stabbed me in the stomach while shouting, "Die, Antichrist, die!" I pushed her away and ran, my mind not registering what she had done to me. She followed me, still brandishing her knife and yelling at me like a Cossack warrior. I felt my legs weaken and decided to turn and face her. I spotted a thick wooden stick by my feet and used it to beat her back until fellow villagers arrived and took her away.'

The woman was an ex-prostitute whose face had been ravaged by syphilis. She had no regrets and likened her attack to a holy duty, saying she had decided to kill him because he was a false prophet and an agent of the devil. Rasputin suspected she had been sent by one of his biggest enemies, the monk Iliodor, and I must say I agree with him on this. Regardless, her act would have consequences as dramatic and far-reaching as that of the assassin in Sarajevo. Her blade would incapacitate the one man in all of Russia who could have kept our great nation out of this savage war.

The nearest doctor was a six-hour ride away. Rasputin hovered between life and death for days. And when he finally recovered, after weeks of care, he was not the same.

The tsar ignored the telegrams Rasputin sent from his hospital bed, in which he implored him to avert the war. In his last plea, my master warned the emperor of 'an immeasurable sea of tears' before concluding that 'everything will drown in great bloodshed.' The tsar didn't listen. Russia went to war, a war that would engulf the entire continent and beyond.

Rasputin was now a changed man. In constant pain from the attack, he took to heavy drinking – not just Madeira and Champagne, but vodka, and lots of it – and his character turned foul. He was now shamelessly taking vast amounts of money from all kinds of unsavory supplicants on whose behalf he intervened with the government. The chronicles of the police agents charged with his surveillance now referred to him as 'The Dark One.' As his strength returned, the wanton debauchery resumed with a vengeance, now combined with drunken revelry and violence. And as the empire sank further and further into war, he sank with it.

He couldn't speak out against the war when everyone seemed fervently delighted by the bloodletting. The tsar was away running the campaign, while, back at the palace, the tsarina needed constant uplifting prophesies to keep her spirits up. The public outcries against Rasputin across all of Petrograd – for that is what the capital is now called, St. Petersburg having been deemed too German – resumed with a new ferocity. He feared for his life, and he was plagued by doubt and disillusionment.

And that was when I made my biggest mistake.

I told him about the developments in my work. About how I had refined my device's powers and greatly extended its range.

'Show me what it can do,' he said, a feral animus radiating out of his deep-set eyes.

I could not refuse.

As I write this, after our return from those most horrific of days in the Urals, I am lost as to what I should do.

The words of Rasputin, the ones that shook me to my very soul as we stood outside the doomed mine and contemplated the result of our cursed deed – they still haunt my every waking moment.

'How?' I remember asking him. 'How does this monstrous crime that we've just committed ensure the salvation of our people?'

'They won't listen to me anymore,' he said, his tone guttural but unusually coherent. 'They want war. They want bloodletting. They think that is the righteous path that God wills. Well ... if they want war, I'll give them war. I'll show them the true glory of savagery. We will ride to the front, you and I. And we'll ride right up to the enemy's lines and stand back and watch as they slaughter each other at my command. And when these fools see this, when they see the extent of my power ... the enemy will beg for mercy, and the tsar will grant me anything to carry my favor.' He smiled and directed his mesmeric gaze into me. 'He will even grant me the throne.'

I am lost in a maelstrom of torturous thoughts.

'Everything drowns in great bloodshed,' he had told the tsar in his warnings against the war. Now we are the ones doing the drowning.

I fear my old master has lost his way. He has fallen into a state of grave spiritual temptation. The purity of soul needed to prophesy and heal has turned into a dangerous gift now that he has succumbed to the Antichrist.

I have to do something to stop him. To save Russia.

I have to do something to save his soul.

54

I was like a caged animal all afternoon, with competing feral instincts battling inside me.

I felt we were really on to something with the van and my theory and wanted to keep pressing ahead with it. At the same time, I felt Kurt had given me a real opportunity to get closer to Corrigan than I'd managed after months of trying, and it was an opportunity I might not get again.

I had to juggle both, if only for a few hours.

We checked on and debriefed Ae-Cha at the hospital, then got back to Federal Plaza and went straight into a video conference call with, of all people, an analyst at the CIA.

They'd gotten a hit on the voice print of Ivan that we'd sent across to them and to the NSA. No ID, sadly. Not a name, or a photograph. But it did tell us a couple of things. One was that they'd heard his voice before, on a couple of occasions. Once in a wiretapped conversation in Dubai, shortly before the disappearance of a Ukrainian businessman who was a growing force in the opposition movement to his country's Kremlin-backed regime. And in Marbella, a few days before the drowning of a senior Russian banker.

Ivan got around.

The other was that while they didn't have a name for him, they had a code name. 'Koschey.' From a character in a Russian folk tale. Also known as 'Koschey the Deathless.'

Terrific.

They wanted him, of course. So did several governments around the globe. Beyond that, there wasn't much they could tell us, nor was there much we could add to their wafer-thin profile. It wasn't like we needed any confirmation about the guy's competence or his ruthlessness.

I also got the info Kurt sent me via a dead-drop Yahoo mail account he'd set up. The hotel's address and a picture of Kirby, just as I'd asked. There was nothing in the photograph to suggest that he was anything other than a middle-aged, middle-rung professional with a middle-American life. Albeit in a slightly more sensitive line of work than your average salary man. He did, however, have few wrinkles and a full head of hair, which considering he was in his early fifties, was no mean achievement. Maybe his illicit trysts were keeping him young.

I checked my watch, then went online and looked at airline schedules. There was a flight leaving JFK at 5:15 that landed at Washington National Airport at 6:40. Assuming it left on time, it would give me enough time to grab a cab to Georgetown and be there when Kirby and his playmate arrived at their secret assignation on M Street. I wondered how the hell he managed to pay for four nights a month at a fancy boutique hotel like that and not feel the pinch. Maybe I'd ask him about that, too.

By four thirty, it was time for me to make a decision. I'd be taking a huge risk. A potentially irresponsible one. Koschey was still out there, with Sokolov and the van. We had an APB out on the latter two. But we didn't have anything else to go on, and I didn't think we'd be having any more Kevlar moments with him. Larisa had suggested we lean on Mirminsky together, but the Sledgehammer was no longer with us, and I couldn't think of any other avenue we could still pursue, anything we could do besides wait and stay sharp and hope something broke.

On the other hand, this was the best chance I'd had to get a bead on Corrigan. I couldn't waste it. I couldn't rely on that opportunity still being there in a week, or whenever this situation with Koschey had run its course. I had to grab it, I had to put everything at risk to try and find him. I had to do it for Alex, even if it did mean I was risking my job – and quite possibly, a jail term – by doing it.

Besides, I wouldn't be gone for more than five or six hours.

A tough call, but I decided to do it.

Which meant I had to tell my partner.

'I need you to cover for me,' I told him as I closed the door to the empty conference room. 'I need to be somewhere for a few hours.'

He stared at me curiously. 'Where and to do what?'

'I can't tell you.'

He snorted. 'You can't tell *me*?'

'Yep.'

He studied me curiously for a moment, then his eyes narrowed with suspicion. 'You got something going on with our Russian hottie?'

'Of course not.'

He grimaced with faux-annoyance. 'Yeah, I didn't think so.' He turned serious. 'What's going on, Sean?'

'I really can't tell you.'

Aparo got angry. 'Hey, this is me you're fucking talking to.'

'I can't. Not now.'

'Not now? When then?'

I had to go. 'Soon. Look, it's better this way. For your sake.'

That really pissed him off. 'You're giving me deniability now? Seriously? Since when did I care about that bullshit?'

'It's just for tonight,' I insisted. 'Let me do this. If something comes out of it, you'll be the first to know.'

As I reached the door, he asked, 'This about Alex?'

I stopped. We hadn't been partners for ten years for nothing. 'I gotta go, man. Anything breaks, call me.'

'At least tell me where the hell you're going?'

I kept my hand on the door handle, then I said, 'DC.'

I heard him mutter, 'Shit,' then I left the room.

It was time for a break. More important, it was the pre-agreed time for Koschey's follow-up phone call.

He escorted Sokolov back to his familiar holding spot on the floor by the radiator and tied him to it. They'd made good progress in dismantling the gear from the inside of the van, but there was still a lot of work to be done.

Throughout, Koschey had gotten Sokolov to give him a running commentary about what he was doing, what each component was, how it all worked. Working alongside him, he gained a firm grasp of Sokolov's ingenious invention. He'd also told Sokolov to divide it into two separate stacks instead of just one. Moving it to yet another vehicle, or packing it into crates, would be easier that way. It wouldn't all need to be dismantled again.

He left Sokolov in the small office and stepped outside by the vehicles to make the call.

His Saudi contact took the call promptly, as he'd expected.

'Do you have an answer for me?' Koschey asked in Arabic.

'The answer is yes,' the man said, 'provided you can guarantee that none of this will come back to our doorstep. You can guarantee it, yes?'

'Nothing will come out from my end because no one else is involved but me. But I can't guarantee what slips out from your end.'

'Our end is secure.'

'Then there's no problem. What about my package?'

'It should be with you within the hour. The other half will be paid on completion, as you proposed.'

Koschey smiled. The promise of a hundred million dollars tended to have that effect on most men. 'Make sure it's not delayed.'

'It'll be there,' the man said. 'Good luck.'

Koschey clicked off. Luck – he scoffed at the notion. He made his own luck.

He'd known the Saudi's people would go for it. Not the government, of course. In his experience, governments were a waste of time. They made terrible partners. The decision-making process was slow and convoluted. Discussions and consultations had to be undertaken. Foreign pressures had to be taken into account. And decisions by committee were rarely unanimous, which meant there would be dissenters, and dissenters were prone to create problems. To say nothing of leaks. Which, given how subservient the Saudis were to the Americans, would be immediate.

Fortunately, there were now people on the planet who made far better partners when it came to decisive action. Billionaires who were as wealthy, and as politically motivated, as any government. Oligarchs, oil sheikhs, media tycoons, and a varied collection of massively successful businessmen who held highly strung views about the world they lived in. Megalomaniacs with staggering riches had the means to fund their own initiatives and shape the world in their vision, whether by initiating advertising and PR campaigns to alter the course of elections, channeling weapons to opposition movements, or funding private armies of mercenaries to overthrow regimes. Bin Laden had been the most notorious of them all, but there were many others and they came in many guises. And Koschey had direct connections with several such players, in all corners of the globe, players whose agendas were as yet unfulfilled, players who could be tempted with the right offer. The kind of offer Koschey had made to his Saudi contact.

An offer that would cause huge problems for the Saudis' arch-enemies – Iran – while giving Koschey the immense satisfaction of delivering a crushing blow to the Americans he loathed.

It was now time to make another phone call.

With another such offer.

This one would be to a Lebanese car dealer, in Beirut. A man who had a direct and secure pipeline into the upper echelons of Hezbollah, who in turn had a direct and secure pipeline to Tehran.

This man could take Koschey's offer to the most radical elements among those in power there.

Koschey was about to make the biggest play of his life. But to do so, this call needed to be handled differently.

For this call, Koschey had to adjust some of the settings on his phone.

This was a call he needed certain people to hear.

He switched off the highest-level encryption, making it possible for his conversations with the car dealer to be picked up and deciphered by the NSA's Echelon eavesdropping software. Not too easily, but possible. And highly likely, given the key words he was going to use in order to snare the attention of the server banks at Fort Meade. Then he added a layer of distortion to the outgoing segments of the call, giving his voice a new frequency range and ensuring it didn't match any voice prints the Americans or anyone else had on record for him.

He also made sure his phone was set to record their conversation. Just in case the trail of evidence he was planting to implicate Hezbollah and their Iranian patrons wasn't enough. Sometimes, more was more. Especially if you were trying to frame a foreign government for a major terrorist attack.

He made sure the settings were all in place. Then he made the call.

Shin hadn't moved for hours.

He was still there, curled up on a bench in Astoria Park, hungry, thirsty, scared, muttering to himself and eyeing everyone suspiciously. The schoolkids and the health freaks running around the track, the carefree dilettantes on the tennis courts, the chess players and the bums. They were all threats.

After last night, everyone was a threat.

After last night, his whole world had changed.

He still couldn't make sense of what he'd witnessed out in Brighton Beach. Even with his extensive knowledge, even with his perceptive and analytical mind, he still couldn't process it. Even worse was the shoot-out. Watching his friends die. And knowing that all the sinister forces of the world had to want this thing and would do anything to get their hands on it.

How he'd made it this far, he didn't know. He couldn't justify or rationalize it. Jonny and Bon hadn't made it, and they were the pros. They had the street chops he never possessed, they were the cool cats, the survivors. And yet they were gone and he was still here.

What to do from here on, though, was another matter.

He hadn't dared go home to Nikki. Sure, she had to be worried sick about him. But she was probably more angry than worried. She was already royally pissed off at him for going out to meet Jonny like that in the middle of the night. Nothing good could possibly come out of that kind of meeting, she'd told him. Jonny was nothing but trouble, they both agreed, and Shin had made her a promise, after all. A promise to drop a life that he knew wasn't made for him.

She was right, of course. And he couldn't face her. Not now. Not like this. Not when he didn't know who might be waiting for him there, watching their place, ready to pounce.

All the sinister forces of the world had to want this thing, he reminded himself.

He didn't dare go to the chop shop either. He couldn't confront the others. By now, they had to know that Jonny and Bon were dead, and given the contempt they felt for him, something they'd never been shy about, there was no point in him going there. Hell, they might even suspect him of having sold their buddies out. No, the chop shop was out of bounds. Besides, it was the obvious place for any agents to be lying in wait for him.

He had to keep his head down until things settled – if they ever did. Wait and watch from the sidelines, and hope that at some point he'd be able to resume his less-than-charmed life and act like last night had never happened.

One thing kept preying on his mind, though. The bad guy. The *gae-jasik* who'd shot Jonny and Ae-Cha.

Shin knew where he was. Where he was last night, at any rate. But it seemed to be his hideout, his safe house. His lair. And Shin knew he might be the only one to possess that information.

Information that could lead to the man's capture.

He'd been debating it all day, and had yet to reach a conclusion. He wanted to call it in, but at the same time, he didn't want to get involved any more than he already was. An anonymous tip – surely, there was no harm in that. But with all the sophisticated tracking technology, nothing could be taken for granted anymore, and the last thing he needed was for them to figure out who he was and find him.

Better to keep your mouth shut, he told himself.

Then Ae-Cha's smiling face assailed his mind's eye, Ae-Cha who he'd had a crush on from the moment he'd first met her when he was twelve, Ae-Cha who'd never taken notice of him but who he still fancied nevertheless, and he wasn't so sure of keeping silent anymore.

55

I landed at Reagan and was in a cab less than ten minutes later. Since wheels-up, Ivan or Koschey or whoever he really was had receded out of my system, and my thoughts had zeroed in on Corrigan. I didn't know how this thing with Kirby would play out. Either way, there were still several burning hoops to jump through, but the hairs on the back of my neck told me that I was about to be closer to him than I had been at any point since Corliss blew his own brains out.

I pulled out my phone and started reviewing what Kurt had sent me, and as the Washington Monument drifted into view, the leviathan himself called.

'*Konnichiwa*. Thursday night is poker night.'

Not exactly what I needed to know. 'Well, good luck then.'

'No, not my poker night, man. His poker night. You seriously think I play poker? Even the online version is for losers. Why flush virtual money on blackjack when you can spend it on proficiency points for your Blood Knight?'

I had to stay calm and remind myself he was coming through for me. 'So that's Kirby's alibi?'

'That's what I reckon. On three of the last fifteen Thursdays, he's charged cigars to the shared credit card. On five, he's charged a crate of beer.'

'They take turns.'

'Exactly. Just four dudes drinking the undrinkable and smoking the unsmokable.'

I glanced at my watch. We were good. 'What about his companion? Anything on her?'

'She's a mystery. Hotel doesn't have enough cameras to track guests to and from each room, and they only keep CCTV footage for a week at a time. Kirby arrived on his own last week. Same with leaving. They're very careful.'

I chewed on his info for a moment. 'All right. Stay put. I'm going to try and borrow her purse or her cell phone, like we discussed.'

'Sure thing, dude. I'm not going anywhere. Not in Newark, anyway.' He laughed like a high school kid. 'Oh, and by the way. The guy has taste. She's a 36E with medium-sized thongs. The dream combo, assuming there's no silicone in there.'

I had to get him and Aparo together. They'd have a blast. Then again, I'm not sure the women of New York would ever forgive me.

My phone buzzed. I had another call coming in.

From Federal Plaza.

At least it wasn't from Aparo's cell, but it still sent a jolt of alarm through me.

'Consider me overinformed and underbriefed,' I told him. 'I'll let you get back to your lovely Pandaren. *Sayonara* till later.'

I swapped calls, and breathed out. It was Wrightson, from the computer analysis and response team, and he didn't sound urgent.

'I've looked at your pictures,' he told me, referring to the shots I sent him of the electrical junk pile we found at Sokolov's garage. 'It's nothing weapons-grade, if that's what you're worried about. It actually looks like your guy's into some high-end microwave technology. He's got strip line, cavity and dielectric resonators in there, transistors, low-power diodes.'

None of that meant anything to me. 'What's it all used for?'

'I'd say he's been tinkering with some kind of microwave transmission device. Some of these circuits you'd find in any cell-phone tower, but others are more specialized.'

This wasn't in line with what I'd been thinking. 'I thought cell-phone towers were huge?'

'Not at all. They're tall, but that's to get the best transmission. The components themselves aren't that big.'

I don't know where the question came from, but I asked, 'Small enough to fit in the back of a van?'

'Sure. Everything in microwave tech is small because the wavelengths themselves are so short, and that includes everything from consumer Wi-Fi to satellite comms. Microwave tech doesn't use your standard electronic circuitry – what electrical engineers call 'lumped-element' circuitry. It uses distributed circuits that are generally pretty minute.'

I focused on the part where he said it could fit in a van. I still didn't see why Sokolov would do that. 'Anything else you can think of?'

'I couldn't say for sure,' he said, 'but it looks like he was trying to increase the range and penetration of his signal through multiple resonator clusters.'

'What sort of range are we talking about?'

'Depends on the power supply and how the resonators were laid out. Anything from ten to a thousand yards would be my guess.'

I'd been hoping for something else. This was all sending me on a tangent that didn't make sense.

'Sorry I can't be any more help,' Wrightson concluded. 'Let me know if you find the kit. I'd love to see what he's been up to.'

I was angling for the same thing.

The traffic was running smoothly and it wasn't long before we were crossing over the Potomac and hitting Georgetown.

You'd never know from the view that you were leaving Virginia and entering the nation's capital. The parkland along both sides of the river and the low skyline always looked more to me like a Midwestern town than the part of the city that housed the seat of government. I asked the driver to drop me off at the corner of M and Thomas Jefferson so I could cover the last couple hundred yards on foot. I needed to know who Kirby was seeing before I confronted him, and that meant being there when she arrived. It also meant attracting as little attention as possible. Since I wasn't carrying an iPad or a Kindle, I had no choice but to fall back on doing this old-style and use a newspaper, the classic cover for discreet surveillance. I bought a copy of the *Washington Times* from a vending machine, then I walked the single block to the hotel.

At around twenty minutes to eight, I entered the hotel and took a quick look around. The lobby had a tony, classic elegance. Plush velvet sofas. Richly veined woods and chrome. Several hundred dollars'-worth of fresh flowers. And darkness. A lot of darkness. The whole place screamed 'Not for Kids,' which was just as well, seeing as what Kirby and his companion used the place for.

There was a small niche by the entrance for the concierge. A couple of guests were clearly putting his local knowledge to the test. At the other end of the lobby were two separate desks and armchairs in lieu of the traditional reception counter. Much more personal. The desk on the right was empty. A overly primped receptionist sat behind the other one, typing away at his computer's keyboard.

I sat in a leather armchair with a perfect view of the hotel's entrance and hoped that nothing had made Kirby alter his weekly routine tonight. I opened the newspaper and affected the casual air of someone waiting to meet a hotel guest.

About ten minutes later, Kirby walked in.

He went straight past me and across to reception. He was carrying a small gift bag from Biagio. The lady was clearly more than partial to chocolate.

He checked in with the minimum amount of fuss and was already on the way to the elevator before I had finished folding my newspaper.

The second the elevator doors had closed, I walked over to the reception desk. There were no other guests there. Some situations called for an FBI badge, but others called for dead presidents. Given why I was here, this was definitely one of the latter. I pulled out a hundred and slid it across the desk.

'Stan Kirby. Just checked in. What room is he in?'

The clerk glanced at the bill somewhat haughtily, then looked up at me. 'Sir, I can't—'

'Sure you can,' I interjected while peeling off another hundred. I held both bills cupped discreetly against the desk.

He gave me an uneasy squint. 'You a private detective?'

'Something like that.'

He considered it for a moment, then adjusted his immaculately trimmed eyebrow with a finely manicured finger and said, 'The guy pays me fifty every week to ensure discretion. That adds up over time. You'll need to go considerably higher.'

I leaned in. 'I'll let you in on something. That streak – it's over. So you might as well take this and hang on to it until your next gravy train pulls in.'

The clerk thought about this. Maybe this was Kirby's last Thursday. I clearly knew about the affair. Why else would I be there?

He reached over and, grudgingly, took the cash.

'Four fourteen,' he mumbled.

I gave him a smile. 'Good call.'

He looked bummed, and proceeded to shuffle papers aimlessly across his desk.

'One more question,' I said.

He raised a stiff hand. 'The woman?'

I smiled again.

He glanced down at his now-open palm, pointedly.

I pulled out another hundred and gave it to him.

'Long black hair. Spectacular body. You can't miss her.'

I nodded. 'Appreciate it.'

I was heading back to my chair when a noticeably attractive woman with long dark hair, a short dress, and four-inch pumps came in and went straight for the elevators.

To the untrained eye she could have been a high-class escort, but everything was a bit too perfect and considered. This was a woman who genuinely cared about the impression she gave, rather than giving an impression because she was paid to.

I already knew she wasn't Kirby's wife, since some of the pictures Kurt had taken off Facebook and sent me had Mrs. Kirby in them. To be doubly sure, I pulled them up on my phone. It wasn't her. Then something clicked in the periphery of my memory, and I scrolled through the other shots. Our mystery woman was in one of them, standing next to Kirby's wife, the two of them all hair and heels with big smiles all around. They were friends.

I called Kurt.

56

I t didn't take Kurt long to call me back. He sounded out of breath.
'You're going to fucking freak, dude.'

'Go on.'

He said, 'She's his sister-in-law. Inès Alcalde. His wife is Sofia Kirby, *née* Alcalde. Inès is three years younger, single, a realtor with a very healthy business. No kids, I don't think she can have any. It's like a movie of the week, dude. I hate those.'

'You hacked her medical records?'

'Nope. Facebook again. Seriously, Zuckerberg's gonna put us all out of business.'

This was good. Really good. 'All right, thanks. I'll take it from here. Consider your free pass well and truly earned. Just don't use it anytime soon.'

'*Sayonara.*'

I now felt armed with more than enough to bring Kirby around to my way of thinking. But that didn't mean that he'd agree to my terms.

I took the elevator up to the fourth floor, found 414, and knocked on the door.

It took a few seconds to get a muffled 'Yes?' from Kirby, who was standing by the still-closed door.

'Mr. Kirby? Hotel security, sir.'

There was a moment's hesitation, then he cracked the door open. He was in a dressing gown.

'What is it?' He was seriously annoyed.

I decided the direct approach was best. 'Do you think your wife would have a problem with the fact that you're screwing her sister?'

His face exsanguinated faster than in any vampire movie I'd seen.

I nodded comfortingly. 'It's OK, Stan. It's going to be fine. She doesn't need to know. But I'm gonna need a few minutes of your time. So why don't you throw some clothes on, tell Inès you won't be long, and come down to the bar with me. Given your line of work, I'm sure she'll understand. Hell, play it right and she might even get a kick out of it.' I added a conspiratorial wink for good measure.

Kirby was having difficulty processing what I was telling him. In fact, for someone who had been caught committing a catastrophic error, it was apt that his brain appeared to be shutting down altogether.

I moved closer to him. Lowered my voice. 'Take a breath, Stan. I'm giving you a way out, and it doesn't involve money or pain or betraying your country. You can even keep seeing the lovely Inès if you want to, though I'm not sure I can heartily recommend it.'

It took a while for this to sink in, but when it had, he seemed to regain control.

'Give me a second,' he said.

We took a booth in the even-darker bar.

I ordered a Coke. Kirby asked for a double whiskey, which I thought was entirely justified.

'Who the fuck are you?' he asked, nervously spinning his iPhone around on the table.

'Not really relevant right now. You just need to focus on keeping me happy and this will all blow over real quick.'

The drinks arrived. He let go of his phone and knocked back both shots within a second of his glass hitting the table. 'What do you want?'

'I want you to find someone for me.'

'Find someone?' He studied me, then asked, 'What are you, a fed?'

I ignored his question. 'Again, not relevant. I just need to put a real name to an alias. A Company one.'

He got my drift immediately, and his eyes went wide. 'This is someone at the Company?'

'Yes.' I looked straight at him.

'I thought you said this wouldn't involve anything like that?'

'It doesn't. This is personal. And if you do it carefully enough, no one needs to know it ever happened.'

'This is fucking blackmail. I could report you and have your ass thrown in jail.'

I felt a lurching in my gut at the word, like I'd just hit the lowest point on a roller coaster less than a second after being at the highest. But I couldn't pull out now. 'Sure. Go ahead. Tell them everything. But you go down that road and you're quickly gonna find yourself in one hell of a custody battle and looking down the barrel at ten years of crippling alimony while trying to find women in singles' bars who won't mind going back to your dump of a one-bedroom apartment without the promise of chocolates or flowers 'cause you're still paying for your son's braces and your daughter's riding lessons and you can't even afford a new shirt, let alone gifts for your lover. How does that sound to you?'

I waited for all that to sink in. It didn't take long.

'You're an asshole,' he muttered.

'Extreme measures, pal. Not by choice. But don't doubt my commitment for a second.'

He glared at me, trying to find some measure of hope in my expression. I stared back like a sphinx. Then after a painful few seconds, he broke.

'So who is it?'

This was the point of no return. Once Kirby had the name, the risk that he would go back to Langley and flag it became very real, with unknowable consequences for me and my family. But I couldn't let go of it. Not when I might be one small step from dragging Corrigan out of the shadows and into the light of day.

'Corrigan. Reed Corrigan. It's a cover. That's all I can tell you about him. There are other things, but knowing them may prejudice you, so all you get is the name.'

He studied me for a beat, then asked, 'What did he do?'

'When I said it's personal, I meant it. But one thing I can tell you. He's a piece of shit. Makes you look like a saint. Keeping the bastard's real identity a secret is not worth you losing everything you've spent twenty years building, and you should be able to get me what I need without anyone finding out. And that would be the end of it. You have my word. Get me the name – his *real* name – and you'll never hear from me again.'

'What if I can't?'

'Then all bets are off. So your best course of action is to find a way because I *really* want to find him. And the sooner you do it, the sooner I'm out of your life.'

'When do you need it by?'

'It can wait till morning.'

Kirby grimaced painfully, then he shook his head and nodded.

'Is that one "r" or two?'

Koschey interrupted Sokolov's work again, secured him in the small office, and stepped away to make another call.

The Lebanese car dealer answered after the first ring.

'Have your people made a decision?' he asked in Arabic.

The man said, 'They're interested, but they're nervous. They fear the potential retributions.'

Typical, Koschey thought in silence. *All bluster, no guts.* Still, he knew they were close to biting. He just needed to press some more and be more convincing.

'Tell them the retributions are coming at them anyway, whether they do anything or not,' Koschey told him. 'You know the Americans and the Israelis are gunning for them as well as I do. It's only a matter of time. They're not going to let them keep their reactors and their centrifuges. They're never going to let them into their exclusive club. But if we do this,' Koschey said, using the 'we' to include himself in the circle of interested plotters, 'we'd be hitting them first. And we'll have something to threaten them with that'll make them think twice about retaliating. Attacking them like this is the best defense. And after Stuxnet and Flame,' he continued, referring to the sophisticated US/Israeli cyberattacks that had been wreaking havoc on Iran's computer networks and crippling its uranium enrichment programs, 'the irony of our method won't be lost on them. Even if they won't be able to prove it.'

'Since when has that stopped them from doing anything?' the man grumbled.

'We have a small window in which to do this. I'll need an answer by morning.'

'I'll let them know,' the man said. 'I'll have an answer for you by then.'

Koschey ended the call and stared at his phone in silence. He knew they'd find his offer hard to resist. He was giving them a chance to strike at the Great Satan in a way they would have never imagined possible. And even that wasn't the whole truth.

Koschey hadn't told them who his real target was. They would have never agreed to that. They would have been too scared. But if they did accept his proposal, as he expected, his conversations with them would be enough to frame them for what he really had in mind, and they were hardly in a position to plead their innocence while acknowledging that they'd agreed to bankroll a different terrorist strike on US soil.

Everything was in place. Koschey's central concern was now time. He needed to do it quickly. Pressure would be mounting and the noose around him would be tightening with every hour now that the Americans realized what he had. Which would make his disappearing act all the more difficult the longer he waited.

He nodded to himself, then turned to retrieve Sokolov and finish what they'd started.

The second hundred million dollars, a new face, and a new beginning were only hours away.

57

Miraculously, Thursday night had come and gone without us having to call in another convoy of coroners' wagons.

I'd made it back from DC on time and spoken to Aparo on my way home. He'd confirmed that nothing noteworthy had happened while I was out of town. He pressed me on how my trip had been and when I was going to let him in on 'Whatever the hell it is you're getting yourself into,' as he put it. I'd said we'd talk about it in the morning and driven home to Mamaroneck, where I managed to grab some quality time with Tess before she glided into sleep and I mulled over whatever the hell I'd gotten myself into.

Then Alex had woken up, just before five a.m., with another nightmare. This time, he'd run into our bedroom, straight to Tess's side of the bed. And yet again, it frustrated me to no end was that I couldn't do anything to comfort him. Yet again, I was crippled, worried it might only make things worse, given what they'd seeded about me in his head. I hated the feeling. Truly, madly, deeply, hated it.

Tess knew it. I didn't have to say anything. Not any more. She knew, just from my breathing.

'I've got this,' she said as she leaned over and kissed me softly.

I didn't say anything back. I just nodded to myself and stared up at the ceiling.

I'd spent the rest of the night – both hours of it – churning over the day's events, a pointless exercise once you've been over it two or three times. Tess had spent them in bed with Alex. She was great at calming him down. I was truly lucky to have her in my life.

It was seven-thirty and all four of us were in the kitchen, wolfing down pancakes – with slightly more elegance than Kurt had that day at IHOP, I hoped – along with a small mountain of raspberries and blueberries.

Alex seemed fine, as if the terrors of the night were in full remission.

I glanced at him and looked faux-pensive.

'I think these are pretty good pancakes,' I told him. 'Pretty, pretty good,' I repeated, saying it the way Larry David did, which usually got a small chuckle out of Alex. 'In fact, they might just be the best pancakes on the planet. I think they are. But you know what?'

'What?' he asked.

'We need to make sure. We need to be absolutely sure. Which means we need to try out the pancakes that are, so they say, truly, definitely awesome. It might be a drag. The place that serves them isn't particularly near. In fact, we might have to take an airplane to get there. But I think we should. I think we need to have the great pancake bake-off before we can crown Tess champion. What do you say? You up for that?'

He looked at me curiously, then glanced at Tess, like he wasn't sure. She didn't seem to know what the hell I was talking about either. I flicked a look over at Kim. She gave me a knowing look and a small nod.

'Look, I know, it's a hassle. But let's do this, for Tess, okay? I mean, even if it eats up a whole weekend. I'm sure we can find stuff to do down there.' I swung my gaze up at Tess. 'There's stuff to do there, right?'

She spread her arms and her mouth went all round and open. 'What on earth are you talking about?'

'You know. Those pancakes everyone's always talking about. The ones they serve at Disney World.'

I glanced innocently at Alex, and his face lit up with sheer delight. And right then, for that brief moment, everything was perfect in the world.

A little over an hour later, I was back at Federal Plaza, and the ants in my pants were on tenterhooks, both from the frustration I was feeling regarding our lack of progress on tracking down Koschey and from wondering when I was going to hear from my favorite libertine.

As far as Koschey was concerned, we were at a standstill. Apart from hoping the APB on the van paid off, the only thing we could do was keep monitoring for any relevant chatter or hope for an NSA intercept that could clue us into his current movements. Homeland Security had a major lock on airports, ports, and border crossings, based on the assumption that Koschey had to be getting ready to get out of Dodge, with

Sokolov and the van in tow. If not the whole van, then at least whatever it was Sokolov had put in it. But we live in a big country, and it's not that difficult to smuggle something or someone out of here if you really put your mind to it.

By ten, I needed some air and some decent coffee and Aparo needed to hear what I was up to, so we stepped out of the building, did a pit stop at my favorite food cart, and took a bench across the street by the African Burial Ground monument.

Aparo didn't take it too well.

'Jesus, Sean,' he said when his blood pressure finally settled enough to allow him to speak coherently. 'You could go to jail for this.'

I shrugged. 'I know. But what the hell. If it all gets that messy, maybe that's how I'll finally get to the truth.'

'You know that's a pipe dream as much as I do. They can clam up and claim national security and lock your ass up faster than you can say patriot.'

'You have a better idea for how I can find him?'

Aparo frowned at me, shaking his head slowly from side to side. 'Let's hope this Kirby really wants to hang on to his wife. 'Cause from where I'm standing, it's not something I would gamble on.'

I was thinking about what he said when an unfamiliar ringtone warbled in my immediate vicinity. It took me a couple of seconds to realize that it was coming from the prepaid phone I'd bought before flying down to DC, the one I'd purchased specifically so I could give Kirby an untraceable phone.

You work in law enforcement long enough, you learn a few tricks from the criminals you spend your life chasing. Basic, in this case, but handy given my current predicament.

'It's him,' I told Aparo as I flipped open the flimsy plastic clamshell phone. At least, I hoped it was him and not some CIA security officer calling to get a lock on who and where I was before the troops swooped in.

'You know what you've asked for isn't exactly easy to access,' he said. His tone was hushed and clearly irritated, which was hardly surprising.

'If it were, I wouldn't have needed you, would I? Do you have the name?'

'Reed Corrigan is mentioned in three case files,' he said. 'All three were flagged, but I managed to pull them without tripping anything. Two of them are dormant and one's active.'

I was crushing the phone with my grip. 'His name, Kirby. What's his name?'

'I can't access it. These files are redacted. I can't get to the clean ones without authorization, which means I'd have to tell them why I want them. And anyway, his name wouldn't be in them. They would only ever mention his code name.'

A charge of fury went right through me. 'That wasn't our deal,' I hissed.

'Hey, nothing was "our" deal,' Kirby shot back. 'It was all *your* deal. It wasn't open to negotiation, remember? Anyway, this is the best I can do. At my clearance level, anyway. If I get promoted tomorrow, maybe you'd be in with a chance. But I wouldn't hold my breath.'

I tried to push back the searing sense of frustration that was engulfing me. 'Send me the files.'

'I can't,' Kirby said. 'I can't take them out of here and I can't leave that kind of electronic trail. The e-mail would get blocked before it even left our servers.'

'Put them on a USB stick then,' I suggested gruffly.

'Same thing,' he countered. 'Any copying is immediately logged by the system. What do you think this is, Dunder Mifflin?'

I was burning up inside. All that effort and risk, for nothing. I don't know why, but I really wanted the damn files. Even though Kirby had already said they wouldn't give me Corrigan's real name.

'The files. Are they paper, or on your screen?'

'Screen. Any old paperwork's been scanned in.'

'You have your phone with you, right? Use it. Take pictures of your screen. Message them to me.'

'They're big files.'

'I don't need all the cross references,' I told him. 'Just the main body of each report.'

I heard him let out a long exhale. 'Then we're done, right?'

My turn to exhale. 'Yeah. We're done. But I need those screen grabs now.'

'Fine,' he said grudgingly. 'And by the way, you're a real asshole, you know that?'

I killed the call without replying.

*   *   *

I can't stay like this forever, Shin thought.

He'd been there for more than twenty-four hours. Sticking to the immediate vicinity of the bench, watching life wind down and start off again. Living off any scraps he could find in the park's garbage cans.

A fucking PhD, he lamented. *What a joke.*

By this point he was dizzy, tired, and weary. His mind was starting to play tricks on him. One minute, he was imagining men in suits and dark glasses hustling his Nikki from their apartment and doing horrible things to her. The next he pictured her sipping Champagne and laughing it up in a luxurious hot tub with a rich, handsome dude in there with her.

He had to put an end to this nightmare. There was no point in living if it meant living like this.

He decided he'd make the call. An anonymous phone call. Tip the cops off to the Russian bastard's location. Who knows. If they got him, maybe it would all go away. Maybe he'd have nothing left to worry about.

He'd do it for himself. For Nikki. And for Jonny and Ae-Cha.

He pushed himself to his feet and shuffled off to find a phone booth.

Koschey was by the door of the warehouse, watching life resume across the industrial park. Today would be a big day. A long one. A challenging one.

He was ready for it. He'd spent most of the night planning the hit. He'd checked the schedule, laid out his timetable, and used the extensive resources available online to research the venue and everything around it. It would be tight, especially on such short notice, but it was doable. And the opportunity was too great to pass up. Besides, he was used to operating under pressure, and quick decisions and swift planning made leaks and last-minute changes less likely.

He would also be enjoying the benefit of a significant tactical advantage.

He checked the time, then made the call.

The Lebanese car dealer told him his bosses in Tehran wanted to go ahead. Just as Koschey knew they would.

Koschey confirmed their arrangements, asked him to thank his bosses for their confidence, then hung up.

He glanced at the SUV. It was ready. But he'd need to try it out first. Make sure Sokolov had done his work properly.

Once that was done, there'd be no stopping him.

Until the next opportunity arose.

58

Kirby's JPEGs were soon pouring into my phone. Lots of them.

I was at my desk, e-mailing them on to myself at my personal Gmail account, and going through them on my laptop as they arrived.

The first file, though heavily redacted, was interesting. It concerned an assignment code named Operation Bouncer and was marked SCI – sensitive compartmented information. It involved the interrogation and subsequent assassination of a Bulgarian psychiatrist who had been torturing prisoners in El Salvador. From what I could make out between the words and lines that had been crossed out with a thick black marker, Corrigan was a field agent working for the CIA's Office of Research Development. In El Salvador, the cover he'd used was a Boston-based CIA front called the Scientific Engineering Institute. All of this didn't come as a surprise to me, given the reason Corliss had reached out to him.

Apart from these two institutions that I would need to look at more closely, the file didn't offer me anything else. Too much of it was redacted to give me any more insights into who 'Reed Corrigan' really was. Not that I expected it to. Code names were there for a reason.

Which was why I wasn't feeling hugely hopeful when I turned my attention to the second file.

It concerned an assignment code named, of all names, Operation Sleeping Beauty. It was also marked SCI and its pages were also heavily redacted, more so than the first file. From what I could gather, it was about a Russian scientist, code named Jericho, who had managed to make contact with our people in Helsinki while attending a KGB-sponsored conference there. He claimed to be working on a highly classified program of psychotronic weapons.

I paused there. I'd never heard the word. I opened a browser window and looked it up and discovered it was a term the Russians had coined for a new generation of weapons.

Mind-control weapons.

I straightened up.

The report mentioned Jericho as a neurophysiologist and described how he had substantiated his claims by revealing details about the organizational structure of the KGB's S Directorate and its Department of Information-Psychological Actions. Frustratingly, the information about what technology he was actually working on was heavily blacked out. From the information that was still readable, it had to do with something called entrainment and was of 'paramount importance to the national security of the United States.'

Again, I paused and called up the browser window and typed in 'entrainment.' The word was used in several contexts, but one of them darted off the screen and sent a charge through me.

Brainwave Entrainment.

I skimmed a couple of articles that explained it. They described it as using an external stimulus to alter the brain state of the person being 'entrained.' Broadly, the concept was that you could make people feel or behave in a certain way by using auditory pulses, flashing lights, electromagnetic waves, or other stimuli to 'entrain' their brains into particular states.

My nerves crackled as I sped-read through the history – about how the scientific concept of brainwave entrainment or synchronization dated back to 200 AD, when Ptolemy first noted the effects of flickering sunlight generated by a spinning wheel, and how humans have been using sensory entrainment throughout their history. Then in the 1930s and 1940s, technology made it possible to measure brainwave entrainment after the invention of the EEG in 1924. This created a flurry of research in the area, including looking at the effects of introducing frequencies into the brain directly through electrical stimulus.

I dug deeper.

I read about how entrainment influences brain function beyond visual and auditory stimuli because of a phenomenon called the *frequency following response*. If the human brain receives a stimulus with a frequency in the range of brain waves, the predominant brain wave frequency will move toward the frequency of the stimulus. The most familiar side effect of entrainment was the way in which strobe lights at an 'alpha' frequency could trigger photosensitive epilepsy.

Then in the early 1960s, at the height of the Cold War, a neuroscientist called Allan H. Frey discovered the Microwave Auditory Effect, which is caused by audible clicks induced by pulsed/modulated microwave frequencies. There'd been a huge increase in radar coverage in the 1950s, and pilots had started to complain about a clicking in their ears when they flew directly into the path of the microwave radiation on which the radar systems were built. Frey discovered that these clicks were generated directly inside the human head and were not audible to people nearby. Research showed that this effect occurred as a result of thermal expansion of parts of the human ear around the cochlea, even at low power density. At specific frequencies, it was thought that these clicks could cause entrainment.

The US embassy in Moscow was famously believed to have been bombarded with microwaves for several decades starting in the 1950s in an effort to confuse, disorient, and even harm its staff. Anecdotal evidence exists of many embassy employees dying in the ensuing years because of the damage that was done to them, although as was usual in these cases, I imagined the real truth was buried in some long-shredded documents or in the graves of those insiders who really knew what had happened – or of those who had been its victims.

I found references to a scientist from Yale called Delgado in several articles. He had implanted electrodes into the brains of animals and humans in order to send highly specific electromagnetic currents into targeted areas. In his most infamous experiment, he wired up a bull, then, in front of several colleagues, Delgado stepped into the bull ring armed with no more than a remote control. He hit a switch that made the bull furious, then as the bull charged at him, he hit another switch that stopped the big animal in its tracks and turned it into a docile pussycat. Delgado was quoted as saying that if he could do these things by implanting electrodes in the brain, he believed it was only a matter of time before he'd be able to do it from outside the brain, using a very precise electromagnetic field.

And if all that wasn't enough to trip all kinds of circuits inside me, another article revealed that the same Microwave Auditory Effect was found to be inducible with shorter-wavelength portions of the electromagnetic spectrum. The shorter the wave, it seemed, the more energy and information it could carry. The article then described how microwave pulses from modern cell-phone network towers could theoretically cause this effect. These behavioral changes had to do with chemical responses in the brain. The external stimuli triggered the release of neurochemicals that caused various reactions in the brain, resulting in remotely heightened emotional and intellectual responses such as calmness, trust, lust, or aggression. The difficulty, and the key to achieving this, was believed to be in pinpointing the right combination of frequency, wave form, and power level to bring about a specific reaction.

Microwaves. Cell-phone technology. Altering human behavior remotely. Aggression.

The bloodbath at Brighton Beach. The gear we found in Sokolov's garage.

MK-ULTRA.

I couldn't read this last section fast enough, and I could already feel my heart kicking in my neck before I saw this:

Russian and American psychological warfare programs are believed to be actively researching the sonic, electromagnetic, and microwave spectrums for wavelengths and frequencies that can affect human behavior and exploring the viability of using entrainment, both to control their own population as well as to use it as an advanced weapon. The Russians are widely acknowledged to be well ahead of their American counterparts in this field. A handful of independent scientists are also actively researching brainwave entrainment, with the more outspoken stating that it could theoretically be used to cause subjects to commit acts of extreme violence and even kill on a massive scale by activating extreme paranoia and predatory survival impulses inside them.

My insides twisted.

I went back and checked the first date in the report.

November 29, 1981.

My eyes went into tunnel vision, and everything outside those words and numbers went all blurry as a fury of connections and implications lit up my mind.

I had zero doubt about it.

This file was about Sokolov.

Leo Sokolov was 'Jericho.'

And he was connected to Corrigan.

59

Sokolov was Jericho.

And everything started to fall into place.

Sokolov develops some kind of radical entrainment technology in Russia. Decides to defect for some reason. Maybe he doesn't want his bosses at the KGB to have it. Maybe he doesn't want his brain-manipulating technology in the hands of the most ruthless oppressors in history.

Or anyone else, for that matter.

Because as it turns out, he doesn't trust us with it either.

Soon after he lands on US soil, he gives his CIA handlers the slip. It happens at a hotel in Virginia. He's taken there by the agents who spirited him out of Europe from under the KGB's nose. Somehow, he manages to smuggle in a powerful tranquilizer with him. Easy enough to do, I suppose. All he would have needed was a small sachet of powder. He slips the two agents a Mickey and by the time they wake up, he's disappeared.

They lose track of him. End of file.

Except that we now know what happened to him.

He lies low, takes menial jobs, and gets himself a fake identity as Leo Sokolov. Marries Daphne. Gets a job teaching at Flushing High. Lives happily ever after. Or should have. Except that, evidently, Leo couldn't keep his inquisitive mind in check. He builds something, whatever it is he's got in his van. Why he would do that – could be for any number of reasons. But regardless, he keeps it a secret. And, as we discovered, it works – which made me wonder if he'd ever tested it. He had to have done that. I made a mental note to look into it.

Somehow, the Russians track him down, all these years later.

I pored over the next JPEGs from Kirby.

The code names of the two agents who smuggled him back from Europe and lost him in Virginia were Reed Corrigan and Frank Fullerton.

Which triggered all kinds of questions in my mind.

Corrigan was the point man on Sokolov all those years ago. Then I get assigned to Sokolov's case.

No need for electromagnetic or other stimuli to prod my paranoia. Was this just a coincidence? Or did Corrigan have anything to do with my being assigned to the murder at Sokolov's apartment? And if so, why?

Was Corrigan still working the Sokolov case?

Was he still after the man who had slipped out of his fingers and most likely caused him all kinds of headaches and embarrassment inside the Company?

Was he playing me? Had he been doing it from the get-go? And if so, why?

Kirby had said the case file was live, and I needed to know if the updates mentioned any activity from Corrigan.

The first entry was dated just over a week ago, a few days before Aparo and I were sent to Sokolov's apartment. It was marked EYES ONLY: DDS&T – a reference to the director of the CIA's Directorate of Science and Technology – and, in cold and urgent prose, it warned that Jericho's current identity and whereabouts had been discovered by the Russians. He'd been conspicuously noisy and rambunctious at a protest outside the Russian consulate in Manhattan. They'd realized who he really was and tracked him down, but the identity he'd been living under was a closely guarded secret and whoever filed the update couldn't get hold of it.

A second update said Moscow had assigned its top SVR agent in New York, Fyodor Yakovlev, to bring Jericho in.

I scanned the reports, looking to see who had authored these updates. It sounded to me like they were written by someone with a solid inside track into the Russian consulate. They could simply have been the result of electronic eavesdropping, but I'd seen such reports and their format would have been different. There'd be all kinds of references on there that these updates didn't have. Alternatively, the updates' author could have a mole inside the consulate. But in that case, I would have expected the mole to be referred to as the source of the information. The third option was that the updates were written by the mole himself. Which meant a CIA agent working inside the consulate – a double agent.

The blood vessels around my eyes pulsed with anticipation as I checked who was credited on the reports, but there was no mention of Corrigan. Instead, the header ascribed them to Grimwood, no first name, reporting to FF – Frank Fullerton, Corrigan's CIA partner back during Sokolov's defection fiasco. 'Grimwood' had to be the agent's code name, which reinforced my mole suspicion. Then I flipped screens and saw that there were further updates. The first one was five days old and related that Yakovlev had died in a fall from Jericho's apartment.

The next one had my name on it.

Well, if not my name, my initials. Because it said that 'FBI SACs SR/NA' (meaning Special Agents in Charge – me, and NA, or Nick Aparo) 'assigned to investigate FY death' (meaning Fyodor Yakovlev).

Then it said something curious.

It stated 'Scene indicates physical struggle with no clarity on how Jericho managed to overpower FY. Unlikely FY would have accepted drugged drink. SR to follow up autopsy tox report.'

SR to follow-up autopsy tox report?

I wasn't sure how many shocks my system could take.

Grimwood had to have been there. In Sokolov's apartment. The morning Aparo and I first showed up, four days ago. The report was written by someone who'd visited the scene. Someone who knew I was going to follow up on the coroner's report. My mind flashed back to the apartment and to who had asked me that. Then to that late meal at J. G. Melon's when it had come up again.

I knew who Grimwood was.

And he wasn't a 'he' at all.

Koschey sat in the Suburban with his engine running and watched as the youths battled it out on the basketball court.

He couldn't hear any of it, of course. The bulky ear protectors were blocking out all the screams and grunts, giving the savage outbreak an eerie and even more surreal tinge.

Given everything he'd seen and done in his life, it took a lot to impress and even shock him, but this did. One minute, they were just a bunch of average neighborhood guys, some with their shirts off, some not, dribbling and blocking and jump-shooting away, all sweaty and committed, letting some steam off. Then Koschey started hitting the presets on the laptop.

The first one was like hitting them with a massive dose of tranquilizer. They slowed down and went all sluggish. Some of them sat, others laid down on the rough concrete of the court. Some wandered around aimlessly with dazed expressions on their faces. They all seemed lost and disoriented.

The second was more graphic. They started retching and throwing up as they hugged their stomachs in pain.

Then he hit the third setting, and they began laying into one another with fists and kicks and anything they could get their hands on.

The speed with which it took effect, the intensity and commitment of the savagery it triggered – it was as if the youths were suddenly facing a desperate life-or-death situation, one in which the only way they could survive was to make sure everyone else was dead.

A sharp knock burst through the ear protectors and startled him. He turned to see a crazed teen with wild eyes and a bloodied nose pounding his side window, shouting wildly, trying to break through the glass and get at him.

It was time to end the test.

Koschey reached over to the open laptop on the seat next to him and struck one of the keys. The kid by his window hammered it a couple more times, then his fist relaxed and he stared at Koschey with a look of utter bewilderment.

Satisfied that it was all working properly, he put his Suburban into gear and pulled away. There was no time to waste. He needed to pick up Sokolov and hit the road.

History was waiting.

60

I had to be sure.

I snatched my phone off the desk and called Larisa.

'Agent Reilly,' she answered, sounding surprised.

'We need to talk.'

She hesitated. 'OK, but – sounds like it's urgent? What's happened?'

I just said, 'Can you come down here?'

'Sure. Where and when?'

Half an hour later, I went downstairs to receive her and took her across the street, to Foley Square, opposite the steps of the State Supreme Court Building.

I dove right into it. 'I know all about Jericho and I know who you are. I've seen your updates in his case file. You've been playing me all along and for what? Just to help you track him down? You could have told me. Things might have turned out differently if I'd known what we were dealing with and how important he is.'

She eyed me with a look of total confusion. 'You're – you've lost me.'

She was definitely good, but I really didn't feel like wasting time. 'OK, you know what?' I pulled out my phone. 'Let's call the consulate. Let me ask your boss there what he thinks. See if he thinks my theory that you're a CIA double agent has any merit. What do you say?'

She was still staring at me like I was a crackpot, but something had changed in her expression. A couple of worry lines had cracked her pristine face.

I just held up my phone with a questioning look. Then I moved to dial the number. 'Here we go.'

She watched me for a second or two – then she lunged for my phone. 'Don't be stupid,' she snapped.

I held the phone out innocently, like, 'What?'

'Hang up, dammit,' she insisted. 'This isn't a joke.'

I put the phone down. 'I never said it was. But you guys seem to love playing games.' I stuffed the phone back in my pocket. 'What the hell's going on?'

She stared at me, her face flaring with annoyance. 'What do you think? We're trying to find Shislenko before he gets shipped back to Moscow.'

Now we were getting somewhere. 'Is that Sokolov's real name?'

'Yes.' She nodded grudgingly. 'Kirill. Kirill Shislenko.'

'And you're one of ours?'

She nodded again.

'Code name?' I had to make sure. 'Grim—'

'Wood,' she completed it pointedly.

She couldn't have known that any other way. Which meant she was working for us. I wasn't sure where her ultimate allegiance lay, of course – who really did, with double agents. But she was on the Agency's payroll and she damn sure didn't want her Russian bosses getting wind of it.

'How'd you find out?' she asked. 'How do you know about Jericho?'

'Confidential sources,' I said tersely. 'So why not let me in on it from day one?'

'You need me to tell you what they'd do to me if the SVR ever found out?'

I didn't need to answer that.

'I can't risk anyone blowing my cover,' she continued. 'It's a very tightly held secret, even inside the Company.'

I guess I could understand that. 'So how'd that happen? What made you come to our side?'

She shrugged. 'It was my plan all along. I never bought into the big lie.'

'What do you mean?'

Her expression took on a distant, steely tinge. 'My father was a diplomat. He was also KGB, and a brute. Both to me and to my mom. But we lived well. We had a privileged life, with nice houses and chauffeurs and all the food we wanted. His being a diplomat meant I got to see the outside world and live in all kinds of places. Beirut, Rome, London. So I also got to see the outside world for what it really was, which was nothing like the lies the Soviet propaganda machine was pumping out when I was a kid. I grew to hate everything my father and the rest of them stood for.'

She paused, gauging my reaction, a little internal debate clearly going on about how much to tell me.

'Then after the Wall came down,' she continued, 'it became even worse. There's this great myth here in the West that the fall of Communism was a people's revolution. Nothing could be further from the truth. I mean, sure, it was a revolution – but the people doing the uprising had no idea who was really pulling the strings and making it all happen. The whole thing was prodded and nursed from within. It was all stage-managed by the KGB.'

'You're saying the KGB helped bring about the downfall of Communism?'

'They didn't just help bring it about. They orchestrated it.'

'Why?'

'Because they didn't have a choice. And because they wanted to get rich. Look, the last guy to rule the Soviet Union was KGB. Our current president-for-life? Also a KGB officer. What does that tell you? Who do you think are the richest people in Russia today? The ones who were running the show before the Wall came down. That's why they were able to plunder the country's natural resources and siphon off these colossal fortunes for themselves. Because, like my father, they were the only ones who were allowed to see what was going on outside our borders. They were the only ones who could travel and read foreign newspapers and see for themselves, and they weren't stupid. They understood that the game was over. They knew Communism was dying. So they prepared for its imminent demise. They set up their own version of democracy, their own version of capitalism.

'People like my father and his friends at the Kremlin partnered with the only people who were doing business under Communism: the black-market bosses, the only people who understood how to actually make money at a time when it was a crime to do so. They all positioned themselves to reap the rewards together when the system collapsed. And they got it right. You think these gangsters were happier before, when a life of privileged luxury meant some crappy Volga limo and a dacha in a remote forest by a frozen lake? Or now, with mansions in London and hundred-million-dollar yachts in Monaco? The collapse of the Soviet Union was the biggest robbery in history. These guys make Al Capone and Don

Corleone look like pickpockets. You think you have a problem with your "one percent"? Come to Moscow. See how our "one percent" live. And how they really make their money.'

'And you want to bring them down?'

She laughed. 'I can't bring them down. No one can. But if I can help turn the tide a little bit, if I can score a small victory here and there ... at least I'll have done something.'

I nodded. I was starting to like her. 'Tell me something. Your people and us, this constant struggle between us. Is it ever going to end?'

'No.' No hesitation there.

'Why?'

She shrugged. 'We will always be jealous of you. Jealous of your economic and industrial success, and frustrated by Russia's lack of it. Look at everything around you. We don't produce anything except for basic natural resources that any third-world country can produce. We don't create anything world-class that we can take pride in. Cars, planes, computers, mobile phones, wine, watches, you name it – we don't make any of those. The only thing we're world leaders in is the creation of spam. Spam, theft, and fraud. That's us.'

'Sounds promising,' I said.

'It's not,' she grumbled. Then the edges of her eyes creased. 'The massacre at Brighton Beach. That was Sokolov, wasn't it?'

'He wasn't there. But it was his handiwork. His machine.'

She asked, 'What is it?'

Which surprised me. 'You don't know?'

'No.'

'Who does?'

'I don't know. Obviously, some people in Moscow must know. The ones who saw his work before he defected. But I don't know if they've shared specifics about it with my boss.'

'What about Langley?' I was dying to throw Frank Fullerton and Reed Corrigan's names at her to see her reaction, but I held back. Referring to them by their code names – the only names I had for them – would be the wrong move at this point.

'I'm sure some people know more than they've told me, but as far as I know, no one really knows what it is or how it works. We just know it's bad.' She paused, then asked, 'What do you think it is?'

I hesitated, unsure about how much to share with her. How much to trust her. But I figured she'd already revealed herself enough to be able to go a bit further.

'He's built some kind of device in his van. I think it has something to do with manipulating the brain using microwaves. But that's about all I've got.' It was time for me to park my Corrigan quest, as I needed her help on something that was far more important – and urgent. 'Who is this "Koschey" we're dealing with? What can you tell me about him?'

'Not much. He's good.'

'That, I know.'

She frowned. 'He's a top FSB agent. A lieutenant colonel. He works alone. Takes his orders straight from the general in Moscow. We're instructed to give him any support he needs if and when he calls.'

'We need to find him if we're going to get Sokolov and his van back. Who's his contact at the consulate?'

'Vrabinek. The consul. But right now, it's a dead end. Koschey hasn't been in touch with him since Wednesday.'

I felt a jab of unease. 'So not since he grabbed Sokolov?'

'Exactly.'

This didn't sound good. 'He could already be gone.'

Her glum look mirrored my sinking feeling. 'Maybe.'

This felt like a total catastrophe. Like we'd only seen the tip of the iceberg with this thing.

Then my phone rang.

And everything changed.

61

I couldn't believe it.

An anonymous tip.

A warehouse out in Jamaica.

Larisa could see something major was going down.

'What?' she asked. 'What's going on?'

I told Aparo I'd meet him at his car and hung up. 'I've got to go.'

'What's happened?'

'I've got to go. I'll call you.'

She reached out and grabbed my arm. 'Talk to me. Don't cut me out. We're on the same side.'

'Oh, so *now* we're on the same side?'

'Come on,' she said, her eyes all fierce. 'I couldn't tell you. And I wouldn't have told you if you hadn't figured it out by yourself. But now that you know, you also know how useful I can be. Let's help each other. Neither of us can afford to let this guy run off with Sokolov or the van.'

I didn't have time for this. Aparo was rushing down to meet me. A dozen SWAT guys were gearing up and getting into their vans. Every second counted.

'Fine. Come with me.'

'What's happened?' she said as she sprinted across the street alongside me.

The warehouse was in a rundown light-industrial zone close to the LIRR station, just south of Liberty Avenue. There wasn't much around in terms of activity – a lot of the warehouses and commercial structures had 'Available for Rent' signposts outside them. It was clearly bust time in the old cycle, and the loading zones around here looked like they'd been hit hard. Which made it a perfect place for someone like Koschey to find himself a quiet little corner from which to sow his mayhem.

The caller's information had been good enough to match up to a particular warehouse, the one we were currently staking out. Me, Aparo, Kanigher, Larisa, and twelve highly trained members of the Bureau's SWAT team. The four of us were all suited up in Kevlar, windbreakers with big letters on the back, earpieces in and weapons out, poised to raid the place. The SWAT guys looked like they were ready to storm hell itself.

A thermal-imaging scan showed only one person in there and no heat signature from a warm car engine. The lone figure was on the ground with his back against the wall and wasn't moving, which meant he had either dozed off or he was tied in place. It didn't guarantee he was alive. At this distance, the FLIR camera couldn't tell us what his temperature was, and the human body didn't cool down that fast.

With nothing else moving in there, we decided to go in.

The SWAT-team leader – Infantino again, from the shoot-out at the docks – led his team in. They battered the door down and streamed in with breathtaking precision and smoothness, like storming a place was an Olympian synchronized sport. We went in right behind them. I heard a lot of 'Clear,' then someone's voice burst through my eardrums and I followed the instructions and cut through the large space to a small office in the back corner and a face that I was very familiar with by then, even though I'd only seen it in photographs.

It was Sokolov, on the floor, his hands tied to a radiator behind him.

He was very much alive.

We freed him and I had him whisked out of there by three of the SWAT guys while the rest of us checked the place out. The van was there, its back doors wide open, only it was empty. And that was it. There was nothing else there.

'He's got to be coming back,' I told the team. 'No way he'd leave Sokolov like this. He's coming back.'

'Then we'd better get ready for him,' Infantino said.

I left Kanigher with the SWAT guys to help set up a perimeter, and Aparo, Larisa, and I set off to talk to Sokolov.

*   *   *

Koschey scowled as he eyed the two parked SWAT vans and the Bureau sedan from a discreet position behind the edge of a building a block away.

So they had Sokolov. And they were lying in wait for his return.

Chyort voz'mi, he cursed inwardly.

He was angry at himself. Livid. He should have taken Sokolov with him on his test run. He'd considered it, but then he'd decided that Sokolov could be a liability, out in the open. The schoolteacher knew Koschey planned to kill him. He knew he had nothing to lose. And people with nothing to lose could do reckless things.

He hadn't wanted to terminate Sokolov either. Certainly not before he was sure that the device still worked properly. He wasn't sure when he'd pull that trigger, if at all. Sokolov could still be useful if he didn't become too much of an encumbrance. But at the moment, that was academic. The scientist was in the hands of the Americans. And there were too many of them there for Koschey to wade in with his guns blazing – assuming Sokolov hadn't already been spirited away to some secure location, which he probably had been.

He watched some more, an unpleasant feeling tugging at his chest – then he thought of the laptop and an idea blew the feeling away. Not just any idea.

A deliciously ironic one.

We found Sokolov huddled in a SWAT support van a block away from the warehouse. Four of Infantino's guys were locked and loaded and watching over him.

He stood up, all jittery and anxious. 'Is Daphne OK? I keep asking and they won't tell me she's OK.'

'She's fine,' I assured him. 'We have her in protective custody till this all blows over.'

I watched as relief flooded his face. 'Does she know you have me? When can I see her?'

'Soon, I promise.'

He was a bundle of nerves. 'Can I at least talk to her? Please?'

'Not just yet,' I had to insist. 'But soon. Just as soon as we have everything well in hand. It's as much about your safety as it is about hers.'

He nodded, his eyes blinking nervously. 'All right,' he mumbled. 'All right.'

He seemed shaken and looked weary and haggard, but at least he was unhurt and in reasonably good shape. We gave him a bottle of electrolyte-rich water, sat him down, and asked him if he needed any medical attention, food, or anything else. He said he was fine. We then quickly went through what he knew about Koschey's current whereabouts. He told us they'd moved 'it' out of the van and into another vehicle, a black SUV. A Chevy, he thought.

I was about to pass that on to Infantino when an urgent sense of foreboding ripped through me. 'Wait,' I asked Sokolov, 'this "thing," your machine – it's in another car and it's operational?'

'Yes ...' He hesitated, unsure as to what I was getting at.

'We've got to get out of here,' I blurted. 'We've got to get everyone out of here. He could use it on us.'

62

I hit my comms mike. 'Alpha One, this is Reilly.'

Infantino's voice burst through my ear. 'I'm here. No sign of him yet.'

'We might have a problem. Get your men ready to pull out. Might have to do it real fast.'

He clearly didn't like this. 'What's going on?'

'Just be ready to do it if I tell you to.' I turned back to Sokolov, thinking this could get really bad in a heartbeat. 'Your machine. It takes over the brain, doesn't it? It can make us turn on each other?'

Confusion and utter horror flushed across his face. 'How do you know? Have you – has someone used it?'

'Yes. Look, I need to know, is there anything that can block it? Is there anything we can do to protect ourselves from it?'

His eyes were darting left and right, his mouth was stammering as he tried to calm himself and focus on my question. 'Yes, there's – I had some ear protectors in the van, but he's got them in his car.'

'Ear protectors?'

'Yes, like earphones. The kind they wear on construction sites. I've modified them, of course. With wire mesh and Kevlar plating.'

My mind was racing. 'So it comes through the ears? Is that how it works?'

'Yes.' He nodded furtively. 'It heats up the inner—' – he caught himself – 'it goes through the ear canals,' he said, conscious of the urgency.

'What about earplugs?' I pulled out my comms piece and showed it to him. 'What about these?'

He turned it over in his fingers and examined it, then shook his head.

'No good. They'll provide a bit of protection, but not much. And that's only if you have them in both ears.'

This wasn't going to work. I couldn't imagine the SWAT guys had enough comms sets for everyone to have two ear buds in anyway.

I could feel the seconds sprinting away. It was maddeningly frustrating. We needed to stay put – this was our one chance to get the bastard – but at the same time, we were sitting ducks.

'What about the helmets?' I asked him, pointing to the SWAT agents in the van with us. They were decked out in drab green fatigues, thick body armor that included a large crotch panel and an FBI patch across the chest, goggles and helmets. 'They're Kevlar,' I told him.

'It's not enough. You need the mesh to break up the microwaves. Think of it like a phone signal. It can get through.' He saw my frown, then added, 'If they're on tight around the ears, they'll offer some protection,' he said. 'But they won't block everything out. I'm sorry.'

It wasn't much, but it was still better than nothing. I turned to the SWAT agent. 'You got any extra helmets or comms units in the vans?'

He shook his head. 'No. We load up in full gear.'

I looked at Aparo, then at Larisa. The three of us, plus Sokolov, were totally unprotected.

The others weren't much better off.

Koschey was back in his SUV, with the open laptop on the seat next to him. He had the engine running, and his finger was hovering over the laptop's keyboard.

Maybe it was time to test Sokolov's machine a second time.

And this time, on a far more deserving audience.

He stared ahead, deep in thought, debating using Sokolov's invention to get the Americans to do his work for him.

All it would take was one tap of his finger to switch it on and turn the whole warehouse area into a kill zone. They'd destroy one another. They'd also kill Sokolov. Which was better than letting them have him.

One tap and it would all be done.

He thought about it for a minute, picturing the scene in his mind, weighing the pros and the cons.

Either way, he needed to act.

* * *

We had to get out of there, and fast. Which meant everyone had to get out. I wasn't leaving Infantino and the others to face it alone.

I thumbed on my comms mike. 'Alpha One. Our guy's got some kind of brain scrambler in his SUV. It comes in through the ears. It'll make us turn our guns on each other. Only protection is to have plugs or comms in both ears and have the helmets strapped on real tight. But it's no guarantee. What do you think?'

It took him a second to process it, then he asked, 'You serious?'

''Fraid so,' I told him. 'Look, we want this guy real bad, you know that, and this is our chance to take him down, but there's no guarantee the helmets will work and if they don't, it's going to turn into a bloodbath.'

'How confident are you about the helmets?' he asked again.

I waved over the SWAT agent closest to me and checked the padding around his ears. It looked pretty tight. And the Kevlar was designed to stop most bullets. But it didn't have the mesh.

I weighed it all up, conscious of the ticking clock in my ears.

I didn't think we were going to get a better chance. But we couldn't all stay.

'All right,' I said. 'I can't force anyone to stay. But I'm staying. Alpha One?'

'You bet,' he said without hesitation.

Aparo said, 'Hang on a sec—'

I cut him off. 'Take the car. Get them both out of here, now,' I said as I motioned to Sokolov and Larisa, then I turned to the SWAT agent. 'Give me your helmet. Take your team and one of the vans and escort them back to Federal Plaza.'

Aparo started with a 'Sean—' but I cut him off again.

'Sokolov's the priority. Get him out of here. And with a bit of luck, we'll take Koschey out too and we can all catch up over a beer later.'

He shook his head at me, but he knew it was the right call.

'Let's go,' he told Sokolov and Larisa.

I took the SWAT agent's helmet and strapped it on tight, then watched as they all mounted up.

Larisa glanced at me for a second before she got in the back of Aparo's car, her eyes clearly telegraphing the concern she felt. I acknowledged her look with a slight nod. She nodded back, hesitated, then climbed in.

The car and the van drove off, leaving me and Infantino's team to face the unknown.

63

It was a really, really weird feeling.

Huddled there behind the Dumpster, looking down the alley toward the warehouse. Keeping a nervous eye on the SWAT agents who were scattered in various positions all around me. Not knowing if something was going to zap us and turn us all into trigger-happy, bloodthirsty zombies.

Waiting there and wondering if my mind was going to be taken over was truly disconcerting. It didn't help that I had all the time in the world to brood on it. My mind was having a field day imagining how it would play out. I wanted to believe I would be above it, that somehow I possessed such strength of character that I would be able to resist it and valiantly rise out of my foxhole and put a bullet right between Koschey's shocked eyes. I found it really hard to accept the idea that, in truth, I would succumb to it as quickly as the next guy, and the notion that something could take hold of me and make me do stuff over which I had zero control was more than unnerving. It was actually terrifying. I knew, there and then, that getting Koschey and making sure no one ever got to use Sokolov's invention again was the most important thing I was ever going to do in this life.

Even worse, another disturbing thought weaseled its way into the quagmire my mind was caught up in. I found myself thinking about Alex, and about how I desperately didn't want him to grow up without a dad. He'd lost his mom already. I had to make sure I was there for him. I'd lost my own dad, in circumstances that weren't any less traumatic than what Alex went through when Michelle died. I was only ten when it happened. I came home from school and walked into my dad's study to find him at his desk, sprawled back in his big chair, and lifeless. Not from some heart attack. He'd stuffed his Smith & Wesson .38 in his mouth and pulled the trigger. In my shocked state, I hadn't turned away. I'd walked up to him in a curious, numbed daze. I'd seen the back of his head missing, the wall behind him splattered with gore, images that would haunt me forever. Alex already had his share of those. I wanted him to have as normal and, well, happy a life from here on as I could possibly provide for him. And part of that included keeping myself in the picture.

I kept Alex's face in mind as time slowed to a crawl and I sat there and waited, wondering if Koschey was going to show up or if I would even be aware of what could be my last moments of life.

Koschey's finger caressed the Command key on the open laptop.

Time was running out. He needed to make a decision.

They were there, in his grasp. At his mercy.

One tap.

He hesitated – then, quietly seething with anger, he decided against it.

He wasn't even sure Sokolov was still there. That was the clincher. And even if he were, Koschey couldn't be sure that the SWAT-team members' protective gear – their helmets and their earpieces – wouldn't dampen the device's effect enough to pose him a threat. If they did, then he'd be putting himself in danger.

He couldn't risk it. He had bigger fish to fry.

Koschey drum-tapped the body of the laptop and settled on his decision. It was a major setback, no doubt, but their having Sokolov wouldn't affect his immediate plans. Nothing Sokolov could tell them would matter. They wouldn't be able to stop him this time. He certainly didn't like the idea of the Americans having Sokolov. They'd know the technology's secrets and its weaknesses. They could get Sokolov to build them a device. But that would take time.

Then he saw something that confirmed he'd made the right call. One of the vans and the unmarked sedan drove off, in tandem. They turned out of the estate down the road from him and set off toward the city.

Sokolov could be riding in one of the vehicles. Well protected. On his way to a serious debrief.

Koschey considered driving after them. Maybe using the device to attack them at a traffic light. Again, he decided against it. Too many unknowns. Too risky.

Getting Sokolov back – or killing him – would have to wait.

Bigger fish to fry, he reminded himself. Time to move on.

With rage pulsating silently through him, he put his car into gear and drove away.

Half an hour or so later, two more SWAT vans arrived. I think I must have dropped a couple of pounds in sweat by then.

They'd brought extra earpieces and helmets with them. And while they deployed and set up a containment perimeter around the warehouse, I left Infantino in charge and got one of the agents to drive me back to Federal Plaza.

I was disappointed that Koschey hadn't shown up, but glad to get the hell out of there. And right then, I was really hoping Sokolov would be able to tell us something useful. And hoping I wouldn't experience those sweats again.

Within twenty minutes, I was in a windowless interview room at Federal Plaza with Aparo, Larisa, and Sokolov.

'No luck with Koschey's SUV,' Aparo told me as I sat down, then motioned at Sokolov. 'He says he had its plates covered the whole time they were working on it.'

I asked, 'Why would Koschey do that?'

Larisa said, 'Plan for the unexpected, especially when it's that easy to do.'

Clearly, the instructors at the SVR knew their stuff.

I shared Aparo's frustration. It was too vague to put out an APB on it, though it was still worth relaying to the SWAT team at the warehouse.

I called Infantino. Then we got down to Sokolov's past and to what 'it' was.

'It all started with my grandfather's memoirs,' Sokolov told us.

He talked about his youth, about finding the old journals in the cellar of the cottage he'd grown up in. He was an efficient storyteller and hadn't dwelled too long on detail, which was good. I could feel a ticking clock bearing down on us all, given that Koschey was still out there, with the device. Sokolov then hit some visible reticence and went silent. We offered him food and drink, which he declined. Then after an uncomfortable moment, he seemed to reach some kind of internal resignation, and he told us what was in the diaries.

64

Misha's Journal

Karovo, Kaluga Province

DECEMBER 1926

It was a night that would long be remembered. The night that would change everything.

Not just for me, but for everyone in the empire.

And to the end of my days, given everything that followed, I shall wonder whether or not I should have stopped it from happening.

That winter, ten years ago, back in 1916, was bleak and harsh. The war against the Germans was raging on, and eleven million of Mother Russia's faithful sons had already been sucked into its bloody embrace. Horrific losses increased by the day, and the army's supply of weapons was virtually depleted. Across the land, there was great hardship and suffering. With food and manpower diverted to the front, there was widespread starvation. The people were angry. Trouble was brewing.

In Petrograd, we were all living on a knife's edge. Rasputin was, as always, oblivious to the danger bubbling around us. His mind was elsewhere, strategizing for our grand intervention at the front. I was playing along while desperately searching for a way out of my quandary.

My old master was, by then, in continual fear for his life, and with good reason. He was loathed by all of Petrograd's society, if not by everyone in the empire. The nobility and the bourgeoisie were outraged at how this sinful peasant had brought shame to the court and how he seemed to control the royal couple as if they were his marionettes. They blamed his meddling for the disastrous mismanagement of the war – it was at his behest that the tsar had relieved Grand Duke Nikolai of his command and taken over the war campaign himself. It was leading to an inevitable revolution that would cause them to lose everything.

It was in that turbulent environment that on a fateful day that December, Rasputin received an unexpected invitation. Prince Felix Yusupov, the young heir to Russia's biggest fortune, wanted Rasputin to join him and some friends at his palace. The Yusupovs were descendants of the Tatar ruler Khan Yusuf and, it was believed, of the Prophet Mohamed himself. The prince's ancestors had ruled over Damascus, Antioch, and Egypt before ending up in Russia at the time of Ivan the Terrible and converting to Christianity a century later. Their palace fronting the Moika Canal, one of many they owned across the empire, was a sprawling edifice that rivaled the Alexander Palace in its grandeur. It had ballrooms, bathing pools, and a private theater where Liszt and Chopin had performed concerts. Much later, I would hear that long after the revolution had wrecked the empire and the Yusupovs had fled Russia on board a British warship, the remains of a corpse were discovered in one of the palace's many hidden rooms. The bones turned out to be those of Felix's great-grandmother's lover. This was a family whose history mirrored that of Russia. On this occasion, it was fated to influence it one final time.

Felix and Rasputin had become more than acquaintances over the last year, but Rasputin had never been to the Moika Palace, nor had he met the prince's wife, Irina, who was the niece of the tsar and was, according to Felix, feeling unwell.

He asked Rasputin if he wouldn't mind treating her while he was there, and offered to send his driver to pick him up.

Irina was young and attractive. I couldn't help but think of the poor woman as yet another lamb being led to the slaughter. But perhaps something else was afoot.

Rasputin knew that Yusupov, as Russia's richest heir and a key member of the nobility, harbored the same hostility toward him as the rest of his enemies. He suspected Yusupov and his friends had other intentions regarding him. Malevolent ones. It was already insulting that the prince couldn't be seen to receive him during the day and had asked that he visit them in the middle of night.

Still, he decided he would go to the meeting. He wanted to know what they were up to.

'We'll use the device,' he told me. 'You will set it up outside the Moika Palace before I go in. And once they're under its effect, I will know what they really have planned for me.'

I harbored the same suspicions, but I had a different plan in mind. I decided I would find out on my own, before he went there.

Not knowing anything about the layout of the palace was going to be a problem. I didn't know where to set up my device, and I didn't want to risk riding out there on the cart with the larger machine, the one we'd used at the mines. The only alternative was to use a coat with the conductors sewn into its sleeves, the one Rasputin had used the first time he treated the tsarevich. It would be more powerful than that earlier version, of course. Many years had passed, and my work had greatly evolved. Still, it was a risk, but one I felt compelled to take.

If nothing else, Rasputin had definitely turned me into an adventurer.

I showed up at the Moika Palace the next day and, reining in my nervousness, I presented myself as the personal envoy of Rasputin and asked to see the prince. Felix, curious as to my presence, agreed to receive me. The liveried Ethiopian manservant led me past rooms of astounding opulence, past a library lined with shelves that held what must have been every book ever written, and down a steep staircase to a charming basement room. It had a vaulted ceiling and was divided into two parts. One was a cozy dining room that had a roaring fireplace. There was a magnificent inlaid ebony cabinet beside it that seemed like it was made up of thousands of tiny mirrors, with a splendid rock-crystal crucifix sitting on it. The other part was a sitting room that had a settee facing a large polar-bear skin. The only windows were small and set high in the wall on one side, just under the ceiling.

Before long, the prince joined me there. He was slim and unprepossessing, his features thinly drawn. He reeked of elegance and of breeding, but I found his manner phlegmatic and rather effeminate. As a youth and during his years at Oxford, he was known to enjoy dressing up in women's clothing and going to nightclubs disguised as such, and I could easily picture him in that attire. Rumors abounded about his liaisons with Grand Duke Dimitry Pavlovich, the tsar's tall, ruggedly handsome young cousin who lived nearby.

Once we were alone, I switched on the device and waited until I felt the prince was under its influence. Then I began by asking him how he felt about Rasputin.

'That scoundrel is the root of all evil and the cause of all our problems,' he hissed, his eyes bulging angrily. 'He is single-handedly responsible for all the misfortunes that have blighted Russia. If he isn't stopped, he's going to bring down the monarchy and bring us down with it. Do you know what he did last month?'

I probably did, but I replied, 'No.'

'He offered to get me a senior posting in the government,' Felix scoffed. 'Me, Prince Felix Yusupov. This illiterate peasant from the armpit of Siberia was offering me a job. In my uncle-in-law's government.'

'What did you reply?' I asked.

'I took on a humbled air and told him I felt I was too young and inexperienced to serve at such a high level, but that I was immeasurably flattered and gratified by the thought that someone as discerning as he had such a lofty opinion of me.' He looked at me in disbelief, then he burst out laughing.

I waited for him to settle down, then I asked him, 'So what is to be done?'

He fixed me with a surprisingly chilling glare and took in a deep breath, then, almost under his breath, he said, 'Only the complete destruction of Rasputin will save Mother Russia. It is the only way to release the tsar from his vile spell and allow him to lead us to a decisive victory against the Germans.'

He then told me what they had planned for Rasputin.

They had chosen the date, December 16, because of something I had forgotten. 'It is,' he said coldly, 'the fifth anniversary of that failed attempt on the depraved scoundrel's life. You remember it, yes? The day that prostitute with no nose stabbed him in Tobolsk.'

I remembered it well. It had been the catalyst to darker times, although I suspect they would have happened with or without the syphilitic whore and her dagger.

I made sure the setting was strong enough so that Felix wouldn't remember our chat, and left him.

I didn't tell Rasputin any of it.

That night, I huddled in the shadows outside the Moika Palace, as Rasputin had asked, awaiting his arrival. But I had no plans to use the machine. I didn't even bring it with me.

It was a mildly cold evening, a few degrees above freezing, and a light, wet snow was falling. At around half past midnight, the canvas-topped motorcar I'd seen earlier returned and pulled into the yard outside the palace. The driver, whom I knew to be Lazovert, the military doctor who was acting as the prince's chauffeur, came out first, dressed in a long coat and an Astrakhan cap with ear flaps on it. He opened the rear door. Prince Felix stepped out first. Then I saw Rasputin emerge, looking regal in his fur coat and his beaver hat.

Rasputin stepped up to the house as if it were his own. What a journey, I thought. What a long way we've come since our days in the austere cells of the monastery at Verkhoturye.

They disappeared into a doorway. I kept watch.

For about an hour, nothing visible happened, not from my vantage point from behind a large hedge. But in my mind's eye, I tried to picture what was happening in that basement. The prince had described their plans to me in great detail. Years later, it would be hard to glean what exactly did take place. Several of the participants have described the event in their published memoirs, but they were all contradictory and, knowing Rasputin as I did, seemed rather fanciful.

What I did know was that Felix would be entertaining Rasputin in the basement dining room. The servants had been told they wouldn't be needed for the night. The other plotters would be waiting upstairs in the prince's study: his friend and lover Grand Duke Dmitry Pavlovich, who had been raised in the tsar's household and loathed Rasputin for all the calamities that had befallen his family; Vladimir Purishkevich, a monarchist member of the Duma who had repeatedly denounced Rasputin; Lieutenant Sukhotin, a soldier who had been wounded in the war and believed Rasputin to be a German spy; Dr. Lazavert, a friend of Purishkevich; and two women: Vera Karalli, a ballerina who was also a lover of the grand duke; and Marianna Pistolkors, Dimitry's stepsister. Felix had not wanted his wife to be there.

I pictured Felix and Rasputin sitting around the table or on the settee, by the bear skin, a log fire crackling in the hearth. Rasputin would have on one of his prized silk shirts, the ones embroidered by the tsarina. It would only inflame the young prince even more. I imagined Felix offering Rasputin the pastries that they had laced with chippings of potassium cyanide, and offering him a glass of wine that they had spiked with a vial of the same poison. They had opted to use poison to avoid the noise from gunshots. A police station stood directly opposite the palace, across the Moika Canal, not fifty meters away. Gunshots in the dead of the night, even inside the palace, would be heard.

I knew Rasputin wouldn't eat the pastries. He still didn't eat sweets. The wine, though, he would happily drink.

And drink he did. But nothing happened. They had prepared four glasses, two of which were laced with the poison. Rasputin downed them, and kept on talking, unaffected. He downed the third glass. Then he smiled at the young prince before his brow darkened around his ice-blue eyes and his face took on a look of terrifying hatred.

'You see,' Rasputin told Felix. 'Whatever you have planned for me, it won't work. You can't hurt me, no matter how hard you try. Now pour me another cup, I'm thirsty. And come sit close to me. We have a lot to discuss.'

Felix was perturbed. Rasputin had drunk all the poison and although he seemed a bit drowsy, he was still as fit as he was when he came in. His fellow plotters upstairs were also getting impatient and rowdy. Rasputin heard the noise and remembered he was also there to treat Irina.

'What's all that noise?' he asked.

'It's Irina and her guests. They're probably leaving. I'll go take a look.'

Felix left Rasputin and hurried up the stairs to his study. He told the others what had happened.

'What should we do?' he asked in a panic, but before anyone could answer, he saw Dimitry's Browning lying on the table and grabbed it.

He went back down to the basement, where he found Rasputin standing by the fireplace and studying the richly inlaid cabinet next to it.

'I like this cabinet,' Rasputin told him.

'I think you'd do better to study the crucifix and pray to it,' the prince told him. Then he raised his gun.

At about half past two, still standing outside, feeling heavy-headed and shivering from the cold, I heard a single gunshot. The detonation roused me like a slap to the face, and I felt my pulse quicken.

Was he dead? Could that possibly be the end of Rasputin? It seemed such an unfitting finish for him. I never imagined he would leave this world in such a prosaic way.

True to form, he wasn't going to disappoint me.

He had fallen heavily onto the bear skin, with Yusupov standing over him, the gun in his hand. The men all rushed downstairs. They moved him off the rug and onto the tiled floor, then left him there, switched off the lights, and went back upstairs to toast their success.

Less than half an hour later, a detachment of police officers walked past my position and knocked at the palace's main entrance. I saw some light spill out onto them as the front door was opened. I couldn't see or hear what was said, but they didn't go inside and left shortly after. Moments later, I saw another car arrive. It stopped near the small footbridge that faced the palace, and four men climbed out of it before it sped away. As they trudged past me in the snow toward the side entrance, I recognized two of them. They were Fyodor and Andrew, the brothers of Felix's wife, Irina. They disappeared inside the house.

Seeing them, I felt a sense of finality. Rasputin had to be dead, surely. Felix must have summoned the young princes to gloat over his achievement and give them a chance to savor the pathetic sight of their dead nemesis before his body was disposed of. I knew Felix would find it hard to keep his mouth shut about what he had done; he would use it to stifle any questions about his manhood and gain some of the respect he desperately sought from his brothers-in-arms in the Corps des Pages.

When Felix led them back down to the basement to show off his prize, they were all stunned to find that Rasputin was still breathing. Not just breathing – he was trying to sit up. The men then all attacked him and beat him mercilessly. I know this, for I heard the commotion and decided to risk a look for myself. I crept up to one of the windows that sat low, just off the ground level of the courtyard, and peered in. It was steamed up from the inside, partly obscuring my view, but I could still see the men – I couldn't count how many – taking turns punching him, kicking him, stabbing him with a candelabra and hitting him with truncheons and bats. I wanted to tear my gaze away, but I couldn't. I managed to catch a glimpse of Rasputin's face when one of them turned him over. One eye had come out of its cavity, and his ear was hanging awkwardly, partly detached from his head. I also saw a large, dark stain on the side of his white shirt, and it confirmed what I'd suspected, that he'd been shot.

Then, mercifully, they stopped. They stood over his supine body, then left the room in a cheerful, uproarious mood.

I took one last look at him before I scurried back to my hiding place, worried they might come out at any moment. But they didn't. In fact, nothing further happened for several hours. I was chilled to the bone and desperate to leave and find some shelter and warmth, but I couldn't tear myself away. Not yet. I needed to see it through to the very end.

With each passing hour, I felt my consciousness wane. It was a struggle to stay awake, but I couldn't let myself fall asleep, not out in that cold. My eyelids now felt like they were made of lead and were inexorably forcing themselves shut when the side door creaked open.

I couldn't believe my eyes. It was Rasputin, on his feet, staggering out of the palace. Impossible, surely – but no, it was him, still alive, still breathing. He wasn't wearing his coat and faltered as he moved across the yard, heading for the gate, his feet plodding heavily in the sloppy, wet snow.

I felt an urge to rush out and help him. We'd been through a lot together, and seeing him wounded like that pained me. But before I could step out of my hiding spot, before he'd even managed ten yards, the door burst open and male silhouettes spilled out into the night, rasping, 'Get him,' and 'He's getting away.' Then I heard two other gunshots and they were on him, pulling him to the ground. One of the men, a man I didn't recognize and who wore a Russian Army gray coat, pulled out a revolver from under his coat and shot Rasputin in the forehead point-blank.

They carried him back inside.

About half an hour later, I watched as another car drove into the courtyard. Several men, their breath coming out in swirling white puffs, emerged from the house carrying Rasputin's body. They stuffed it into the car. Three of the men climbed in, and the car sped off. The whole country would later hear how they drove his body to a bridge and dumped it into the freezing river.

The autopsy on his body would reveal that he was still alive when he hit the water.

Even in death, my old master would continue to mesmerize the country. His death became the stuff of legend: he was poisoned, beaten, and shot several times, and yet he still lived on.

Only a devil could manage that.

It was time for me to disappear.

First, I made sure I destroyed everything. The machine. All my equipment. My notes and my books, all burned.

A whole lifetime of work. Gone.

It had to be done.

Then I left Petrograd and the brewing rebellion and wandered the land for months until I settled here in the Kaluga Province, in a small village called Karovo. It is a remote, idyllic place of birch forests, picturesque bluffs, and lush meadows by the Oka River.

I have found work as a farmer. I masquerade as a barely literate fool with no past and no future.

I plow the soil and keep to myself in the quiet hope that, one day, I will find a way to atone for my sins.

65

I asked Sokolov, 'And your grandfather destroyed the machine?'
'Yes,' he confirmed. 'The machine. All his notes. Everything. All he left behind were the journals.'

I was puzzled. 'So you don't know what it was? How it worked?'

'Not exactly. But there were clues in what he wrote. He mentioned things like it was powered by batteries, then the piezoelectric transducer—'

'Hang on, batteries?' Aparo interrupted. 'We're talking early nineteen hundreds, right? They had batteries back then?'

'Batteries have been around for over two hundred years,' Sokolov said. 'That "Ever Ready" Flash Light my grandfather referred to? The first one came out in 1899. They've even found clay jars in Iraq that are over two thousand years old and that are believed to be primitive electric cells.' He waved it off. 'Anyway, my grandfather also talked about having studied drumbeats and church organs and how they affected us. He said he needed to put wax in his ears when he used it, whereas he was surprised that Rasputin didn't need to, that he had trained himself to be immune to it – which meant its effect came through the ears. He mentioned Heinrich Wilhelm Dove and his "magic." Dove was no magician. He was a Prussian scientist, and it became clear that the magic my grandfather was talking about was actually what Dove had discovered in 1839: binaural beats. All pieces of the puzzle. And gradually, they all fell into place. I figured out how he did it. I suppose part of his hubris couldn't resist leaving some trace of his work, teasing his reader and alluding to his genius.' He dropped his gaze. 'Perhaps we all suffer from it.'

Sokolov told us about his journey, from his local village to the technical school a long bus ride away and on to Leningrad University.

'Manipulating neural circuits was a big priority back then,' Sokolov told us. 'They were recruiting the best minds from universities across the USSR, and I was lucky in that I came to it all at a time when technology was opening up all kinds of possibilities. It was an exciting time. Subliminal messages, inaudible commands, radio-frequency radiation, infrasound, isochronic tones, transcranial magnetic stimulation of specific areas of the brain ... all kinds of new approaches to psychic driving and psycho-correction, all of us looking for the Holy Grail: the ability to influence thoughts, perceptions, emotions, and behavior. To control people from a distance.'

'And you figured it out.'

He nodded. 'When they transferred me from Leningrad University to the KGB's Department of Information-Psychological Actions in 1974, research into microwaves hadn't progressed much beyond attempts to disorient and confuse by aiming a broad range of wavelengths at the subject. That's where I started. And I discovered other frequencies and settings that could do a whole lot more.' He let out a ragged sigh, then said, 'I worked on it for eight years before we finally tested it on human subjects.' He shook his head, visibly pained by the memory. It took him a moment before he could resume his story. 'Mujahedin rebels the Army had captured in Afghanistan. They never knew what hit them. They turned into killers within seconds. We just watched them butcher each other to death. Dozens of them.'

He looked up at me, his eyes imploring for some kind of empathy. I nodded, encouraging him to continue. It was a strange feeling to be sitting there with him. And it was oddly satisfying to finally hear him tell us what had happened, even if his entire story appeared to be filled with death.

'So you defected,' I said. 'Why?'

'All those deaths. It woke me up. Before that, I was naïve. I was too caught up in my own ego, in the science of it, in this extraordinary possibility of controlling people's emotions and desires. My fellow researchers and I, we had these big conversations about what it would mean to create a completely psychocivilized society. It was fascinating and addictive. But I didn't dwell on the fact that it could also program people to kill on command. Then when it happened ... it was a huge shock to me. The implications of what I had invented … And I knew I had to do something. I couldn't let something like that happen again. I couldn't hand it over to them. Not after everything they'd done, everything I knew they were capable of. I mean, they'd just tried to kill the pope. *The pope* … There was nothing they wouldn't do."

'The pope?' My mind rushed back to the attempt on the life of the great Polish pope, back in 1981. 'You mean John Paul?'

Sokolov nodded. 'You know about that, right?'

It was before my time, but I knew that back then, the CIA had its suspicions. His Holiness had become a major problem for the Kremlin. John Paul was known in intelligence circles as a man of indomitable courage. As a priest, in his homeland, he had confronted Nazis, then Communists, and as pope, he was determined to lead his people to freedom. At the time, Brezhnev had been threatening to invade Poland in order to put a lid on the influence of the burgeoning Solidarity movement. John Paul had challenged him on that openly. In August of the previous year, he'd sent the Russian leader a handwritten letter. One single sheet of stationery that bore the papal coat of arms. In it, he told Brezhnev how concerned he was about his homeland. Then the pontiff added something remarkable: he informed Brezhnev that if the Soviets invaded Poland, he would give up the Throne of Saint Peter, abandon the Holy See, and move back to Poland to lead his people in their resistance.

Nine months later, a lone gunman shot and critically wounded the pope in front of a quarter million stunned pilgrims in St. Peter's Square. The shooter, a Turk by the name of Mehmet Ali Ağca, was captured. He was portrayed as a crazed, lone madman. The truth – or, in any case, the intelligence community's suspicion – was somewhat different. He'd been working alongside members of the Bulgarian Secret Service. CIA and Italian intelligence doctors who examined him after the hit found traces of amphetamines in his blood. He had multiple injection bruises on his body. They were convinced he had been medically prepped for what they believed was a mission – essentially, that he'd been brainwashed. A real life *Manchurian Candidate*.

Sokolov nodded ruefully. 'It helped me make up my mind. I couldn't let them have it. I contemplated destroying the device and all my research and killing myself. But I was too cowardly to do it. So I chose to run … after sabotaging it and making sure all my paperwork was destroyed. Without me, they couldn't rebuild it.'

'But you didn't want us to have it either,' I said.

'I decided no one should have it. No one could be trusted with it. No one.' He fixed me with a hard look and asked, 'Do you disagree?'

I held his gaze, then I glanced at Larisa. I couldn't read her look, but I know where my mind was heading on that question. And I hadn't even seen its effects firsthand.

'So you drugged our guys and took off?'

'I brought some powder with me, something we'd developed,' he explained. 'Powerful, tasteless, and harmless. We toasted our success after we arrived here. And I ran. Took on a new name. Got married. And you know the rest.'

'But you couldn't turn off that part of your mind,' Larisa said.

Sokolov rubbed his eyes. He looked weary.

'I tried, of course. I actually managed it for quite a few years. But then I read this article about all the developments in cell technology, and I didn't sleep for a week. It was the ideal delivery system. I needed to know if I could build a more sophisticated version of what I'd built in Moscow.' He looked at us ruefully. 'I had to try. I couldn't help myself.'

'And you stayed below the radar. Until the protest outside the embassy last week,' I said. 'Why did you go there? What made you draw attention to yourself?'

Leo nodded to himself, his face lined with regret. 'After I left, they came down hard on my relatives. I had three brothers. They took them all away, sent them off to work camps. It was years before I found out they had died there, and the only reason I did find out was because one of my brother's sons became a big political activist and they wrote about him and his family in the Western press.'

'Ilya Shislenko was your nephew?' I asked.

Sokolov nodded. 'When they killed him … when they murdered him, it just gutted me. Two of my brothers weren't married, they never had any children. Ilya was my only nephew – as far as I know, anyway. And his death, at their hands … it was too much to take. I lost control.'

'And here we are,' Aparo said.

'Here we are,' Sokolov grumbled softly.

I watched him for a moment. 'So,' I asked, 'how does it work?'

Sokolov took a slug from the bottle of water I had handed him. 'Do you know what entrainment is?'

I told him what I'd only just read.

He nodded thoughtfully. 'Everything we feel, all our emotions, from happiness and elation to depression and aggression,' he said, 'it's all triggered by electrochemical events in our brains.'

Years as a high school science teacher kicked in as he patiently explained how the brain instinctively experiences a variety of strong emotions in response to rhythmic stimulus.

'You've got one hundred billion neurons in the three pounds of flesh between your ears,' he said, 'and they're connected by a hundred trillion synapses. That's a huge network with limitless potential, and we know very little about it. But one thing we do know is that our brains are able to perceive things below our ability to consciously be aware of them or identify them. And that's what I was tapping into to manipulate the neural circuits that govern states like euphoria, trust, fear, anxiety, depression. Even physical side effects like nausea and disorientation. And I discovered that we can effectively and selectively induce them.'

'With microwaves?'

He scrunched his face. 'It's very complicated and, honestly, you'd need PhDs in math and electrical engineering to understand it in any meaningful way. But basically, my discovery was that multiple alternating cavity and dielectric tubes combined with heavily customized magnetrons can create a targeted field of microwaves at stable wavelengths that can be fine-tuned precisely to control the vibrations in the inner ear so as to entrain the brain through its entire range of frequencies.'

This was the 'basically' version.

He shrugged. 'An anthropologist at Yale recently proposed the idea that our susceptibility to entrainment is due to natural selection,' he added. 'Those of our ancestors who could achieve a state in which they didn't feel fear or pain, but were instead united in a collective identity ... they were more likely to survive against grassland predators – and against other tribes.'

'Sounds a lot like Communism,' I remarked. 'And we all know how that turned out.'

Sokolov smiled grimly. Then he added, without a shadow of pride in his voice, 'But this susceptibility to entrainment has a very dark side. My machine can do everything from put you to sleep to make you kill your children.'

A cold nail slid down my spine.

He couldn't have said it any more simply than that.

I could see why everybody wanted him. Having access to that kind of technology – especially if you were the *only* one who possessed it – would give you immeasurable power over both your own people and your enemies.

Aparo asked, 'What about the man who came to your apartment Monday morning? How'd you manage to overpower him? What kind of Jedi mind trick did you use on him?'

Sokolov didn't seem to get the reference. He looked a bit confused, then said, 'I had put some monaural beats on a CD. Basic, but effective. I kept it ready for just that kind of emergency, in case anyone ever came looking for me.'

'What does it do?' Aparo asked.

'It makes you confused. Dizzy. Nauseous. You lose focus. Makes you amenable to suggestion. To answering questions truthfully.'

'But it didn't affect you?' he asked.

'Like I said, it's more basic. Much less potent than what's in the van. I know what it does and how it does it, and I'd trained myself to resist its effect.'

Aparo just said, 'Wow.'

I remembered the neighbor and his suddenly aggressive dog. 'A neighbor said his dog attacked him at around that time. Said it had never happened before.'

'Animals react differently from us. And when they get scared, some of them attack.'

I wondered how many other neighbors had been affected by the brief burst.

'Apart from the earmuffs,' I asked, 'is there any way to protect against what you've got in the van? Anything that can block it?'

'Not really. And if you're too close to it and especially if you're in its direct line of sight, even the ear guards can't block out the more aggressive frequencies. The only way is to be standing behind enough insulation to stop the microwaves from reaching you. We're talking at least an inch of iron or several feet of concrete or even a screen of very fine wire mesh to disrupt the waves. The mesh is actually the most effective, but it has to be very fine to disrupt the wavelength. They use it widely these days to block cell-phone reception.'

Aparo asked, 'What about jamming it? Like with a cell-phone-signal jammer.'

'It might work if the jammer is powerful enough and broad enough to block out all frequencies,' Sokolov said. 'The different settings have different frequencies, so you'd need to kill the full range of signals to make sure nothing gets through.'

'What range are we talking about?' I asked.

'Depends on the power source. In the right conditions, it could reach over half a mile with full line of sight. But ultimately, you could say the range is limitless. Think of how a cell network provides seamless coverage for your cell phone. Theoretically, the same thing could be done with this. If you can get a phone signal, this can reach you too.'

I felt like I'd been dropped on a bed of nails. 'Are you saying you could link it to a network of cell-phone towers?'

He nodded. 'Theoretically, yes. You couldn't just plug my version into one, though. I don't know how network control centers are set up. It would take some figuring out, but, basically, it's doable.'

'Jesus.'

The amount of damage that one psychopath could do with this technology at his command was staggering. You could take out a whole city with it. Maybe even more than that.

I looked at the faces around me and could only state the obvious. 'We need to stop him.'

66

My relentless little nag was kicking and screaming inside my head, insisting we were missing something.

I turned to Larisa. 'Why isn't he in touch with your guys? If only to say "mission accomplished." Why has he gone dark?'

'I don't know,' she said. 'Maybe he doesn't trust our setup at the consulate. Maybe he thinks he can do a better job at getting the device out of the country.'

'Maybe, but … why rebuild it in the SUV once it was dismantled?' I asked. 'Why not document Sokolov taking it apart, film him doing it using any smart phone, then pack it all up in some crates and ship it out? Easier than trying to smuggle a car out with all that stuff in it. And why test it now?' The most obvious answer was troubling. 'He's planning to use it. Here. Soon.' I turned to Sokolov. 'Tell me again. You said he was asking you about range, power.'

Sokolov nodded. 'He wanted to know how strong it was. If it could go through walls or glass, or reach a basement.'

I asked, 'And? Can it?'

Sokolov shrugged. 'It's microwaves. Like I said before, if a phone signal can get through, so can this.'

I didn't like where this was going. It was all sinking in with alarming clarity. 'He's gonna use it. That's why he wanted to set it up in a clean car. That's why he's asking about what it can get through.'

'That's not what he was tasked with,' Larisa said.

'How do you know?'

'Come on. We're not at war. And using something like this, here – that's terrorism. That's an act of war.'

'Maybe he's been tasked by elements within the Kremlin or in the intelligence services who have a different agenda,' I countered. 'Or maybe he's decided to go rogue and work freelance. I can think of several countries and groups who'd love nothing more than to unleash this here. And they'd pay handsomely for it.'

'He's an agent of the state,' she insisted.

'You're saying he can't be bought?'

She didn't have an answer.

'You need to call your people,' I told her. 'Find out if he's still dark. And if he is, let them know what we're thinking. Tell them they need to do all they can to help us shut him down. Warn them about the consequences of him using it. Ask them if they really want to start a war.'

Larisa pulled out her phone and hit her speed dial.

Koschey pulled out of the Hertz lot at Newark Airport in a silver Dodge minivan. Within minutes, he was back on I-95, heading south.

It didn't take him long to move the bulky equipment out of the Suburban and into the people carrier. He'd just told the overworked and harassed car-rental attendant that he needed to swap his stuff over from the old car to the new one, and did so in a quiet corner of the lot without attracting any undue attention. To any passing onlooker, it would have looked like he was a record producer moving some studio gear around, or a computer geek ferrying around some servers.

He'd need to connect the power cable to the engine, but he would do that later. Then he'd do one last test to make sure he'd done it right, but that was easy enough to accomplish.

There would be plenty of potential guinea pigs en route.

Larisa hung up and looked at me, grim-faced.

'Koschey's still dark,' she said. 'No one's heard from him. Not even at the Center.'

'As far as you know,' I remarked.

'My feeling is, there's no plan.'

I asked, 'Would they tell you if there was?'

'I have no way of being sure,' she said.

I fumed. 'If he's gone, there's nothing we can do about it now. But if he's not gone, if he's still around – then my gut says he's planning to use it.' I looked at Larisa. 'You tell me. You really think he's on his own?'

She nodded. 'I do.'

'Then we can worry about the geopolitical implications later. Right now, we need to find him and stop him.'

'How?' Aparo asked. 'What are we going to do? Get Homeland Security to raise the threat level to red and check every black SUV in the country? Assuming he hasn't moved it into some other vehicle?' He turned to Sokolov. 'He can do that, right? Now that you've done it once, he can do it again?'

Sokolov nodded. 'Yes. In fact, that was part of the exercise. To make sure it could be done quickly. Which it can; it's just a matter of putting the right plugs in the right sockets. The only fixed connection to the car is for the power supply, which is just one cable.'

'Which convinces me even more that that's what he's up to,' I said.

I could see the problems we'd be facing in getting other agencies to react to this.

'We have another problem,' I added. 'We'll need to convince the suits that this is real. Which isn't going to be easy.'

'My guys know it's real,' Larisa offered. 'I need to call my handler at Langley. They can help track Koschey down.'

Which brought up another problem. 'Do they know we have Sokolov here?'

'I had to tell them.'

I tightened up. 'I'm amazed they haven't swarmed in here already to take him off our hands.'

'They will,' she said, though her tone didn't seem thrilled at it. 'Any minute now, I imagine.'

My insides were roiling.

I couldn't let that happen. We might need him. And I didn't want him to end up under their roof. But I had more pressing matters to deal with at the moment.

Aparo said, 'The threat's still too vague to act on. We need to hone it down.'

The possibilities I was picturing were endless, and each new one seemed more terrifying to imagine than the last.

'He could use it anywhere,' I said. 'A concert at the Garden. A big sports event in a packed stadium. Rockefeller Center. What are the big events in town this weekend?'

'He could go for Wall Street,' Aparo added. 'The New York Stock Exchange. A hit like that would crash the markets big-time.'

Then I thought that if this was going to be a terror strike, there was a far more crippling set of targets he could go for. 'The Capitol,' I suggested. 'The White House.'

Sokolov's attention perked up. 'He asked me about bulletproof glass,' he said.

'What?'

'He asked me if it could go through it. Something about three-inch glass.'

'Blast-proof. The kind they use in major government buildings in DC,' I said.

I could already see it. A packed session on Capitol Hill – then, out of the blue, senators and congressmen start ripping one another's eyes out with security officers shooting indiscriminately, the whole thing broadcast live on C-SPAN.

Or even worse.

A Secret Service detail going haywire during a press conference on the White House lawn and gunning down everyone in sight, including the president of the United States.

'I need to call someone,' I said. 'We can't just do nothing.'

'Who?' Aparo asked.

I thought about it, then said, 'Everett.'

Will Everett was a SAC at our DC field office and ran its counterterrorism division. We'd known each other for a few years and worked well together. I needed someone with a bit of an imagination for this. Someone who knew me and knew I wasn't prone to flights of fancy. Someone who wouldn't think I was stoned when I told him what was going on.

As I reached for my phone, I wasn't even sure I could be fully open with Everett. I thought it might be better if I sounded him out first. Just let him know something was in play, could be nothing, could be serious. And play it by ear depending on his reaction.

The conversation ended up being much shorter than I anticipated. He was having a busy day. A lot of liaising with the Secret Service and DC police.

The White House Correspondents' Dinner was taking place in less than three hours' time.

67

For a psychopath who was out to strike at the heart of America's identity – an identity defined by freedom of expression, meritocracy, and a free press's access to the highest levels of state – I couldn't think of a more significant target than the White House Correspondents' Dinner. Especially when this target came with guaranteed maximum media exposure.

They call it the nerd prom, hashtag and all, which is appropriate if you consider George Clooney and Sofía Vergara to be nerds. More than two and a half thousand of the nation's most influential people – politicians, Hollywood celebrities, journalists, business leaders, and Supreme Court justices, among others – would be packed into the ballroom of the Washington Hilton for an evening of high-octane glamour that had all the glitz of the Oscars but without the interminable running time, the false modesty, or the embarrassment of cut-short acceptance speeches.

And not even the Oscars could boast the president of the United States as its guest of honor.

The gala had been broadcast live on C-SPAN for years, but in the last few years, with politics in America more polarized than ever and political humor more pointed than ever, it had become a huge mainstream event. Multiple entertainment outlets on television and online would be covering it due to its high-wattage celebrity host and attendees, who were all there as guests of the Association's members.

The more I thought about it, the more I thought this was too potent a target for Koschey to pass up, even at such short notice.

He'd have plenty of other opportunities where the president would be present, of course. Welcoming speeches for foreign dignitaries on the

White House lawn, cultural events at the Kennedy Center, major state functions – there was something big going on every week in the capital. But this one bested them all. Any attack on the president would be disastrous enough, but an attack that struck at the heart of not only the world's press, but of the entertainment industry – and that also hit some of the most outspoken and influential voices in America – would be any terrorist's perfect storm. Not to mention the implicit reprisal it would be for the 2011 dinner, which would always be remembered as part of the narrative that led to the killing, one day later, of bin Laden by SEAL Team Six.

It was tight, but if Koschey was going to do something, this felt like one hell of a night to do it.

'We've got to get down there,' I told them, then turned to Larisa and gestured at Sokolov. 'And he's coming with us.'

She didn't hesitate. 'So am I.'

I wasn't sure about that. I raised a stern finger. 'You can't give your guys a heads-up. I don't have time to lock horns with any welcoming party when we hit DC.'

'There won't be one,' she said. 'You've got my word on that.'

68

I looked out the window of our Bureau chopper and watched, with mounting anxiety, as the Statue of Liberty glided by in the late-afternoon light.

The president was scheduled to arrive at the Hilton in a little over two hours, and we'd be stuck in here and belted to our seats for more than half that time. It didn't help that I knew that Koschey probably already had his plan all sorted out, whereas in our case, I wasn't at all sure how we were going to handle this.

For starters, I couldn't see how my talking to the Secret Service about this was going to work out, even with Everett there as my character reference. What was I going to tell them? 'I have this hunch that there's a clear and present threat from one man, but we have no description, name, or prints to give you. Oh, and he's going to use some kind of microwave transmitter to turn you all into killers and have one of you gun down the president.'

That was going to be a fun conversation.

Not only could I see them not believing me, I could picture them detaining me for questioning, wondering what the hell I was playing at and what motives I had for making such an outlandish claim.

I wasn't even sure we should tell them about what was going on, given that it was all based on a hunch. Then again, we couldn't *not* tell them. Not with what was at stake. Worst case, nothing would happen and they'd think I'm ripe for a pink slip and a straitjacket. Best case, we save the leader of the free world. No contest. But the more I thought it through, the more I realized that we were probably going to be on our own. They weren't going to give it the attention it deserved.

In a perverse way, deep down, I was hoping Koschey would be there, trying to pull this off. Despite the huge risk, despite my fear that the night could turn out to be a disaster of epic proportions for our country, at least we knew what he was up to and had a chance to take him down. If I was wrong and he wasn't going to be there, if he wasn't planning what I thought he was planning, then we would have no idea where or when he, or whoever he delivered the technology to, would surface again and use it. It could be in a day, a week, a year … Could be anywhere. We'd be clueless. And the disaster we would face in that uncertain future would be far more likely to succeed since we would be completely unprepared for it, and because of that, its outcome could be far worse. Far worse because it could also be much bigger. At least at the correspondents' dinner, Koschey wouldn't be able to hook it up to a whole network of cell towers. Or at least I hoped he wouldn't be able to. But that would be a real possibility in the not-too-distant future, as Sokolov had confirmed. Which was another reason I was hoping we'd have a chance to take him down right away.

I glanced across at Sokolov. I felt bad that we hadn't been able to get him together with his wife yet, and it hadn't been easy to calm him down and get him to accept the fact that there was no time for it. All I'd been able to give him was a quick phone call to her just before we got on the chopper. He didn't look any calmer and was busy fiddling with the helmets we'd grabbed from the SWAT desk before getting on board. Our tech lab had also given us what little wire mesh they could get hold of at such short notice, and Sokolov was fitting it inside the Kevlar helmets. For such a sweet old guy, he had created something with truly monstrous potential. It was easy to understand why he pulled his disappearing act on our guys – which got me thinking about Corrigan again. He was one of the agents to whom Sokolov had given the slip. I was dying to ask Sokolov about him. Maybe he could tell me something about him that would help me out. A description, something, even after all these years. But now was not the time. It would have to wait.

I turned away from Sokolov and saw Larisa watching me.

'You all right?' she asked, her voice coming through the headset.

I shrugged. She slid off her headset and gestured for me to take off mine. She obviously wanted to have a private chat, away from Aparo, Sokolov, and the pilot. On choppers, all the headsets are linked to the same radio setup.

She leaned in close and spoke directly into my ear.

'Sokolov saying he didn't think anyone should have it. Where are you on that?' Larisa asked.

I flashed on what her role had been in all this. I turned to her ear. 'Your guys want him. That's why they asked you to shadow me, to keep tabs on the investigation and let them know when to swoop in and take him off our hands.'

She didn't seem that proud of it. 'That was the plan.'

I didn't say anything back and just looked at her.

'That doesn't fit in with your game plan, does it?' she asked.

'Let's just say I've seen the kind of stuff your guys don't have a problem doing, and the idea of Sokolov's baby ending up in their hands doesn't exactly warm me up inside.'

'We do what we have to do,' she said. 'We're fighting many wars. It can get ugly.'

'Yeah, but messing around with a four-year-old kid's brain to flush out some Mexican drug baron. . . that's not war. That's just sick.'

Her face clouded with confusion. I guess she hadn't been privy to my file yet, but from my tone and the way she looked at me, I think she realized that it had been something major for me.

'Am I missing something here?' she asked.

I wondered if Corrigan was still active, if he'd been pulling her strings all along. If he'd got me assigned to Sokolov's case, maybe he'd chosen her, too. Which meant there was a chance that she knew him.

I just said, 'Why don't you ask your boss at Langley about that.' I was going to add, 'And tell him I said I'll be seeing him soon,' but I held back.

It would also have to wait.

69

I checked my watch as we landed at the helipad of the *Washington Post* Building, which was the one nearest to the Hilton. It was already edging past six-fifteen. The president would be arriving in about forty-five minutes.

Everett was waiting for us at the helipad, ready to whisk us up to the Hilton, which was a ten-minute drive away.

'I spoke to the director of the Secret Service,' Everett told me as we set off. 'He didn't exactly embrace this.'

'I didn't think he would,' I replied.

We blew past Dupont Circle and up Connecticut Avenue, but it wasn't long before the traffic hit a standstill. It was wall-to-wall limos, one long stream of Lincoln Town Cars and the like ferrying the glamorous attendees to the big event. Media vans were parked to our left all along Connecticut Avenue, satellite dishes deployed. I flashed at how ideal one of those would be for Koschey and wondered if hooking up Sokolov's machine to those dishes could be done, but based on what Sokolov had said, I discounted it as something Koschey would not have been able to set up this quickly. If anything, this was an opportunistic move on his part. He'd be keeping it simple. Not that it was going to make it any easier to find him.

'Roadblocks and diversions have been up all afternoon,' Everett told us. 'They've got a major red-carpet thing going. It's a zoo. And a big headache for us, especially since we're playing second fiddle.'

I knew what he meant. The dinner had been designated a National Special Security Event by the secretary of Homeland Security. This meant the Secret Service was running the show as lead agency for the design and implementation of the NSSE's operational security plan. They'd be working in partnership with law enforcement and public-safety officials at the local, state, and federal levels, but it was still their show, and they weren't shy about showing it.

Everett badged us through a police roadblock to get onto T Street and we came to a stop behind a big gray Mobile Command truck, about a hundred yards south of the hotel's main entrance.

I glanced at the hotel. It was a huge, sprawling, curved structure, about twelve floors high. It had a '60s vibe going, what with its two semicircular wings and its façade of white rectangular modules. I asked Larisa and Sokolov to wait by Everett's car while Aparo and I followed Everett to where a cluster of senior agents were engaged in heated debate.

As we reached the group, a tall suited agent with short graying hair and seemingly devoid of a single ounce of body fat cocked his head to one side and answered a question, his tone dripping with sarcasm: 'I'm not going to stand around any longer talking hypotheticals. We'll know soon enough whether the feds are wasting our time. I've got things to do.'

He raised his wrist to his mouth – no doubt to issue a stream of instructions – and started to walk away when Everett intercepted him.

'I've got Reilly and his partner here,' he told him, using his thumb to point us out. He turned to me and said, 'Gene Romita,' tilting his head at the director of the Secret Service.

Romita cocked an eyebrow in my direction, then gave me a once-over like I was an attraction at a freak show. Everett shook hands with another one of the men and introduced him to me as Assistant Commissioner Terry Caniff. Caniff was a stocky, gray-bearded man wearing a look of permanent rancor, a look not helped by what Romita had said as we were coming in. I didn't envy him; it can't be easy running the police force in a city where every single military and civilian law-enforcement and intelligence outfit either has its headquarters or a significant operational presence.

'Everett tells me you're playing a hunch,' Romita told me gruffly. 'So tell me what you've got, but make it quick.' He checked his watch. 'POTUS leaves the White House in forty minutes.'

I gave him a brief rundown of what Sokolov had created without getting into the nitty-gritty of how it worked. I then told him about Koschey having it in an undetermined car, and how I thought he might be about to use it.

'That big bust-up at that bar in Brighton Beach,' Aparo added. 'You saw the reports, right?'

He nodded.

'That was it,' he told Romita.

'You know that for a fact?'

I said, 'We came pretty close to getting hold of the van that night. It didn't work out.'

Romita mulled it over for a second, then said, 'Here's my problem, Reilly. I don't know what to make of your story. I don't know if there's some Russian rogue running around with some kind of oversized Buck Rogers stun gun. Fact is, even if that were possible and he was out there, we don't know for a fact that he's coming here, do we?'

'No, we don't.'

He didn't really need my confirmation. 'Look, we take any threat – any threat,' he repeated, emphasizing the 'any,' 'to the president's life very seriously. But we also have to use our better judgment if we're not going to keep him locked up inside the White House twenty-four-seven. 'Cause as you know, we do get threats. And we have to take a view on how credible each threat is. And my problem with this is, there's no credible intel. There's nothing credible about it and nothing to indicate a targeted threat to this event. It's all just based on your hunch. And if I was going to hustle POTUS into his bunker every time someone had a hunch, well, then I'd say those bastards have won. You understand me? They've won if they can get us to run for cover that easily. And I'll be damned if I'm gonna give them or any two-bit terrorist wannabe the satisfaction of knowing they can get the president of the United States to scurry for cover just because they said boo. Show me something credible and I'll lock him down. But it's gonna have be more than a hunch.'

He jabbed a forceful finger in the direction of the hotel behind him. 'We've got this place locked down tight. The entire perimeter is secure from a block away. Nothing comes in or out without our say-so. We've got roadblocks and we've got sharpshooters on the roofs. And you're telling me this guy has some kind of brain zapper that doesn't need line of sight and has an indeterminate range?' He said it like he didn't believe a word of it, which didn't really surprise me. 'So what do you suggest? You want us to keep the president in the bunker permanently until we get this guy? We talking about a week, a month, a year? 'Cause that's what you're saying, isn't it? He could strike anytime, anywhere. From a distance. What do you want me to do, exactly?'

I wasn't sure what I was suggesting anymore.

'I hear you,' I said. 'All I'm saying is, factor it in on the off chance that I am right. Let's make sure we do everything we can and take whatever protective measures are available to us, just in case.'

'Like what? You said this thing can't be blocked out without specialist gear?'

I nodded. 'Get hold of as many ear buds and helmets as you can. Hand them out and tell your men to keep them close at hand. Anything weird starts happening, make sure they put them on as fast as they can. And stay close to POTUS and be ready to evacuate him to the deepest basement in the hotel if it happens.'

I spread my arms like, 'That's all I've got.' Because it was and, realistically, he was right. We couldn't lock down the whole country. And president or not, a strike at an event like this would be devastating, and it wouldn't necessarily be the last we heard of Koschey.

Romita frowned, unhappy with being put on the spot like that. 'You got it.' Then he scoffed. 'I'll also hand out some rolls of aluminum foil. Maybe we can wrap some around our heads for added protection.'

He strode off, remora-like agents in his wake.

Like I said. We were going to be alone on this one.

I glanced at my watch. Half an hour to go.

'We don't have much time,' I told Everett and Caniff. 'Show me the setup.'

70

I followed them into the Mobile Command Center, with Aparo, Larisa, and Sokolov in tow.

A bunch of agents were manning various posts, eyeballing a plethora of screens while communicating with the agents on the ground outside.

'Show me the layout,' I asked Everett.

He got one of his techs to pull up an aerial view of the hotel and its immediate surroundings.

'Is this live?' I asked.

'No,' the tech said. 'We haven't tasked a bird, not for tonight.'

From above, the Washington Hilton looked like a scribbled lowercase 'm,' kind of how Alex would draw a bird in flight. The tips of the wings were aligned just off the east-west axis, with the main entrance at the center of the left-hand concave scoop. Four circular flower beds were arranged asymmetrically on a large oval of grass that formed the center of a turning circle that fed the entrance. The right-hand scoop cupped a sun patio and gardens and provided no access to vehicles. A large pool sat at the end of the eastern wing tip. Screened from its neighbors by a line of trees, a narrow access road ran along the dual convex bulges of the hotel's northern façade.

Everett pointed at the screen and gave me the virtual tour. 'The president's motorcade will drive up the same way we did, up Connecticut. He comes in through the main entrance here, then heads down to the ballroom.'

'Where's the ballroom?' Sokolov asked.

Everett hesitated before answering, but I gave him a slight nod to let him know Sokolov was fine. 'It's in the basement under this area right here,' he said, pointing to the grass oval outside the left wing.

'What do you think?' I asked Sokolov. 'Can it reach there?'

He stared at the screen and shrugged. 'One basement, no building overhead. I'd say yes, if he has it turned on full blast.'

'What about ideal positioning?'

He studied the aerial view. 'Obviously, facing the front would be the most effective. But again, he could put it anywhere.'

Koschey may not have had the same level of technical knowledge as Sokolov – no one did when it came to this – but he was clearly exceptionally clever and had the ability to grasp complex ideas quickly. He was also a highly trained killer. He would be perfectly capable of gauging line of sight in urban terrain, in addition to factoring in multiple variables.

I asked Everett, 'You've got the whole perimeter locked down?'

'We've got roadblocks on all the approach roads. No one gets in but residents and not without having their vehicles checked.'

I looked at the screen. The Hilton had a lot of open space in front of it, which was good as it provided a natural barrier. There was a large building across from it on T Street, behind us. To our left was a Marriott, a building that housed a FedEx office and an apartment building. I pointed at the building opposite the tip of its northwest wing. 'What's that?'

Everett said, 'The Russian Trade Federation.'

I gave Larisa a dubious look.

She pursed her lips. 'He'd have access to it, of course. Then again, he'd be incriminating the Kremlin pretty clearly if he did it from there.'

'Maybe that's what he wants.'

The rest was what looked like apartment buildings, behind the hotel and east of it, between Columbia Road and Nineteenth Street. There was also a big building behind the northeast tip of the hotel that Everett said was a school. It had a basketball court, a playground, and a parking lot for buses.

There were plenty of places someone could park a car and shower the hotel with microwaves.

'And nothing suspicious to report?' I asked Everett. 'Everything's been smooth?'

He nodded. 'Yep.'

I checked my watch. Twenty-five minutes till kick-off.

'All right. Best we can do is run a perimeter sweep on foot and hope I'm wrong.' I turned to Aparo and Larisa. 'Front, northwest corner, northeast corner. Pick your zone.'

'I'll take northwest and the Russian Trade Federation,' Larisa said.

'Front,' Aparo said.

'OK,' I said. 'We need comms and ear buds,' I told Everett. He issued a quick command, and one of his techs hooked us up within seconds.

I held up my helmet and buds to Aparo and Larisa. 'First sign of any discomfort . . .'

They nodded.

I turned to Sokolov. 'Stay here and online in case we need you.' Then I asked Everett, regarding Sokolov, 'You look after my man for me?'

'Go,' he said.

71

With a comms bud in one ear and a helmet and earplug in my hand, I trotted off along T Street, away from the hotel's entrance, leaving the limo parade and the attendant media bustle behind. I had the massive curving façade of the hotel beyond the landscaped green to my left, a tall office building looming over me to my right.

The roads had all been cleared of parked cars, and despite the hubbub behind me, the street ahead had an eerie, empty feel. I passed the office block and banked onto Florida Avenue, where I encountered the first police roadblock. It consisted of two patrol cars blocking the road, with four officers directing the few cars that had ventured this far to turn back. I surveyed the wide intersection, but couldn't see anywhere that Koschey and his vehicle could be lurking, so I kept going.

I turned off Florida onto Nineteenth Street, with the hotel still to my left. Its loading bays were there, underneath the large elevated deck where the pool was. There was a lot of activity there. Catering trucks and other suppliers were parked in the half dozen bays, with a lot of staff milling around. A lot of mouths to feed in there. I was approached by a couple of cops and showed them my creds.

'Anything to report?' I asked them.

'It's all good here,' one of them said.

I checked the bays as I passed them, but I couldn't see anything out of place. There were too many people working the loading area for Koschey to risk using it as his approach.

I got back on the street and advanced north on Nineteenth, the hotel's rear elevation curving away from me. The street was pretty and lined with lush trees. To my right was a series of three- and four-story redbrick town houses and small apartment buildings. No cars parked on Nineteenth, no cars moving, either.

Larisa's voice came through my ear bud. 'Reilly?'

'Where are you?'

'Moving northeast on Columbia,' she said.

I called up the map in my mind's eye. We were moving in parallel up the two angled, intersecting roads that flanked the hotel.

'Trade building clear?' I asked.

'Yes,' she said. 'I spoke to the guard at the gate, in Russian. Everyone left early to avoid the traffic and no one's been in all afternoon.'

'OK. Nick?'

Aparo came in. 'So far, so good.'

'Copy that,' I said.

I was starting to wonder if I'd gotten it wrong, and was uncomfortably conflicted about how I felt about that. Despite all indications to the contrary, my gut said that Koschey was around, and I wanted him to be here. I wanted to take him out of the game and put Sokolov's machine back in its box.

I could hear some sirens in the distance, and glanced at my watch. Five to. The president was about to arrive.

I reached a T intersection, where Vernon Street went off to the right. There was another white squad car parked there, blocking the street, two uniforms beside it talking to a woman and a kid. To my left was the edge of the school, a three-story redbrick structure built on a brick podium with stairs leading up to it. A sign told me it was the Oyster/Adams Bilingual School. It looked deserted.

'Falcon arriving at Roadhouse' a voice announced in my comms. 'Repeat, Falcon arriving.'

Outside the Hilton's entrance, Everett watched as the police squad cars that had been escorting it peeled away on Connecticut Avenue while the rest of the presidential motorcade pulled into the hotel's circular driveway.

Secret Service agents quickly slipped into their positions as the two massive armored Cadillacs rolled to a stop outside the lobby. More agents spilled out of the support vehicles that formed the tail end of the convoy.

Everett's entire body tightened up as he watched the president emerge from his limo. The crowd beyond the cordon clapped and cheered wildly, and the president and his wife, who was there alongside him, waved back and smiled graciously. Everett couldn't stand it. He was on edge, standing there helplessly, willing them to move on, wanting them to head inside despite knowing that they weren't necessarily any safer there.

He saw Romita in the scrum. He was, as always, totally focused, overseeing the president's transfer, issuing crisp orders and asking for updates over the comms. Romita looked his way and their eyes met. Romita was radiating confidence. He acknowledged Everett with a quick nod, like 'Everything's under control.'

Somehow, Everett didn't feel as confident.

My stomach tightened at hearing the Secret Service code names for the president and the hotel. I pictured him getting out of his limo, surrounded by armed agents whose instincts and training had primed them to shoot to kill.

Not ideal. Not in these circumstances.

Aparo's voice came through my ear bud. 'I'm done with my sweep. All clear.'

'OK,' I replied. 'Get back to the command unit. Stick with Sokolov.'

'Roger that.'

Two possible angles of attack left. Larisa's side. And mine.

I went up to the cops with my creds out.

'Everything okay here?' I asked.

'Nothing to report,' one of them said.

'No one's gone through,' I asked. 'No black Suburbans or some other SUV in the last couple of hours?'

The other cop laughed. 'Black Suburbans? You kidding me? That's all you see around here.'

I felt a flush of worry. 'You let any through?' I asked.

They glanced at each other questioningly, then shook their heads. 'Nope. A couple of locals, family cars, no SUVs though.'

'Okay.' Then I added, 'Stay sharp,' somewhat pointlessly.

I started to head off when I heard the woman say, 'Well, make sure you let me know if you need any more pills or if I can get you a cup of hot soup or something.'

I don't know why, but that made me stop in my tracks.

I turned to hear the cop reply, 'We'll be fine, but thank you. Very kind of you.'

I approached them again. 'I'm sorry, what was that about?'

They looked at me curiously.

'The pills? The soup? You feeling okay?'

They all did a double-take, like this was such a weird query.

'Talk to me,' I prodded.

'We're fine,' the cop said. 'It's just, maybe an hour ago. We both had a dizzy spell.'

'Nauseous,' the other cop added. 'Felt like my head was going to cave in.'

'I think you boys have been standing out here too long without anything to drink,' the woman said. 'And you too, young man,' she added, addressing her son. She looked up at me. 'Sammy here fell off his bike earlier.'

'Mom,' the boy groaned, like she was embarrassing him.

My mind was hurtling elsewhere. 'When was this, you said? An hour ago?'

'Around then,' one of the cops said.

'Any cars drive by at the time?' I asked, my pulse rocketing.

'I can't remember,' he said. 'We were both kind of out of it. Not for long, but—'

'Didn't that minivan drive past then?'

'I can't remember.' He smiled sheepishly at me. 'I was busy trying to hold it together.'

My whole body went rigid. I turned away from the cops and hit my comms. 'Leo, you there?' I hissed. 'Leo.'

It took a couple of seconds, then his voice burst back. 'Reilly?'

'Leo, that thing you used on the Russian at your apartment, when he came for you. You said it fogged his mind and made him feel sick? Can the machine in your van also do that?'

'Yes,' he said. 'There are five different presets I've programmed into the control screen on the laptop. One of them is that one.'

My heart was like a battering ram in my rib cage. 'Did you tell Koschey about the different settings? Does he know what they are?'

'Yes,' Sokolov said.

I was already sprinting away from the cops, heading up Nineteenth, my fingers tight against the helmet.

'He's here,' I blurted into my mike. 'Nick, you copy? Koschey is here and he's gonna use it.'

72

I charged up Nineteenth, my eyes scrutinizing every parking bay and every driveway, but I already had an idea of where he'd be.

It was Everett's voice that burst into my ear. 'Can you see him? Do you have confirmation?'

'No,' I fired back. 'But he's here. He used it to get past one of your roadblocks on Nineteenth Street.'

'Where? Are you sure?'

It was pointless. I knew Romita wouldn't act based solely on my assumption. Besides, maybe it was too late. There wasn't much they could do. Rushing the president back out of there might expose him to even more danger, what with the heightened tension around him and the agents' readiness to draw weapons and fire.

I brought up my wrist mike. 'Nick. Where are you?'

'Just got to the command unit,' he replied. 'I'm with Sokolov.'

'Find Everett. Help him convince Romita this is real. They need to get POTUS to safety.'

'Got it.'

I found the entrance to the school's parking lot tucked away by the far side of the building, in a gap between some trees. I crossed the street and tucked into it.

He was here. He was definitely here.

Moving briskly, I shoved the extra ear bud into my ear before slipping on the helmet and strapping it on tightly. Then I pulled out my Hi-Power, flicked the safety off, and chambered a round.

I was hugging the building, focused on the open area beyond the alley that sat directly behind the hotel. I could see some parked school buses at the far end of the lot, to my right. I couldn't see what was beyond the building, to my left, the area that backed up to the rear of the Hilton.

Everett's voice came back in my ear.

'Reilly. The president is inside. I repeat, the president is inside. All federal agents are maintaining the perimeter. Romita is inside and coordinating from the ballroom.'

'Copy that,' I said, low, into my mike.

'Do you have confirmation yet?'

'No,' I replied tersely. 'But it might be too late by the time I do.'

'Standing by,' was all he came back with.

Dammit.

I crept up to the corner of the building and looked out. There was a playground to my left. It led to the basketball court. Then on the far side, right at the edge of the property, by the wall of a low-rise apartment complex, I saw a silver minivan. It was facing the buses, its tail end facing the rear of the hotel.

Its rear door was slung upward, wide open.

I could also see a silhouette in the driver's seat.

Koschey.

A deathly quiet had descended on the area around me while my comms bud was crackling with rapid-fire chatter of agents reporting positions and statuses.

'Everett,' I rasped into my mike. 'I can see him. He's here. Do you have POTUS locked down?'

'Hang on,' Aparo replied. 'He's with Romita.'

I pictured Everett arguing with the director of the Secret Service while the president and his guests were having a whale of a time as the proceedings got under way, none of them having a clue that they were only a hair's-breadth from being turned into murderers, from having their humanity stripped away and being turned into nothing but instinctual beasts waging close-quarter warfare until the last man was left standing.

'Everett, get him locked down, goddammit,' I hissed. 'Get those helmets on.'

'I'm trying,' Everett shot back.

I quickly ran through my options. There was about forty yards of open terrain between me and the minivan. Too far to score a hit, too wide an area to cross. Koschey would take me out before I got halfway there.

I had to try it.

I leaned out, scoping the terrain, picking out potential cover I could use on the way. Then I saw Koschey's hand edge out of the car's side window and, almost instantly, a bullet punched into the brick wall inches from my face, spraying debris all around me.

I sprang out and put three quick rounds in his windshield and ducked back into cover—

Then I felt something happening inside my head.

73

At first, it was like an electric pulse had danced across the inside of my skull, like a tiny Taser had reached in and tapped my eardrums and gone in deeper. Then I started to feel dizzy and I felt my eyes going in and out of focus.

Koschey had switched it on, and I was too close to it.

Sokolov's makeshift protection wasn't blocking it all out.

Koschey wasn't shooting back, nor was he coming for me. I knew he was in no rush. He assumed I'd soon be under the effect of the device. It would make me mad with rage, irrationally aggressive. And in my crazed state, I wouldn't be thinking tactically. I'd just break cover and rush him mindlessly – literally – and he'd be able to pick me off without even looking while the Hilton ballroom would be turning into a shooting gallery, with the president on the podium being the grand prize.

I had to focus. Concentrate. Try to block it out. But I couldn't. It was the weirdest feeling. I could feel my consciousness draining away, Sokolov's waves just choking it out of me.

In a matter of seconds, I'd be under its spell.

At the edge of the Hilton's ballroom, Aparo felt the discomfort in his ears as he clutched his helmet and watched the intense argument going on between Everett and Romita.

Reilly was right, he thought. It was happening.

He scanned left and right, his mind racing, desperate for a way to stop the inevitable. He knew Romita would be a hard-ass, knew Everett would have a tough time getting him to do what he needed to do – and even if he did, the odds were against them. The killer signal would still, in all likelihood, get through.

He needed something else and he needed it fast, otherwise he and everyone else around him would soon be dead.

He had to help Reilly. That was the only thing he could do. Help him take down Koschey.

He ran up the stairs and out the lobby and was about to radio Reilly to find out the quickest way there when he spotted something he'd missed.

A black Chevy Suburban, part of the presidential motorcade, just behind the two Cadillacs.

Not just any Suburban.

This one had two big collinear antennas mounted on its roof.

Aparo dashed toward it.

I could sense an anger swelling up inside me, a primal anger at nothing specific, and yet everything at the same time. I was desperate to block it out, desperate to do anything to keep control of my senses, but I was helpless and could only wait for control over my mind to be ripped away from me.

I didn't dare think of what might be happening in the ballroom.

I forced myself to focus on the situation again, my besieged mind racing for a solution. I couldn't charge him, not given how good a shot he was, not given his tactical advantage. He was manning his fort, and I was a foot soldier looking to charge across the trenches. Never a winning strategy. I needed something else. Something to bridge that advantage gap.

I scanned around, seconds flying past.

The buses. Sitting there about thirty yards away from me.

There was a low wall separating the parking lot from the playground, around halfway to the buses. I figured I could break the journey in half by taking cover there.

I also heard some shots fired from beyond, along with a solitary shout. Then another. The microwaves were starting to have an effect.

It was time to stop thinking and just move.

I sprang to my feet and darted across the open asphalt, shooting for cover before slamming into the side of the wall and crouching low. I caught my breath and was about to cover the second leg when several bullets slammed into the wall around me. They weren't coming from Koschey. Confused, I spun and raised my gun, panning across to where I thought they'd come from. And I saw Larisa coming up the driveway from the street, gun raised, advancing toward me – and still firing.

She was wearing her helmet, but it wasn't doing its job. Sokolov's hasty efforts in the chopper were obviously not keeping the signal out, not as well as mine was. Either that or she just wanted to kill me.

'What are you doing?' I yelled out.

She kept firing. A bullet scraped my arm, sending a jolt of pain up through my shoulder as she loosed two more shots.

I stared at Larisa, had her in my sights – something inside me wanted to kill her, right there and then. I wanted to blast her to bits, to empty my whole clip at her, and it took all the resolve and willpower I could muster to resist pulling the trigger. She had a blank expression, like she was in a daze. It had to be the signal, and I couldn't just cut her down.

Worse, she would soon be in open ground and in Koschey's sights.

I fired at her feet, hoping to stop her, to get her to stay behind the wall. But she didn't react, didn't go for cover. It was like she'd lost the ability to defend herself. Rage superseded everything else. All she could think of, all she was programmed to do at that moment, was to kill.

I couldn't wait any longer. I had to kill the machine.

Repeating this thought over and over in my head and using it as a mantra to try to keep control over my consciousness, I raised my gun and emptied the clip toward Koschey as I dashed toward the nearest bus.

I kept mouthing it to myself as I pulled the driver's door open and jumped in, hoping Larisa was still standing. More rounds drilled into the side of the bus, which told me that Koschey hadn't hit her. I tucked my weapon into my waist and yanked the ignition wiring out from under the dashboard, immensely grateful for old-school buses and their antiquated, easily hot-wireable electrics.

Three seconds later, the big diesel engine in the back grumbled to life.

'Kill the machine. Kill the machine.' I was shouting it now.

I glanced out the side window. Koschey's Dodge minivan was lined up almost directly behind me.

Now or never.

I slammed it into reverse and floored the pedal.

The big bus lurched backward and shot across the lot, its engine whining like a wounded beast. I made a couple of micro-adjustments with the steering wheel before bracing myself just as the yellow mammoth plowed into the minivan. It kept going, pushing it through the mesh fencing around the basketball court before crushing it against the side of the school building in an earsplitting crunch of metal against brick.

Then it all went quiet.

I drew my weapon and pulled the helmet off my head. Waited for a second.

No buzzing, no internal Taser sensation. Nothing.

I scrambled around to the back of the bus. The minivan was all mangled up and accordioned against the side of the building. The front section was crushed right in past the front seats.

Koschey wasn't in there.

I heard a rustle behind me and spun to face it, but before I made it around, I heard three quick, successive rounds that whipped the air and shattered the serenity of the empty school grounds.

The side of Koschey's skull erupted outward and he collapsed onto the asphalt of the basketball court. And at the edge of the open ground, Larisa was standing in full shooting stance, her gun still held tight in front of her in a straight-armed, two-fisted grip.

It was aimed right at me.

I leveled my gun at her, unsure as to whether she had fully regained her senses. I wouldn't get a chance to fire if she took the first shot – she seemed to be a decent-enough shot to take me down with her first pull. But I couldn't fire first. She'd just saved my life. I just stood there, with every tendon in my body taut to breaking point, sweat gushing out of every pore in my face, staring down the barrel of my gun at the one that was facing me, wondering if a bullet would come whipping out of there and punch a hole into me, trying to gauge her expression, hoping I'd get a split second of a heads-up before she pulled that trigger and blew my skull to pieces.

Each second felt like it stretched forever. I could hear my own pulse pounding away between my ears, each thump taking an agonizing eternity before ushering in the next.

She just stood there, rigid, a stalled killing machine – but she didn't fire. She finally lowered her gun and I saw her face all scrunched-up with confusion.

She looked around, then, slowly, walked over to me. 'What happened?'

I smiled. 'You saved my life,' I told her.

'But ... what about ... ?' She was staring at the wound on my arm, still foggy-brained but wondering, like maybe some part of her memory had registered that.

'It's over,' I told her.

I sucked in a deep breath. Larisa took off her helmet.

We wandered over to where Koschey had fallen. He was dead, two to the chest and one to the head. Larisa was definitely a good shot, and Koschey's soul – if he ever had one – was taking the slow train to an eternal sentence at a Siberian gulag.

'Nick,' I said into my comms mike. 'It's done. Koschey's dead. We're clear.'

Nothing came back.

'Nick. Come in.' Nothing. 'Everett? Anyone?'

Nothing.

I looked at Larisa. She seemed as spooked as I was.

I had a really bad feeling about this.

We stood there for a minute, in silence. Wondering about what had happened. I tried to raise them again, but the radio was still dead.

Then I heard loud footfalls coming our way. I tensed up, swung my gun up and aimed it at the edge of the wall, waiting to see who was going to show up. They couldn't still be under the machine's effect now that it was in pieces. But for a split second, I found myself wondering if its effects lingered even after it was turned off.

Then I saw Aparo appear from behind the corner, rushing toward us, with Everett close behind. They had their guns out.

I leveled my gun at them – then Aparo shouted, 'Sean, whoa, it's us. It's us.'

I hesitated, then brought my gun down.

'What happened, man?' he asked as he reached us and took in the crashed bus and the squashed minivan.

I said, 'He's dead. It's over.'

He slapped me on the back. 'Glad to see you're still in one piece, buddy.' Then he smiled at Larisa. 'You too.' Then he added, with a grin, 'Even more so.'

I swallowed hard, then I asked, 'What about POTUS? Is he OK?'

'Yeah, he's fine,' Aparo confirmed, laconic as always. 'Confused, but fine. They've got him locked down in some storage room in the basement.'

I breathed out with relief and for the first time in days, I felt my entire body unclench itself.

'What about everyone else?'

Everett said, 'We had some punch-ups and four agents outside took bullets to their vests, but they're OK.'

Which, if true, was a much better outcome than I expected. 'So the signal didn't make it into the ballroom?'

'Oh, it did,' Aparo said. 'We heard the shots over our comms and we felt it all right, but before anyone inside was affected enough to pull any weapon, I came up with a Buck Rogers trick of my own.'

I was lost. 'Come again?'

'The electronic countermeasures van,' Aparo said, beaming. 'I don't know if it did the trick or not, but I got them to switch on every jammer they had full-blast when it all started to go weird.'

I smiled with relief and nodded to myself, feeling exhausted. A key component of the presidential motorcade was a Chevy Suburban that was used to counter any remotely controlled attack. It had powerful barrage jamming equipment on board that was designed to kill any kind of phone, radio, or electromagnetic signal in order to block any remotely controlled bomb threat.

'And Sokolov?' I asked.

'He's fine. The guys in the command unit didn't really feel anything. Might have something to do with the amount of electronics they have in there,' Aparo said.

'I'm guessing we're all staring down the barrel of a week-long debrief, at best,' Everett chortled.

'I can't wait,' I told him, pulling my ear bud out.

There was something I needed to check.

'Give me a sec,' I said. Then I glanced at Larisa. She understood.

I headed back to the crushed minivan. Larisa followed.

It was battered beyond recognition. Front to back, it couldn't have been more than six feet long. I walked around to the back of it, which had slammed into the brick wall. Among the twisted debris, I could see various electrical components, all busted up. Like someone had chucked a stereo from a fifth-floor window.

Still, I didn't want to take any chances.

I pulled back a couple of bent panels and climbed into the wreckage. I found three components that didn't look completely damaged. They were the size of stereo amps. I also found the laptop, closer to what used to be the front of the minivan. It didn't look as badly broken as the rest. A small travel case was also relatively unscathed. I pulled it out and opened it. I found some clothing and men's grooming items inside it. I also found a hidden compartment in which Koschey had stashed several passports and credit cards as well as a decent bundle of hundred-dollar bills.

I set the three components down on the asphalt, then I looked around until I found a more-or-less whole brick that had come off the wall.

I looked at Larisa. 'You okay with this?'

She studied me, then nodded. 'Seems like the reasonable thing to do.'

I raised my arm and battered them with the brick until they were unrecognizable. Then I tossed the components back into the wreck.

I picked up the laptop. 'I'll need to dispose of this properly.'

'What about Sokolov?' she asked.

'Yeah,' I said. 'Might need your help on that.'

74

There was nothing I wanted more just then than to be back home with some Joss Stone in the background, a cold beer on the nightstand, and a warm Tess in my arms. But that would have to wait.

There was a monster issue I needed to sort out first, and it had to be done quickly and carefully if it wasn't going to get me trussed up in an orange jumpsuit and thrown into a dingy cell.

I needed help, but not just anyone's help. This had to be someone I could trust implicitly. Someone who had the resources and the strength of character to make the impossible happen. Because what I needed was the impossible.

My monster issue was called Leo Sokolov. Or Kirill Shislenko, take your pick. Either one led to the same headache.

There were only three options. One was for him to die. That was one way to guarantee that his horrific discovery wouldn't rise out of the carnage of the Oyster/Adams Bilingual School's playground and unfurl its cloak of pain and suffering again. Inconveniently, Leo had survived this whole debacle, and I didn't really have it in me to put a bullet in his head. Plus, I'd grown to like the guy in the short time we'd spent together. Yes, he had blood on his hands. But I didn't think he deserved the gas chamber or a 115 grain jacketed hollow-point slug penetrating his brain at 1,300 feet per second.

Option two was to hand him over to Larisa's people at the CIA. He'd be well looked after. They'd probably sort out a wonderful life for him as a member of one of their protection programs. Slight hitch, though. Remember what I said a few seconds ago about that nasty cloak of pain?

Option two pretty much guaranteed that Leo's machine would be reborn – bigger and nastier, too, no doubt. And I didn't think I could ever forgive myself for unleashing that on the world in which Kim and Alex would grow up. It was already screwed-up enough as it is.

Option three was for him to disappear. I liked that option. It also felt like the fairer one to Daphne, who hadn't really deserved any of what she'd been through so far. Problem was, if Leo was going to disappear, he had to really disappear. I mean, disappear disappear. Never-to-be-heard-from-again disappear. And that, as Osama bin Laden and countless others would testify if they were still around, was pretty tough to pull off.

But I thought I knew one man who could help me make it happen.

We'd avoided the post-event briefings and flown the coop, taking the chopper right back to New York City, the four of us – me, Aparo, Larisa, and Leo. It was around ten o'clock by the time we landed at the East Thirty-Fourth Street heliport. Aparo's charger was there, where we'd left it. But what I was going to do next, I need to do alone. For Aparo's sake, and for Larisa's.

'You guys know what to do?' I asked.

They both nodded.

Leo went up to them and thanked them warmly. Then it was time to go.

'I'll see you in the morning,' I told them, then looked at Aparo. 'You gonna be able to keep Miss Tchoumitcheva here entertained until then?'

I could almost see his blood pressure rise as he struggled with a controlled grin. It was like waving a red rag to a bull.

Larisa sidled up to me.

'You sure you want to do this alone? You still don't trust me?' she asked. Then before I could formulate an answer, she leaned in and kissed me on the cheek. 'I love watching you squirm,' she said. Then she nodded at Aparo, turned, and walked away. He followed her, flicking me a wave of his hand.

Leo and I got in the charger. We bypassed Federal Plaza completely and drove straight across to Brooklyn and then to the 114th Precinct in Astoria, where we sprang Daphne with minimal obstruction from the overworked and underpaid desk sergeant.

Seeing Leo and Daphne hug each other tearfully only confirmed my feeling that these two deserved to be left alone to enjoy the rest of their lives together. Whether we'd get away with it – that was another matter. But it seemed like a gamble worth taking. And like I said, options one and two – not really options at all.

Next came the hard part. Where to stash them.

I explained it all to Daphne. How if we went ahead with this, she would never, ever be able to communicate with anyone in her family again. Not her sister, who she was close to. No one. We'd let the sister know they were OK. But that break would have to be final. That was the only strictly non-negotiable condition she had to accept.

It's never an easy one for anyone to accept. But after some painful moments when it finally sank in, she said she would do it.

I knew she would.

That time of night, and with my lights spinning, we made it to the Canadian border in five hours.

We talked a lot on the drive up. I got to listen to Leo tell Daphne his whole amazing story. Daphne was in turns stunned, fascinated, shocked, but to her credit, she took it all well, considering. He'd had quite a life, by any standard. I was glad that the worst part of it would soon be over.

I asked him about Corrigan, of course. He couldn't give me much more than a general physical description, which was pretty broad – no one-armed distinctive trait for me – and thirty years out of date. It killed me that I couldn't sit him down with a sketch artist back at the office and get him to draw up a portrait of my ghost, which we could then age appropriately using our software. I couldn't use the Bureau's resources on this, nor was there time for that. I had to make Leo and Daphne disappear quickly, before anyone noticed they were gone.

We hit the border, and I was able to badge my way through. A few minutes later, we were in the parking lot of the Best Western at Saint-Bernard-de-Lacolle.

True to his promise, Cardinal Mauro's people were waiting for us there.

I didn't want to know where the Church would hide them. It was safer that way for everyone. What I knew, though, was that the Vatican would ensure the Sokolovs' safety. They'd be fine. Mauro assured me of that. As the Vatican's secretary of state, basically the pope's right-hand man, he had the power to make pretty much anything happen. And I knew he'd be true to his word. We've been through a couple of seriously intense experiences over the last few years, both related to Templar secrets, the most recent of which was a couple of years ago, when Tess had been kidnapped. He owed me, I owed him. We helped each other out.

Daphne gave me a long, tight hug, Greek-style. I loved every second of it.

'*Efkharisto poly,*' she said into my ear, thanking me. 'You'll be in my prayers, always.'

I reached into my jacket's inside pocket and pulled out the wad of cash I'd found in Koschey's bag, and handed it to Sokolov. 'Take this. It might come in handy.'

He flushed, then nodded. He reached out and gave me a firm, warm handshake, cupping my hand in both of his – then he pulled me in for a big bear hug himself.

'Thank you,' he said, not letting go. 'Truly.'

I nodded.

He paused and studied me for a moment, as if deciding whether or not to say anything. Then he said, 'You know, your people are researching this too. Who knows? Maybe they've already figured it out.'

'God, I hope not,' I told him.

'They could already be using it in ways you can't imagine,' he added. 'The thing is … this is going to be the century of the mind. The technology's finally here for it. And these discoveries … they'll have the ability to either free us to explore our minds and reach higher potentials that we never dreamed about – or they're going to enslave us. And it's going to be very tough to explore the first without opening the door to the second. I wish you the best of luck in keeping that door firmly shut.'

'I think we're going to need it,' I smiled. Then I watched them get into the car and disappear into the early dawn.

75

By the time I caught up with Aparo and Larisa at the French bistro in Chelsea, it was almost noon and they looked wrecked.

Which was the idea.

We'd be showing up at Federal Plaza sometime soon, looking like someone had slipped us some serious mickeys. Which is what we needed everyone to believe. After all, we would have allowed one of the government's most wanted prizes to slip through our fingers, and if we were going to hang on to our careers and avoid prosecution, we needed to have a solid story. One that we all agreed upon and would be able to give individually without being caught out.

It wouldn't be too difficult. It was an easy tale to tell. After all, Sokolov had done it before. And there was no reason for us to know about it.

Predictably, the debriefs took a while, but it was all handled without too much aggravation. Sure, they were pissed off that he'd gotten away. FBI, CIA, you name it. But then again, the president was alive and well, and he wanted to meet us personally to thank us for what we'd done, which helped. A lot.

I managed to extricate myself from that first session at around seven and was home in Mamaroneck about an hour later. It felt great to be back and even greater to have Tess in my arms.

I polished off the leftover roasted chicken she'd made for dinner and we both had a laugh watching Alex and Kim taking Super Mario through space on the Wii, then we all hit the sack. I was exhausted and couldn't remember the last time I'd had a solid stretch of sleep. My body demanded a respite, and it was finally going to get it.

I showered and was on the bed putting my phone on its charger when I remembered something. I'd never gotten around to reading the third Corrigan file that Kirby had sent me. The JPEGs were still sitting in my message inbox.

The lure was stronger than my exhaustion. I couldn't resist a peek.

I padded into the study, downloaded the files, and pulled up the first image.

The file was massively redacted. There were more lines blacked-out than there were unmarked. It was about an assignment code named Operation Cold Burn and was marked SCI – sensitive compartmented information. It involved something called Project Azorian. In my tired state, I just skimmed past it and cast a weary glance on the page before clicking on to the next page, also heavily redacted, then the next one that was just as mutilated.

I was about to switch it off and head back to bed when two unredacted letters on the page caught my eye. CR. Something inside me flinched, something at the very edge of my consciousness, a minute stab of recognition.

CR.

Could be anything, normally. Except that in this case, the two anodyne letters weren't just anything. And it was because of the context. It was because of the word I'd passed over lethargically only moments earlier. Azorian.

It was a word I'd seen before. And in that instant, prompted by the two letters, I remembered where I'd seen it. And heard it. And asked about it.

It was a long time ago. Back when I was ten years old.

I'd seen it on CR's desk. Heard him say it. And when I'd asked about it, he'd said it was someone he worked with who had a silly name, a name they'd laughed about at work. The Mighty Azorian. We'd joked about it before he brushed it away and we moved on to something else.

CR was Colin Reilly.

My dad.

The dad I had walked in on all those years ago, when I was ten, to find him at his desk, slumped in his chair, with a gun on the floor by his side and a wall of blood splatter behind his head.

Sitting there on the edge of my bed, exhausted beyond reason, I found myself frozen, my mind focused on two questions:

Did Corrigan know my dad?

And given all the mind-control mumbo-jumbo Corrigan was involved with ... had my dad really killed himself?

AUTHOR'S NOTE

There is so much research material on Rasputin out there, it was hard to know when to stop. Even better, a lot of it is first-hand. A huge trove of letters and diaries of many of the key players still exist. Most striking are those of the tsar and the tsarina: their letters and telegrams to each other, and their diaries, all of which have been carefully preserved, give us a clear and incredibly detailed insider's look at their lives and their dealings with Rasputin. All the main players testified to the Extraordinary Commission in 1917, a few months after Rasputin's death and after the tsar's abdication. The monk Iliodor wrote a book about him from the comfort of his new home in America. Even his murderers published their memoirs long after fleeing Russia, although their versions of the events surrounding that infamous night have glaring, self-serving inconsistencies. Rasputin himself wrote – or, more likely, dictated, to Olga Lokhtina – several works, most notably *The Life of an Experienced Wanderer*, which was published after his death. All of which allowed me a phenomenally intimate look at what happened in those final turbulent years of the Romanov dynasty.

Remarkably, every event described in this book's historical chapters actually happened – with one caveat: Misha and his discovery are, of course, my invention. Rasputin really did everything described in this book, and as far as I know, he achieved it without a shadow like Misha helping him out. Which is astounding. He did keep the tsarevich alive long enough for the young boy to face an executioner's bullet three weeks short of his fourteenth birthday. He bedded countless aristocratic women, culled from the highest rungs of St. Petersburg society. His influence over the tsar in affairs of government was mind-boggling and contributed in no small amount to the fall of the monarchy and the onset of the revolution.

How did he do it? There's little doubt that he was a remarkably brazen and cunning man who exploited the gullibility and superstition of those around him. In that respect, the tsarina was his prime dupe. Throw in a touch of hypnosis (which has been medically demonstrated to reduce the amount of clotting factor needed by hemophiliacs to stop bleeding) and a young heir to the throne who hovered close to death for most of his short life, and Rasputin's bewildering rise to power is easier to understand.

As for entrainment, the scientific basis for Leo's machine exists. Entrainment is real. The grid box and the zombie room are real, as is the huge grinder at Lefortovo Prison. The Yale scientist and his remote-controlled bull are real. In the spring of 2012, the Russian Defense Minister publicly announced that research into building mind-bending 'psychotronic' weapons that can turn people into zombies had been given the green light by the Krelim. The potential to induce and control different emotional states has been achieved by implanting electrodes into the brains of animals and, it is rumored, of humans too. What hasn't been achieved – yet – is doing it wirelessly.

I wouldn't want to bet against it becoming a reality in the not-too distant future . . .

ACKNOWLEDGMENTS

There are two very different sides to writing these books: one is uncompromisingly solitary, while the other is social and collaborative. I enjoy both – locking myself away with my characters and getting lost in their worlds; and bouncing ideas and plot threads off friends and colleagues along the way. Both sides feed one another, and I'm lucky to have a great bunch of people around me for the latter.

For this book, I'd particularly like to thank Jessica Horvath, Jemima Forrester and Jon Wood for their inspired editorial guidance. I'd also like to thank my friends and agents old and new, Eugenie Furniss, Jay Mandel, Michael Carlisle and Richard Pine.